THE FAR CALL

"In the sixties and seventies, Gordon R. Dickson was one of a cadre of science fiction writers who regularly traveled to Cape Kennedy to witness the blastoffs of the Apollo and Skylab launches, and the early days of the Space Shuttle. A lot of us wrote newspaper and magazine articles from the experience (so NASA would let us keep coming); and a few nonfiction books resulted from it, too. But to my knowledge, only one novel was written directly about that thrilling experience: Gordon R. Dickson's *The Far Call*.

"In *The Far Call,* Dickson has projected his unique experience into the far future, writing about an international quest to put the first men on Mars. A novel of character as well as adventure, *The Far Call* traces the actions of dozens of people—politicians, administrators, and spies, as well as pilots and scientists—whose lives are changed forever by this epic undertaking. A lot of careful thought, as well as recaptured passion, went into this novel, one of the best ever by a true master of science fiction."

—Joe Haldeman,
    award-winning author of THE FOREVER WAR

GORDON R. DICKSON

THE FAR CALL

A TOM DOHERTY ASSOCIATES BOOK
NEW YORK

THE FAR CALL

Copyright © 1973, 1978 by Gordon R. Dickson

Portions of this work have previously appeared in *Analog* magazine in
different form.

A TOR Book
Published by Tom Doherty Associates, Inc.
49 West 24 Street
New York, NY 10010

Cover art by Kotzky

ISBN: 0-812- 53544-8   Can. ISBN: 0-812-53545-6

First Tor edition: December 1989

Printed in the United States of America

0 9 8 7 6 5 4 3 2 1

This book is dedicated to the following individuals, who supplied professional advice and criticism upon the many occupations, technologies and places treated in its pages.

Joseph Green
Ben Bova
Keith Laumer
J. W. Shutz
Ann Cass
Clifford D. Simak
Eugene Aubry
Clarence Morgan
Samuel Long
Major Jerome Ashman
Robert Asprin
John Bailey
Roger De Garis
Igor Mojenko

He and the others—the image formed itself in Jens Wylie's mind suddenly, out of his state of light-headed exhaustion—were like nothing so much as mindless ants crawling about on the monstrous toy of some giant child, with toy and child alike beyond their understanding. He, with the other five diplomatic representatives of the six nations involved in this International Manned Expedition to Mars, was dwarfed now to less than insect-size by this great vehicle named the space shuttle on which they climbed.

Uncomfortably aloft on the spidery gantry of the launch tower that embraced the shuttle with its steel arms, the six of them stood crowding closely about the tall, postlike, gray-haired figure of Bill Ward, Launch Director for the Expedition. They were supported on a small metal platform between the unshielded sky and the massively curving hull of the shuttle itself. Even at as close as arm's length, in the explosive brilliance of the Florida afternoon, through Jens's dark glasses the others looked black and tiny against the white-painted hull, like barnacles on the belly of a whale.

"Ordinarily, we could go further up," Bill Ward was saying, "but the elevator to the command section of the shuttle is currently undergoing general decontamination procedures before the launch tomorrow. . . ."

Jens saw no eagerness in those about him to go up. On the faces of several, and in particular on the heavy, white face of Walther Guenther, the Deputy Minister for Space from Pan-Europe, Jens read the clear feeling that this third level of the gantry was already too high a perch for them. He did not mind the altitude. He found the vast windy emptiness about them a healing relief. The stiff breeze blew away the last blurring of the wine that had been served at lunch, and left him alone with the words of the marsnaut who would be Commander of the Expedition; words about the experiment workload.

". . . but what can *you* do about it?" Tadell Hansard had asked.

"I can talk to the President," he had answered without thinking.

Now he turned away from the rest. For the first time since he had eagerly accepted his appointment as U.S. Undersecretary for the Development of Space, he found the title a hollow thing to consider. Tad did not really understand his position. He could talk; whether the President would listen was something else. He turned his back to the steady buzz of Ward's lecturing and the gargantuan vehicle itself, and looked out over a red-painted steel railing at the National Aerospace Administration's Kennedy Space Center, spread over Cape Canaveral.

Below and all around, the view of the calm, flat Cape land, green with tangled brush, soothed his jangled thoughts. It stretched away on all sides, uninterrupted except for the scattered NASA buildings and the blue water in the canals that would find their way to the more distant Indian River. At the farthest visible point to his right, Jens could just make out the Atlantic Ocean, a dark line on the horizon. Almost within arm's reach by comparison loomed the towering Vehicle Assembly Building, capable of holding four Apollo vehicles, each nearly double the height of the shuttle. The VAB stood less than four miles off, dwarfing all the other man-made constructs—tricking the eye into a belief that it was half as big as it was, and half again as close, because no structure could be so huge. Overhead, there were only a few stray clouds, white as the flanks of the shuttle, under the searing bowl of the sky, and some restlessly soaring seagulls.

Jens turned once more to his five diplomatic counterparts, and saw Bill Ward already herding them back to the elevator that would take them down again. They were real—he was not. Jens followed them into the latticed shadow of the openwork elevator, almost stumbling against the giant, craggy shape of Sir Geoffrey Mayence, the British deputy minister.

"Hold up!" said Sir Geoffrey, catching Jens's elbow as he tripped. The bony, lined face stared from six and a half feet of height down at Jens. "Heat getting you?"

"It's the sun," said Jens thickly. "I couldn't see."

"God, yes. And the heat. We could use a drink."

The elevator sank under them, with Bill Ward still talking steadily. Jens rested his eyes in the relative dimness of the elevator shaft. Alinde West had been due in this morning, but she had not shown up. For the first time in the four years he had known her he felt a longing—more than a longing, almost a desperate need—for her. He forced his mind away from her nonarrival and back to the immediate place and moment. Below was their bus and air conditioning, cold drinks and a phone. Jens's stomach ached and felt hollow.

The elevator touched bottom. They emerged on the landing pad and walked, sweating, down one of the parallel concrete ramps that had supported the treads of the massive crawler when it had carried the shuttle here from the VAB. At the foot of the ramp, their hoverbus was waiting.

Its front door swung open as they reached it. They pushed into its dimly seen long shape, like a loaf of bread with its upper half all tinted glass coming down to floor level. The self-adjusting gray coloration of that polychromic glass was now so dark in response to the sunlight outside that only indistinct, dim shapes within hinted at seats, attendants, and the driver.

Here, suddenly, everything was reasonable again. The white-bright sun outside and the stark contrast of light and shadow in the natural landscape were toned down by the adaptable gray tint of the glass to plausible sources of original or reflected illumination. The rediscovery of coolness around them was like a technological benediction.

Blinking against the dimness, Jens turned to the outline of a uniformed figure standing to his left as he reached the top of the steps. As he did so, he came abruptly to a decision.

"Phones?" Jens asked.

"At the back, sir," the answer came. "To the left of the bar."

Jens turned and went down the length of the bus toward its rear, his vision adjusting as he went. The ordinary seats on this vehicle had been replaced with heavy lounge chairs that swiveled or slid about according to the desires of their users. Most of his fellow diplomats had already seated themselves. At the back of the bus, seeing clearly now, Jens shook his head at the white-jacketed security man behind the small, semicircular bar and stepped over to the row of three v-phones along the wall at his left. The polished surface of the wall gave him back his image—thirtyish, tall, a gangling body with a lean, bone-plain face above it, in a short-sleeved white dress shirt and gray slacks.

He sat down before the first phone and put his hand on the code buttons. They were cool under his fingers and for a second he hesitated. No one had ever given him authority to go to the President in this way. . . . He shook off the twinge of a feeling very like cowardice, and began deliberately punching for a long-distance call to the White House number he wanted. As the first button was touched, a transparent sound baffle slid silently out from one side of the phone and curved around, enclosing him and his chair. With the last button a chime-tone sounded, but the v-screen before him retained its pearl-gray blankness.

"Scrambling," he said. He took his pocket scrambler from the inside pocket of his borrowed jacket and slipped it into the slot at the base of the phone. A different note sounded but the screen stayed blank.

"Scrambling," said another voice, a woman's, hard-edged and on guard. "Who's calling, please?"

"Undersecretary for the Development of Space Jens Wylie," he answered. "I'm calling Selden Rethe."

"One moment . . ." There was a pause. "I'm sorry, Mr. Rethe can't answer right now. Would you like to call back?"

"I'll wait." Jens leaned his hot forehead against the deliciously cool plastic of the phone booth wall above the instrument.

"It may be several minutes."

"I'll wait."

"Very well."

Silence, filled by the slowly oscillating tone that signaled the connection was still unbroken, but on hold.

Jens closed his eyes and breathed out deeply. This was the

sort of situation that would have been so clear-cut to his father that the sensible choice to be made might have been etched by acid on metal. He could hear Horace Wylie's voice now, telling him to back off from the whole situation.

"You've got to think, kid."

The voice of his father's ghost sounded now in the back of Jens's mind. That had been the Senator's favorite remark to his son. According to Senator Wylie, Jens had never stopped to think. He had not thought, nearly eight years ago, when he had made the decision to pass up the fellowship he had applied for—the Charles Evans Hughes Fellowship at Columbia Law School—in order to choose newspaper work, instead of taking a path that would have followed his father into politics. Nor had he thought when he had grabbed the chance to move from his St. Paul newspaper job to the paper's Washington bureau. Nor had he been thinking, by his father's standards, when he had considered leaving the bureau to do the book on the history of the space program—as a purely speculative, free-lance venture. The one thing he had done in the last eight years that the elder Wylie would have approved of was take advantage of the President's friendship with his father, immediately following the senator's death, to get this appointment as Undersecretary; and his father would consider that done for all the wrong reasons, since Jens had seen it as valuable experience before doing the book, not a step toward fame and fortune.

No, the senator would not have approved what Jens was about to do. He had loved Jens as much as any father might be expected to love his only offspring; but Jens had understood early that to the senator there was something unmanly about a son who let his feelings get in the way of his thinking. The only time the senator had ever really made an attempt to protest what Jens did or change Jens's mind by arguments had been after Jens had turned down the law school scholarship. For the first time, then, the senator had walked the floor, and a great many things had come out of him that Jens had only suspected. One was the senator's own feeling of helplessness at having been left on the death of his wife to raise his son alone. The other had been that Jens's attitude toward the world was not only one the senator did not understand, but one he could never understand. It was an attitude that Jens's mother had had, and that Jens now had and that the Senator stood somehow walled-off from.

Basically, it was the feeling that there was a right thing to do in any situation to which every right-thinking person would respond instinctively. To the senator, instinct was something that had been superseded by the conscious mind. To the senator the mind would examine a situation, tot up the advantages and disadvantages of each course possible and choose the one that gave the most attractive total. Once you made such a choice, whether the course chosen was instinctively or emotionally, or even morally attractive, was irrelevant. The senator was not a bad man in any sense of the word, but his ethics were pragmatic, and he assumed that a practical world threw up practical choices—others did not exist.

Jens had been aware of this since the time of his mother's death. He had wanted, like most sons, to have his father understand him—even to be like his father. But he could not, any more than the senator could understand him. And because he could not, and because he could not defend what he was or explain it to the senator's satisfaction, he was left with a low opinion of himself, a consciousness of his own impracticality in the Senator's eyes, his uselessness, what the Senator called in that one outburst, his "lightmindedness."

He had never been able to change himself from that; and he had never been able to justify the fact that he was as he was. His father had disapproved; and his father's ghost would be disapproving now, of everything that his son had done since getting this appointment—from the business of Lin to Jens's other love affair, the one with space. Jens, deliberately sticking his neck out into forbidden territory, as he was about to do, would have sent his father through the roof—

"Jens?"

As the voice sounded from the instrument, the pearl-gray oblong of the screen dwindled suddenly to a dot and disappeared, to show a lean, pale face, the face of a trim middle-aged man in a neat blue office jacket, sitting at a desk.

"Hi, Jens," said Presidential Private Secretary Selden Rethe. His eyes were a neutral tone—almost colorless.

"Sel," said Jens, "you know I've got special permission to go direct to the President in an emergency."

He waited. Selden raised his eyebrows but said nothing.

"I think I need to talk to him now," Jens said. "I think it's something he ought to hear personally."

Selden sat for an additional second without speaking.

"I don't know, right now," he answered at last. His speech was precise, northern, and like his eyes, colorless. "He's on his way to Philadelphia for the William Penn Memorial dedication. You'll see him tonight at his reception down there, as scheduled."

"That's not going to be in time." Jens stopped to take a deep breath. Selden watched him with unmoving face. "This is something important, Sel. It could even wreck the Expedition."

"Oh?" said Selden. The eyebrows were still up.

"Yes," said Jens grimly.

"What is it all about, Jens?"

"I think I ought to tell him myself."

Selden nodded slowly, and the eyebrows descended.

"Well, as I say," he said. "There's no way for you to catch him before tonight at his reception down there at Merritt Island."

"Will he talk to me then?"

Selden frowned slightly.

"I couldn't promise." His long face under its neatly balding middle-aged skull looked out from the three-dimensional depths of the holographic screen without emotion. "You're sure you don't want to tell me what it's about?"

"I'd rather talk to him. It may be touchy."

"I see . . . maybe tomorrow morning, then."

"That's almost launch time. It'll be too late."

"I'm sorry, Jens," said Selden. "I don't know what else I can do."

Jens sagged a little.

"All right, then." he said. "I'll tell you. Tadell Hansard just talked to me—"

"Who?" asked Selden.

"Tad Hansard—the Expedition Commander. Our own U.S. marsnaut. He's upset over the number of experiments they keep adding to the workload of the Expedition. Every country's been fighting for as many of its own pet experiments as possible to be part of the program; and the whole program's got too heavy."

"He thinks so, does he?" Selden said. "What do the others think?"

"Others?"

"The other marsnauts," said Selden, patiently. "The Pan-European, the Japanese . . ."

"Oh. They agree, of course."

"Are they saying the same thing to their own government people?"

"I don't know," said Jens. "For Christ's sake, Sel! Tad only had a moment to speak to me alone at the lunch the 'nauts gave us today at the Operations and Checkout Building here."

"I see," said Selden. "Well, Jens, you know we've got no control over what the other participating countries want."

"But the President ought to know what's going on!" said Jens. "Tad thinks the results could be serious. It could cause real trouble to the Expedition."

Selden sat for a second.

"I'm sorry," he said. "I don't know what can be done at this time to arrange a talk for you."

"You know God damn well what can be done!" Jens lowered his voice. "Damn it, Sel, we're scrambled aren't we? This is me, Jens! Don't try that bureaucratic polite-evasion stuff with me!"

"Well, I can pass along what you've said, of course."

"Sel," said Jens. "I want to talk to the President at the earliest possible moment, on an emergency matter. That's an official request from me as Undersecretary of Science for the Development of Space."

"All right," said Selden calmly. "Of course, Jens. I'll get on it right away and do the best I can, naturally."

Jens stared at him.

"Sel," he said. "For God's sake, Sel, I tell you this is important!"

"Don't worry about it, Jens. I appreciate your concern and everybody else here will too. Make sure the VIP Message

Center there can locate you at any time. I'll call you just as soon as I have some kind of word. Good-bye.''

Selden's picture disintegrated into a crazy quilt of color which swirled away like water down a drain shrinking to a single bright dot. The screen was left pearl-gray, quiescent.

"Good-bye," said Jens emptily, to the pictureless surface before him.

He pulled his scrambler, put it in his jacket pocket and walked toward the front of the bus, passing Sir Geoffrey, who was now at the little bar, a drink looking tiny in his great hand.

"You?" he asked, raising his glass as Jens passed.

"Thanks. No, I guess not," said Jens, going on.

The bus had risen on the cushion of its air jets some seconds since, and was sliding along the asphalt roadpath away from the shuttle launch pad. Jens sat down in one of the three heavy lounge chairs that had been pulled together to form a group. In the chair beside him was Bill Ward, listening with brisk, controlled patience to the Soviet Deputy Minister for the Development of Space, Sergei Verigin. Their conversation clattered in his ear.

"'. . . your brother," Verigin was saying. "A doctor of veterinary medicine, I understand?"

"Yes," Bill Ward said. "He's on the faculty at the University of Minnesota Veterinary School—"

He broke off, standing up as the bus slid almost imperceptibly to a halt.

"Excuse me," he said to Verigin, and turned to raise his voice so that it could be heard through the whole of the bus. "We're going to stop out here for a moment so you can all see the shuttlecraft and the launch pad as a whole. We'll be about half a kilometer from it, but still close enough so that you can get a good look, overall."

They were indeed quite close. It was the opposite side of the bus from Jens that faced the launch pad, but the bus itself was so sparsely passengered that he could see clearly between the opposite lounge chairs without needing to stand up or move.

The bus had halted some three hundred yards from the platform holding the space vehicle. The two joined shuttlecraft that made it up could now be seen as essentially an upright two-stage vehicle, such as the earlier Saturn rockets had been. Awaiting launch, the shuttle rested, as the Saturns had done, in vertical position; but, unlike the Saturns, it looked like one heavy-bodied small aircraft—the orbiter—glued to the back of its big brother, identical in appearance but scaled larger, like a remora self-attached to a shark. The mobile launch structure from which the diplomats had just come down pressed against both skyward-pointing craft.

"The orbiter will ride piggyback on the booster, as you see it now," Bill Ward was now saying to the deputy ministers, "to about two hundred thousand feet. By this time we're about three minutes past lift-off. Then separation occurs—"

Someone broke in with a question. His mind still occupied with the problem of the experiment overload and the image of shark-remoralike partnerships, Jens only belatedly recognized Guenther's voice, and lost the sense of the question entirely.

"No, the booster lands like any other aircraft—slides in, actually, on its belly skids," Bill Ward answered the Pan-European deputy minister. "Just the same way the orbiter itself does, when it comes back. Both are piloted. Meanwhile, after it separates from the booster, the orbiter proceeds to climb into the parking orbit of the Mars craft. . . ."

Staring out through the light-reducing glass which covered the top half of the bus, Jens found it difficult to believe in the reality of what he saw. Here, only a few hundred yards from the launch pad, the two parts of the shuttlecraft loomed impossibly large. There was something about them reminiscent of the eye-tricking size of the huge Vehicle Assembly Building, which the diplomats had been taken through before lunch. All these structures and machines were too big to be real, too titanic not to be a mock-up by some moviemaker whose only aim was to awe an audience with his film.

Jens closed his eyes.

The truth was, he thought, Man had now moved up into a scale beyond the small dimensions of Earthside reality. But still, there were people—people in power—who had not yet recognized this and were still trying to play their usual small business-as-usual games, as if the familiar, safe conditions of Earth were to be found everywhere in the universe. In the case of this manned expedition to a planet that was a next-door neighbor, how far was Mars, really? How far? How far was a world in the neighborhood of fifty millions of miles distant, when downtown Cocoa Beach was only seventeen miles? How deep was the ocean of space . . . ?

Jens felt an inward shudder at his momentary vision of the cold depths of infinity stretching away all around him.

"We've just finished mating the orbiter to the booster," Bill Ward was saying. "The prelaunch checkout is still going on. It's a matter of checking innumerable little details. . . ."

. . . *With our own tiny world circling its little sun, lost way out on the spiral arm of our galaxy, which is itself lost among other and greater galaxies, in a universe that goes on without end . . .*

Jens woke suddenly to a firm grip on his forearm, and saw the face of Verigin only a few inches away, looking at him with concern on his round, aging features. He realized suddenly that he was a little dizzy, that he must have been swaying.

"Are you all right?" Verigin was asking in a remarkably gentle voice. "You aren't ill?"

"Ill? No!" Jens pulled himself upright. "Tired . . . that's all."

"Oh, yes. Yes," said Verigin, letting go of his arm. "It is always tiring, this sort of thing."

Bill Ward finished speaking and sat down again in the chair from which he had risen earlier. Verigin turned almost eagerly to him, again.

"Your brother, you were telling me," Jens heard him say, "is on the faculty of the School of Veterinary Medicine, at this University?"

"Joel—oh yes," said Bill. "Yes, the last six years."

"I wonder," Verigin said. "Do you know if he's been involved in any work or research on nerve degeneration in animals? I have a dog at home, a small dog—"

"Afraid I don't know anything about that," said Bill. "He doesn't usually tell me much about what he's doing."

"It's not important, of course," said Verigin. "I hardly

see the dog, these days. But to my wife—we only had two children, adult some time since of course. The older, the boy, was a test pilot. In fact Piotr and Feodor Asturnov, our marsnaut on this flight, were test pilots together. Not that they were close, you understand, but they knew each other. Unfortunately Piotr's—a plane my son was testing came apart in the air and he was not able to get out in time."

"Oh. Sorry," said Bill, restlessly and uncomfortably, sitting stiffly upright in his seat.

"And his sister, our daughter, is married and lives in . . . well, you would not know the name, one of the new towns of Siberia. My wife and this dog—we call him Chupchik— are alone most of the time; I have to be away so much. Chupchik means a great deal to us."

"Ah . . . yes," said Bill, glancing past the Russian's head at the road still separating them from the landing space where the VTOL—Vertical Takeoff and Landing—aircraft waited to take the deputy ministers back to their hotel on Merritt Island.

"Chupchik's hind legs, lately, have been failing him—he's not a young dog. Ten, twelve years old, I think. Yes," said Verigin, "twelve years old. When he was young, he was hit by a truck; but he seemed to recover very well. It's only this last year it's become harder and harder for him to walk."

"That's too bad," said Bill Ward. "That's a shame. You've had a veterinarian look at him before this?"

"Oh, of course," said Verigin. "But—so little seems to be known about dogs, in this way. They tell us Chupchik is just getting old; and we're not veterinarians ourselves. We can't argue. But Chupchik got along so well with those back legs all those years . . . I thought, perhaps, if someone over here was looking into nerve troubles, or whatever causes paralysis like this, in dogs . . . your brother might have heard of something . . . ?"

Jens saw the fingers of Bill Ward's left hand twitch on the arm of his chair.

"I can drop him a line. Be glad to," he said.

"Would you?" said Verigin. "I'd appreciate it greatly."

The bus pulled up at last at the landing area; and the VTOL plane waiting there took them into its interior, which was hardly less spacious than that of the bus. A moment later, the plane lifted smoothly, elevator-fashion, to about five hundred feet and flew them to the landing area on top of the Merritt Island Holiday Inn that had been partly taken over by the government for VIP quarters.

Jens headed for the stairs, thankful at the prospect of a chance to lie down, and call the desk. There might be a message from Lin that had come in since he had been gone. As he went toward his own suite on the floor just below the landing area on the roof, which had been set aside for the deputy ministers and undersecretaries representing the six nations cooperating on the Expedition, he heard Verigin being hailed by Guenther, who, with the representative from India, Ahri Ambedkar, intercepted the Russian as he turned into the central lounge area leading to his suite.

2

"Sergei, have you a minute? Stop and have a drink with us," Walther Guenther called in Russian as Verigin started off toward his suite.

The Pan-European's command of the language was good enough, but obviously required some effort. Verigin faced about and went to join the other two, answering in much more fluent German.

"Thank you," he said. "That's a pleasant invitation, now that we're off duty for an hour or two." He seated himself in one of the heavy, overstuffed green armchairs by a circular table of the lounge area. "I believe we are free until the President's reception at eight?"

"I believe nine P.M." said Ahri Ambedkar. "There has been some delay in making the arrival of President Fanzone on time. The official hour of the reception remains, but we are quietly informed to consider nine our hour of beginning."

It was immediately apparent that the Indian deputy minister's German was effortful as Guenther's Russian. Verigin switched again, this time to French.

"I didn't know that," he said.

"We just heard it," said Ambedkar in French and with obvious relief.

"Yes," said Guenther easily in the same language, "the pilot of the 'copter that will take us there was just now telling us. What will you have, Sergei?"

"Cognac," said Verigin, "since we've ended up where we have."

The other two smiled. *Ahri is really an old man*, thought Verigin, studying the brown, round face next to the middle-aged white, square one that was Guenther's, while Guenther delivered the order into the telephone grid on the table beside him. *I spend most of my time dealing with old men—men my age—and I forget that most of the world is younger. The world is run by old men—necessarily, of course, since the young have not yet learned. . . .*

"It's a relief to sit back and relax, as you say," said Guenther, after the order was in. "By the way, I am a little surprised, I thought Fanzone would have made an appearance here before this."

"He's somewhat above our rank, of course," said Ambedkar.

"Politically, yes," said Guenther. The cognac was brought in by a young U.S. Air Force corporal who was on duty in the lounge; and the conversation paused until he was gone again.

"Politically, yes," said Guenther again. "The chief executive of a nation like this; and ourselves only deputy ministers for the Development of Space." He smiled. The others smiled. "We won't talk about political antecedents, our own—or his."

Verigin chuckled politely. But Ambedkar looked interested.

"There is, indeed, then," he asked, "some truth to this

noise about underworld support having helped him gain the presidency of the U.S. ?''

Guenther waved a square hand.

''No, no. I hardly think so, really,'' he said. ''Not that it's important. They're all half-gangsters at heart, these Americans. But they never let that stand in the way of business.''

''You might say,'' agreed Verigin, sampling the cognac, which had been brought, sensibly, in a snifter glass, ''that the U.S. is such a fat dog it doesn't really mind a few fleas. It would feel lonesome without its gangster element.''

''But,'' said Ambedkar, ''if gangsterism should be a factor in their political consideration at this moment—particularly in regard to this international mission . . .''

''I think we can ignore anything so minor,'' said Guenther. ''It's the obvious elements in Fanzone's thinking that are worthy of concern. The private agreement was that he would not be here for the actual launch, so as not to disturb the balance of unity at that time. Now an accident makes him late for his reception the night before. I merely wonder if another such accident might not delay him here until the shuttle actually takes off?''

''I doubt that,'' said Verigin.

''Perhaps you are right,'' said Guenther. ''There's a natural tendency to speculate about changes in schedule, all the same. But then, he does have Wylie here on the spot.''

He put his glass down on the low coffee table between them and lowered his head in the process. Above that head, the eyes of Verigin and Ambedkar consulted each other.

''I'm afraid I don't follow you, Walther,'' Verigin said. ''We're all aware that Wylie is, both by experience and situation, in rather a different position from the rest of us. Has there been some change in his condition? Is he doing something we don't know about?''

''Oh, nothing I know of,'' said Guenther, looking up at both of them. ''Perhaps I'm letting myself become unduly concerned about things.''

Ambedkar looked at Verigin again.

''What do you think, Sergei?''

''There's always a cause for concern, of course,'' Verigin

said, "particularly when dealing with the American mind. Of all such capitalist organs—no offense, my friends—the American mind is the most self-centered and therefore the most unpredictable. But I find it hard to believe even an American president—" he hesitated slightly "—or his representative, would risk his country's image by any obvious move to shoulder the representatives of other nations aside."

"But perhaps we should keep the possibility in mind," said Guenther.

"Oh, yes," said Verigin. "By all means we should keep the possibility in mind."

In his own suite down the hall from the lounge area, Jens, having put off for the moment his plans to lie down, was once more speaking to Selden Rethe over a scrambled circuit.

"Look," Jens said patiently, "if he can't talk to me will you ask him at least to talk to Tad at the reception tonight?"

"I'll ask, of course," said Selden. "But this reception down there where you are is strictly a stage appearance, Jens. I believe you know that. The last thing a president can do in a case like this is give the impression of being partisan toward you or the American astronaut."

"Marsnaut, damn it, Sel!" Jens interrupted. "They're proud of the name marsnaut—why can't people understand that? They're the only ones there are."

"If you like, Jens—marsnaut, then."

"Look," said Jens, "this concerns everybody involved with the Expedition, all the countries, every 'naut—not just Tad. But if you could just explain to the President that since Tad's senior captain for the Expedition, he knows what he's talking about when he says the work schedule's too heavy with tests, particularly on the outgoing leg—"

"But there's a reason for that, of course," said Selden. "The Mars Expedition's going to be at its biggest as news during the first nine weeks. That's why you national reps are all staying on here that long, and that's when what's most needed will be the 'nauts reporting they've just done this experiment that Hamamuri of Nagasaki wanted done, or that experiment for Miller at Bonn University, and so on . . ."

"All right. All right," said Jens, keeping his voice down.

"But the thing is, there's too much now for the crew to do; and not enough time. Tad's point is, what if they get up there and have to skip some of the experiments, or some of the tests get bungled because they're trying to work too fast? All he wants is for the President to drop a word to the deputy ministers of the other countries, here—and this late, he's the only one who can do it—so that everybody concerned agrees to cut their list by one experiment, or two. There's more potential dynamite in letting them go off this way than there is in facing the thing now."

"That's only his opinion, of course," Selden said calmly. "Besides, if he's so sure that's the case, why can't he just handle the priorities for the experiment list himself once they're on their way?"

"Man!" said Jens, staring into the screen with Selden's face printed on it. "Oh, man! When you want a scapegoat you don't fool around, do you? You just shout out his name, rank, and serial number and wait for him to take three paces forward. Tad's a marsnaut. They're all marsnauts—not politicians!"

Selden stared back at Jens from the screen without speaking for several seconds. When he did speak, it was with a new remoteness.

"We've all got our jobs to do," he said. "Including me. As I said, I'll pass on what you've said to the president. That's all I can do, pass the word to him. However, I wouldn't expect anything much, if I were you."

"Sure," said Jens.

"All right, then. Unscramble." Selden broke the circuit.

Jens sat back in the chair beside his bed, slumping. He felt as if he had just been punched in the stomach, drained of strength and a little sick. The phone buzzed again. Automatically he stabbed it to *on;* and a woman's face, oval, brown-eyed under chestnut hair, appeared.

"Hi!" it said, affectionately. "If you'd stay off your phone for five minutes, maybe somebody could call in!"

A sudden deep feeling of gratitude and relief wiped out the battered feeling.

"Lin!" he said, happily. "Where are you?"

"Here. Downstairs, that is," Alinde West said. "I was

going to come up and just knock on your door; but evidently you've got security guards around you, five ranks deep. I told one of them I was your common-law wife; but it didn't move him. He's watching me now while I phone you from the lobby."

"Who is it?' Jens asked. "Gervais? Black man, middle-aged? Slim and sort of stiff—looks like a Roman senator?"

"With a scowl."

"Let me talk to him."

There was a short pause; and then the face of Security Department Agent Albert Gervais took over the screen.

"Sorry if I've been holding up someone I shouldn't," Gervais said. He did not look sorry at all. "She said something about being your wife; and according to our records you're not married."

"Not exactly, no," said Jens. "She's a very old friend, though; and she's had White House clearance to accompany me before. If you put a call in to Selden Rethe's office, you ought to find authorization for her to visit me."

"Just a minute, Mr. Wylie." The screen went blank with a holding light. Jens sat waiting for several minutes, thinking that Gervais could at least have put Lin back on while the check was being made. Then Gervais himself appeared again. "Yes, sir. There's White House record of clearance for her. It's been reactivated on a twenty-four-hour basis. If you want it extended beyond that time, they ask that you call them."

"Thanks," said Jens. "I will."

He felt a sudden sympathy with Gervais, who was a professional. Lin's visit represented a complication and an increase in the duties of guarding the international representatives attending the launch. "I promise she'll go directly to my suite up here and directly from it," Jens said. "And I'll let you know as soon as she leaves the area."

"Thank you, Mr. Wylie," said Gervais, with no more emotion than he had shown before. "I'll have her escorted to you now."

One of the agents, whom Jens had seen around but whose name he did not know—a square, blond young man with a New England accent, brought Lin to the suite. It was incredibly good to hold her—a trim, vibrant woman-shape, long-limbed and firm-muscled in a tan and green pantsuit with only the hint of some clean, light perfume about her.

"When I didn't hear from you this morning, I thought something had come up to keep you from getting here," Jens said as he let her go. "Hey, what would you like to do first?"

"Sit down and have a drink," she said. "Oof! All the first-class flights were booked and I had to sit in economy with fifty pounds of recording and transcribing equipment in my lap, all the way down."

She walked over and dropped into one of the suite's armchairs. Jens went to the little bar to make them both a Scotch on the rocks.

"But how was it you didn't get here this morning?"

He handed her her drink, and sat down himself on the sofa opposite her armchair.

"Thanks. The magazine decided to make the time pay. So instead of taking it off, while I'm down here I'm to do a piece on the marsnauts' wives—how they adjust their families to the idea that dad's going to be gone three years in outer space."

"There's not a lot of wives for you to ask," said Jens. "Feodor Asturnov is a widower. Both Anoshi Wantanabe and the Pan-European 'naut, Bern Callieux, have wives who decided to stay home with their children and not come for the launch. Bapti Lal Bose, the Indian, isn't married. That just leaves Dirk Welles's wife and Tadell Hansard's."

"You've met them, haven't you?" Lin asked. "The wives of those two, I mean?"

Jens nodded.

"You'll like Wendy Hansard, I think," he said. "She looks something like you. She's the sort of woman you'd kind of expect an astronaut to marry. Dirk's wife, Penanine—Penny, he calls her—I don't know as well. But she seems likeable, too. Big, young girl. Sort of more English than Dirk. Blonde."

"Can you help me get to see them tomorrow?" Lin asked.

"I can try. You shouldn't have any trouble, once the launch is over. Before, there's no chance, of course. Look—" He came over with the drinks, put them on the table before the couch and sat down, turning urgently to her. "There's a presidential reception for all of us to go to this evening; and it's not the sort of thing where I get you on the invitation list. But if you think you can wait here, I ought to be back about eleven—''

She got up, leaving her drink behind and thumped down beside him on the sofa.

''Idiot!'' she said, putting her arms around him fondly and nestling up against him. ''Of course I'll be here when you get back—waiting. Why do you think I managed to get down here anyway?''

''I didn't know that you were going to manage it all,'' he muttered, feeling peculiarly lighthearted and rather warm inside.

She let go of him, but she did not move away.

''Now, let's not get off on that right away,'' she said. ''I said I'd be here for the launch, and here I am.''

''I know,'' he said, ''and you couldn't come at a time when I wanted to see you more.''

She looked at him narrowly.

''I thought you seemed wound up about something,'' she said. ''What is it?''

He shook his head.

''Oh, just this job.''

''What about just the job?'' she asked.

''Well,'' he said, heavily, ''the Expedition to Mars is one thing. The international politics behind it is something else. You wouldn't believe that end of it.''

''Try me.''

''It's all the nations involved, pulling and hauling against each other to see who gets the biggest piece of the publicity involved—the most credit—and, above all, the most of the marsnauts' time for their own experiments. That last, in particular.''

''You mean the science experiments they're going to do on the flight to Mars and back again?''

''I mean those,'' Jens said, ''and the end result of it all is that the marsnauts are overscheduled. They've got too much to do. Oh, on paper, it works out. But all it'll take is some small thing going wrong, one of them being sick for a few days or some such thing, and the work load is going to get on top of them. And you can figure that on an Expedition like this that's never been done before something is bound to come along to interfere with their doing everything clickety-bang.''

"What's the problem?'' Lin asked. Her face was suddenly interested. "Don't the governments involved know this? Can't they just get together and settle on a reasonable experimental load?''

Jens laughed.

"The governments in this can't get together on anything," he said. "To begin with, it's all the rest against the U.S.—''

"All the rest?''

"Sure, Lin. Which of them can use Shared-Management Technique as profitably as we can? The only nation it really works for is us. Or rather, it works so much better for us that it might as well work *only* for us.''

"All right,'' said Lin, "but they're all supposed to be co-operating on this Expedition, aren't they?''

"The cooperation's all in the public relations end,'' said Jens. "For us, too.''

"What do you mean?''

"I mean it's the U.S. which stands to get the most out of the publicity from this flight. Why do you think we're in it? We're only putting in one crew member, just like the other nations; but our government can still point its finger at the fact that the lion's share of everything that goes to Mars, except the people, is either U.S. hardware or U.S. technology.''

"Pretty expensive stunt,'' said Lin.

"Well, we need it.'' Jens frowned again. "As I say, this Shared-Management Technique has been looking too much like it's God's own gift to His favorite United States. We need something to take the shine off that. We're just too rich-looking, as things stand right now. It's us who've got the most factories in space, for making the parts that make the Computer Communications Network possible. Without the industry we had to start with, we'd never have been able to produce a network like that in a little over three years, with a terminal on every desk in the country; and without a business and industry pattern geared to conference-style management, the whole process of being able to lay your fingers on just the right consultant at a moment's notice wouldn't have done any good.''

"Maybe," said Lin.

"No maybe about it, damn it!" Jens said. "That's what nobody in the street seems to realize! Lin, without that input of consulting information and the improvement in decision-making, would our gross national product have quadrupled overnight the way it has? No wonder our efficiency's going right off the top of the charts! But look at it from the standpoint of any of the people-rich, industry-poor countries. If it doesn't look to them like a clear case of the rich getting richer hand over fist, I'll eat it. What this whole Expedition can do is lightning-rod some of the bitterness from people who see it just that way.''

"All right." Lin half-turned on the couch so that she was facing him more squarely. "But what's all that got to do with too large an experiment load? And above all, what's it got to do with you, personally?''

"The marsnauts are worried about the load, and it looks like I'm the only one who listens to them," muttered Jens. "They've talked to everyone else they could to hold the work load down. Today, at lunch, Tad Hansard dumped it in my lap.''

"Why you?" Lin frowned. "It's not your responsibility.''

"But I can talk to the President—maybe." Jens shook his head. "Though so far I haven't had much luck doing it, I've been trying to get to Fanzone through Selden Rethe.''

"You can't get hold of Rethe either?''

"Oh, I got to him, all right. But he keeps finding reasons why Fanzone can't see me.''

Jens reached for his drink absentmindedly, then took his hand away again without lifting the glass from the table where it stood.

"But Fanzone's coming in to this diplomatic reception tonight; and I ought to be able to corner him there, with or without permission. The marsnauts are going to be there too. That's what the dinner's for. It's a case of us national representatives to the launch entertaining the 'nauts, and Fanzone is due to put in—theoretically—a surprise visit.''

''I still don't follow you,'' said Lin. ''Why should you have trouble talking to the President? You're the man he appointed, aren't you?''

Jens laughed a little bitterly.

''Oh sure,'' he said, ''but I'm a fake!''

She stared at him and suddenly, he found himself telling her—the whole story.

''That's what I am,'' he said grimly. ''You weren't too far off, Lin, back when you told me if I took this appointment I'd be nothing but a sort of token diplomat. Not that I'm regretting I took it. It's still going to be worth its weight in gold when I sit down to serious writing and do the book. But the truth is, since the Launch and Expedition Control are both here at Merritt Island, in this country, a national representative to the launch from the United States doesn't mean a thing. The real U.S. representative to this Expedition is the President, himself. So I'm just stuck up here like a straw figure on a pole to fill the quota, but look harmless—above all, to look harmless. You ought to see my opposite numbers. They're the best tough old political infighters the other countries could send. Compared to them, I'm like a puppy among wolves.''

Lin laughed, then sobered. She put down her drink and slid her arms around him, holding him.

''I'm sorry,'' she said. ''I didn't mean to laugh. But it struck me funny, you being a puppy among wolves. Are they all wolves, Jens?''

''Yes. Well—'' said Jens. ''Sir Geoffrey Mayence isn't so bad. In fact, he's a pretty good old character. But he's as sharp as any of the rest of them. Maybe more so.''

''Well,'' said Lin. ''If they're all together against the U.S., they ought to be able to get together themselves on reducing the experimental load.''

''It's not that simple, though,'' Jens said. ''There're divisions and factions among them, too; and what it boils down to is every nation for itself. The only thing holding everybody together is the fact that each country's got its own interests in space-based industries.''

"Well, the others may not have as much in the way of factories in space as we do," said Lin, "but what about this other system that's supposed to work for them as well as the Shared-Management Technique works for us—according to what I hear, anyway? What's that *'Belle-Petite'* thing called in English? Oh, yes, the Incremental Production Theory. Can't they get together in the name of that?"

"I don't think so. Propaganda aside, it is all very pretty, the idea of putting a piece of a factory in everybody's home, using the same kind of computer communications hookup we're using for Shared-Management. But the countries trying it never did have an existing business pattern like ours to build on. To get that's something that's going to cost them five to ten years of programming first, before they can really put their system into effect. When they finally do, of course—" he grinned at her "—all those nations with tremendous populations like India and China may sweep us off the face of the Earth, but right now we're the only ones who're getting our GNP quadrupled, and that may put us so far ahead by the time they come on line—" He broke off suddenly, making an effort to push the whole problem away, at least temporarily. He looked at her and suddenly he did not want to talk any more.

"But why are we sitting around discussing all this?" he asked.

"She grinned back at him.

"I don't know," she answered. "Why?"

"I thought as much," he said. "You don't know, either. In that case, let's not. It's high time we got on to more important matters."

3

The thin face under the receding black hairline looked out from the phone screen at Albert Gervais.

"I just got word," it said, "you let someone named Alinde West up to Jens Wylie's suite, on the National Reps' floor."

Gervais watched the face. Amory Hammond and he had been trainees together. But Hammond had been on loan to the Air Force for two years now, and the recommendations the Air Force had given him had pushed him up the ladder. He had been moved back to Washington and put in charge of Gervais's section from there.

"I checked," said Gervais. "She had clearance."

"Yes, I know, Albert," said Hammond. "But she's not a relative or anything. She's just some bed-partner or other."

"I checked with the White House," said Gervais. "They okayed it. She's had clearance to be with him before."

"I know. I know." Hammond looked aside from the screen for a moment and then back into it. "But what you don't know is, she's media. She works for *New Worlds*. It's a large, slick, women's sort of magazine."

"I assume the White House knows that," Gervais said.

"Of course they know it!" said Hammond. "And they don't care. But they're not the ones on the spot. If anything goes wrong, it's us who'll get the blame."

"I don't know what could go wrong," said Gervais. "Besides, what do you want me to do about it? When they gave her clearance I couldn't turn her away."

"All right," said Hammond. "But it's not good. If any kind of a fuss should come out of it . . . These women's magazines are worse than anything else when it gets into anything they can call scandal."

Gervais sat for a second looking into the screen at the other man.

"I repeat," he said at last, slowly. "What do you want me to do about it?"

"Well, watch her, for God's sakes!" said Hammond. "Try to get her out of there, one way or another."

"How?"

"How? Can't you think of something?" Hammond's face twisted.

"No," said Gervais. "I can't."

"Albert," said Hammond, "Albert, you aren't cooperating."

Gervais did not move or speak. Not a line in his face altered. He sat as still as a monument.

On the screen, Hammond looked away from him abruptly, and lit a cigarette. The thin man puffed the white cylinder alight and dropped the hand holding it to the desk. The lit cigarette trembled slightly between his fingers.

"I'm sorry," he said, looking away again. "That's a little hasty. I didn't mean that, Albert."

Gervais said nothing.

"Look!" said Hammond, facing him from the screen once more. "I'm sorry. It just popped out. You don't know what the pressure's been like here. I'll get down there myself just as soon as I can clear my desk off a little. But you know there's things that can be done!"

"No,' said Gervais, "I don't know what you mean."

"All right!" Hammond snubbed out the cigarette. "All right. That's all right. I shouldn't have gotten hasty. It's my own fault. But, damn it! If this woman, whoever she is, ends up writing something unpleasant for that magazine she works for, then it'll be our necks on the block, all of our necks."

Gervais waited.

"You'll do what you can, anyway?" Hammond asked, finally.

"Of course," said Gervais.

"Well, all right then. That takes a load off my mind."

Hammond punched off.

Gervais stayed gazing at the dead screen for a long second. Then he sat back in his chair and breathed slowly. There was no such thing as a slip of the tongue that did not count, no such thing as stepping by mistake for a second over the line, then pulling back and never stepping over it again. Once stepped over, the line moved in the direction of the step, and the next violation moved it a little further in the same direction and so on. Anyone stepping over the line at all, even by accident, could expect a reaction.

Hammond, like anyone else, had understood that, once. But Hammond had always been weak, and now the Air Force had spoiled him, made him dangerous as well. Gervais rubbed his chin thoughtfully and began to think.

Jens drifted gradually back to consciousness, without really being aware of the moment in which he became fully awake. Lin lay sleeping on the big hotel bed beside him.

The most ancient tranquilizer in the world had had its effects, and he felt clearheaded and calm for the first time in days. The overall exhaustion from the excitement and the heavy social pressure of those days was still with him, but now it had moved off a small distance. The steam cloud of emotion enveloping him had blown away, and his thoughts were now bathed in the clear cool sunlight of practicality.

Lying there, with some little time yet before he had to get up and dress and go to the diplomatic dinner, he found himself at last in a position to stand back from everything and take a long look at the situation in which he was caught up—the situation of the Manned Expedition to Mars and all the concern of a world with it.

It was like standing on a high mountain and looking down at a landscape spread around the base of the mountain. The mountain itself was the fact of the Expedition, the effort to reach Mars, the whole theory of cooperation of six nations. But the flat landscape stretching to the horizon from the base of this mountain was divided into differing territories, into special kingdoms, all concerned in their own way with the Expedition, but seeing—really only seeing—one face of the whole mountain.

Those on the mountain could not see its entirety, either. Only at the very peak, standing on the topmost crag, where the marsnauts stood and some of the NASA people, and—

yes, possibly himself—could the whole territory be seen, mountain and surrounding territories, all at once.

Jens looked down now from the peak of the mountain at the territories, imagining them laid out in different colors, like the colors of countries on maps. How many colors was it that were necessary—three or five? At any rate, there was some finite number that made it possible to do a map without ever having two areas side by side with the same color. A matter of topology. The colors he looked down at now would be five; because there were, in effect, five main groups of people, five human territories concerned with the Mars Expedition.

One of the territories was the mountain itself, the mountain of the marsnauts, of NASA, of the actual Expedition. Of the other four at the mountain's feet, one was the territory of the diplomats and the politicians. Another was the territory of the technology people, the engineering companies and all the rest who supported the building of the spacecraft and all else that was physically necessary to support the Expedition and make it possible. A third was the territory of related people; the whole local human community, including the wives and children of the marsnauts, who were connected with the Expedition in a human sense. Finally, there was the territory to which half of him still belonged. The territory of the newspeople and their public—the men and women on the streets of the world to whom the newspeople were responsible.

In fact, now that he stopped to think about it, what placed him on the peak of the mountain, along with the marsnauts and a few others, was the fact that he was not wholly of any of these kingdoms, but partly of all of them. Part of him was still newsman. Part of him, by present occupation, was politician/diplomat. Part of him, by sympathy—a would-be wish to be what he could never be—was a marsnaut; and he was at once both one of the people in the street watching, and someone who had been immersed for some years now in a study of the technology, the world-wide industrial pattern that had made this whole thing possible.

What was now happening, what would happen tomorrow at the launch and in the days and months to follow, would not be just the matter of the two ships of the Expedition falling on their long curved path through space to rendezvous with Mars nearly ten months later. It would be this plus all the interaction of the kingdoms back here on Earth who had a stake in it one way or another—from the third-world villager reaching out toward whatever could be touched of the rich life that could be seen in the more favored parts of the Earth, to the men and women caught up in the machinery of the politics of the most powerful of the human communities, the people who were at the very top and controlling the machinery, yet caught up in it at the same time.

But no, you couldn't have it. Each territory was set off separately. The kingdoms overlaid each other and interacted, forming intricate designs, each mingled with the others. Out of the back of his mind came the image of a medieval tapestry he had seen once in a chateau in the south of France; a room-wide cloth, crowded with scenes of workmen, noblemen, foresters, savage beasts, and mythological creatures. Above them, the greater fantasies of the sky, and the great wheel of the Zodiac—an attempt by centuries-dead hands to crowd the magnificence of creation and man's place within it into one magnificent sweep of fabric.

As he remembered it now, the image of a tapestry in which he and everyone else were individual threads grew and focused in his mind. He was caught up in its pattern. It was weaving itself and being woven by each and every human act as he watched. Countless threads like his own made up the background, individually invisible but each necessary, the brighter ones deftly woven together to create the elements of the grand design. Those brighter threads would be the movers and the shakers among the people; the politicians, technicians, the missionaries—Jens himself, Lin, even people like that security man, Gervais, and who knew else, among those crowding Merritt Island and the Cape. Yet none of them in the final essential were any more than a single thread, no matter what their color or their position. They were meaningless, except as they were woven with the other threads, in this effort now going on to break out of the eggshell of Earth's atmosphere.

The clash between the mental images of tapestries and eggshells was enough to rouse him momentarily from his introspection. The image of Earth as the eggshell from which humans as a spacegoing race must hatch was powerful and real enough. But it did not catch at him like the image of the great unrolling tapestry, which now took over his imagination again. It was real and it was there, stretching off into eternity and infinity; and it seemed to him now to float before and over him. He searched out again the thread in it that was Jens Wylie, and thought he saw it there with its part in the tapestry, whole and clear, trending toward some certain end, interweaving with all the threads about it; and with that thought, still imagining, still dreaming, still tracing himself into the overall pattern, he fell asleep.

4

Fourteen levels below, on the ground floor, the cavelike interior of the cocktail lounge was almost uncomfortably cold. A black-haired man in his early thirties, named Malcolm Shroeder, went toward the dimly-seen ridgeback shape of the bar with his hands held a little before him in automatic self-defense against obstacles. He touched the bar, groped for a bar stool, and climbed on to it.

"What'd you like?"

The woman behind the bar was also in her early thirties and not bad-looking, but a little thin. Her dark brown hair was cut short and curled closely about her head and neck. She wore a short-sleeved burgundy-colored outfit, tight about the breasts and waist but with a full, short, ruffled skirt. To Malcolm's Philadelphia ear her voice had only a trace of southern accent. He gazed past her at the ranks of softly-lit bottles climbing the face of a mirror.

"Tom Collins," he said, then remembered it was only mid-week and said, "No. Beer. You've got Schlitz?"

"We sure have."

She went away. His eyes were adjusting to the dimness now. Not as thin as he'd thought. Down near the rounded far end of the lounge, a heavy man with brown, curly hair and a tough, clown-cheerful face, about forty years old, leaned on the bar.

"Nurse!" he cried faintly, slyly. "Oh, *nurse* . . ."

"Thanks," said Malcolm, smiling at her as she brought his beer. "Got a patient down there?"

"Oh, he's one of those press people. His name's Barney Something."

"Nurse . . ."

"Press people?" said Malcolm quickly, though he knew what she meant. Maybe it was only her way of showing the calling man that she wasn't going to run at a word; but it seemed to Malcolm she was inclined to linger here with him.

"You know, newspeople," she said. "The Press Center's just across the street."

"Oh," said Malcolm, still smiling at her, though it was obvious she was going off now. She smiled back and went.

"Martini on the rocks again?" he heard her say to the man named Barney.

It would not be impossible to get to know her, Malcolm thought, looking after her. He smiled as he thought of the sweat deal he had worked. A whole month on his own down here, while he settled into the new job and looked around for a house. Myrt hadn't liked it much, but he had pointed out that it was important to get the right place, and you couldn't rush that. Especially, he thought, looking again at the bartender, if you made damn sure not to hunt too hard for it. It was too bad he had never been able to move fast with women. Every time he had tried it, he had made a fool of himself. It was a better technique to smile and hope, anyway, he told himself. He had a good smile, after all. He was fairly tall and not bad-looking—still lean, dark-haired. No, smile and sit tight. Calling out *"nurse"* . . . well maybe some could make it work . . .

He sipped his beer to stretch it out. Here, that nurse-caller had caught her again, and she was talking and laughing with him. Maybe the management required her to put up with press people, for the sake of publicity or some such. . . .

He went back to thinking. Money was the problem.

Suppose he sent a wire—better yet, called long distance—back to their bank with something about needing a few hundred dollars suddenly in connection with hunting for a new house? They could take it out of the savings account, wire it to him, and Myrt would never—no, don't be a damn fool. Of course she would, at the end of the month when she made the regular deposit to the account. Besides the bank might not . . . after all, he was leaving their area and going to be switching everything to some new bank down here, after the house was bought and he was in the new job. They might even phone Myrt to check, when he called them asking for the few hundred. Wouldn't that be nice?

The bartender came back. There were only four other drinkers at the bar now, all men. She began to slice some limes by the small sink behind the bar—quite close to Malcolm.

"Work you pretty hard, these launches?" he said, as sympathetically as he could.

"Not bad now. Later on—but I'm off at four. Five through closing, it'll be a madhouse."

Four P.M.

"I can imagine, with guys like that one down there hollering 'nurse' at you all the time."

She laughed.

"He's not that bad. Some of them—but not him. It's just the launch, you know. Everybody thinks it's a great thing—and it is, of course."

"I think it's a great thing, too," Malcolm said, quickly. "When I was young I built model rockets. We had a club. I'm being transferred to a job in Orlando, and I told myself I had to come over and see the launch. I didn't realize there wouldn't be any motel rooms, though. Oh, well."

"I suppose you could call it great." She finished one lime, and started on another, the last of those she had laid out to slice.

"You don't . . . ?"

"Two, three days and then everybody's gone again. And

when's there going to be another launch? Six months? A year, maybe? The space program was supposed to bring in all kinds of industry and business. You see the empty office buildings up and down the street out there?''

''Well, yes. But I thought people around here were all for it.''

''Nobody's against it. It's just that for us it's not the prize package it's made out to be, that's all. And what can ordinary people like us do about it? Nothing. We just have to live with the world they give us.''

''I know what you mean . . .'' he began, but she had just finished slicing the last lime, and now she half-turned to put the dish with the slices an arm's length away, on the service counter behind the bar, with the cherries, olives, nuts and other solid material for drinks. The movement pulled her burgundy-colored dress tight against the side of her body. Following her movement with his eyes, with a little shock he realized that the newsman and everyone else in the bar had left. Freakishly, on this busy day, for a moment they were alone together.

Now was the chance. His heart beat. Go on, you gutless . . .

''It's too bad you aren't one of that press crowd,'' she said, turning back to face him and wiping her hands on a bar towel, ''and you'd print what I said. Not that you would. Now Barney—the one who was just in here—is pretty good; but most of them just want to stand around drinking and sending their papers the stuff the NASA people hand out across the street.''

Too late, he thought. Well, maybe it was all right, still, in the long run. He smiled his best smile at her.

''You know that's all they do, don't you?'' she was saying. ''They don't even make up their own stories. The NASA publicity people do it for them. I could tell them a few real things to print, but they don't want to hear that sort of stuff.''

''I bet you could, too,'' Malcolm said.

''Do you know we've got twelve percent more unemployment here in Brevard County? That's nearly three times the national average. Money's so tight around here nobody's making any of it. And this is the place they take off from to go to the moon and Mars, and places nobody ever heard of 'til twenty years ago. All right, let them. They can go right ahead, if that's what they want. But they could find some work for the local people while they're at it, and bring some money for the local businesses. They could do that if they wanted to."

"Washington always messes up on things like that," said Malcolm. "In Philadelphia, where I live—"

"Just a minute."

She went off to serve a tall, lean man with a deep tan who had just come in. To Malcolm's disgust she started talking with him and did not come back. The bar began to fill again; and soon she was busy.

Malcolm looked at the inch of flattish beer in the bottom of his bottle. Carefully, he poured it into his glass. He could get her attention by ordering another beer, but there were too many people around now, anyway. And money really was a problem. He drained his glass and stood up. She was not even looking in his direction; and she would not notice his going.

He went out. Outside it seemed even hotter and the sunlight was as cruel as life in general. It was not true that he had not been able to find a room. All the good motels like this Holiday Inn had been sold out months in advance. But the little independent places with no national reservation service had not done so well. He had found a unit—one of five behind a filling station about ten miles out on the road to Orlando; and it was even air-conditioned. But it was a small concrete box with a single lamp by the bed. Still, he could buy a six-pack of beer and a paperback book and kill time fairly cheaply. It would not hurt to drop back here at a quarter to four in the afternoon when she got off. Anything might happen.

5

About the same time Malcolm Shroeder was carrying two six-packs of Schlitz out to his three-year-old sedan, James Brille was getting ready to leave the home of the bartender to whom Malcolm had talked. Her name was Aletha Shrubb, and Jim had been staying with her for eight days now, ever since he had met her, his first evening on Merritt Island.

Jim's appointment with Willy Fesser was for two o'clock in the afternoon, from which Jim gathered there would be no meal of any kind involved. Accordingly, he had just finished a liverwurst sandwich and a bottle of root beer, and tidied up after himself in Aletha's kitchen. He noticed now that the garbage sack was almost full. He toed the foot lever that flipped the garbage container's top back, lifted out the nearly full sack and tucked in an empty one. The brown paper crackled pleasantly as he spread it out to fill the inside of the container, and the letters ER GOOD FOOD caught his eye for a second before they were pressed firmly against the inside of the metal container. Jim nodded approvingly at the letters. He liked doing things in the house. Finished, he flipped the lid closed again and took up the full sack. Carrying it out across the driveway to the two garbage cans standing in the shade of a willow tree, he waved to Mrs. Wocjek, Aletha's neighbor on the left, who was setting out the long length of a fat green soaker hose on her lawn.

"Takes a lot of water?" he said, nodding at the close, bright green of the lawn.

"That's all right," said Mrs. Wocjek. "It's free."

"Free?"

He put the garbage in the one garbage can that was still empty and fitted the metal cover firmly back on to it. Then he went over to Mrs. Wocjek, who was now turning the handle of a faucet on a pipe that seemed to go directly down into the lawn.

"Aletha didn't tell you?" Mrs. Wocjek said. "There's water under all this land here. You just drill down and tap it."

Jim was agreeably surprised. He looked with approval at the hose, then turned his gaze back to the woman. Sara Wocjek was no more than half a dozen years older than Aletha, square-jawed, big-boned, not fat, and nearly as tall as Jim himself. She must be five-eight, or even nine, Jim thought. He liked her. In fact, he liked people generally; which was one reason he had been able to get on good terms with most of the neighbors here, even in these few days. The area was a bedroom neighborhood of Merritt Island with houses now in the forty-thousand-dollar range, but which had probably originally sold for a fifth of that; and during the day it was populated mainly by women and children.

"And there's enough pressure there to make it work?" Jim asked.

"You see," Mrs. Wocjek said.

He nodded.

"You have any luck with a job yet?" Mrs. Wocjek asked.

"I'm seeing someone today."

"Good job?"

"I don't know," he said. "You can't ever tell with sales. I won't know until I talk to whoever it is."

"You get it, and it's a good job, you and Aletha give us a ring. Harry and I and you two'll go out and celebrate."

"Aletha'll be ready to celebrate, anyway," he said. "I've been on her hands some days now."

"Don't you think it," Mrs. Wocjek said. "It's not easy for someone as young as Aletha after a divorce. I wish more of her family'd drop by and spend some time with her."

"Maybe they will," Jim said. He looked at her and she stared back frankly and cheerfully. It was perfectly clear that she understood Jim was not Aletha's cousin; but, liking Aletha—and now, him—did not give a damn.

"I guess I got to go," he said. "Let you know how it comes out."

"You do that."

He turned and went back into the house, locked the two doors and put on his suit coat. Spreading the collar of his yellow sport shirt above the collar of the brown sport coat, he checked his general appearance. All in all, he was not getting old too fast. He still had the round face and the black, curly hair, though the hair was getting just a bit thin. Also, his sport coat was becoming a little tight; but the tan slacks, now that Aletha—no, it had been Betty Rawls, last month in Houston—had let them out, they were quite loose and comfortable. He smiled at himself experimentally in the mirror. OK—wouldn't frighten any kids, yet. Good enough for being forty-two.

He went out to his rental car, feeling a genuine regret at leaving. He might not be coming back. It would have felt good to cut the grass before he took off; but that would be going too far. Every time he did something like that, he left a piece of himself behind.

Mrs. Wocjek was back inside her house, and none of the other neighbors were in sight. He turned the Gremlin into Larch Avenue, off Laburnum, and drove toward the causeway.

His destination was at the far end of Merritt Island. He approached it about twenty minutes later, down a winding, two-lane asphalt road. A heavy stucco gateway with the name "Kelly" spelled out above it in black wrought-iron framed a single lane of asphalt leading in to a close stand of pine trees festooned with Spanish moss. What was beyond the trees could not be seen from the road. A sawhorse had been set across the driveway, blocking it. Jim pulled his car to a stop at the sawhorse, got out, saw no one, got back inside and blew the horn of his car.

A moment later, a big, middle-aged man in white shirt, police-style cap and olive trousers, armed with a short-barreled revolver, came out of the trees and up to the car.

"Yea-ah?" he said, putting his face down to the open window of Jim's car.

"My name's Brigham, William Brigham," Jim said. "I think I'm expected."

"Mr. Brigham? Why, yes, sir." The man straightened. "Straight in. You can park down by the garages, there."

"Thanks," said Jim. He watched the man lift the sawhorse out of the way and then drove on through. Beyond the pines, he went for a short distance through an orange grove, its trees looking somewhat neglected, and then through a further screen of pines, heavy with Spanish moss. He emerged at last on a curving driveway that divided a very large expanse of neatly mowed lawn from a massive house of gray-brown brick. Wide steps led down from a half-pillared porch to the driveway; and farther on were a cluster of smaller buildings with a large circle of asphalt before them, where several cars, newer than his, were parked.

The lawn, he saw as he passed in front of the house, was not as flat as it had first looked. There was a considerable crest to it and hidden by that crest, lower down in front of the place where the cars were parked, he discovered a large, rectangular swimming pool, with some umbrella-shaded tables and chairs alongside. In two of those chairs a man and a woman were sitting, doing something with what seemed to be a stack of papers.

One of the smaller buildings, Jim saw, had a wide door lifted, showing several more cars inside. Jim parked his car beside one of those in the open circle, got out, and looked around. There was no one about to tell him where to go, and it seemed to him that the people at the poolside table were looking at him expectantly.

He walked down toward them. The two turned out to be a young man, his black hair cropped short, holding a pen and clipboard in his hands; and a lean, tall, still good-looking woman in her sixties with reddish-brown hair, wearing a yellow lounging robe that contrasted with the deep tan of her strong-boned face.

"Dear lad," she said in a husky, near-baritone voice, when Jim got close, "who are you, anyway?"

"Bill Brigham," Jim said. "I'm here to talk to Willy Fesser."

"Oh. Willeee," said the woman, nodding, drawing the last syllable of the name out. She looked at the young man. "Dear lad, where *is* Willy?"

The young man scowled.

"Library, I think," he said. He passed a paper across to

the woman. "Here's the caterer's estimate for the post-launch party."

The woman took it and held it out several feet from her eyes.

"So expensive," she murmured.

"I did my best."

"I know you did. Dear lad—" She broke off, looking at Jim again. "Didn't you hear? The library!"

Her free hand flipped at the wrist, commanding him toward the house. He turned and went.

The front door, when he reached it, was not only unlocked but ajar. He stepped into a high-ceilinged entrance hall with a wide staircase at its far end. Closed, heavy oak doors were spaced at intervals down both sides of the hall. One of the doors opened and two slim, dark-haired men, dressed in identical, sharply pressed white slacks and white short-sleeved shirts, came out, arguing in Spanish. They ignored him, going on toward the far end of the hall where a corridor disappeared under the wide stairs.

"Hey," said Jim. "Where's the library?"

They stopped, looked at him, considered his clothes, and one pointed toward the third door from the entrance, across the hall.

"Is there, sir."

"Thanks."

"You welcome."

Jim went to the door and knocked on it. There was no answer. He opened it and went in, to find a long, book-lined room scattered with sofas and easy chairs, and Willy Fesser at its far-end in a plum-colored wing chair by a bay window, a notepad and pencil in his hands. Jim went toward him.

"Hello," he said.

"Sit down," Willy grunted, nodding toward a mate to the chair he was in. He had acquired a touch of middle-European accent since Jim had last seen him.

Jim sat. Willy, he saw, was showing his age. He could not have been more than four or five years older than Jim, but he had put on even more weight in the past nine months than Jim had. The double-breasted dark-blue suit he wore was creased by its tightness. Of course, thought Jim, Willy liked to eat and Europe was full of good restaurants. But the extra flesh was soft and sagging, and Willy's face was drawn, rather than full. The gray hairs combed over his balding skull no longer seemed worth the effort of their careful arrangement.

"You've got some reason for being in the area, here?" Willy asked.

"I'm hunting a sales job, of course," Jim said.

"You quit that job of yours selling farm machinery in Denver?"

"What do you think?" Jim said. "I'd leave loose ends? Besides, I can get it back any time I want to."

"Better not," Willy said. "Better not go right back there after this. Go some place like up the east coast and live for a half a year or so. All right, from now on, you only talk to me by phone."

He tore off a sheet from his notepad and passed it across to Jim.

"Got it." Jim glanced at the notepaper and tucked it in his pocket. "I'll learn the number and get rid of the paper. But, where'll I get in touch with you if I need you in a hurry? Here?"

"You don't need to know where I'll be."

"The hell I don't," said Jim. "Things happen. You know that as well as I do."

"All right." Willy glanced out the window. Jim, looking out also, saw the swimming pool, the baritone-voiced woman and the black-haired man. There was also now a figure in white slacks and shirt, offering them a tray with glasses on it.

"All right," said Willy, again. "Here. But the Duchess doesn't know anything about anything—you remember that. And she actually doesn't."

"What good does that do?" Jim said. "Everybody knows she rents space to anybody in the business."

"All right, she's useful," said Willy. "You never mind about the rest of it. There's got to be some place out in the open to talk, and she makes it with these parties of hers. Just follow the rules."

"It isn't as if she needs the money."

"Never try to figure who needs money," said Willy, heavily. "You need it. That's all I want to know. Now, here's your job. The federal representative to this Expedition business is the U.S. Undersecretary for the Development of Space. His name's Jens Wylie. You want to put a tap on what he says to his own people. He's staying with the other diplomatic reps to the launch, at the Holiday Inn. The three top floors there are all theirs."

Willy broke off, leaned sideways in his chair to enable him to get a hand into his right trouser pocket, and came up with a short key, which he handed Jim.

"Data, equipment," he said. "It's all there for you in the bus station locker that this fits. Four hundred a week."

"Come on, now," said Jim. "We talked five. That's why I left Denver."

"I'm sorry." Willy shrugged briefly. "It turns out the money's just not there after all. Four hundred."

Jim got up.

"I think I'll go get my job back," he said.

He turned and walked away. When he got to the door, Willy had not stirred. He still sat in his chair, once again writing in his notebook. Jim turned again, walked back and sat down.

"Fuck you. All right," he said.

"That's good," said Willy, not looking up. "Hang on to that bus locker key. It's a duplicate. After midnight, every Saturday A.M., your money'll be there for you. Look out for a federal security number at the motel named Albert Gervais. He's sharper than most."

"Got it." Jim rose to his feet. He paused. "Nothing down?"

"There'll be some expense money in the locker with the other stuff."

Jim nodded, turned and went out. Outside the building the Duchess and her social secretary—or whoever—still sat by the pool. Jim got in his car and drove slowly out through the orange grove and past the massive gateway, trying to make himself appreciate the fact that everything was set.

As usual, once he was into it, he had a slightly sick feeling in his stomach, a sort of wonder that life could have turned out this way for him. It was the illegal part of what he had to do that worried him. God knew it was all nonsense—anything Willy was engaged in had to be. Jim had never been mixed up in anything important, and undoubtedly never would be. People like him existed only to supply routine information for people like Willy to sell to other people who needed it to justify themselves to other people higher up yet. All of it done with the appropriate cloak-and-dagger stuff, but still nonsense. Each time he finished one of these jobs, Jim swore it was the last time. There was almost no risk . . . but still. Things could blow up, and he could get sacrificed—for the sake of somebody's appearance, if nothing else. What he would be doing was technically illegal, and . . . jail would kill him. It was not that he was not tough, in his own way. He could still handle himself in most rough situations. But inside, gut-wise, he was too easygoing. In a federal prison they would find that out.

All the trouble came from the fact that, somehow, he could not hold on to money. Sales had trained him all wrong, he thought. He was just good enough at it to make a steady, small living, but not good enough to make it big. He had reached the point of just drifting. He had been at that point when Willy had contacted him the first time, half a dozen years ago. Jim had been selling electronics then; now he made it a point to sell anything else but. The first time he worked for Willy had been just to see if he could do it. After that it was for money. Not that much money either, but more than he could pick up selling. Each time a small stake. Enough for the moment, but not enough to build on; so that when Willy contacted him again some months later he was flat and ready to try one more time. If only he could break it big once, if he could just take the money this time and put it into something that would pay as much as five times over. But he had tried that. All that happened was that he lost, each time. Better to live it up while the extra money lasted. At least, that way he picked up a few memories.

But God, for some money . . . real money. He was not really a criminal and criminal ways were closed to him. What he did for Willy was just nonsense. But God, for some *real* money. He wondered how much Willy had, one notch up from him, from brokering the information people like Jim passed on. He wondered how much the Duchess had, moving around the world for thirty years now, running a traveling flea market for all the small shady dealers in international politics. Enough, anyway, to rent that estate during this launch and throw her parties.

Or maybe they were both as broke in their own ways, Willy and the Dutchess, as Jim was himself. One thing, though. If so, they were broke on higher levels than he, and he envied them that.

He headed back into the center of Merritt Island. He could stay with Aletha safely for a while yet, he thought. One thing for sure, Willy would not actually be living at the estate. He might have a bedroom there, but his real hole would be somewhere else. Willy had lied about that—after this many years Jim could tell when the other man was lying. Willy was too old a hand to let anyone know where he was stashed. He took care of himself, first. That meant that any hope of getting hold of him in a hurry if things did blow up was pretty faint. Jim would be out on a limb by himself if anything happened; and Willy would fade discreetly into the sunset.

Oh well, there was nothing for it now but to play the hand he had just bought.

As soon as he saw Jim's Gremlin pull out of sight, Willy went to a phone on a nearby library table and called a cab. Forty-five minutes later he was seated at a pay phone in the air-conditioned lobby of the motel in which he had a room under the name of Robert K. Larsen. He dropped a coin in the slot, punched out a number, and listened as the phone at the other end was picked up.

"Hello," said a male voice. It was not the voice of Walther Guenther, but Willy ignored that fact. If the Pan-European diplomat was not himself listening in at this moment, he would be rehearing the conversation verbatim within minutes.

"Hello," Willy said. "This is Alan Grover, at Overseer Employment. I just wanted to let you know that I've already sent out that new gardener you needed. He should be busy at work shortly."

"I'm sorry," said the voice at the far end. "You must have the wrong number." The line clicked and hummed, disconnected.

Satisfied, Willy got up and headed across the lobby into the bar.

"Yes, a martini," he said to the bartender. "Straight up, Tanqueray, lemon twist."

When the drink came, he sipped at it gratefully. A couple of these and then dinner, a good dinner even if it was a little early for one. A little celebration. The wheels were turning now. He had made certain that Guenther was hiring him out of his own pocket. A private matter. That meant a gamble on the part of the Pan-European representative that might pay off in personal political advantage back home. A little money spent on the chance that this Wylie, inexperienced as he was, would either do something foolish of which Guenther could take advantage, or that the surveillance would uncover something else that Guenther could make use of, to hint that Wylie was not the innocuous political cardboard cutout he seemed.

That made the situation very comfortable for Willy. It was always better to work for individuals than deal with organizations. Easier to cut loose, if necessary; and there was the long-shot chance of stumbling across some information that would later turn out to be valuable.

At any rate, he deserved a good meal now—aside from the fact that if he waited until the regular hour, as a single diner in this launch-crowded town he would have to tip somebody out of all proportion just to get a table.

6

Shortly before nine P.M., the marsnauts and their personal guests went by VTOL aircraft from the Operations and Checkout Building to the landing pad on the roof of the Holiday Inn. The reception was held in the private dining room on the ninth floor; and with security guards manning the elevators, the guests were taken from the roof down to it. The representatives were already there; and President Fanzone arrived less than ten minutes later. Jens caught Selden Rethe's eye as the President's private secretary entered the reception room a few steps behind the stocky, dark-haired Fanzone. Selden shook his head, briefly.

Jens felt cold. If that meant that the President had already turned him down, without excuse or explanation . . . for a second he toyed with the idea of resigning. Then he came back to common sense. Far from resigning, he knew that he would fight to hold on to this job if anyone tried to take it away from him. There was no need for anyone to remind him that as a newsman-turned-diplomat he was a paper tiger, but the Mars Expedition represented everything in which he had ever believed and he wanted to be part of it.

But the reception had gone tinny and hollow on him. He had skipped dinner in order to spend the extra time with Lin; and that had been real and solid enough. But now, with a glass of champagne in him that had gone directly from his empty stomach to his head, he was back in the quicksand of politics again. Standing with his refilled glass in a corner of the reception room, he had a moment's disorientation in which he felt like a character in a bad play. All the other people present seemed to be going through a ritual social dance, making expected gestures, speaking expected commonplaces, and murmuring expected replies.

In the midst of all this, however, he caught sight of Wendy and Tad Hansard and the world clicked back to reality. As he had said to Lin, she and Wendy were alike physically; and the sight of Wendy turned the cardboard stage figures back to flesh and blood. Returning from his momentary slip into fantasy, he was struck with an idea. He moved across the room and spoke quietly in Tad's ear.

"Got a second?"

Tad, a wide smile still on his tanned, wedge-shaped face for the wife of the Air Force general to whom he and Wendy had been talking, turned casually to face Jens. Together they took a step away from the others, and once again Jens was touched by a feeling of incongruity in the fact that this man who would lead the Expedition to Mars should be half a head shorter than himself.

"What is it?" Tad asked.

"I haven't had any luck getting through to the President about the experiment schedule," Jens said. "Why don't you have a shot at getting him alone yourself?"

Tad smiled bleakly.

"I don't know how to talk to a president," he said in his soft southern voice. "How do you do it?"

"The same way you talk to anyone else."

"All right," said Tad. "But don't hope for anything. I never made the debating society back in high school or college."

"It isn't a debate," said Jens. "You know your business. You're the astronaut—I mean, the marsnaut—the man who knows. Just tell it to him like it is."

"I've got nothing to lose. So I'll try it," said Tad. His voice sank into a drawl. "But I got a hunch it ain't a-gonna work." The tone of his voice was light but the skin around his eyes was drawn tight.

He turned back to the general's wife and Wendy. Jens faded away, mingling until he found the group that included Selden Rethe. He stuck with them, hoping to get a second with Selden, alone. But when the group dwindled to four, Selden excused himself and moved away so abruptly that Jens could not follow without making it obvious he was doing just that.

He kept his eye on Selden after that, and made a couple of further attempts to get close to the man. But it became obvious that Selden was determined not to be trapped in any situation where Jens could speak to him privately. Later, however, Jens caught a glimpse of Fanzone and Tad, momentarily isolated. Tad was speaking and the President was listening and nodding.

The reception ended at ten-thirty with a cold buffet supper. Jens found himself eating like a starving man; which, he suddenly decided, he was. With food inside him, optimism and courage returned. He was turning over in his head several wild scenes of insisting on talking to Fanzone before the President left, when he felt a tap on his elbow. He turned around, still holding his fork and plate, to look directly into Selden's face.

"If you'll step into the back room over there without attracting attention," Selden said, "he'll talk to you after everyone else has gone—for a few minutes."

He turned away without waiting for an answer. Jens stood, mechanically cleaning up the food that was left on his plate, feeling a fierce determination and hope lift in him. Fanzone had been nodding when he talked to Tad. Perhaps Tad had got through to him, and this decision to talk to Jens was to get substantiation of what Tad had said. The argument might be won, after all.

Jens held grimly to that hope. The last five years of statistics on world conditions had made him a believer in the need to explore space. It was incredible how no one else seemed to realize how a breakdown now, at this point in the Expedition, could delay the move to space beyond a point where it could be achieved in time to save big trouble back here on Earth. Blindness is always the enemy, he thought. Everyone wanting to go their own way selfishly with business as usual— while all the time the house was burning down around their ears. *"Not I,"* said the pig . . .

He did as Selden had said. Twenty minutes later the last of the voices from the reception room faded into silence. A moment after that, Paul Fanzone, followed by Selden, strode into the attached bedroom where Jens had been waiting, sitting in the room's one armchair. Selden carefully closed the door behind them and Jens scrambled to his feet.

Fanzone ignored the armchair. He stayed on his feet, halting in the center of the room as Jens came up to him, so that when Jens reached him and stopped, they stood facing each other like two fighters in a ring.

"It's good of you to see me, sir," Jens said. "I can't tell you—"

"Don't thank me," said Fanzone. "You've got nothing to thank me for."

The swarthiness of his skin, which masked the signs of tiredness well enough from the television cameras, did not hide them in this softly-lighted room as he stood a few feet from Jens. Fanzone's face had sagged slightly even in the six months since Jens had seen him to accept the position of undersecretary. There were little heavinesses of flesh at the corners of his mouth and under his eyes. Almost as tall as Jens then, he now seemed somehow shorter; his football player's shoulders were rounded and humped, contracting his neck and giving his head, with its alert and questing eyes, something of the aspect of a turtle's. For a man in his early fifties, he still looked good; but not as good as he had six months ago.

Jens gazed at him with the odd feeling of mingled respect and sympathy. Because of Fanzone's long friendship with Senator Wylie, Jens had known this man who was now President since he himself had been thirteen years old. There was no one Jens had admired more during the last ten years. The elder Wylie had become a state governor with wealth and family behind him to help him to almost anything he wanted. Fanzone had made it from nowhere to his present office solely on faith in himself and in what he wanted to do.

"The President," said Selden, who had come up from the closet door to join them, moving silently over the rug of the room, "only has about a minute, Jens. This visit was supposed to be purely social."

"He understands that, Sel," said Fanzone. He spoke abruptly to Jens. "You're standing in for me. That means you're supposed to say my words and think my thoughts.

You're not some independent liaison between me and the 'nauts."

"I realize that too, sir," said Jens. "But the Mars Expedition itself is important to the United States; and I thought you'd want—"

He was interrupted by Fanzone's weary exhalation of breath. The President walked around him and sat down in the armchair, motioning Jens to a seat on the edge of the bed, facing the chair. Jens sat down.

"Look, Jens," said Fanzone, leaning forward in the chair. "You're not a son-of-a-bitch diplomat. You're not a politician. I could have had my pick of either to put in your shoes down here. All the other nations sent experienced people as their deputy ministers. Don't you know why I picked some bastardly amateur, an ex-newspaperman?"

"I understand it was because you wanted someone who knew the press and could work with it—"

"All right, that too," said Fanzone. "But that was a bonus. The main reason was to put a representative of mine in with the other representatives who was obviously some amateur none of them needed to worry about."

He looked at Jens for a minute.

"I think you knew that," he said. "But if you didn't, and the information bothers you, Jens, it shouldn't. I'm not suggesting you can't get the job done. I'm just saying you're a damn amateur among professionals—put there deliberately so that the professionals will know they don't need to compete with you—or me."

"Yes, sir," said Jens. "I knew that. And I'm not upset about it. I never was."

"I planned on you stumbling over your feet here a little," Fanzone went on. "Hell, I wanted you to! Just to reassure people like Mayence and Verigin that you weren't a wolf in sheep's clothing. I wanted them to be sure they had a U.S. president who'd be absent from the scene; and a U.S. undersecretary who was obviously nothing to worry about. But do you know why I wanted that?"

"No, sir," said Jens, since it was plain that was the answer Fanzone wanted.

"Too right you don't!" said Fanzone. "And the reason

you don't know is because you're from our country. You're like everybody else. You take everything that's American about this mission for granted, as a natural right—just as if we owned space personally. But if you were from Pan-Europe or Russia, or any one of the other countries involved here, you'd understand in one second. More than any other head of government involved here, I've got to lean over backward to keep from looking as if I'm trying to run things.''

''I understand that, sir,'' said Jens. ''But—''

He stopped. Fanzone had risen and was striding toward the door. Jens got hastily to his own feet.

''You tell him, Sel,'' the President said. ''And make sure he understands.''

He disappeared through the door.

Jens turned back to Selden Rethe with an emptiness in him that was not helped by the food now filling him. Selden had not moved from where he stood since the President had entered the bedroom.

''The trouble is, Jens,'' Selden said, ''you're looking at only a corner of the picture.''

''I'm looking at the lives of *six men*, for God's sake!'' said Jens. ''I'm looking at the success or failure of the Expedition, if they start to break down. Damn it, Sel! Don't you realize it could actually come to that?''

''The Expedition itself's only a corner of the picture,'' said Selden remotely, his voice unchanging. ''You heard the President tell you we have to lean over backward to keep from looking as if we're running the Expedition. It's how the whole thing looks that's important.''

Jens looked at him for a moment.

''You can't mean that,'' he said. ''That looks are the first thing.''

''Of course I mean it.''

''You talk—'' said Jens, and found his throat was dry. He swallowed and began again. ''You talk as if there's nothing to this but politics.''

''In a sense there isn't,'' Selden stood, watching him. ''It's international politics, of course, which isn't anything like the politics of the newspaper cartoons, or the election speeches or the stage shows that have fun with what goes on in Washington. You may think the Expedition's a great thing, Jens—"

"I do," said Jens.

"Well, you're wrong then," Selden said. "The great thing is setting up alliances here on Earth so people can work together to survive. I know it makes very pretty reading, how we need to do things like study the sun from space and come up with fusion power before we run out of fuel, and so on. But that sort of thing's only read by a small bunch of intellectuals and scientists. Most people aren't interested in hearing about an energy crisis until their lights go out and there's no fuel for the fire."

"Look," said Jens, "I know what you're talking about, Sel. I've been around Washington myself for ten years, remember? But it's too late for playing politics, even international politics, at this point."

"No," said Selden. "At any point, we have to be practical. We've got to deal for example with the woman who isn't interested in pollution until the food she buys poisons her children; or she goes to the supermarket and there's nothing there for her to buy at all. Don't tell me that most of the people in the world don't have supermarkets, because that's not what I'm talking about. I'm talking about a sort of attitude that's common in all populations. Most people are people who want practical answers, because their first impulse after ignoring oncoming trouble is to turn around and shoot the first person they can put the blame on, once they've admitted the trouble's there. The 'nauts and people like you, Jens, might be able to afford having stars in your eyes. The rest of us have to be hardheaded and realistic."

"Damn it, but I'm *being* hardheaded and realistic!" said Jens. "The Expedition's got to work to make the sort of working together you talk about work!"

"Hopefully, yes," said Selden. "But there's really nothing you or I can do about the Expedition being a success. That's up to the marsnauts. Our job is to concentrate on keeping the lid on here at home—and that's not easy. As it happens, the governments cooperating in this effort are all under a great deal of pressure, economically and otherwise, on their home fronts right now. If we could have handpicked the time of the launch, things might have been a good deal easier, politically. But we're tied to this launch window because the scientists and engineers say so—''

"You mean, because a moment when Earth, Mars, and Venus are all going to be lined up just right only comes when the planets make it available," said Jens. "Let's not put it on the scientists and engineers."

"Put it any way you want," said Selden. "I'm trying to talk sense to you, Jens, but you're making it very difficult. The fact remains that this launch comes at an awkward time, internationally. Landing on Mars won't butter anyone's bread immediately. But the chance to demonstrate the role we can play in international cooperation could lead to new agreements, a breakthrough—a new world alignment that could lead in turn to a cutback on defense cost and more butter for everybody the day after tomorrow."

"And what about next week? What about next month, next year—" Jens broke off. It was no use, with Selden. Jens was wasting his breath and as well risking the loss of this job he still wanted.

"We'll always have crises, of course," Selden was saying. "And we'll meet them as they come up, naturally. That's the cross governments have to bear. Of course, we all like to dream of the far future; but some of us have to deal with the present and that includes you, Jens. The facts right now are that the President can't afford to look as if he's using U.S. muscle on the other cooperating members, over some little thing like this scheduling."

Jens stood, empty of words.

"He really feels you're the right man for the spot here, you know, Jens," said Selden. "I think so, too. But he needs to feel you understand the real priorities. Now, I believe you do. But I want to be able to go to him and tell him you do. Can I?"

There it was, in a nutshell. Everyone—and that meant everyone—was washing their hands of the work overload problem. The message to Jens was plain—do the same or turn in his papers. No! There was a bitter taste in his mouth. He would hang in there at any cost, including eating crow, here and now. All right, thought Jens grimly. All God damn right!

"Of course you can," he said. He forced himself to stay calm. "I goofed, asking to talk to him about this. I can see that now."

"Then there's no problem," said Selden.

He turned a little toward the door of the room.

"Don't get the idea there was anything wrong with your being concerned about the Expedition, Jens," he said. "It's just that the suggestion can't originate with us. You see that now?"

"I see that," said Jens. The food he had eaten was sour in his stomach.

"Good. There's nothing wrong with pointing out a problem; it's just a matter of making sure it's done by the right people, at the right time."

"Of course," said Jens. He stepped toward the door himself and Selden fell in alongside him after they had passed through it into the now-empty dining room with its many tables thickly littered with the remains of cake and fruit and emptied champagne glasses.

"You know, Jens," said Selden, as they went toward the front door of the suite, "the President trusts you. That's the real reason he put you in here. He needed someone he could count on to do the right thing without obvious instruction all the time; and because he's known you most of your life, he's been sure you'd do just that. He knows your instincts are sound. You understand what I mean?"

"Sure," said Jens.

He thought of the man he had known since his own father had been in the governor's office in St. Paul, and Fanzone had been the brand-new state attorney general. If Fanzone had known Jens long enough to know him well, Jens had also been acquainted with Fanzone long enough to know the other equally well; and Jens had always been sure there was a sincere dedication in the man, the dedication of someone who believed in giving his lifetime for a purpose. But that had been looking at Fanzone from a distance. Now they were down in the trenches together and standing close enough to smell each other's sweat.

"At the same time," said Selden, "as the chief executive he has to do what the conditions call for and he needs people who'll follow him without question. He doesn't have time to stop and explain every step of the way to those of us who fetch and carry for him.''

''No,'' said Jens.

They went out, with Selden carefully shutting the door behind them, into the corridor which was icy cold from the air conditioning and very clean.

7

Barney Winstrom, head of the camera team for the Southwest Cable TV Network, came back to Merritt Island after checking the power lines running out to the van parked in the vehicle lot below the press stands; and after some searching, he found a parking spot at the motel. It was the Holiday Inn just opposite the Press Center, and, like all the large chain motels, was jammed when a launch was imminent. The only reason Barney and his team had rooms here was because Southwest Network had some local clout. Even six months before, all room reservations here had technically been filled.

He left the panel truck and, entering the Inn, glanced at his watch. Only a little after ten. He turned into the cocktail lounge and found a seat at the curving bar. Again, lucky. Most of the people here must still be trying to get fed in the dining room. Another hour and they would be three deep, at least, around the bar. Right now there were half a dozen seats empty.

The night bartender was some ten years younger than Aletha Shrubb.

''*Nurse*,'' called Barney when she came by. ''My medication, nurse, please!''

She laughed as she went past to serve the drink she was

carrying, then came back to make him a martini on the rocks.

"Don't you get tired of that?" she asked when she brought it to him.

"My medication? Of course I do," said Barney. "But I know it's good for me, so I take it anyway."

She laughed again. She was small, blonde, and good-looking, without being pretty enough to trade on her looks for a better job than this. She had the unfettered laugh of a sixteen-year-old, Barney thought, suddenly hearing again the laughter of Jessa, who would be eighteen now, but whom he had not seen in three years, since Wilma had taken herself and the two kids to live in Spain.

"You drink too many of those you'll see how good it is for you."

"Never," said Barney coming back to the present, to wink solemnly at her. "Only what the doctor prescribes."

She was called away. There was a man in a green cloth jacket helping her bartend, but Barney noticed that she was still serving three-quarters of the customers in the chairs on either side of him, as well as the table waitresses' station.

He sipped the martini, which tasted like all other martinis, and tried to see himself between the bottles hiding the mirror behind the bar shelf. He could catch a glimpse of brown curly hair and a section of incipient double chin—that was all. However, his eyes were now adjusting to the dimness of the cocktail lounge and he looked around the curve of the bar. Beyond the man in the chair at his left was an empty seat and beyond that his eyes collided with those of a dark-haired woman in her late twenties, smoothly dressed and with a good body, if a little cold of face.

Hooker, Barney thought automatically. As if he had said the words aloud, she turned her face abruptly away from him. He ran his eye over the rest of the bar and saw no familiar features—no faces of newspeople, anyhow.

The martini was beginning to spread its soothing fingers through his insides. Relaxed, he picked up the sharp odor of sweat from the man on his left. He looked and saw that his neighbor, a slim, black-haired, thirtyish man in a gray suit, was rolling his empty Schlitz beer bottle back and forth between his palms and sneaking occasional glances across the space of the empty seat between him and the dark-haired woman.

The sight saddened Barney, because it occurred to him automatically that once it would have irritated him. If the sucker wanted her, Barney would have told himself then, why didn't he just move over and tell her so? But that was the way he would have reacted, watching them in his twenties. Now he was wiser. He himself had got over being self-conscious by the time he was in tenth grade; but now, nearly thirty years later, was aware that most of the men and women in the world never did. It was the reminder of his own advancing age that saddened him.

Well, well . . .

The martini was almost gone from the ice in his lowball glass. He picked up the olive to eat it before ordering another, and felt a tap on his right shoulder. He turned.

"Jens, you old bastard!" he shouted delightedly, dropping the olive back in the glass. He remembered suddenly to lower his voice. "Who let you out of the cage? Don't you know you diplomatic fairies aren't allowed out without an escort?"

They gripped hands.

"Nobody worries about me in my off hours," said Jens. "Look, Barney, one of your engineers up in your suite told me I might look for you down here, if you weren't out at the press site. Got a minute?"

"Hell, I got the whole night," said Barney. "Just a second."

He turned back to the secretly sweating individual on his left.

"Excuse me," he said loudly, breathing in the man's ear, "would you mind shifting over one seat so I can talk to my friend, here?"

"What? Oh. Why, yes." The other glanced at him startledly, suspiciously. "Not at all. That's all right."

He moved. Half-grinning, Barney looked after him for a second.

"Sit down, Jens," he said, turning his head back. "What'll you have? Nurse!"

"Anything," Jens said. The bartender was coming up inside the bar.

"Nurse," said Barney. "More medicine for me. And a dose of the same for my friend, here."

"Christ, no! Sorry, Barney," Jens said. "It's a good thought but I've just finished being floated in champagne at an official dinner. Make it Scotch and water."

"One scotch and water, one medicine," said the bartender, turning away.

"Such gentle hands," Barney crooned to her departing back. He turned to Jens once more. "What's up? You just decide to take the rest of the evening off?"

"Would you have a match?" the dark-haired woman was already throatily asking the nervous, black-haired man. He fumbled in his pockets.

"Not exactly," said Jens. "I've got a favor to ask of you. There's a girl named Lin West I'd like you to give a ride to, out to the press site tomorrow in the van."

"Van's already out there and wired in," said Barney. "That's why I just came back from the site. But there's other wheels. She got a press pass, or do we have to take her in under a tarpaulin?"

"Don't worry about that," said Jens. "She's with *New World* magazine, down to do a feature on the wives of the 'nauts."

"We can take her out in the panel," said Barney. "Only that'll be leaving here about nine in the morning, so she better be good at getting up early. Just tell her which our rooms are, here. She can knock on any of the three doors."

"Thanks, Barney," said Jens. He gulped hastily at his drink.

"Slow down," said Barney, watching him. "Sit and talk a spell. Didn't I always tell you, never rush your drinking? Only amateurs rush their drinking, afraid it'll all be gone before they can get their share. Later on you learn there's always somebody to buy you a drink. It's getting somebody to buy you a meal that's hard. Sit and tell me how it's going. How do you like it up there where the air's thin and expensive?"

Jens let his weight settle back in the bar seat. The back of it pressed against the lower part of his spine solidly, almost comfortingly.

"It's great to be part of this thing," he said. "It really is, Barney."

"I believe you," said Barney, and broke off to beam at the bartender, who had just come up to deliver another round of drinks. "Just in time. I could feel a seizure coming on."

"Sure," she said tolerantly.

Barney watched her move off for a second.

"I believe you," he said again. "But what I asked you was how you like it up around the smell of Fanzone's cigars."

"I'm not actually around the smell of his cigars," said Jens. "This is my beat, here. I've only been in the White House twice; once when I was hired, and one other time."

"But you see the man."

"Occasionally, when he comes down here. Usually, the only one I see or talk to is State Department or Selden Rethe—and I do that mostly on the phone."

"Rethe?" said Barney, sipping his martini. "He's a cold-assed bastard."

"Why," said Jens, looking at him, "what did Sel ever do to you?"

"Nothing," said Barney, "I never let him get close enough to do anything. I just don't like cold-assed bastards."

He took a little more martini.

"Bastards," he said lightly, "yes. Cold-assed bastards, no."

He had said more than he had meant to, but he thought he could count on Jens not to press it; and, sure enough, Jens shifted conversational ground.

"It's hard to tell, sometimes," Jens said, slowly, "who's really running the show. That's the only real trouble with a job like I've got now."

"Shouldn't be hard," said Barney. "There's only one boss running the show. There's only been one boss since the world began. The general public."

Jens shook his head.

"I used to think that," he said. "I know better now. The public's too far away from the power seat. A small handful of people really run things. The only question is which one of them is actually in charge at any one time."

"Bearcrap," said Barney. "Those characters of yours get to pull the wires for a little while, but either things work out or they don't. If they work out, they get to stay a little while longer and pull. If things don't work out, the public eats them for breakfast. I don't care if it's a democracy, a republic, a Soviet, a commune, a what-the-hell-you-want. When things go wrong, everybody else eats the bosses for breakfast."

He sat for a second.

"Timber wolves do it, too," he said, "when game runs out. It's an instinct in us animals."

"Tell me," said Jens, "from what you've seen of it, how's the general public taking this Expedition to Mars?"

"It's a piece of candy," Barney said. "It's a circus. They like it."

"No, Barney," said Jens, "you know what I mean."

"All right," said Barney. "Three-quarters of the people in the world either aren't hearing about this or are too busy keeping themselves alive to pay any attention. Of the other quarter, ten percent are against it as a waste of money or effort, or something man wasn't meant to do, and fifteen percent are caught up in the idea; only less than five percent of those have really got some understanding of what's going on. Of course, even down at five percent you're talking in the hundreds of millions and it's true that it's out of that same five percent that your wire-pullers come, and ninety-nine percent of those that run the machinery and the economies."

Jens shook his head, but said nothing.

"Damn it, Jens!" said Barney. "What do you want? I know you think this space thing's a necessary step; and maybe I feel the same way about it. But what we think or feel isn't going to matter, because it's not going to work. They're going to mess it up. You can count on it."

"Not necessarily," said Jens.

"Yes, necessarily! Anything like this always gets messed up. It has to, because the machinery that's supposed to make it work is always out of whack one way or another. It's always got crooked cogs and bent wires in it, so it ends by chewing up what it's supposed to produce instead of turning it out whole. Ever see a camel—"

"I know," said Jens. "A camel is a horse designed by a committee."

"Dead right!" said Barney. "And a committee's a sweet-running piece of machinery compared to any government, let alone six governments trying to work together."

"Maybe," said Jens. "But they don't have to always go wrong. Maybe this is the one time the odds will pay off and things go right."

"No, it won't," said Barney, shaking his head. "It can't. You tell yourself that, Jens, you're letting yourself in for getting kicked in the teeth when it does go down the drain."

He stopped talking, emptied his glass, and catching the eye of the bartender, held up one finger.

"Now there you go," he said. "Getting me to talk seriously."

"I guess you're right," said Jens. "Well, I asked the question."

"You did at that," said Barney. "Well, it doesn't hurt to be serious now and then, just so it doesn't get to be a habit—thank you, nurse. And one more Scotch and water for my friend, here."

"No thanks," said Jens, finishing his glass. "I've got to get going."

"Right," said Barney. "Look, after the launch let's get together sometime for an evening and talk."

'I'd like to do that. In fact, I'd like to sit around and talk now."

"Somebody waiting?" asked Barney—and then wished he had bitten his tongue off before he said it.

"You could say that," said Jens, grinning tiredly.

He got down from his seat.

"Thanks for the drink, Barney," he said. "And the seriousness. I'll see you before too long."

"Live well," said Barney, and watched him go out of the cocktail lounge.

Of course there was somebody waiting for him, Barney thought. It would be this Lin West, no doubt; and nobody to deserve it more. But what was getting into him, that he couldn't keep his mouth shut? It couldn't be the martinis, after all these years. The funny thing was, he'd known he shouldn't say it even before he had opened his mouth, and then he'd gone ahead and said it anyway. Giving himself away, giving himself away . . .

It was the bit of remembered poetry that had made him blurt it out like that—the tear-jerking lines that had jumped into the front of his mind the minute Jens had talked about going. He had almost quoted it to Jens. Thank God he had held back that much. He said the lines to himself now, under his breath, the couplet from Kipling's *McAndrews' Hymn*:

> *There's none at any port for me, by driving fast or slow,*
> *Since Elsie Campbell went to Thee, Lord, thirty years*
> *ago . . .*

Not that Wilma had gone to any Lord. She had taken the girls and gone to Reno, and then to Seattle, and then to Spain . . . well, it didn't matter. In an age of poetry, unlike this twentieth century, there might have been room for one more bad poet. Then everything might have been different for him. Maybe.

Hell, he was getting maudlin. He shook the mood from him.

"More medicine?" asked the bartender, stopping in front of him. The bar was jammed now; there was perspiration on her upper lip, and it was good of her to ask.

"No thanks, nurse," he said. "I've had my dose for now. Thanks anyway."

She went off. He looked after her. It was pleasant, kidding with her; but he didn't want anything more than that. Not tonight, anyway. And besides, she was too damn young. He got down from his seat at the bar.

He would go upstairs and let the engineers chew on him for a while with their own worries about the cameras and equipment and everything else to do with tomorrow. It would be another kind of medicine.

Seated at a desk under the bright lights of the lobby-floor motel room that had been set aside for security headquarters,

Albert Gervais had neatly laid out before him two sheets of cardboard cut from a box of typewriter paper, a roll of Scotch tape, a stapler, and a heavy manila envelope. At his elbow was a small green paper sack with the three-planets emblem for the Mars Expedition printed in white on it.

He reached for the sack and upended it on the desktop, sliding two identical paper knives into view. They were eight inches long with black plastic handles. Printed on one side of each handle in silver were the words *Kennedy Space Center* and on the other the silver outline of the paired shuttle-craft.

He took one of the knives and fastened it to the center of one of the cardboard sheets with short strips of the tape. His long brown fingers were delicate and precise in their movements. When the paper knife was securely fastened, he laid the other cardboard sheet on top of it and stapled the two together with staples driven in around the four edges. Then he put the stapler aside, took a slim silver pen from the inside pocket of his suitcoat and wrote on the top piece of cardboard:

Ronny:
   A souvenir of the Mars Expedition, for you to keep.
                                        Your loving Father

He signed the note, slid the card with the paper knife between into the manila envelope, sealed and stamped it with stamps from the desk drawer, and addressed it to his home post box in New Orleans. He picked up the other paper knife, held it for a second thoughtfully, then pushed it unwrapped into the inside breast pocket of his suit coat. He was busy putting the Scotch tape and stapler away when Kilmartin Brawley, one of the agents on the night shift, came into the office.

"I thought you went off duty," Brawley said. He had a faint Maine accent.

Gervais finished clearing the desktop and looked up at the square form of this young man, whom some day soon he must get rid of.

"I had a few things to take care of," he said. "How's it going?"

"Quiet. Want to make a check?"

"No." Gervais shook his head. "They're all in, aren't they?"

"Yes," said Brawley, then added, "—except Wylie."

"Wylie?" Gervais sat for a moment, perfectly immobile with his hands relaxed on the desk, thinking. "Go see if he came in while you've been talking to me here."

"He couldn't have. I just left the lobby—"

"Go look."

Brawley went out. He came back less than a minute later, and said, "He must have walked in the second I left. He's up in his suite now, with that chick."

"If they've got clearance, they aren't chicks," said Gervais. "Does the book show he said where he went, when he went out?"

"He didn't leave word, evidently."

"Yes." Gervais got to his feet. "I'll be in at oh-eight-hundred. Try and get him to say where he's going, after this. And Kil—"

"What?"

"Leave the local punks alone. Save your fun and games for when you're off duty and back in Washington."

Brawley stared back, across the room. He was a young, stocky man with a boyishly cheerful face that now looked slightly sullen.

"What d'you mean?" he said. "You know I'm married now."

"I've heard that before, too," said Gervais. "I know how much marriage means to you left-handers, whether it's the real thing or your version. Besides, that's something else you'd be smarter not to mention out loud around here."

"I tell you, you've got nothing to worry about!"

"I'd better not," said Gervais, unexcitedly. "The next time the local law calls me about some half-dead dickybird, I'm going to leave your white ass high and dry for them to come along and collect. I've already made sure we can cut you off safely from this end if we have to—a word to the wise."

He got to his feet and went out, humming to himself almost

inaudibly under his breath. Outside the motel and a block down, he stopped at a mailbox to post the paper knife. He went on to a short order restaurant and turned into the parking area around it. There was a waiting line and it was a few minutes before his turn came with the hostess.

"How many in your party?"

"Two," he said.

She led him to one of the booths; then, turning, saw he was alone.

"I thought you said two?"

"Someone's meeting me here." Gervais smiled at her. "He'll be along any minute."

"Well . . ." She hesitated. "Singles are supposed to go to the counter."

"He'll be along," said Gervais.

"Well . . . all right."

She went off. He sat down and the teenaged waitress brought him a menu.

"Iced tea," he said, glancing at it. "And the fried clams on the dinner. Does the fish chowder come with that?"

"No, it's extra," said the waitress.

"I think I'll have it anyway. Oh, by the way," said Gervais. "Somebody's meeting me here and he ought to be along in a minute or two, but would you start me with the iced tea and soup, now?"

"Sure would," said the girl, and went off.

Left alone, Gervais took out his address book, flipped through it and got up to go over to a pay phone on the far wall of the restaurant. He put in a dime and punched.

"Operator," said a voice.

"I'd like to make a collect call, please," he said. "Station to station. My name's Jackson."

"One moment."

After a second there was a chime-tone at the far end, but the screen still remained blank.

"This is long distance," said the operator. "I've got a call for anyone from Mr. Jackson."

"I'll take it. Hello," said a man's voice.

"It's me," said Gervais. "Who've you got immediately, at home right now, in Merritt Island, Florida?"

There was a short wait, then the voice spoke again.

"Try four six eight, three four seven two."

The line went dead. Gervais fished out the dime the long distance operator had returned and used it to reach the number he had just been given. The phone chimed several times, was answered and for several seconds the screen remained blank and silent before a man's tenor voice spoke tentatively.

" 'Lo?''

"This is Jackson," said Gervais. "I'm at a place called The Island Kitchen. Get over here as fast as you can."

"I . . ." the voice wobbled. "How I . . ."

"Tell the hostess when you get here that you're meeting a friend; and he's already here, holding a booth down for the two of you."

Gervais hung up and went back to the booth. He had just finished eating when the hostess brought to the booth a thin, nervous-looking black man well past his forties. She went away and the thin man slid into the booth facing Gervais.

"You've got a car?" Gervais asked, spooning up the last of the chowder.

"Pickup."

"All right. There's a place toward the bottom end of Merritt Island, called the Kelly Estate—you know about it?"

"Everybody know that place."

"Good." Gervais studied him for a moment. "I want photographs of everyone who goes in and out of that place in the next few days. You get them for me."

"Hey. How I—"

"Get yourself a camera. Try not to take their pictures around there if you can help it. Follow them somewhere else and snap them anyplace but close around the Kelly place if it's possible."

Gervais looked at the other thoughtfully.

"Find somebody who'll develop them for you while you wait. Then, every day about six, you bring the finished prints in an envelope to the Holiday Inn and leave the envelope at the desk there with the name of Jackson printed on the outside. That's all. You understand? Any questions?"

"Hey . . ." The man stared at him for a long moment. "Hey, but what f'me?"

"What for you?" Gervais smiled a little and leaned forward across the table. "You do a good job and I'll give a good report on you to some people in Willermore, so maybe you don't have to go back there, you get a little out of line. What did you expect?"

The thin man swallowed.

"I got to take time off work. Then there's the money for gas—"

"So you take off from work," said Gervais, still smiling, "and you find money for gas. And you be there tomorrow morning—won't you?"

The other swallowed once more, swallowed a third time, and nodded.

"Good," said Gervais. He pushed the menu across the table. "Order something and eat. Better pick what you can afford. You're paying for that yourself, too."

He got up from the booth, picked up his check and walked toward the door. After paying the check, he stepped outside into the hot night air. As he got into his car, he thought with a certain amount of satisfaction of the wheels he had just now set in motion. There would be nothing important going on out at the Kelly mansion. But there would be something he could use; and anything at all would make a beginning, a start to serve his purpose. There was always something going on; and when that something was known, it could always be made to serve a purpose.

8

Wendy Hansard came awake without rousing Tad, who continued to sleep quietly beside her, and lay there looking at the unfamiliar darkness of the ceiling in the room of the Operations and Checkout Building, remembering something her grandmother had said.

"You must like lumps in your bed or you wouldn't have made it up that way."

Wendy had remade her bed after hearing that, without lumps; but the words had stayed with her. Now they were back in her mind again. She must like her life the way it was, or she would not have made it this way.

Certainly there had been nothing deliberately hidden about Tad, or about what she would be getting into, when she married him. She had known what he was like then, and liked him as he was. Tom, now thirteen, was going to be just like his father, a dedicated adventurer. But an adventurer with a purpose. Cassy, younger than Tom, was more level-headed. She was less likely to gamble everything on one strong impulse; and little Jimmy was going to be different from his father and his sister and his older brother. He was more sensitive and cautious, more internal in his dealing with life.

Perhaps the same sort of terrible determination that was in his father would surface eventually in him, too. But for the present, at six, he showed none of it. It was evidence of how Wendy had matured in the fifteen years since she had married Tad that she now appreciated how deep that determination ran. While she had known of it in the beginning, she had not really measured it—necessarily, because it was something so foreign to her own nature. She could be devoted enough to the things that mattered to her. But Tad's utter commitment to an abstract idea, the near-deathwish urge in him to give everything for an idea or a cause that was such a part of his nature and could never be a natural part of hers, was something which all her efforts to understand had been able to bring her only to acknowledge, not to accept.

Lying awake with her thoughts, she faced at last the direction in which they were taking her. There had been a darkness alongside everything in her mind these last few months, a shadow she had resolutely refused to look at or even admit was there. But time had run out and there was no ignoring its presence any longer. Now, she found herself turning squarely to face it; and the facing after all brought a feeling almost of relief.

She had seen Tad go into many things that were dangerous, particularly in his test-pilot days. She had lived through them and stood up early to the understanding that at any of these times an accident could happen. Suddenly, all at once it could be over—all the years she had had with Tad, all the children had had with him. It could happen as abruptly as the fire had on the Apollo One training mission, when three astronauts like Tad had died in seconds. It could erupt as unpredictably and unpreventably as the blowout of the overpressurized oxygen tank that had threatened to kill the men of Apollo Thirteen out in the ocean of space between Earth and moon.

But such possible strokes of fate she had learned to live with. What she now faced fully for the first time, as she turned at last to go down into the dark chasm that had been waiting for her these past weeks, was something much harder to accept. It was something she could not be sure that she would ever be able to live with. It was not the thought that some deadly accident might suddenly take Tad from them all. But that Tad, this man sleeping beside her, the father of her children, might in answer to the terrible urge for commitment inside him deliberately and calmly choose to walk into death for the sake of one of those abstract causes—this space-wish for which he lived.

She had to accept that now, because it was no longer only in Tad that she could see it. The same trait was visible in all the astronauts. They were all, in some way, a breed apart. She had not believed this about Tad—she had refused to believe it—until this Mars Expedition had forced her to face it during the last half-year. Before then she had clung to the notion that what she saw in him and the rest of them was a function of the similarities in their backgrounds, the fact that almost all of them had been pilots, that a certain body type found it easiest to qualify physically for space, that these and other things in the particular culture that was America made them alike in that particular way she sensed but shied away from naming.

Then this international Expedition became a reality, and she could no longer fool herself. It did not matter where they came from, what language they spoke, what their individual histories were. They were all 'nauts—and that meant they were different from everyone else in this one undeniable way. They all had something no one else on Earth had—the real chance to go where no one else could; and that chance had stolen them from the common pattern of humanity. They alone were different. Their scale of values was not the scale everyone else used; and they would do things for other reasons. So open-faced, so normal and everyday as soup, as they all appeared to be—still they were not so at all. They had given themselves to something no one else had; and now what mattered so much to the rest of the world mattered little or nothing to them, compared to their own special dream. Their eyes looked outward, and would not be turned back. She knew them now . . . and she knew Tad at last.

Her knowledge of him was certain. If the proper combination of circumstances should put themselves together, then his response would be a foregone conclusion. He would not think of her or the children at that time, or if he thought of them at all, the thought would not be enough to hold him back from self-sacrifice. The cruelty of his decision, the robbery of her and the children that such self-sacrifice would be, was what she had been avoiding in her thoughts all this time since it had become certain that Tad would not merely be one of the men on this expedition, but would be senior captain. Because it was the position of responsibility that increased the chances of a situation in which he might do what she feared.

He would leave her. He had already left her, never to return. She was abandoned, with their children—and she had no faith in her own courage now that she was finally, irrevocably alone.

She lay on her back in the darkness, dry-eyed, staring at the shadow-bound ceiling and feeling the knowledge that was inside her like a sharp-edged chunk of something heavy, unnatural and undeniable. Beside her, after a little while, Tad stirred, muttering something sleep-distorted to unintelligibility, reaching out to her.

She turned to look at him; and saw his face blurred in the darkness. The hardness inside her was suddenly not there. It had not evaporated. It would be back. But for the moment it was no longer there. Automatically, she put her arms around him.

Aletha Shrubb woke thirsty a little after midnight. It was the wine they had drunk at the Wocjeks' after coming back from dinner. She got up without disturbing Jim and put on her green robe. Going into the kitchen, she filled a tall glass at the sink with cold water, drank it down, then filled the kettle and put in on to boil.

While the water heated, she sat down in a chair at the kitchen table. It was only at odd times like this when she woke in the middle of the night, or found herself alone on a Sunday morning, that she made tea. Normally she was a coffee drinker. But tea had been a medicine and a sort of symbol for everybody in her family, back home. Something for sleep. Something for private, quiet personal times when the doors were locked and the cat put out for the night.

She sat waiting for the kettle to boil, not really thinking. After several minutes, a few wisps of steam began to come from the kettle's capped spout, and shortly after that the first thin reedy sound of the whistle that was built into the cap began to sound. She got up and took the kettle off the burner before the whistling could sound through the house and wake Jim.

She put a teabag in a cup, filled it and took it into the living room, turned on the light by the green armchair and settled down into its slightly hollowed, overstuffed cushions.

She was still not thinking. There was a peace in her; and she wanted the peace to stay, holding her as long as possible. For the moment the world was all it should be. She was private, but not lonely. She could feel Jim's presence now under her roof, like the fire in the fireplace, warming her; and at the same time, without his knowing it, she was off by herself in her own world.

She looked at the room about her in the soft lamplight. The carpet, the pictures on the wall, the furniture, were all hers and all familiar. She wrapped the sense of the room around her like a warm quilt as she sat sipping the hot tea.

Enclosed and protected here, by the hour and by what was

all hers, she began to think, finally. But her thoughts were slow, easy, without pain or hurry.

She had not told herself any fairy stories about Jim. She was old enough now to be unable to believe in such self-made dreams, anyway. She had learned to accept the good things that came along in the same way she had learned to live with the bad. When things got mean, you waited them out. Then, when things were good, you could let yourself enjoy them all the way, without stirring into them the bitter taste of the bad that might happen afterwards.

Sitting in the chair, she pictured Jim as he would be now, sleeping in the bedroom. It was a special small pleasure to imagine him, knowing she could go and find him there if she wanted. He would be lying on his side, sleeping quietly in pajamas a little too small for him, small enough so that the pajama jacket rode up on his chest and his stomach showed, flattened out against the surface of the bed. The sight of that stomach moved Aletha almost more powerfully than anything else about him. She had an impulse to pat it tenderly, as she might have been tempted to pat a baby's bottom. So far in the time she had known him, she had held herself back from doing so, not wanting to wake him. But someday she would be there when it was time for Jim to get up anyway, and she would be able to give in to the urge with a clear conscience. That is, provided he stayed around long enough for her to have the chance.

Because she knew him for what he was, she knew there would be no use trying to hold on to him if he decided to leave. He was too good to be true, in bed especially. Someone like that had known too many women to be the settling-down kind. Either he would finally want to move or things would happen to move him, because he was the sort of person he was. There would be no point in her trying to move with him, either. Aletha had seen men like him before; and whether they made their lives do to them what their lives did to them, or whether it was that their lives did it to them because they were the people they were, did not matter. The point was that in the end they moved on, or were moved on, and the result was the same. Anyone having to do with them was left behind.

She was one of those who knew that she did not control—one of the people life handled, instead of letting itself be handled by them. She knew it and she did not complain about it much, or often. But at moments like this, when she thought of loving something or someone like Jim, the unfairness that she should be so helpless came on her like a keen inner-body pain.

Why should it be that people such as she should not have a right to make their own happiness? The pain was on her now, but resolutely she pushed it back. Time enough for that when it came, she told herself, grimly. Now was not yet that time. Now was good. Enjoy it while it was here.

Lin West was also awake, thinking.

Jens had come back to the motel room, and she had expected him to want her again. But he had only made a clumsy, almost reflexive, motion or two toward her, and then fallen into a profound, exhausted sleep. Knowing Jens, she knew that he would wake tomorrow, and, alive once more, damn himself for a clumsy idiot and think that she had been disappointed, if not disgusted, with him. But she really did not mind. She did not mind his falling asleep like that at all. Jens had never understood that she could enjoy just having him there at certain times—not that there were not other things, too—but Jens saw everything from his own point of view and assumed that if he would have been disappointed, she must have been also.

She had done a lot of thinking from time to time about how serious he was about her. It was a problem to know just how she should handle him. Once she had soberly considered never sharing her life permanently with any one man. But even then, in theory she had approved of marriage, and wanted children. More than one. She had been a single child herself; and while there were great advantages to both parents being able to concentrate on a single offspring, there was no doubt it was better, healthier even, to have more than one. Two, possibly three. Not more than three, though, except in extraordinary circumstances; nor was her opinion on that merely a concern for the overpopulated world. With too many children sharing the same household, individualism would be submerged. She would want her children to grow up strong and independent, as she had. She could thank her parents for that.

But she would always make it a point—she thought now—to be closer to her children than her parents had been to her. They had loved her, of course, and they had tried to be close; but they were too respectful of each other's privacy to be really intimate—with each other or with her. They were, in fact, a little stuffy; a pair of people who intermeshed without ever really interlocking, and she had been conscious of the fact that it had been something of a relief to them when she had grown up enough to go away to Princeton.

College had been the best time of her life. She had painted herself into a tailspin, but it had all been marvelous. Some day she would get back to painting. She had something to say with her shapes and colors, and one day she would say it. Dad and Mom had been respectful of her art and approving of her doing it; but they had never known what it was to love something like that as she did. Yes, she would come back to it eventually. Meanwhile there were other things to be done.

Luckily she had found this out early. She thought back now over the eight unsuccessful fall and winter months she had spent as a beginning artist and illustrator in New York, trying to break in. Then luck had dropped in her lap the chance for an editing job at Walthon Publishing. Not that an eventual position as an editor there had been what she really wanted; but four months of that work had opened her eyes to what actually would suit her; she had been smart enough to start writing on the side and selling freelance articles to magazines like *New World*.

It was nearly ten months later that the chance of a job on the staff of *New World* came, and she was able to get it, with the double leverage of her editorial experience and the success she was beginning to have as a writer. From then on the road had been open.

Her instinct had been right. It was the double- and triple-threat people who moved up the ladder fast. She was Editorial to begin with, but since she could also write—and, somewhat to her own surprise, the writing turned out to be her most marketable ability—and because of her *cum laude* in art at Princeton, she could also talk with the art department at *New World*. Two years ago they had made her a staff writer and for the last half-year she had been able to suggest assignments for herself. Two or three more years would put her in the top ranks of the magazine's staff writers. Then, either at *New World* or on some equivalent magazine, she intended to hold down a top editorial job for several years; after which, having proved herself, she would retire to do book-length nonfiction until she had built up a tidy income from royalties. Then back to painting and watching her children grow up.

It was an ambitious program; but she had already proved, if only to herself, that she had the talent and drive to make it work. The only question was, how was it all to work with Jens? She definitely wanted him as part of it. She wanted him very much, enough to give up more than part of the program for him. But giving up part of what either one of them wanted would not be right. It would not be right, even if she did not end by storing up resentment against him because she had had to limit her life just to include him in it.

He was well worth including. He had talent himself, not only that of a newsman and writer, but a knack for ending up at the center of where things were going on. But the matter of his drive—that was something else. He was nearly seven years older than she was; and at the age she was now, he had been a nothing in the Washington bureau of his hometown newspaper. The main trouble with him was that he did not seem to *want* enough—or at least he did not seem to want enough for himself. He had turned down a chance at a law school fellowship to go into newspaper work; and not just any fellowship—the Charles Evans Hughes Fellowship at Columbia had been created for students with a special interest in the economically and racially disadvantaged. As the son of a senator, of course, it would had been a fellowship without stipend. But it was just the sort of fellowship that Jens, with his crusading spirit, would have done well with; and what an asset it would have been as part of his record—later on when he did end up in politics.

He had told her about that—and she had hardly been able to believe him when he told it. Just by a simple decision to take the fellowship he had originally applied for and go through law school, he could have had his life made for him at one stroke. There was no doubting his capacity to get through law school. He could have graduated easily with fine grades, gone into practice with an established firm that had deep ties of friendship with his father, who was then living. After a few years of practice he could have gone into politics and found that career open for him all the way, because of his father's experience and presence. Right up until his father's death that option had still been open to him. Possibly even something could be done now, particularly with this appointment of his, this present appointment, as something to build on. But, just as he had turned down all the reasonable offers that life had made him, he seemed determined to turn everything else down now, except the wild fancy that moved him to do something with the space program. It was not that he did not have the capacity to work for something, to really *want* in her terms; for something like this Mars Expedition, with which he had plainly fallen in love, he could want like cold murder. But always, it was for something outside of himself.

That was his problem. He was too unworldly, not strong enough in practical ways. She liked the fact that he needed her—but he should not need her so much. He should not so easily be able to leave all the practical relationships with the world in someone else's hands. And the worst of it was . . .

Her lashes were suddenly, unexpectedly wet with tears and the shadows of the ceiling blurred. Something within her broke. It was not fair. He could have anything he wanted from her. Any time he really wanted to he could reach deep inside her and touch her . . . he could touch her . . . and she would do whatever he wished. And he did not even know it. Her only defense against that great power of his was to hide from him the fact that he had it. But what kind of a blind idiot was he that he could not see it for himself?

And it was *not* fair. It was not right that he should be able to reach so casually right into the very middle of her and take hold of her life as if it was some small, crouching bird in a large, calloused hand, its tiny bird's heart racing with excitement and fear. It might be right if things were the other way around—if she could depend on him for the practical things, the ambition. It was intolerable that he did not know of his advantage, even though she lived with the fear that he would one day find out.

The gush of emotion ebbed and left her calm again. She stared at the ceiling, seeing it in focus again with dry eyes. It was all right. He had no suspicion at all of his power, and there was still plenty of time. A lot could happen. If things went well with this fake government job, perhaps he would get a chance at one where the demands were real and important. He might then rise to the occasion and grow into responsibility and reliability. He could if he wanted to . . .

9

Delbert Anthony Terrence awakened in the dark to the ringing of the telephone.

"I just got to sleep!" he said furiously, out loud to the unseen unit.

The telephone rang on.

"Aren't you going to answer it?" asked the voice of Jonie Wextrum.

"Just what the hell choice do I have?" He groped in the dark at the unfamiliar nightstand beside the queen-size motel bed, found the phone and picked it up. "Hello!"

"Del?"

"Yeah."

"This is Al Murgatroyd. Look, I know I'm calling late—"

"Late? It's—" Del rolled over on his back with the phone still at his ear and held his other wrist up before him in the blackness. The luminescent numbers on its dial glowed a few inches from his eyes. "Jesus, it's two forty-six!"

"I know. But I've got to talk to you. We just ran another test on the guidance system for the lasercom—"

"Now? Al, why for shit's sake another test *now*?"

"Because I decided we wanted one, damn it! And I think you and I better talk about some of the results we got."

A coldness formed suddenly just behind Del's breastbone.

"Beyond specs?"

"Not exactly. But—"

"Then *Christ*, Al—"

"Sorry, Del." The voice at the other end seemed to take a step backward and firm up. "But I want to talk to you. Now."

"All right, Al. Of course. Where are you?"

"I'm calling from a phone booth halfway back into town from the Space Center. Look, there's a food place called The Happy Pig that stays open twenty-four hours. I'll meet you there."

"An all-night food joint? Al, what the God damn hell's going on? Why not your place as long as you're coming back into Merritt Island anyway?"

"Because my place's lousy with relatives and friends of my kids, in for the launch!" Al's voice had a touch of hoarseness. "There's no place to stand there, let alone sit and talk. You know where The Happy Pig is?"

"I know."

"Meet you, then, in half an hour."

"Right."

"All right. I'm sorry to get you up, but there's no choice."

"That's all right, Al. Part of my job." Del struggled to smooth his voice out. It was fantastically improbable that Al would really have found something to worry about; but . . . "See you in half an hour."

"Half an hour."

Al hung up. Del put his phone back in its cradle.

He felt around behind the phone, found the switch at the base of the nightstand lamp and turned it on. The motel room around him sprang into existence. Jonie was up on one elbow, lying on her side facing him, the covers slipped off her bare shoulders and down to her waist. The brown hair framing her small, round face looked darker than usual in the sudden, soft yellow light. Del felt contrition stir in him. He ought not to take it out by yelling at her. He had met her eight months ago when he had reacted violently to a wasp sting and Al had rushed him to the Brevard County hospital. Jonie had been a nurse on duty there and they had had time enough together since then so that he knew she bruised easily.

"It's work," he said, as gently as he could. "I've got to get up and go."

"Now?"

From the change in her face he could tell that she was no longer thinking of how he had snapped at her, but about how it must be for him—having to leave a warm bed and a warmer body at this time of night to go back on the job. He felt a small spasm of deep affection for her. She was something to look at, right now. She had been one of those small town girls who got married right out of high school to a kid who didn't appreciate what he had in her; and with only the short times Del had had to spend with her on his trips down here to the Cape, she had really blossomed.

"That's what Laserkind hires me for," he said. "A factory rep's got to keep the local engineers happy, even if it means getting up at three A.M."

He was climbing out of bed as he answered, and reaching for his clothes.

"What is it?" she asked him.

"The guidance on the lasercom."

"Oh, you were worried about that."

"No, I wasn't, damn it!" he snapped. "Not *worried*!"

There was a moment's silence as he continued to dress.

"Will you be back still, tonight?" she asked.

"God knows," he grunted, wrestling into his shirt. "If we talk more than an hour, it won't be worth it. I'd just have to hit here, turn around and walk back out again."

She watched him finish dressing and start to leave.

"Tell him how tired you are," she said, as he started out the door. Del laughed in spite of the way he felt.

"He'll be kind of tired himself," he said. "Somehow, I don't think that kind of statement's going to move him, this particular morning. 'Bye, knockers."

She pulled the covers up to her chin quickly, and lay back down in bed, gazing at him over the edge of the blanket and her two fists.

" 'Bye," she said.

He laughed again and went out feeling, for the first time, nearly awake.

Riding down in the empty, smoothly humming elevator, he caught sight of his own lean face under its dark cap of hair in a strip of mirror set vertically on one wall. He needed a shave already; and the chances of getting anything like that from here on out were, to say the least, remote. Well, he wouldn't be the only one on launch day with twenty-four hours' worth of dark beard.

The Happy Pig, when he pulled into its parking lot, was busy, an island of bright light behind the large expanses of polychromatic wall glass that nowadays went to make up most of any eatery less than five years old. With the sun gone from the sky the glass was on full transparency. Beyond it, Del could see hurrying waitresses, full stools and booths. The crowds of Merritt Island on the night before a launch were restless. Most of the visitors had nowhere to sleep except for a car, parked somewhere along the causeway in a spot from which they hoped to be able to see the launch across some fourteen miles of water.

He went in and looked for Al, spotting him at last in a booth, alone. Either Al knew someone working at the place, or he'd greased somebody's palm to be able to hold a booth by himself, like that. More likely the former. Al was not the world's greatest tipper.

Del caught the other man's eye, waved to him, and went toward the booth. Al was sitting hunched over a cup, a large capped and insulated coffee pitcher of green plastic handy at his elbow. His open-necked white shirt clung damply to his large upper body, although the air-conditioning in the place was good. The lines in his face were deeply grooved. He was a big, soft bear of a man, with reddish-gray hair and large, freckled hands, a good two inches taller than Del's six feet, and he had been around the Cape since the old Vanguard days.

There was silverware and another clean cup, empty, on the

gaudy paper place mat before Del's seat at the table. Del reached for the insulated pitcher as he sat down, and poured black coffee into the cup.

"You could use some sleep yourself," he said, looking at Al.

Al shook his head as if the suggestion was a fly buzzing around his ears.

"Listen," he said. The hoarseness in his voice was more noticeable here, face to face, than it had been to Del's ears over the phone. "I'm sorry about getting you up. I tried to get hold of you earlier, but they said you were out—gone over to Orlando—"

"Yeah. I'm sorry," said Del. "I had a PR man from Disney World to talk to. Forget it. I'm ready for a full day anyway. The only thing that bites me is places like this, the night before. I'm geared up enough already without all this light and noise and rush."

He glanced around him. It was true. Eating joints like this got on his nerves under the best of conditions. He looked back at Al and made himself grin.

"Too bad all those houseguests of yours crowded us out," he said. "At least at your place we could have put our feet up and been comfortable."

"My two oldest brought in about six people we weren't counting on, Cissy and me," said Al. "Otherwise we'd have had at least the living room free."

"There's more want to watch, each launch," said Del. He shook his head at a waitress who was swooping down on him, menu in hand. "No food for me. Al?"

"No. No, thanks," Al turned his attention to the waitress. "Just coffee, Rhoda, for both of us."

"Cream, please, though," said Del.

"Sure. You take your time," said the waitress. "Hear, Al? You just sit back and drink your coffee."

"Thanks," said Al. She went off.

"College friends?" asked Del, spooning sugar into his coffee. In spite of the cream and sugar, he knew, the contents of his cup would taste like wood ashes in water, this time of the morning.

"Rhoda, here? Oh, you mean the bunch my Tib and Moira

brought in to watch the launch? Who the hell else would they be? Lucky the two youngest are still in high school here, or Cissy and I'd be out of our skulls by this time. Look, Del; as I said, I'm sorry about getting you up but I've got some figures from this test I want you to look at.''

He reached into a briefcase on the booth seat beside him, brought up a sheaf of computer printout, and pushed it across the table at Del.

Del took it. He had to make what amounted to a physical effort to shift his mind into the gear necessary to translate the numbers on the sheet before him. They had apparently, once more, run a standard operating test on the direction equipment of the laser communications system installed on both spacecraft. The waitress, Rhoda, came with two little plastic cups of imitation cream and Del poured the contents of both absently into his coffee cup. The test had necessarily been run by radio command from Communications Control here at the Cape, since there was no one now aboard the two Mars spacecraft up in orbit, and would not be until the 'nauts boarded them late tomorrow.

The vague concern that had sat brooding at the back of Del's mind began to evaporate as he went through the sheets. It was replaced finally by a gust of anger. There was nothing wrong. Nothing at all.

Al had been senior engineer on the Spacecraft Equipment Evaluation Group that had originally considered contracting for the laser communications system for the two Mars Expedition spacecraft. The system was Laserkind's baby, their own development. No one else had anything like it; and there had been some division of thought in the NASA Group Al had headed, about using it as a primary communications system for the craft rather than as backup to radio. But the freedom from interference in the laser system was so superior that Al himself had been solidly sold; and he had sold the rest of the Group. Now, with the launch right upon them, for the last week Al had been sweating out his own earlier decision.

It was part of his being a G.S.-15 with four kids and twenty-odd years here at the Cape, Del thought, looking across the table at the other man. Nailed down by job, family, and community, Al had forgotten how to take a reasonable chance. It was things like this that turned Del off any idea of marriage whenever anyone like Jonie began to turn him on. How the hell could you call your guts your own if your soul was shared out among half a dozen other people? Imagining himself in just that sort of box, Del could see that he would be likely to wake up a factory rep at two-thirty in the morning because he had two kids in college two more yet to go, and was not sure he had done the right thing two years before.

At the same time as he was thinking all this, however, Del was making an effort to keep the anger bottled up inside him. It might be perfectly true that Al was just chewing his fingernails for his own reasons; but at the same time Al was Chief of Onboard Equipment for the launch and Expedition, and had a right to run as many tests as he wanted or query as many factory reps as he chose.

"I don't see anything," said Del, carefully, letting the paper drop to the table top before him.

"This is the third time this week we've run a check and each time we're getting a little more slop in the system," Al said, tightly.

"Slop?" Del picked up the sheets and hunted back through the figures, although he already knew what he would find. "You had to fine-tune in from only twelve seconds of arc. That's well within specs."

"That's slop, damn it!" said Al. "Five seconds is what we ought to have. We were getting five seconds down here on the ground, no more. Now that we've got it on the craft up in orbit, we're getting a fucking eight to twelve. Why?"

"Jesus Christ, Al," said Del, trying to make the tone of his voice reasonable, even amused. "There could be eighteen dozen little things throwing it off a bit like that. You're doing a remote, man. Even radio interference on the way up—"

"A bit!" Al hunched his shoulders, leaning forward above his coffee cup. He lowered his voice, which had raised on the last word. "That's God damn double what we'd like—more than double!"

"And it's just barely more than God damn half what the specs allow for!" Del felt his temper getting away from him after all, and took a firmer grip on it. "What you'd like is no more than twenty-five percent of what's permitted. You got it to begin with, for Christ's sake; and because of that, now you're acting like it's the spec limit. Relax, Al—you're going to kill yourself over this and there's absolutely nothing wrong!"

"Maybe not yet." Al sat back heavily. "I don't like it, I tell you."

"Look," said Del, "you know what that system can do. If it was going to show trouble, it wouldn't be some shitty, tiny increase in fine-tuning requirements, like this."

"I don't know," Al muttered, staring down at the printout sheets.

"Well, I know," Del said. "Believe me, Al, if there was anything really to worry about with the guidance system, I'd be half a block out ahead of you sending up rockets over it. But there isn't. There damn well can't be—particularly not with figures like this. All this proves is that the system's working the way it's designed to work. Now, you've got to know that as well as I do. Don't you?"

Al breathed out heavily. He picked up his coffee cup in one large hand, put it down again and shoved it away from him. He rubbed his fingers over his eyes.

"I don't like it," he said. "It's slop—and we shouldn't have it like that."

"Al . . ." Del spoke as gently as he could. "You know what you're doing right now, don't you? Of course you do. You've been through enough of these launches. You know how everybody finds some particular thing to sweat about at the last moment. You're out on your feet, that's the trouble. You're out on your feet and you've got your mind going around and around in one groove, whether there's any sense to it or not. What you need is some sleep. Tell me, you still got a bed for yourself left at that house of yours?"

Al grunted a short laugh.

"I damn well better have," he said. "If Cissy's let those kids talk her into giving somebody else our bedroom, I'm going to kick some strange asses right out my front door!"

"Well, why don't you get back there and get some sleep while you can?" Del demanded. "You've only got a few hours before you're going to have to be back at Operations. Don't waste any more of it drinking coffee and sitting here trying to make me agree there's spooks in the guidance system that you and I both know don't exist."

Al rubbed his hand over his face again; this time, across his mouth and chin.

"Yeah," he said. "All right."

He reached out, gathered in the printout and stood up, out of the booth.

"Good night."

"Good morning," said Del.

Al grunted a second short laugh.

"That's right," he said. "Good morning."

He turned and went out. Del stood up also and looked around for the waitress. She was a few tables away and it was a moment before she saw him and came over.

"Could I have the check?"

He got the check, paid at the cash register up front, and went out into the still, hot predawn. Driving back to the motel, he thought intensively. Damn, damn, damn, *damn*! It would be at the eleventh hour that suggestions of trouble would stick their heads up out of the woodwork. But there was nothing that could be really wrong. It was true there had been some bugs in the guidance control system back in the beginning on the west coast—he should not have bit Jonie's head off when she remembered him talking about it—but those were taken care of long ago. No, it was all nonsense, born in Al's head of too much coffee and not enough sleep.

Thinking of Al again, Del's own thoughts took another term. Al was an old acquaintance, almost an old friend. But Del's first responsibility was to Laserkind. If Al was going to be irrational and maybe end up making some kind of statement about the unreliability of the lasercom equipment, then maybe Del should pass the word back on this possibility to the home office; so that they could start to build up some evidence for counterargument, both on the system and on Al's relationship with the company, earlier.

In fact, the more Del thought about doing just that, the wiser a move it seemed. He would put in a call to Downey as soon as he got back to the hotel. It would be just after midnight there on the west coast; and Jack Sharney, Del's immediate superior, would probably have just tucked himself under the covers. Del grinned, thinking that perhaps the session with Al had not been a complete loss after all. At least he would be able to pass along the experience of being roused out of bed to possible bad news. Old Jack would appreciate that happening to him just about as much as Del had.

10

Tad and Wendy Hansard lay on the bed in Tad's quarters of the Operations and Checkout Building. Light from a moon that was almost down came through the windows along one side of the room, making things in the room visible to them, outlining Tad's lean-muscled frame in contrast to Wendy's soft shape. They lay on their backs, side by side, looking at the moon-painted ceiling and talking, with little intervals of silence now and then.

"How much longer until I have to leave?" Wendy asked.

He turned his head and squinted at the clock on the bedside table.

"Forty minutes," he said. There was one of the little silences, and he added, "To hell with it. You can stay. What are they going to do—fire me?"

"No," she said. She reached out without looking at him and stroked the side of his naked arm with her fingertips. "It'll be a long day; and you won't have any chance to catch up on sleep the first two weeks. They're right. I've got to go."

There was silence again. She took her fingertips away from his arm.

"Jimmy's the one who really doesn't understand," she said. "The older two have an idea, at least."

"Idea?" he said. "About what? What Mars is?"

"No," she said, "about how long you'll be gone. Tom and Cassy have some idea, at least. Only some idea, of course. Three years is a lifetime, even to them. But they can think ahead and measure it by something. Tom'll be in his first year of college when you get back. Cassy'll be a junior in high school. But Jimmy . . . three years is half the time he's been on Earth."

"Little old afterthought, that boy," said Tad, half to himself. "Maybe we shouldn't have had him with a gap like that between him and the other two."

He sensed, without seeing, that she shook her head on the pillow.

"I was happy," she said.

"Me, too," admitted Tad. "Guess we've spoiled him."

"If we have, I'm glad," she said, "now that he's got to go three years without you. Tom and Cassy had you around those years when they were little."

Another little silence came and went.

"Sure," he said. "But it's always the now that counts."

They lay there with the last of the moonlight strong upon them; and the hands of the clock at the bedside crawled onward as the eternal moment of the present ate its relentless way into the future.

Some sixty feet away, in his quarters, cosmonaut Feodor Aleksandrovitch Asturnov dreamed of his dead wife and children. In shadow, his regular, narrow features looked like a bas-relief on an old coin.

They were out on a picnic. They had spread out the picnic things in a meadow that barely sloped for some little distance to the edge of a wide, very shallow river, glinting in the hot summer sunlight; and Mariya was afraid that Vanya, being still a baby, would wander down and fall into the river. He tried to reassure her; but then with the older three children he went off into a little woods nearby to look for mushrooms. Somehow they got separated; and, going back to the meadow to look for them, he saw all five of them—Mariya and all the children, Pavlushka, Kostya, Iliusha . . . even the baby— wading in the river.

It was immediately apparent to him that Vanya, as Mariya had feared, had wandered into the water; and Mariya, with the other children, had gone after him.

"Don't worry!" Fedya shouted to them now, running toward the river. "It's all shallow—quite shallow—"

But as he looked, the current seemed to catch them one by one. One by one, they appeared to step off into hidden depths. He saw their heads bob for a moment on the sparkling water, and then they disappeared. And he was still running, running toward the river . . .

The anguish and terror of the dream half-woke him. He came to for a moment in the unfamiliar bedroom in the Operations and Checkout Building. For a second he was lost. Then he remembered where he was and why; and that Mariya and the children had been dead for over two years now.

"That's right," he told himself, "it was a train wreck, not a river."

Strangely, this correction of his conscious mind comforted him. The dream image of the meadow and the heads bobbing on the water began to fade rapidly. He turned over on his other side and closed his eyes again. In a very few minutes he was deeply asleep and beginning to dream that he had been made sole commander of the Mars Expedition as the result of a last-minute change in plans. It was necessary, however, for him to fill out a number of forms attesting to the competence of the other five marsnauts. He wrote rapidly but clearly, finding it a pleasure to put down on paper their high qualifications and his own high opinion of them.

In the hotel on Merritt Island, the angular, aging, six-and-a-half-foot length of Sir Geoffrey Mayence, Her Majesty's Deputy Minister of Science for the Development of Space, lay hard awake. He had not been able even to approach sleep; and chasing through his brain again and again, were his own words about cross-country running, that day at the lunch with the marsnauts in the Operations and Checkout Building, before they had gone to look at the spacecraft. Remembered, his talk sounded fatuous and egotistic. What had he been doing, talking about cross-country running, nowadays—an old crock like him? A man should outgrow making a fool of himself.

It was his own inflated reaction, of course, to the unspoken challenge of the young men, to the marsnauts themselves. The fact of their well-conditioned presence in the room was enough to prick him into boasting about his own athletic past. Dirk Welles—the British 'naut in particular—must have been laughing up his sleeve.

Sir Geoffrey lay rigid, his long bony frame extended diagonally across the king-size bed, and thought of the sleeping pills in his suitcase. Insomnia. Another feebleness of old age. *No, by God.* . . .

He lay unmoving; and the slow gears of the iron hours ground their way through the darkness until light began at last to show around the edges of the heavy drapes shielding his bedroom from the dawn.

Lin turned on her side to look at Jens in the faint light leaking in around the window drapes from the illuminated front of the hotel. A feeling of deep tenderness stirred in her. He was breathing less raggedly now. He had relaxed in sleep and his face was calm.

It was an ugly, funny face, but a nice one. She reached out and very, very gently lifted back an edge of the top sheet, which had fallen forward from his shoulder to cover his mouth. He had a good chin, she decided, studying him. It would be a good chin to sketch. She should do a sketch of him sleeping like this, some time, and see how it came out. It was not exactly a cleft chin, but there was a definite indentation where a cleft might have been. She found herself wondering if he could understand how important to her that art of sketching might be and then, with a queer sort of vertigo, if that was what *he* felt about . . . She pushed the thought away.

The ticking of the travel clock on the bedside table suddenly made itself noticeable. She looked over at it and saw the hands standing at five-ten. He has wanted to be up by five, but she had turned the alarm off after he was asleep, seeing how exhaustedly he slumbered and knowing that she could set herself to wake at any time without needing an alarm.

It was a shame to wake him. But if she did not, late as it was now getting, he would be upset. In fact, she herself would be needing to get up, too, very soon. She had to make those interviews and get back to New York in three days—that is, unless she decided to take some of her vacation time, after all. It was true that she had cleared the extra time with the office before coming down, but she had let Jens think she had to be back in three days just in case there was some reason she . . .

Yes, it was high time for her to wake him.

Very, very carefully and slowly, she leaned over him, bending down so gradually that when her lips at last brushed his sleeping cheek the touch was as light as that of a butter-fly's landing. He stirred slightly at the feel of it, but did not wake. She lifted her head again, reached out and gathered the edge of the top sheet into a small point. She began gently to stroke across the end of his nose with the tip of it.

His nose wrinkled. He stirred and snuffled. One hand came up from under the covers to rub clumsily and sleepily at the nose. His eyes opened.

"Up and at 'em!" she sang out briskly, cheerfully. "Time to be moving, pardner! Daylight in the swamp!"

Outside, the sun was rising from the ocean horizon, and the air was rapidly heating. All over Merritt Island and north-ward, from air-conditioning units like the one below the sealed bedroom window of Jens's motel suite, the one outside the utility room of Aletha Shrubb's house, and the one on the roof of the Operations and Checkout Building, there was a deepening of the voices of machinery increasing the effort it was putting out to meet the demands the growing day were beginning to put inexorably upon it. Time was on the move, and all things moved with it.

The scheduled launch time was eleven A.M. At five-thirty the 'nauts were awakened by a call on their bedside phones. Tad rolled off the bed and up onto his feet. Fifteen minutes later, shaved if not fully awake, and carrying his two white cartons with morning urine and stool specimens, he joined the other five in the clinic for the last, cursory physical exam.

He did not feel like talking this morning; and as he went through the clinic door, he braced himself against the early chatter of the others. But they were also quieter than normal. Even Bapti Lal Bose, usually merry, was now sober-faced.

They stood, lay down, got up and ran, all patiently for the benefit of the medical instruments. They donated their blood by the way of samples from fingertip and forearm, stared across scant inches of distance into the eyes of the physicians poking and prodding them, and were finally released to get dressed and have breakfast.

To Tad, the orange juice, bacon, and scrambled eggs tasted good; but a very small amount of them seemed to fill him up.

"Sleep well?" he asked Fedya, who was sitting across the table from him.

"I think so," he said. A slight smile on the regular, calm features vanished. "I saw you talking to your President, at the reception."

"Yeah," said Tad. "But don't expect any changes."

"I see," said Fedya. They were talking English, which was the tongue in which the Expedition crew was to operate—in which it had been operating for nearly nine months now, since they had all started training together. For the first time in those nine months, Tad found himself wondering if Fedya was this taciturn in his own language—whether, if they had been speaking in Russian, he would have answered merely, "I see."

"Sorry," said Tad. "I gave it all I had. I guess we're stuck with the full slate of experiments."

"We can still go on strike," said Bapti Lal Bose, rediscovering his normal cheerfulness. "A sit-down strike. Put Phoenix One and Phoenix Two into orbit and sit there, going around and around the Earth until they negotiate."

"All right, Bap," said Dirk Welles. "Strike, it is. We'll leave the organization and the details up to you."

"I will take care of it. I!" Bap struck himself on the chest. "All scabs will EVA without suits."

Fedya had regained his quiet smile, listening to Bap. But now he shook his head.

"We can't afford even one scab," he said. The remark was humorous, but his face had gone serious.

"You can't afford to lose this scab, at least," said Bern Callieux. "Seeing you others are so ignorant about geology."

The round-faced young Pan-European 'naut was so soft-voiced, and his excursions into humor came so seldom, that the other five stared at him for a second before understanding. Then there was a general groan around the table. They had all been forced to sit through hours of classes on rock identification.

"The first boulder I see on Mars, Bern," promised Anoshi Wantanabe, the Japanese 'naut, "that's the one I'm going to pick up and hit you over the head with."

And the talk around the breakfast table began to sound more like the talk there on other, more ordinary, mornings.

Jens, dressed and awake by virtue of shower and shaving equipment and all the habits of arising, sat in an armchair drinking coffee provided by room service. Lin still lay in bed, her face on the pillow, watching him.

"Coffee?" he asked her.

She shook her head.

"Can you eat one of these sweet rolls?"

"Not right now," she said. "I ordered them for you."

"Not this early—not this morning. I'll pick up something along the way." He finished his coffee and put the empty cup down. "Look, I told people you've got a press pass. You've picked it up, already, haven't you? I suppose the magazine got you one."

"Yes," she said.

"I'm supposed to be in the VIP stands," said Jens. "But I had the chance to talk to someone I know last night. Do you know Barney Winstrom of Southwest Network? They're a cable TV group."

"No."

"Well, he and his team have rooms here—the operator can give you his number. You'd better call him about seven-thirty. He's going out with a panel truck to the parking lot at the press stands at nine. I got you a ride with him so you wouldn't have to fight the press buses. You'll be going a little early, but the panel'll be more comfortable. You'll be better off that way than with anything else I can arrange for you. I'll try to sneak over from the VIPs and join you just before the shuttle lifts. All right?''

"All right," she said. "Don't forget to set up the interviews for me, to talk with the Hansard and Welles wives."

"I've got it in mind," he said, getting to his feet. "Now . . . see you later."

"Take care," she said as he went out.

He left the suite, checked in with the security office, got an official car and driver from the VIP pool and directed him first across the road to the Merritt Island Press Center for the launch.

Inside, the building was aswarm with men and women wearing orange press passes; and buses loaded with more of them were pulling out of the parking lot in back at regular intervals. Jens shouldered his way down the long transverse corridor until he came to the doorway next to the credentials desk. He went in to a long room bisected by an equally long desk; and got the attention of one of the women working at a typewriter behind the counter. She came up to the counter, a thin-faced, black-haired, cheerful young girl.

"Is Wally Rice in his office right now?" Jens asked. "I'm Jens Wylie. Would you ask him if I could see him for just a moment?"

She looked at him brightly, obviously not recognizing the name.

"I'm sorry," she said. "This is Mr. Rice's busiest time—"

"I'm the United States Undersecretary of Science for the Development of Space," Jens said softly. "But I'd rather it wasn't noised about I was here. If you'll just tell Wally my name, I think he'll see me. We've know each other for some years."

"Just a minute," she said. She went off. In a few seconds she was back, opening the swinging door at one end of the counter. "If you'll come in . . ."

Jens went through the door and followed her to a small cubbyhole of a white-walled, white-ceilinged office, within which was a short, heavy, tan-faced man standing behind a desk.

"Sit down. Take it easy, Wally," said Jens, as the girl left them. "I'm just sneaking in to ask a personal favor—one I don't want to go through VIP channels for."

"You're looking good," said Wally. His southern accent was similar to Tad Hansard's, and gentle against Jens's hard-edged mid-U.S. They sat down. "What can I do for you?"

"I want to talk to Bill Ward, just for ten or fifteen minutes this morning," Jens said. "Don't jump down my throat, now. I realize he's Launch Director; but if I could just see him for those few minutes. It's important—"

"Well, I don't guess I have to jump down your throat for that," said Wally. "It might be arranged, if you see him before the shuttle goes. It's after that, with the Mars birds, he'll be busy. What's this all about—something governmental?"

"Yes . . . and no. Something personal and governmental both," Jens said. "The personal angle is why I don't want to go through the VIP machinery. Leaving aside the fact they'd diddle around all morning and end up not getting it done."

"That's a fact," said Wally. "We bail them out from time to time when it's something on short notice."

"Do you mind if I don't tell you what it's about then?"

"Well, I don't mind," said Wally. "But Bill Ward's going to want to know why he has to walk away from his consoles."

"I suppose . . ." said Jens, unhappily. "All right. Tell him it's a matter of scheduling."

"Just—scheduling?" answered Wally.

"Do I have to say more than that?"

"Maybe not," Wally nodded. "No, I would guess not. He knows who you are, nowadays?"

"I'm sure he does," Jens said. "You might work it into the conversation if you think he doesn't. But kind of mention, too, the fact that I'd just as soon my seeing him didn't get into the general conversation about this launch."

"All right. Gotcha." Wally reached for the telephone. "Where are you going to be? This may take a little while."

"I'm going back across the way to the Holiday Inn, or wherever I can get in, for breakfast. From there, I thought I'd go out to the press site a little early. I can leave word out there where I'm sitting—that is, if you'll give me a press pass."

"Hum," said Wally, thoughtfully letting go of the phone. "I didn't think of that. You've got a VIP badge. That and a press pass don't go together, exactly."

"One of the reasons I was named undersecretary was because the President wanted my experience and knowledge with the press," Jens said blandly. "I think the White House would want me to have a press pass. Want me to call Selden Rethe right now and ask?"

He reached for the phone. Wally shook his head. "I'll take your word for it. We'd better put 'White House Press Office' on it, though."

He picked up the phone and spoke into it.

"Well," he said, putting it down. "How've you been?" They chatted about things in general until another office girl came in with a press badge made out. Jens pinned it on his shirt, shook hands with Wally and left.

The Holiday Inn restaurant, as Jens had expected, was jammed and people wanting to eat were standing in line for tables. He thought for a minute. As usual at a launch, a million and a half people had flooded the area. Cars were parked solid on the causeways, and any place that served food would have the same kind of waiting line he had seen at the Inn. Jens changed his mind about breakfast.

"Have you eaten?" he asked the driver.

"Two hours ago," the driver said.

"Good," said Jens. "I can skip it. Take me out to the press stands, and I'll turn you loose."

The driver pulled back out into the busy traffic of the street. Jens glanced at his watch. It was nearly a quarter after eight. There really had not been time for breakfast anyhow.

The roads to the Kennedy Space Center area were already full. They soon found themselves locked in line behind a camper that was in turn behind a press bus. However, they managed to move at twenty miles an hour until they reached the entrance to the Center, where the traffic thinned and they picked up up speed. It was twenty-five minutes after nine when they finally got to the press site.

Jens thanked the driver and got out. He watched the white sedan with the official seal on its side turn and go, then turned and walked in over the little wooden bridge to the end of the press stands.

The stands were half-filled; and the first few rows, thronged with correspondents at telephones and typewriters were entirely without empty spaces. Jens came up to the small official building by the end of the stands, mounted three steps and knocked on the door. There was a moment's wait and then the door opened. A thin, harried-looking man in shirt-sleeves looked out.

"I'm Jens Wylie," Jens said. "I'm expecting a message from Wally Rice at the Press Center. He said he'd leave word here."

"Oh yes, Mr. Wylie," said the thin man. "He said to check back here with me about ten. He ought to have some word for you by then. Where're you going to be in the stands?"

"I don't have a seat," Jens said. "Why don't you just call me over your PA system? Only don't use my name—ask for Mr. West."

"Right. Mr. West. I'll just make a note of that." The thin man ducked back inside, closing the door; and Jens started for the stands, then changed his mind and went back across the little bridge to the press parking lot to find Barney Winstrom's van and Lin.

He located it in the first row of vehicles and knocked on the door. It opened, and a blast of air-conditioned air chilled his already damp forehead.

"Let him in!" called the voice of Barney from somewhere in the dark interior. The man who had opened the door stood aside and Jens climbed gratefully up the interior steps into the coolness.

Lin was sitting, drinking a beer in the office section of the van with Barney. Jens accepted a can of beer, but had only managed to half-empty it before the sound of the public address system at the press stand reached his ears.

The noise of the air conditioning and the walls of the van had made the words unintelligible. But Jens got up and opened the door of the van in time to hear the message repeated.

"*. . . Will Mr. West come to the north corner of the stand, immediately?*" the loudspeakers were booming. "*Mr. West, wanted at the north end of the stand, immediately.*"

Jens put his beer can aside and went. Waiting for him at the corner of the stands was a uniformed guard wearing a general pass with a yellow Vehicle Assembly Building tag on it.

"If you'll come with me, Mr. Wylie," said the guard.

They crossed to a NASA sedan that was waiting, and rode over to the four-story building, attached to the VAB, that was the Launch Control Center. Inside, an elevator lifted them to the third floor and Jens's guide took him down a short stretch of narrow hallway to the active firing room.

There, the ranks of consoles on the sloping floor marched away down to the level area filled with other ranks of tall metal cabinets. Jens and his guide came up to the console behind which stood Bill Ward looking over the shoulder of the man seated there, before turning away to talk to two other men in shirt-sleeves standing with him. Jens and the guide stood and waited silently.

Bill finished talking and turned abruptly to face him.

"Well, Jens?" he said. "You said you wanted to talk to me?"

"That's right."

"All right, come with me."

He strode off with Jens, leaving the guide behind. They went back to the door of the firing room, out of it and down the hall to another door. They stepped into a room which was exactly the size of the firing room they had just left, but empty of consoles and with a wall cutting off most of the level space beyond the slope. In the middle of the nearly empty room was a conference table with straight chairs around it. Bill led Jens to this, and sat down in the end chair of the table, stiffly upright. He motioned Jens into the chair next to him.

"All right," said Bill briskly across the corner of the table, as soon as Jens was seated. "What sort of scheduling is this all about?"

11

The sun came up that launch morning in a cloudless sky, and Aletha Shrubb went to work early. It would be a hot day. Jim Brille called the Duchess's mansion for Willy Fesser, and was told that he was not in, but would be given Jim's message and would call back.

Five minutes later the phone rang.

"Hello," said Willy's neutral voice, the voice he used when he wanted to be anonymous.

"It's me," Jim said. "I've looked the situation over. I'll need a room in Wylie's motel on the fourteenth floor and facing west over the courtyard that has the pool."

"A room?" Willy's voice was back to its usual tones. "Don't you know it's launch time? There isn't a room to be had for two hundred miles."

"That's the only way it can be done," said Jim. "There's no other place to put a tap in. That motel's swarming with government people who know what they're doing. Some place else I might be able to get to the main telephone cable; and then, if I could get into this Wylie's room—but there's no chance of either one of those things, the way it is now."

"I don't know how I could get you a room."

"Talk to whoever it is you're dealing with." Jim felt exasperation pulling at him. "Do I have to tell you your own business? Somewhere along the line you've got there has to be someone with hype enough to get me that room. If there's a choice, I want it in the middle of the building on that side. I've got to be able to look out and see at least the top of one of Wylie's windows over the edge of that balcony that runs all the way around the motel on the tower wing.''

Willy's voice was abrupt. ''I'll call you back.''

This time it was more than half an hour before the phone at Aletha's rang again.

''All right, you've got it. You're reserved in the name of Wilson Stang,'' Willy said. ''Don't ask for anything more, though. That pot's dry now.''

''There's nothing else I need,'' Jim answered.

Half an hour later in his room at the Holiday Inn, Jim went to the window and looked out. His location was not in the middle on that side of the motel, as he had hoped. It was nearer the back end of the building. Still, he was able without trouble to pick out the windows opposite and one floor up that he had identified as belonging to Jens Wylie's suite. Only the upper third of their panes were visible; but that would be enough.

He went about moving into the room. From the smallest of his suitcases, he took out some extra clothing, hung two suit coats in the closet, laid shaving materials out in the bathroom, and put some underwear in the drawer. A few other personal possessions he scattered over the tops of the dresser. When he left the room nearly two hours later there was a tangle of equipment on top of a table by the sealed window above the air conditioning unit, looking as if it had been dumped there carelessly, to be picked up later. One end of the tangle touched the window, and within it the rod of a laser unit sent a beam of invisible light through a tiny hole drilled in the window, to bounce off the resonating surface that was one of the panes of glass in the bedroom of Jens's suite; through another small hole the beam from a second laser touched the glass of a window in the suite's sitting room.

Jim paused to look at the carefully arranged tangle with satisfaction before leaving. It was a deep pleasure to him to work with his hands this way. The neatness of it left him with a calm, steady feeling of having done something well. Any voices or other sound within the two rooms of Jens's suite would cause vibrations in the glass windowpanes. The laser beams would read those vibrations, and transmit them back through the tangle of equipment by wire into a converter, and from there into a tape recorder that appeared to be turned off, but was not. Once in the converter, the vibrations would be reconstructed as sound which could be recorded on tape. Literally, from now on, no word could be said in Jens's apartment that would not be recorded by this device as well as if it were connected to mechanical bugs wired into the walls of the suite itself.

Jim went out, locking the door behind him. On his way to the elevator, he passed the glowing exit sign, and on impulse stepped into the stairwell. Narrow, green-painted stairs led upward one flight to the floor above him that was reserved for the V.I.P. visitors and government personnel like Jens Wylie. Jim went quietly up the stairs and tried the entrance door on the floor above. As he had expected, it was solidly locked.

He turned around and went down again to his own floor and out into the corridor. When the elevator came it was empty. Thoughtfully, he pushed the button for the floor above. The elevator hesitated. The downward-pointing red arrow alight on the elevator's control panel blinked out; and the white arrow beside it went on, pointing up. The car rose. The door slid open. Jim stepped out into a small lobby, empty except for a squarely-built man in his mid-twenties, wearing a business suit, reading a paper and seated in one of the half dozen overstuffed chairs that occupied the lobby. He got up at the sight of Jim.

"Were you looking for someone?" he asked pleasantly, in a New England accent.

Jim smiled back at him.

"Just poking around the motel," he said. "I thought there was a restaurant up top here someplace."

"There isn't," said the young man. "Rooms only. Also, I'm sorry, but this floor's private."

"You don't mind if I wander around anyway, do you?" Jim asked. "I always like to prowl around a new motel."

"Sorry," the other answered. "We do mind. You understand that, now, don't you?"

He stepped past Jim and pushed the button for the elevator.

"Oh," said Jim, "of course. But you don't mind if I ask who's on this floor?"

"Sorry," the young man smiled at Jim. Jim smiled back. The elevator came.

"Well thanks anyway," said Jim, stepping into it.

At that moment a female figure came into sight around the corner of the corridor leading to the lobby.

"Hold the elevator!"

She was young and her voice was strong and cheerful. She came toward the elevator with long, rapid strides, and stepped in.

"Thanks," she said impartially to Jim and to the young man in the business suit, who were each holding one of the doors of the elevator open.

"Pleasure to help, ma'am," said the young man. He let go of his door and Jim did the same. The doors closed and they went down.

Her eyes met with Jim's. She was, Jim saw, at least as tall as he was; with chestnut hair, oval face, and the open, competent look of a woman who had never been beaten down, either by the events of own life or the strictures of her own particular niche in society. He smiled at her. She did not smile back, but her eyes looked him over as frankly as he had looked her over. She was, Jim thought, out of his territory. With someone like Aletha he always felt an immediate common bond; but this girl came from a different house on the street. All the same, though, she was female and attractive; and he liked her with the same immediate liking he had for almost every other woman he had ever encountered. He could feel her response to him. It was different—but parallel. She was not the kind to be strongly attracted to him. But she could like him, too, in spite of the age and other differences between them. Under other circumstances they might have been good friends.

As he was thinking this, the elevator reached the lobby. The doors opened and Jim stood aside to let her out first. As he stepped into the lobby behind her, his good feeling went and his stomach muscles tightened. Watching him from beside the reception desk was a black man wearing a solid-gray business suit—five-eleven, a hundred and eighty pounds, in his late thirties or early forties. Jim recognized the quality of the watcher as immediately as he had ever recognized another barfighter in his old beer-drinking days. This trooper would be one of the government security team here at the motel. Not only a team member, but a damned good one. The way he stood gave him an in-charge look, an air of liking his work for its own sake. Only the eyes moved in his dark face, and they continued to follow Jim as he crossed the lobby behind the girl. Clearly the guard on the upper floor had called down and this security sergeant, or whoever he was, had come out to see for himself if Jim was just a casual tourist—or something else.

The woman who had come down on the elevator with him was a half dozen strides ahead of Jim. He lengthened his own steps and caught up with her at the entrance to the lobby restaurant. While the eyes across the lobby watched him, he spoke to her.

"Thinking of having breakfast?" he said.

She turned to face him. For the first time, there was a little smile at the corners of her mouth.

"Coffee," she said. "At the counter. Alone."

"Well, well," said Jim gently. "Have a good day."

"I intend to," she said, turned away from him, and went through the white-curtained, glass door into the restaurant.

He turned and went away from the restaurant toward the front door, in profile to the man who stood by the desk, setting his face into a slightly angry, pouting mask. He was, he hoped, the very picture of some salesman in town for a day or two and on the cruise for a woman, who has just been turned down. He reached the front door and went out.

The Gremlin was there waiting for him. He pulled it away from the curb and headed out in the traffic. A feeling of regret stirred in him, a desire to go back in through the outside door into the bar where Aletha would be at work. But now that the security sergeant had seen him, that particular bar was going to have to be off limits to him, at least when Aletha was around to identify him by a name other than that by which he had registered.

12

The directness of Bill Ward's question took Jens unaware. He had spent too much time recently among political people and their words; he had forgotten this other area of machines and their people—the land of plus and minus, day and night, go or no-go. All at once the pressures of the last few days, the tension, the lack of breakfast and the half a can of beer on an empty stomach piled up on him and made the whole situation seem unreal. He stared at the strange, empty, sloping-floored room around him, half-ready to believe that it was some stage scene mocked up for his bafflement. Even as he looked at the room it seemed to sway and tilt in the fashion of a room in the crazy-house of an amusement park.

"Hold on!" Something caught him strongly by the upper arm and he became aware that Bill Ward was holding him upright in his chair and was talking to him. "What's the matter, Jens? You all right?"

Jens blinked and got his eyes, the room, and himself once more under control. He straightened up in his chair.

"Yes," he said, surprised at the huskiness of his own voice. "Skipped breakfast this morning. I guess it really wasn't the best thing to do."

"You're pretty pale," said Bill sharply. "You'd better just sit there a minute. Let me get you something."

"No, no. I'm fine . . ." But Bill was already gone. "Just water!" Jens called after him. After a minute or two Bill came back with a paper cup half-filled with water.

"May be a coffee taste to it," said Bill, sitting down with him again. "There's no cups around here. I had to get a cup of coffee from the machine and pour the coffee out to fill it with water from the fountain. How do you feel?"

"Fine," said Jens. The water flowed down his gullet, a cool finger of feeling that brought him to. He set the cup down. "Where are we? What is this room?"

"One of the firing rooms," said Bill. "There were four—one never got activated. You still look pretty white. Sure you're all right?"

Jens nodded. "Look, you asked me what scheduling I wanted to talk to you about. It's the experiment schedule for the Expedition."

"That?" Bill's face hardened. "You?"

"I know it's none of my business, officially," said Jens. "But Tad told me the 'nauts think the schedule's too heavy. He wanted me to talk to the President. I did. I even got Tad to talk to him. Nothing doing. So I came to you."

Bill sat in silence for a second.

"Why me?" he said in an emotionless voice.

"It's politics," said Jens. The room threatened to sway again; but with determination he kept it solid and real. "Every nation involved in this wants the largest share of the Expedition's time they can get; and national pride's at stake when it comes to agreeing to cut their share of the schedule. Apparently the President—apparently they *all* believe that the general public in each of the cooperating nations wouldn't stand for the experiments being cut. It's the way they measure their share in the Expedition."

"All right," Bill Ward said, "I say—why come to me with this?"

"You're the Launch Director."

"Sure."

"Well," said Jens, "you're one of the people who're putting those men up there. If their work schedule's too heavy during the first six weeks, or whatever, you have to know it, don't you? If there's something that's going to put them and the Expedition in danger, you'll want to correct it—"

"Slow down," said Bill.

Jens quit talking. For a second they were both quiet; and a healing silence gathered round about them in the empty room.

"What do you expect us to do?" asked Bill, after a little.

"You could kick up a fuss," said Jens, but without the

explosiveness that had been in his voice a moment before. "If you get word from them that they're too busy, or too tired, you can tell them to skip part of the experimental work, can't you?"

"You want the Expedition Director for that," Bill said tightly. "If and when they complain to him he'll order a reevaluation of the situation and take what corrective action seems to be called for."

"I don't know the Expedition Director," said Jens. "You do. If you spoke to him, wouldn't he order a reduction, as long as you and he have to know as well as Tad and the others do that they're overscheduled?"

Bill sat back in his chair. He was thick-waisted enough so that he sat stiffly upright, putting his head higher than Jens's. He glanced briefly at his watch.

"I've got to get back to the firing room," he said. "I'm sorry, I couldn't help you even if I thought you had a point. Even if I wanted to. You're talking to the wrong man."

"Is it the truth that you'd want to?" said Jens, as Bill shoved his chair back.

Bill stopped. For a second he loomed over Jens like a low-hanging thundercloud. Then he relaxed and straightened up.

"Let me tell you something," he said, sitting down again. "I don't think I have to explain this, or anything else, to you, but I'm going to. Do you know what puts men up into space? Other men and woman. And those other men and women have to eat. They've got to make mortgage payments and feed their families. There's got to be a payroll; and the birds don't pay for themselves like a cash register. What they do is bring in long-term benefits that a high percentage of people can't connect with their going up in the first place."

"I know that," said Jens.

"Do you?" said Bill. "Do you know it in the paycheck area? Were you ever personally given the choice of taking a one-quarter or more cut in your salary at a time when you had shoes to buy for the kids and dental bills to pay? Take it or quit your job? It isn't a matter of work—most of the people here work long hours when they're needed, away and beyond what they're paid for in the first place. But they've got to be paid *something*. And we damn near lost that something, that minimum, half a dozen times now.''

''I know that,''said Jens.

''Never mind what you think you know,'' Bill said. ''Just listen a bit. The last time we damn near lost the payroll was two years ago. And if we'd lost it entirely, we would have lost the experienced men behind the work going on here today. As it was, we lost a lot of them anyway. People blame it on the push for poverty programs; but if it hadn't been the poverty programs, it would have been something else. Once the emotional push quits, the people who don't know basic research and don't understand it start to make themselves heard. And those who ought to explain it to them are too busy attending to their own affairs. So something like the space program goes down the drain, along with the skills of the people who've worked in it fifteen to twenty years. And everybody suffers.''

''You don't need to worry now,'' said Jens. ''You've got half the population of the world cheering for you on this mission.''

''Right,'' said Bill. ''And if they quit cheering, it's not going to be because of anything our people did: If we cut that program of experiments while it still looks possible the marsnauts can handle them without trouble, and then one of the cut experiments results in some people here, or India, or anywhere else, dying because certain experimental equipment wasn't tested—what do you think the newspapers are going to say about us when they start reporting those deaths? Well? You were a newsman to begin with. What do you think?''

Jens sat silent.

''You see,'' said Bill, a little more gently, getting to his feet from the chair, ''we're able to make this Expedition to Mars because the public spotlight's on us again. But the price of being in that spotlight is that everything we do is going to be seen, and remembered—and maybe used against us some time in the future when the spotlight's back off. You can be sure we'll reexamine the experimental schedule if and when the 'nauts complain about it. But doing it beforehand—and under the circumstances—doesn't make sense.''

He stopped talking. Jens still said nothing, sitting there not knowing quite what to do.

"Come along with me," Bill said. "I've got to turn you back over to the security man who brought you."

Jens stood up numbly. With his hand resting almost gently on Jens's shoulder Bill led him up the bare slope of the floor and out the door into the corridor. The guard was waiting for Jens outside the entrance to the other firing room. Bill nodded to the guard and disappeared.

"Where to, Mr. Wylie?" asked the guard. "Back to the press stand?"

Jens started and came to. He looked at his watch.

"No," he said. "No. I'm supposed to be over in the VIP area by this time. Better take me there as fast as you can."

But when they got to the VIP area, he and his guide were directed on to the entrance of the Operations and Checkout Building, where the deputy ministers were waiting to watch the marsnauts board the vehicle that would carry them to the waiting shuttle.

Over a period of time, thought Tad, a spacesuit became familiar, just like everything else. The strangeness that came with it, the first time you had it on, and that everyone who had never worn one imagined was always there, was lost somewhere along the way. In the end it was no more than getting taped up and into a football uniform.

Of course, it still took over an hour to get the spacesuits on, even with plenty of help. First came the long underwear with all the sensors wired into it that had to be attached to the skin of the body at various points with a special glue that not even perspiration could loosen. Then, there were tests to make sure the sensors were all working. Then came the climb into the suit itself, and the twisting to get the plug with wires from the underwear sensors into its socket inside the suit. Then more tests to see that everything was working when the suit was plugged in to the recording outlet. Finally, there was the sealing of the suit and walking around in it, the testing to make sure that everything had been done right and nothing had been left undone.

Then you were free to move out to the carryall waiting to transport everyone to the shuttle.

Leading the others, Tad clumped on his heavy magnetic (though presently inactivated) boot soles down the corridor, into the elevator, along the ground-level corridor and out into the sudden glare of August Florida sunshine. His helmet's faceplate darkened automatically, and the temperature control of the suit was undoubtedly stepping itself up to keep him cool, though he could not sense that. Out beyond the entrance, by the green glass-topped carryall, was a small knot of people—the deputy ministers, provided with headsets and phones so that they could talk to their 'nauts. Jens was among them, looking somewhat disheveled, as if he had hurried to be here. Tad stopped briefly in front of the taller man. Jens, he saw, was not looking good; his face had the stupefied, heavy expression of someone overdue for sleep. His lips moved.

"Good luck," his voice said over the circuit in Tad's earphones. The words were overlaid with and made almost unintelligible by the voices of all the other diplomatic people talking at once to their own 'nauts. It was like being on an old-fashioned telephone party line that everyone was trying to use at once. Jens shook Tad's large-gauntleted hand, peering through the sunshaded glass of the helmet to see his face.

There was no way to talk privately. Tad raised his eyebrows interrogatively. Jens shook his head. Tad nodded grimly in acknowledgement of the information and promise of his determination; but the gesture, while successful, was lost in the looseness of the spacesuit. He did not believe that Jens had seen or properly interpreted it.

Someone was tapping Tad on the shoulder. It was time to get into the carryall. He raised his right glove in salute to Jens, turned all in one piece, as you had to do when suited, and went forward and up the steps into the carryall, taking the first large seat to his left.

The other 'nauts entered, heavy-footed, and went past him to fill the double row of seats on either side of the wide aisle. Fedya, as co-commander of the mission, took the other front seat, across the aisle from Tad. The door to the carryall closed and the vehicle rose on its underjets and slid off down the way to the waiting shuttle.

They had fallen into group silence again; and, isolated in the privacy of his suit, Tad welcomed it. He was conscious of the suit as a second skin. He felt the familiar pressure of the EMU urine collection system, front and back about his crotch, the pressure of the shoes against his sole and heel, the weight of his helmet, of the folded fabric pressing on shoulders, arms and thighs, the thickness at his waist and under his arms. But it was a familiar feeling, again like the football uniform—no matter how strange it might feel to someone else. Now, in their suits, all of them in the bus had stepped over the line, and become a different sort of people from all those others on Earth who were waiting and watching. They who were bound for space were set apart by what they did—and by why they were about to do it.

They belonged to Earth, but their business was elsewhere. They were like working sailors. Like deep-sea fishermen. He remembered the age-greened copper statue at Gloucester he, Wendy, and the kids had seen years ago on vacation, the statue of the New England fisherman standing with one knee braced against the wheelhouse, the deck canted under him, the eyes beneath his rain hat looking outward and ahead.

He and the other 'nauts, Tad thought, were like sailors. They must travel out and away. The silence of the suit phones rang in his mind now like the imagined sound of the sea heard when an ocean shell was held to the ear. It was as if it was to the sea he and the others were now going. How did the psalm go? *They that go down to the sea in ships, that do business in great waters . . .*

Jens managed to break away from the deputy ministers. Luckily, the guard and the NASA auto had waited for him.

"Back to the press site," Jens said, getting in. The car pulled out into the empty road.

As he crossed the wooden bridge to the press stand, the loudspeakers were announcing that the vehicle carrying the 'nauts had just reached the shuttle. The big screen in front of the press stand, thirty feet long by ten high, gave a window-like three-dimensional view of the carryall pulling up the ten-degree slope of the concrete launch pad, to halt at the top by the Mobile Launch Tower. Slow-moving because of their suits and therefore more solemn than they might have seemed otherwise, the 'nauts emerged, one by one, from the vehicle and went to the elevator in the MLT.

All this was happening as Jens walked along the front walkway of the stands, looking up into them to find Lin. He found her at last, about halfway up in the far end section, and climbed up the nearest aisle. She had her arm over an empty gray-painted metal folding chair beside her. As he came up to her, she took her arm from it.

"Sit down," she said. "I've had a hard time holding this for you." She looked at him perceptively. "I'll bet you didn't have any breakfast after all."

He shook his head. "Doesn't matter. We'll make up for it at lunch. You'll be ready for lunch yourself, after the launch?"

"Of course," she said lightly. "I always lunch after launch. Did you set up those appointments for me with Wendy Hansard and Penny Welles?"

"I'm sorry," he said. "I just haven't had time yet—" He broke off. She was staring at him.

"Haven't had time!" she exploded. "I mentioned it to you last night and again this morning! Do you realize I've been down here nearly twenty-four hours and as far as the magazine's concerned I haven't done a thing?"

"I really am sorry," Jens said. "But in any case you couldn't get to see them until later—"

"And what if it turns out I can't see them this afternoon? What if it turns out I'm going to miss them completely because they're going off some place?" She was blazing mad. "Do you think I came down here just for . . . just for a holiday?"

"I'll do what I can as soon as I can," he said. "They'll be in the VIP stands right now, watching like everyone else. There's no way I can talk to them until after the launch. As soon as I can, I will."

Lin jerked about, staring straight before her over the rows of heads below, at the large video screen before the stands.

He watched her for a moment, waiting for any answer she

might make. But she made none. He looked at the screen himself. The 'nauts were going up in the Mobile Launch Tower elevator now two by two, and across the catwalk to the shuttle entry hatch, some seven stories above the level of the launch pad. Jens felt empty—a shell of a man, inwardly stripped of energy and muscle, a dull-minded, sweating observer, floating with the too-powerful currents that pushed against him. Lin's burst of anger had cut away his last illusion of understanding and support for the lonely position in which he had placed himself.

Yet this was the moment to which he had been looking forward. The moment in which he had expected to feel something almost mystic, with the larger part of the world's population concentrated, participating in a single action all together, like members of a single family. And, in fact, to a certain extent, the feeling was there.

The stage was set. Before them, beyond the stands and the line of video cameras with their telescopic lenses manned by assorted news cameramen, was the grassy apron of land leading to the deeply dredged canal up which the huge sections of the Apollo rockets had been brought to the Vehicle Assembly Building. The VAB itself stood to their left, still ready and able to handle four vehicles the size of the three-stage Apollos at once, one in each of its high bays. In the other direction, three miles off from the press stand, on the launch pad of LC39, was the shuttle itself.

Above, the relentless August Florida sun beat on metal, concrete, green scrubland, men and women alike. The mingled voices from the press stands of newspeople speaking into telephones and microphones and to each other hummed like the voice of a wasp hive under the amplified tones of the public address system, explaining what they were seeing on the large video screen.

"... and now, last of all, as senior of the two co-commanders of the mission, Tad Hansard is leaving the elevator and boarding the shuttlecraft ..."

From day-brilliance, Tad stepped once more into interior dimness; and once again his faceplate adapted, clearing so that he could see the section of the shuttle in which they would travel. The six gimbaled acceleration couches were arranged three on a side, and the foremost one on the left side was waiting for him. He walked to it, eased himself down into it and plugged his spacesuit's umbilical into the receptor mounted on the metal wall alongside it.

It was like sitting in a circular-walled section of an old-fashioned cargo plane. The shuttle itself was a cargo carrier and the metal framing and walls of its body were bare. The floor beneath the couches was corrugated steel plate, interrupted only by the metal hatch opening in the center and the ladder, leading both down to the cargo sections below and up to the control section overhead. Up there, the pilots and copilots of the shuttle would already be in their own acceleration couches, ready to lift.

Everything around Tad—couches, receptors, even the floor plate—was an accessory to the shuttle's normal interior configuration and could be quickly and easily removed in the case of a flight carrying only cargo to one of the space labs in orbit around Earth. Like himself and the other 'nauts, like the shuttle itself, everything here was utilitarian, replaceable—and expendable.

Anoshi and Bap were talking now over the helmet phone system, joking gently and quietly. Beside him, Fedya was not talking; and Tad did not feel like talking either. Work time was here. They were away from the eyes of the world now, ready to begin their jobs.

A red light lit on the forward section of curved wall facing them.

"Shuttle pilot, here," said a voice in their earphones. "Steve Janowitz, gentlemen. All ready to lift on schedule in eighteen seconds, seventeen, sixteen . . ."

The press stands were half empty. As in the days of the Apollo flights, many of the newspeople had left them and swarmed forward to the water's edge a hundred yards off. Lin had chosen to stay in the stands. She had heard that they literally shook at the moment of launch and she had wanted to experience that.

"I think I'll go down," Jens had said.

"Yes," she had said, somewhat emptily.

She had watched him walk slowly away, becoming smaller with distance and then finally lost in the crowd. He did not slump or drag his feet, but it seemed to her that there was something defeated in his walk. She felt a sting of remorse for her outburst at him at the moment in which he had had so much emotion invested. Not for the first time, she wondered if there was something of a demon in her, something shrewish and destructive. Then she reacted against that worry, and forced herself back to hardness. Jens had to learn. He had to learn, that was all, that the rest of the world would not always adjust its needs to fit his dreams. He might for a while be able to get away with it, having his eyes on the stars and being oblivious to everything else; but other people like herself had to get their nails dirty digging up a living right here down on Earth. It really wasn't the matter of the unmade appointment that had got to her. Lord, she could make her own appointments any time she needed to. But he had to learn, he had to learn, for fear worse would happen to him later on if he didn't. It didn't matter that her rubbing his nose in it made her feel desolately miserable, like this. It had to be.

The lost feeling began to wane a little, replaced by the contagious tension of the crowd as the countdown around her went into its last stage.

". . . five," said the public address system, "four . . . three . . . two . . . one . . . We have ignition!"

Orange flames spurted from the base of the shuttle, shooting out to each side. For a moment the whole space-going creature seemed to stand there unmoved above the flames—then it began to rise. The flames faded to white fire. Slowly, and then more swiftly, the shuttle lifted into the sky; and the thunder of a giant's firecracker reached and rolled over the press stand. As the shuttle went swiftly and more swiftly up into the cloudless sky it was lost to the sight of those below.

They had been right, those who had told her about the stands shaking.

The hand of acceleration lay heavily upon Tad and the others as the shuttle lifted—but not so heavily as in the past. Three gravities for the shuttle as opposed to the ten gravities of the Apollo launches. Tad waited out the pressure that forced him down into his couch, until it finally yielded part way, then ceased altogether. His weight went from him and he floated on the couch. Thirty minutes had gone by and they were now in orbit with the two Mars ships that had been assembled here, away from Earth's gravity.

"Just about there, gents," said the voice of the shuttle pilot in their helmets. "Right nice burn we got. Now a little correction . . ."

Ten minutes later, there was a clanging of metal transmitted through the skin of the shuttle as it docked with one of the Mars ships.

"Phoenix Two," announced the shuttle pilot in their earphones.

Fedya, Dirk, and Bern disconnected their umbilicals, rose and clumped off through the entry hatch of the shuttle that now opened on a docking tube connecting with the entry hatch of the second Mars vessel.

"Now for Phoenix One," said the pilot. The shuttle undocked and moved on.

Ten minutes more and it was the turn of Anoshi, Bap, and Tad to leave their shuttle couches for the tube. It let them through an air lock into the pleasant, white-walled surroundings of the control level—the top of four levels—in the ship that was to be their home for the next three years. They checked to make sure the air lock was closed again behind them.

"All clear," said Tad over his helmet phone to the shuttle pilot.

"All clear. Disengaging," came the answer.

With a clang heard through the metal bodies, the shuttle undocked from Phoenix One. The three of them moved to their control couches and plugged in their umbilicals. They began final checkoff.

The seconds counted down toward launch time. Checkoff was completed. From the two ships Tad and Fedya reported to Expedition Control that all was ready; and Expedition Control entered the last sixty seconds of countdown to firing—to the actual launch that would lift both ships into a Mars-injection orbit.

"Fifty seconds and counting," said the headphones in Tad's helmet as he lay on the acceleration couch waiting. About him he could feel the huge shape of Phoenix One, thirty-three feet in circumference, two hundred and seventy feet in length with two mighty booster engines flanking her. "Forty seconds and counting . . ."

He could feel the ship now as if she were no more than a more massive spacesuit enclosing him. She was his ship, he and she were identical.

"Thirty seconds, twenty-nine seconds . . ."

Earth was nothing, now. This was everything. He could not look back at the planet below, he could not even look back in his mind to his wife and children, in this moment. He could look nowhere but forward, out toward where he was going, like the statue of the Gloucester fisherman peering ahead from under the brim of his rain hat. . . .

"Fifteen . . . fourteen . . . thirteen . . ."

They that go down to the sea in ships, he thought again, *and do business upon great waters*—that had been written for him and the five others as well as for all those who had ever sailed out of sight of land. It was only a mightier ship he sailed, now, out into a greater ocean.

"Ten . . . nine . . . eight . . ."

He thought the psalm should read, They that go out to the stars in ships, and do business in great spaces—

"Two . . . one!"

His gloved finger came down on the backup firing button. A part of what was unseen to him, white fire blared from three great sets of jets; and acceleration jammed him down, down into his couch as Phoenix One, with her sister ship beside her, lifted outward to the stars.

13

Twenty-eight minutes later the pressure of acceleration ceased; and Tad floated lightly on his acceleration couch. On either side of him, Anoshi and Bap would be gravityless as well. A lightness that was from something more than just the lack of gravity seemed to touch him. He felt free and in command at last.

"Phoenix One to Phoenix One booster shuttle pilots," Tad said into his helmet phone. "Is firing completed?"

"Booster Shuttle One," said a voice tinged with the accents of the western plains. "Firing completed."

The free feeling still lifted inside Tad. He pushed it aside. There was no time for that now.

"Booster Shuttle Two," added another voice. "Firing completed."

"Thank you, gentlemen," said Tad. He reached out a gloved hand and changed channels. "Expedition Control. This is Phoenix One. Both booster shuttles have ceased firing."

"Roger, Phoenix One." The voice of Expedition Control came drawling back at him almost before his last words were uttered. "You're in injection orbit, right on the button. Phoenix Two's right there with you. If you want to take a look to starboard there, about ten kilometers, you ought to be able to catch the sun on her."

Tad turned his helmet with some effort to stare out the glass port to his right. For a second he saw nothing but stars against the blackness of airless space. Then there came a slow, bright flash that seemed to burn for about half a second before vanishing. A moment later it was repeated.

"Looks like they're yawing just a bit, there," said Tad.

"Nothing to trouble about, Phoenix One," Expedition Control said. "Phoenix Two advises they're smoothing it out with steering jets. You all ready to say good-bye to your booster shuttles?"

"All ready," said Tad.

"You have the go-ahead, then, Phoenix One," said Expedition. "Effect separation from booster shuttles."

"Roger," said Tad. He returned to the frequency on which he had been talking with the pilots of the two nuclear booster shuttles, strapped one on each side of Phoenix One.

"This is Phoenix One again," he said. "All ready to separate. Shuttle One and Two, also ready?"

"Shuttle One ready."

"Shuttle Two ready."

The answers were immediate.

"Firing release charges," said Tad. "Three, two, one . . . fire!" With the last word his gloved finger came down on the button, setting off the explosive charges which released the heavy bonds banding Phoenix One to her two booster shuttles. There was a dull thud from what seemed behind them in Phoenix One; and Tad reached up to activate a view of the shuttles in his pilot's screen, looking back from a sensor camera-eye mounted near the front of the spaceship.

Full in the sunlight, looking as if they were below the underbelly of Phoenix One, the two shuttles appeared to be falling away, separating as they went. A couple of flashes from farther off signaled the sections of banding, tumbling in the sunlight as they moved away at the higher speed imparted to them by the explosive charges releasing them. The support shuttles themselves were departing from Phoenix only on the small push of steering thrusters. Now, as Tad, Bap, and Anoshi watched, each shuttle slowly revolved end-for-end, so that they faced away from Phoenix One.

The shuttles had lifted Phoenix One to Mars-injection orbit, from which she would now begin her nine-month coast to the point where she would fire her nuclear engines to fall into a close orbit around Mars. Now they were dwindling in the screen, looking almost tiny. It was jarring to think that with their separation, plus the fuel they had expended, the Mars mission had already spent the greater part of its mass—

just for the initial departure from Earth orbit. Tad felt the diminishment almost like a personal loss.

A little over half an hour ago, Phoenix One had weighed approximately one million six hundred thousand pounds. Now, with the departure of the two booster shuttles, that weight was down to six hundred and seventy-five thousand pounds. By contrast, at the time Phoenix One reached Mars, she would have lost only an additional twenty-five thousand pounds—down to six hundred and fifty thousand pounds. Life support and consumables plus fuel needed for mid-course correction would be the reason for the twenty-five thousand pounds that would be spent.

Bap was murmuring something incomprehensible, his voice a low tone over the helmet phones.

"What, Bap?" Tad asked, turning his head to look at the other's couch.

Bap broke off. His helmet was facing toward a port which gave a view of the dwindling booster shuttles.

"What? Sorry," he said. "Oh, sorry. Just—remembering something from the *Bhagavad-Gita—The Song Celestial*. In English it goes something like '. . . Today we slew a foe, and we will slay our other enemy tomorrow! Look! Are we not lords . . . ?' "

"Hmmm," said Tad. The quotation seemed to have no application to the departure of the shuttles or their present situation. But there was no understanding Bap.

I should learn to keep my thoughts to myself in my head, Bap was thinking, a little ruefully. *No point in telling them that what I quoted was part of the speech of the Unheavenly Man, as Krishna delineates him. But it would have made no more sense to Tad and Anoshi if I had. Still, it is true. We are very lordly here with our powerful ships and our Expedition plans, close to Earth. But out there, close to Mars, we will be small and insignificant. No, no point in trying to explain what I meant or felt. To the English anything religious must be immediate or personal.*

Not, Bap corrected himself, *that Tad is English. But no, he is, in the sense I use the word. Tad is distorted English, as Dirk over there on Phoenix Two is undistorted English. And the English do not understand such thoughts as I was* thinking. Neither the English nor the American English understand. Would Anoshi? Not really; and in that sense, he is tinged with an English sort of color also. Even as I am tinged with English, because I am conscious of, though rejecting, what it is to be so colored. Truthfully, we are all alike, Tad, Anoshi, and I.

Possibly that is part of it. I love Tad—nonsexually, of course—Bap grinned in his helmet. One always has to make that distinction when thinking in English. Why am I thinking in English? Because I am thinking about English—rather, about some quality I call "English." No, I have a great affection for Tad. Once long ago, it might have been that we rode to battle on horseback together, swords at our waists. And Anoshi, also. It is not sheer accident that the three swashbucklers among the six of us should find ourselves in one ship. Over in Phoenix Two, they are in common of a different breed and cloth, once one ignores all their national differences. Even Dirk, who is English, is not-English in that sense . . . I am becoming whirled about with words. The words are losing me amongst them. I should stop thinking and return my attention to duty . . .

Outside, the booster shuttles were now pointing away at an angle from Phoenix One.

"Booster Shuttle One to Phoenix One," said the phones in the helmets of Bap, Tad, and Anoshi. "So long, and good luck."

"So long, Phoenix One," said the different voice from Shuttle Two pilot. "Good luck to y'all."

"Same to you," said Tad. "So long."

Bright fire, barely visible in the sunlight of space, spurted from the jets of the two shuttles. They seemed to hang there a moment, not moving; then they began to shrink, at first slowly, then more and more rapidly, until they were suddenly gone.

Somewhere off to the starboard of Phoenix One, Tad knew, the two booster shuttles of Phoenix Two would also be retrofiring to head homeward into Earth orbit.

"Expedition Control," said Tad, punching the console before him. "Our booster shuttles have just taken off. We're now ready to restore Phoenix One to an active status."

"Roger, Phoenix One," came back the voice of Expedition Control. "We copy that. You're now going to restore Phoenix One to active status. Your next communication with us will be sixteen hundred hours, according to schedule."

"Roger. Copy," said Tad. "Sixteen hundred hours. Over and out for now, then."

"Over and out, Phoenix One," said Expedition Control.

Tad switched back to communication with his two crewmates.

"Okay," he said. "Let's get this ship unbuttoned and back in full operation."

He sat up on his couch and the other two rose with him. Still in their suits, they turned to the business of bringing the ship around them up to operating condition.

Primarily this meant restoring the operational and life-support systems of the ship, which, with the exception of the biomedical lab, had been under storage conditions for the last nineteen days, since loading had been completed of the two Mars Expedition ships which had been constructed in orbit. Chief of these systems was the 5 psig nitrogen-oxygen operating atmosphere of those sections of the ship where the three of them would live and work without suits, closely followed in importance by the thermal control systems and the power distribution systems. These and all the related mechanical activities of the ship would enable them to live and work aboard her for three years, until they saw Earth again. In his mind's eye Tad saw the duties to be performed like soldiers at attention, waiting to be dealt with.

The three of them raised their couches into control position, and went to work on the consoles before them where primary controls for all the systems were located. One by one, the small red sensing lights began to burn, signaling that the systems were up to full operational level. Then, one by one, for the benefit of the ship's automatic log recorder as well as for theirs, each of them went verbally through a checklist of the systems he had brought to full activity.

". . . and all systems full on," said Tad finally, winding up the checklist. "Phoenix One in complete active operating status. All right, let's start our visual check of the decks."

He led the others as they got to their feet and headed toward the access tube running through the center of all four of the ship's decks. In the absence of gravity, and still in their spacesuits, they bumped clumsily against each other, opening the door to the tube and entering it. Tad went first, pulling his way along—in the direction that "down" would be, once Phoenixes One and Two were docked together and rotated to provide a substitute for gravity—until he reached the door opening on B Deck. This was the first deck below A, the control deck they had just left; like A, it consisted of a doughnut-shaped space, the outer wall of which was separated from the skin of the ship only by insulation and a network of thermal tubes designed to balance interior temperature between the heat of the side of the ship in direct sunlight and the chill of that side in the shade. The interior wall of B Deck, like that of all decks, was the wall of the access tube.

"Home," said Anoshi, cheerfully, when they had all emerged on to B Deck. And, in fact, that was what it was.

Unlike A Deck, which was all open space with the control consoles and other equipment spaced about its floor, B Deck was partitioned. Three of the spaces enclosed by partitions were the individual cabins, somewhat more spacious and deserving of their name than the individual "sleeping compartments" in Skylab.

"Look," said Anoshi. "Nameplates already up on each door. No danger forgetting where you sleep."

Tad looked. What he saw had not been specified anywhere in the original plans, or part of any of the mock-ups of B Deck he had encountered back on Earth. A solemn black nameplate had been attached to the door of each cabin—a small, almost impish touch on the part of those who had finished off the interior of the spaceship. The nameplates were unnecessary. Long ago, the three had decided which cabin would be whose among the three of them. But they were a little bit of human decoration, a going away present from some of the ground workers. He felt the emotion behind the nameplates in spite of himself; and reading the tone behind Anoshi's words, understood that Anoshi—and undoubtedly Bap as well—was feeling it, too.

"Well, let's check them out," said Tad, breaking the spell. Each stepped into his own cabin, the magnetism of the soleplates on their boots switching on and off with each flexing of the instep above it, so that it was a little like walking across a kitchen floor where something sticky had just been spilled. The rooms checked out; and they met again outside them to step together into the wardroom.

The wardroom—dining and recreation quarters alike for the three of them—took up nearly a third of the space on B Deck.

"I'll check storage and waste compartments," said Tad. "Meet you down at C Deck."

He went next door to the small consumables storage compartment where immediate supplies of their food and drink were packed. The storage compartment checked out, and he moved on to the waste management compartment. The strict utilitarianism of the waste management compartment that had been tested out in the Skylab had undergone some improvement here—in looks, if nothing else. But the basics remained. Equipment had to be available for the biomedical monitoring of the three men's body wastes—although on Phoenix One automatic equipment took over most of the job. In addition there had to be disposal capabilities for a mass of things, from food containers to damaged tools or parts to discarded uniforms, which were easier to throw away than launder under space conditions. Again, happily, automatic machinery took care of the freezing and dumping of these wastes through a channel leading to an air lock in the unpressurized section aft.

With the waste management compartment checked out, Tad went on down to C Deck and the four different lab and workshop sections there. Anoshi and Bap were still checking the equipment. Tad went on alone to D Deck.

The fourth and final deck was packed solid with stores and equipment. Much of the equipment was intended for use in the experimental programs for the Expedition's first four weeks of coasting to Mars, while public interest was still high. Tad looked grimly at the ranked cartons.

These Mars Expedition vessels had been designed originally to carry double the crew they had now—six men per ship. Now they barely had room for three. Part of the crowding was due to proliferation of basic research itself—the larger countries, at least, had finally begun to wake up to the need for it, under the demand by their peoples for new technological answers to massive natural problems of air, water, and land. But the overriding reason for Phoenix One and Two being so overloaded with research equipment and problems was political.

Jens Wylie had failed him about getting the list reduced. That left no one to turn to but himself. And Tad had done some tall thinking in the last twenty-four hours. In fact, he had come up with a possible way of saving the men and the Expedition. Only he would need at least some help—and the only one he could turn to for it was Fedya.

He would talk to Fedya as soon as he could. Meanwhile he shoved the matter from his mind and came back to the immediate job. A quick check took D Deck past inspection— and beyond D was only the Mars biolab, sterilized and sealed at present. From the Mars biolab forward to Control Deck A constituted the so-called "shirt-sleeve" area of the ship. Familiar as he was with it from training with the mockups of the individual spaces, Tad could not help feeling a new sensation of being constricted and enclosed. This was the life zone—these four and a half decks—of Phoenix One. Outside that zone, and its duplicate on Phoenix Two, there was no place where life was possible without a spacesuit between here and the Earth they had just left.

Beyond the biolab and the unpressurized section surrounding it there was only the hundred-and-sixty foot section of the single nuclear shuttle, their main engine, that would not be fired until they had reached Mars and it was time for them to drop into a close orbit around that red planet. Forward of the nuclear shuttle, the life zone plus the unpressurized compartment beyond A Deck holding the unmanned probes and the MEM, the Mars Excursion Module, made up the remaining hundred and ten feet of the spacecraft. In less than fifty-six feet of that hundred and ten, he, Anoshi, and Bap would spend most of their next three years living and working.

It was cramped, it was not beautiful—but it was their ship, it was *his* ship. And he would bring it through. Buoyant, Tad turned and made his way back in the access tube to A Deck where Bap and Anoshi were already waiting for him. The A Deck chronometer showed 1400 hours exactly.

"Visual check of Phoenix One shows everything A-okay," Tad informed Cape Canaveral. It still seemed a little odd to him to be reporting to Canaveral at this point instead of to a Mission Control at Houston NASA. Tad's experience in space dated back before the last and most serious economy cut had reduced the NASA installation at Houston to a shadow establishment. In theory NASA headquarters were still there. In reality, only a few administrators and a planning division still occupied the few buildings NASA made use of at the once-busy installation. Expedition Control for the Mars flight would be at Kennedy Space Center throughout the trip.

"Roger. We copy. Visual check Phoenix One, all okay."

"So," said Tad, "unless you can think of a good reason for us not to, we'll start getting out of our suits now."

"Hold that desuiting for a moment, will you, Phoenix One?" said Expedition Control. The helmet phones fell silent.

"Now," said Anoshi, "they'll send us back to run a white glove around the compartments for dust, before desuiting."

"Not dust," said Bap. "Gremlins. There is nothing worse than gremlins in your control systems. An Extended Gremlin Watch must be kept in operation at all times—"

"Okay there, Phoenix One," said Expedition Control, coming suddenly to life again, "you may proceed with the desuiting."

"Good enough," said Tad. "Copy. We'll begin desuiting."

Getting out of the spacesuits was not quite as much a problem as getting into them; but it was still an awkward and lengthy process that only in theory could be easily performed by the spacesuit wearer alone. In practice, a good deal of helpful hauling and tugging by extra pairs of hands was welcome. Tad, as spacecraft commander, had the privilege of being the first to be helped out of his suit, after which he helped free first Anoshi, then Bap.

The emptied spacesuits went into a storage compartment, leaving the men in the undersuits that were designed to match with the many connections and entry points of the spacesuits.

"Go ahead," Tad told the other two. "I'll be ready to man the first shift." Standing orders called for one of the three-man crew to be dressed and ready to don his spacesuit at all times. The other two were free to shift to CWGs, Constant Wear Garments. Bap and Anoshi disappeared down the access tube; and Tad seated himself in his acceleration couch, now in control position, to inform Expedition Control that they were now ready to begin docking maneuvers with Phoenix Two.

"Roger. We copy that," said Expedition Control. "Have you got position figures of your own yet?"

"In process," said Tad. He was squinting through the sextant lens at the sun, the north star, and Earth, seen simultaneously through three different sensor eyes on the outside of the ship. His right hand twisted knobs until the three lines intersected at centerpoint on the lens. Then he punched for the inboard computer, lifted his eye from the lens and looked at the computer screen.

"I'm in reference grid cube JN 43721, Kennedy," said Tad.

"Copy. Grid cube JN 43721. How's your radar, Phoenix One?"

Tad looked at the radar screen with its sweeping line of light and the intersecting blip in the upper right quadrant.

"Fine," said Tad. "Phoenix Two looks to be not more than sixteen kilometers off."

"Thanks, Phoenix One. That checks with our data. Stand by for plane, bearing, and distance."

"Standing by," said Tad.

While he waited, Bap and Anoshi came back up to the Control Deck.

"Say again?" Tad asked, for the sound of their return had obscured some of the figures Expedition Control had just begun to give him.

Expedition Control repeated itself, giving Tad first the angle to the longitudinal axis of Phoenix One of the plane which enclosed both spacecraft, then the bearing and distance of Phoenix Two from Phoenix One within that plane. Tad reached for the control buttons of the cold gas steering jets used to maneuver his ship. A docking maneuver between the two vessels in space was too chancey to be trusted to any computer.

"All right, Expedition Control, I copy," he said. "Phoenix One to Phoenix Two, if you are holding position, I will approach for docking."

"Holding position, Phoenix One," came back the calm voice of Fedya. "Come ahead."

Tad's fingers descended on the controls of the steering thrusters. Out beyond the glass viewing point to his right, the little reflection of Phoenix Two was lost among the lights of uncounted stars. In the ceaseless glare of the sun, through the airless distance between them, six hundred and seventy-five thousand pounds of Phoenix One tilted, turned, and drifted toward the six hundred and seventy-five thousand pounds of Phoenix Two under the necessity of coming together with a touch so light that it would not have dimpled the bumper of a four-thousand-pound automobile back on Earth.

14

The lights of all the stars visible forward flowed slowly away from the point toward which Phoenix One headed. As they reached the edge of vision they accelerated, disappearing off the edge of the hemisphere of the front-vision screen in the control console before Tad, to appear in the rear-hemisphere screen, slowing gradually once more toward the point of no motion that was directly behind the moving spacecraft.

Phoenix Two was only a brighter point of light for some minutes, then a glare-spot for some time more. Only when Phoenix One was finally quite close did she appear to change suddenly from a light-reflection to a spacecraft. Actually, it was as only half a spacecraft in the forward view screen, because, lying nearly bow-on to the approaching Phoenix One, as she now was, only the half of her length that was illuminated by the sun was visible. The other half was swallowed up in the perfect darkness that was shadow in airless space, so that she looked as if she had been divided longitudinally by an enormous band saw.

Anoshi and Bap sat on their own couches and waited. In Phoenix Two, Fedya, Dirk Welles, and Bern Callieux would be doing the same thing. There was nothing to be done on the other ship, and only one man could do what needed to be done aboard Phoenix One.

The motions of Tad's fingers on the controls of the steering thrusters were practiced, familiar ones. He—and for that matter the other five 'nauts as well—had practiced steering one ship into docking configuration with the other, unnumbered times. But there was always the difference between rehearsal and reality. Tad felt the prickle of sweat on his face and at the back of his neck. He was as conscious of the whole two hundred and seventy feet of craft about him as a man might be of his own car while maneuvering it into a parking place.

He approached Phoenix Two slowly, bow to bow, the great bell-shaped ends of the forward sections, the space probes and their individual MEMs in airless readiness, now creeping toward each other like blind leviathans about to touch in greeting. Beyond the circular metal lip of each of those ends were six feet of the light metal scaffolding enclosing half of the zero-g lab pod and the cryotex tube leading back into D Deck of each ship. The two scaffoldings must take the impact of meeting; and also they must interlock to hold the two ships together. It would be upon their joined structure that the strain would come when the two ships were rotated around their common central point, where the completed pod would sit, to provide a substitute gravity for the men aboard both crafts.

The two ships moved closer to each other, slowing more and more as they approached under the braking jets of the thrusters activated by Tad's fingers. Expedition Control and Phoenix Two were now silent. Bap and Anoshi were silent. Only the faint hum of the inboard air system fans aboard Phoenix One competed with Tad's voice.

". . . Twelve meters from dock-point," Tad was saying aloud for the benefit of Expedition Control. His eyes were no longer on the now completely bow-on image of Phoenix

Two in the forward screen, but on the graduated schematic screen below it, where the outline of both spacecrafts approached each other, square by red-lined square. ". . . ten meters . . . nine . . . eight . . ."

Phoenix Two seemed to loom above the viewers of the forward screen, as if she was falling upon her sister ship.

". . . three meters . . . two. One . . . *docked!*"

What sounded like an unreasonably loud and prolonged clang rang through Phoenix One and Two. But a red signal light, unlit until now, was burning to the right of the console in front of Tad, signaling that the two scaffoldings had locked correctly and were holding.

Tad sat back in his seat with a sigh.

"All okay, Phoenix Two?" he asked.

"All okay," Fedya's voice answered.

"Phoenix One to Expedition Control," said Tad. "Docking accomplished. Are we clear to send a man EVA from each ship now to activate outside equipment and secure?"

"We copy docking accomplished," said Expedition Control. "Tad, will you hold off on EVA for the moment? We'd like to run another position check on the two of you now that you're docked together."

"Be our guest," said Tad.

There was a short period of silence from Expedition Control.

"All right, Phoenix," said Expedition Control, coming back to life again. "Your position shows no discernable drift as a result of the docking maneuver. You may EVA and activate exterior equipment whenever you're ready."

"Roger," said Tad. He looked to his left, at Anoshi, who nodded. "Anoshi will EVA for Phoenix One."

"Dirk will EVA Phoenix Two," said Fedya's voice.

"Roger. We copy. Anoshi to EVA Phoenix One, Dirk to EVA Phoenix Two," Expedition Control agreed.

Anoshi got up.

"Back into harness," he said. He disappeared down the access tube.

Bap touched the button on the communication headband above his ear, cutting off the voice-activated microphone on the slender arm that curved around to the edge of his mouth.

"Good for you, Tad," he said softly. "Anoshi wanted to be first man out. Did you know that?"

"No," said Tad. "Besides, he's first out because he's the astronomer here, the cameras are his."

But it was true about Anoshi—Tad had not known, but he had suspected.

"Sure. Only when you kept your undersuit on, I thought you were planning to be first out yourself," Bap said.

"Standing orders call for a man to be ready to suit up whether there's a man EVA already or not," Tad replied. "You know that."

"Ah, yes," said Bap. "But you could've just told one of us to get back into his undersuit."

A little silence fell. A few minutes later, Anoshi came back out of the access tube, wearing his spacesuit underwear. He went across to the spacesuit locker and got his suit out. Tad and Bap helped him get into it, and fastened to his belt the tools he would need and the film packs for the cameras he would be activating.

"All set," said Anoshi over the communication caps the other two had redonned—also according to standing orders when one of them was to be outside the shirt-sleeve area. He lifted a gloved hand, rose and turned to the access tube. This time, on entering it, he went forward rather than aft, for the distance that would be the height of A Deck; and at the end of that distance he came to the inner door of an air lock.

The air lock let him forward into the airless, though now lighted, space containing the Mars Excursion Module and the unmanned planetary probes that would be sent down to Mars—and in the case of one of them, down to Venus on the trip back. He went forward alongside the two-meter height of the cryoflex tube that would provide a shirt-sleeve conduit to the pressurized section of the zero-gravity pod between the ships. He followed the tube forward and exited through the hatch in the end wall to find himself among the light metal scaffolding that had joined with the scaffolding from Phoenix Two to dock the two ships together.

There was no spacesuited figure from Phoenix Two in sight yet, so Anoshi turned and walked from the hatch, the magnetic soles of his boots sticking and yielding alternately to the outside surface of the end wall, until he came to the actual edge of the ship's hull some twenty feet away. He stepped over the foot-high end rim of the hull onto the cylindrical metal of the hull itself. Above him all the stars of the universe revolved solemnly as he went from the surface he was on to one at right angles with it. It was like stepping around the edge of a box from one flat side to the other.

He walked down the hull.

There were twelve recording star-cameras for him to check out and load, five fixed, three with automatic programmed movements, and four which could be manipulated from inside the ship. There was the laser mirror to erect and align, and the solar cell holders to erect. But, as he walked slowly along the ship, Anoshi was thinking only secondarily of these things.

His mind was filled now, at last, with the great, passive satisfaction of being where he was—here, alone with the ship and the stars.

He had said no word of what concerned him to any of the other five 'nauts; nor had he said any word of it to any other human being. Bap and Tad had perhaps sensed the emotional traces of it through the closeness that had grown up between them all. But even with them, it would be no more than seeing the corona of a solar discharge, without feeling the unbelievable power and heat behind and below it. Alone of all the six now between Earth and Mars, he had been ashamed not to be more than he was. He had wanted to be a true astronaut, a marsnaut, not just a space-going scientist.

There were only two real marsnauts aboard: Tad and Fedya. Anoshi and the other three were merely scientists with astronaut training. For Bap, Bern, and Dirk, this difference did not seem to matter greatly. What counted with them, apparently, was that they were *here*, on any terms. But Anoshi had wanted more than that; and only a trick of timing had forbidden it to him.

Unlike the other three, he had been intended to be a marsnaut—a true marsnaut in the space program of Nippon. But that program had not gotten to the point of developing its own experienced astronauts at the time that this Expedition was conceived and instigated. If it had been, he would have been a space traveler in his own right, instead of, as now, a sort of auxiliary specialist, for all his recent months of training. Only one thing could make him a marsnaut; and that was the very thing he was doing. He was leaving Earth as an auxiliary specialist. But three years from now he would come back, they would all come back, true marsnauts, men who *had* voyaged through airless space between the stars, from one world to another.

That was why it was so important that he be out here alone as he was now—he interrupted his thought and knelt to check and load the first of the outside cameras. His gloved hands worked clumsily but surely and the loading section of the camera opened, black with shadow, before him. He loaded it, closed it, and rose to his feet again. By the time he came back to Earth there would be nothing concerned with the Expedition that he would not have done. Anything any one of the others was to do aboard, he would find a way to do also, officially or privately. That was his goal and he would see it accomplished.

Moving on to the next camera now, he saw that Phoenix Two had disgorged her own spacesuited figure. There was no external identification on this suit, but over the months they had grown used to the way the others moved when suited. Anoshi identified the other figure as Dirk and lifted an arm in greeting. Dirk waved back. He had gone to work on Phoenix Two's outside cameras, and clearly they would work their ways back together eventually to the scaffolding joining the two spacecraft for their final duty of making that joining rigid and secure.

Anoshi finished the cameras and moved on to set up the solar cells in their holder. They made up a square panel standing almost as tall as himself above the hull of the ship. By contrast, when, twenty feet further aft of the cells, he lifted the copper laser mirror into erect position and peeled the protective coating from its carefully polished surface, the mirror stood barely thigh-high and was no more than a square foot in area. Miracle of science, thought Anoshi fondly, handling it. So tiny, to serve eventually as a target for a coherent light beam all the way from Earth to Mars.

The laser mirror was small but massive, with its heavy

cooling fins at the back. He locked it in the upright position and engaged its base with the control housing below it that would enable it to be aligned from within the ship. Then, finished at last, he rose and headed toward the scaffolding and the pod.

He moved slowly forward along the ship since Dirk was still involved with the laser mirror on Phoenix Two. At that, Anoshi still had to wait several minutes after he had reached the scaffolding for Dirk to join him.

The scaffolding consisted of two heavy rodlike sections diametrically opposite each other around the circle of the rim of the end wall of each ship. They held the two vessels a little less than ten feet apart; and had been so designed that the rods of matching sections clung magnetically to those of the opposite ship as the vessels had come together. Magnetism and inertia still held them together, but the spacecraft were merely drifting at the moment. The rods had to be clamped tightly together to take the strain that would come upon them when the two six-hundred-and-seventy-five thousand-pound masses were rotated about their jointure to provide gravity for both ships.

The clamps were built into the rods. Working in silence, Dirk and Anoshi pulled them into position and dogged them down by hand. Then, when that was done, they moved to the center of the space between the now locked-together spacecrafts and began to seal the two halves of the no-gravity pod that was approached by the cryoflex tubes from each ship.

The sealing was a simple matter of intersandwiching several specially treated layers of the rubbery, fantastically strong cryoflex fabric along the lines of jointure. Once these layers were laid in contact, an electric current sent through the fabric from either ship would cause the layers to flow together in a bond more than capable of containing the pressure of the ships' atmosphere. Of course, only one half the pod would have atmosphere and be connected to the tubes that now made a shirt-sleeved passageway from one ship to the other. The other half, beyond its impermeable wall, was to be left airless, enterable only by someone in a spacesuit through a simple hatch in its side.

"Done," Anoshi announced over the common phone circuit of both ships. "Run the current through the pod fabric, pressurize, and you're all set."

"Done, indeed," said Dirk's voice in the earphones. "Phoenix Two, pay no attention to any unofficial reports from Phoenix One personnel. This is your own coworker announcing everything A-okay."

"We copy," Tad's voice said.

"Copy," said Fedya. "Come on back inside, Dirk."

"I," said Anoshi, "am returning inside, Phoenix One. My apologies for taking so long; but there was some bystander in a spacesuit that kept getting in my way."

"Awfully crowded out here in space nowadays," said Dirk.

They waved to each other, turned and stomped off toward the hatches in the end walls of their ships.

By the time Anoshi was back inside on A Deck, Tad had started the ships rotating about their common center to provide the equivalent of about half a gravity at the far ends of both ships, where the main living and working quarters were.

It was not really gravity, of course, but the centrifugal force produced by those same two ends being swung around a common center—the same sort of force that can be felt in a certain type of ride in amusement parks in which people are spun rapidly around on a wheel-like affair. Same force, in fact, that historically allowed the milkmaid to keep the milk in her pail while she swung it completely overhead and back down again.

It was not the same thing; but it would be, it was hoped, a great help in many matters, from aiding utensils to stay on the surface of a table, to keeping liquid in cups. Primarily, however, it was aimed at avoiding the bone loss and other damage that earlier astronauts had reported after long stays in space under weightless conditions.

At the end of his shift, Anoshi gratefully switched off the magnetism in his boot soles. Meanwhile, electrical current had effectively sealed the pod halves and safe atmosphere pressure common to both ships was built up in the tubes connecting them through the pod. Tad, now seated at his console, had finished passing the word to Expedition Control and was inviting Fedya over for a visit.

"We're scheduled for a down period now, anyway," he was saying over the phone circuit. "Come across and spend half an hour with me and a cup of coffee. We'll go over the schedule together."

Fedya nodded, looking back at him from the phone screen. "I'll be over in five minutes," he said.

Five minutes later, punctually, the hatch in the ceiling of A Deck just beside the access tube opened. Fedya climbed easily down the handholds on the outside of the tube until he reached the deck. He looked around.

"Bap?" he asked. "And Anoshi?"

"In their compartments," Tad said, getting up from his console. "They're going to get some sleep."

"Dirk and Bern are down, also," said Fedya. He carried a folder of schedule sheets under his arm. Now he held them out. "Do you want to compare these with yours?"

"No," said Tad. "We can just work with yours. Besides, there's something else I want to talk to you about, privately."

He led the way to the access tube. They climbed down to B Deck and went in to take a table in the wardroom by the dispensers. Tad got them both cups of coffee.

"Something else besides the schedule?" Fedya queried gently, when they were seated.

"No. Really *beside*," said Tad. He looked at Fedya. "You know I tried to get the experiments list cut."

Fedya nodded. "If everything goes without trouble, we should be able to get it all done."

"It won't." Tad lowered his voice, glancing toward the wall beyond which was the first of the sleeping compartments—luckily his own and therefore empty. "It can't. It's too much to expect everything to go perfectly. And if it doesn't, the work is going to spill over into our down time. What's more, it'll be cumulative. Expedition knows we're scheduled too tightly."

"We can only try," said Fedya.

"And make a mess of things when it all falls apart," said Tad. "It's these first four weeks when they've got us scheduled to be working on all the razzle-dazzle research. There's political pressure behind every item on the schedule, you know that."

"As I say," Fedya repeated. "We can only try."

"No," said Tad, "we can do better than that. We can keep the schedule."

"You just said that was impossible." Fedya was watching him closely.

"It is. I've got a notion, though," said Tad. "Only, I'll need a lucky break—from one other man. Maybe I should say an unlucky break."

He looked at the long white fingers Fedya had wrapped around his coffee container.

"Someone on Phoenix Two," said Tad, "would have to have a minor accident—to his hand, say. Enough to bar him from working in a spacesuit."

Fedya's eyes met his.

"Not the sort of accident that would slow him down on his share of duties inside his ship," said Tad. "Just enough to keep him from going out. To make up for what he can't do, the man from our ship would do both, now that they're docked."

"And how will this man find time to do that?" Fedya looked closely at him. "This man—yourself?"

Tad nodded.

"Don't ask me how," he said grimly. "In fact, don't ask anything. Forget we had this little talk. But I tell you the program can be kept and completed, if I just have that one bit of help."

Fedya's eyes held with his. They sat, looking at each other. That Fedya understood, Tad had no doubt. That he would help, was another question. It was up to him; all up to him, now.

15

Jens floated gradually from a dream into wakefulness. He had been dreaming about the moment of the launch itself, and the rest of yesterday, following that. Now, imperceptibly, the dream melted into his actual memories—memories that still had the vividness of the dream-experience, so that he lay, remembering what had happened as if he was reliving it, and without any real awareness that he still lay in bed.

He had been to a number of the earlier launches of the shuttle itself and of the spacecraft that had been parked in orbit waiting for the men of the Mars Expedition to come to them; and he remembered, as a boy, being with his father and watching some of the old Apollo launches from the V.I.P. area at Kennedy Space Center. It had been wonderful enough then, to see the great white-painted towers lift off for space, but it was not until he grew up and was able to come as a newsman that he truly appreciated the launches, seeing them from the press site.

The press site was different. For one thing it was closer to the launch pads than the V.I.P. or the Dependents Area. But, more than that, the fact that the press site was occupied solely by working newspeople gave a different angle and perspective on what was about to happen and what eventually always did happen, as it had again, yesterday.

The first few rows of the stands at the press site were always filled with reserved sections to which telephone and other equipment lines had been run, and yesterday had been no exception. Under the shadow of the roof—the press site was the only one that had a roof, to keep the rain off the papers and other materials on the desks in front of the correspondents—these front rows were always very busy for several hours before the launch with newspeople talking to distant radio audiences, or dictating stories to rewrite people.

Higher up in the stands yesterday morning, there had been less equipment than usual to be seen, but more people. Early, under the merciless Florida sun, ancient buses had brought most of the newspeople out to the site. They had still some hours to kill before the countdown would be completed and the launch could take place; so they were in continual movement, visiting the trailers that sold soft drinks and sandwiches and bringing back their purchases, sitting around eating, drinking, and talking to each other.

But when the countdown began to approach launch time, the air of conviviality in the upper stands had dwindled away into one of purpose and of work. Even on the top levels people were to be seen hammering away at typewriters, making notes and sketches, looking through Questars and Celestrons, as well as ordinary binoculars, at the launch pad three miles off, where the shuttle itself now stood like a monstrous double airplane, twin white plumes fuming softly in the sunlight, as it bled off the excess pressure of the liquid oxygen and liquid hydrogen being piped aboard to be combined as fuel for its flight.

As the countdown went into its final minutes, a gradual exodus began from the stands toward the front edge of the stretch of grassy earth that reached to the edge of the canal leading to the Vehicle Assembly Building. For some time now cameras on tripods had been set up at the canal bank, as close as the photographers could come to the actual bird itself.

Now these cameramen were being joined by a host of other people moving down under the common impulse to get as close as possible to the shuttle at the moment of launch. By the time the final seconds were being counted off over the loudspeakers, the crowd was standing four and five deep at the edge of the water.

Leaving Lin behind, Jens had gone down to the canal edge alone, almost relieved to be solitary in this moment of semi-communion. This was his moment, at last, the moment that paid off for all else. It was what he had waited for all these months, compensation for his position here as a political straw man, and his knowledge that that was all he was, a reward for all he had come to believe in as far as space and man's effort to go out into it went. Now, with the launch of the shuttle, all this and more became worthwhile and proved.

For a moment, like a vague, uncomfortable, gray ghost slipping through the back of his mind came the memory of his self-centeredness and guilt in not making the appointments for Lin. Once the launch was over, he thought, he could probably get over to Expedition Control in time to catch both Penny and Wendy there, before they left. He could talk to them both, then, and set up appointments . . .

But the countdown was almost finished. His mind left the uncomfortable area of neglected duties and came back to this moment that was his personal justification. There were only seconds to go, now. He was only feet from the edge of the water, closely surrounded on all sides. He looked about him.

In the center, the crowd was thickest. He found a place off to one side where there were only two people between him and the shuttle; a tall man and a small, dark-haired girl, talking quietly in Spanish with an Argentinian accent. Once more, as always at these launches, he found himself unable to believe that the massive, double craft he was looking at, perched up on the enormous concrete pad, would really be able to lift itself against the force of gravity, when the moment came. In spite of the many times he had seen it, it was always unthinkable. The construct was too heavy, there was too much mass. It was impossible.

Intellectually, he knew that in a few moments he would actually see it happen. He knew that it would suddenly prove itself—do the impossible—and that in the moment of its doing, everything would suddenly be reversed. The wonder and the glory of it, the great rightness of it, would lift him as well, suddenly making anything possible. But right now it was unbelievable, and he knew it would go on being unbelievable up to the very second in which he finally saw it happen.

About him, in the crowd, he could feel the emotional heat of other reactions similar to his own. The people about him were relatively quiet, speaking to each other only in short sentences and in undertones, as if the shuttle was some huge wild bird that might be frightened by too loud talk in its vicinity and disappear before it was able to do what they had come to see it do. There was tension to be felt in the air all about Jens; there was a feeling of expectancy, mounting to uneasiness.

Jens—reliving the moment now—remembered wondering then, as he always did at these times, that repetition did not seem to be able to dull this experience and make it commonplace. Instead, it was almost as if continual exposure to launches sensitized the individual's emotions to them, in the way the someone might become sensitized to an allergen; so that later launches were more excruciating to the imagination, not less, than the ones experienced earlier, when knowledge had been less and expectation imprecise.

Now, as he stood, he could hear the large clock-board facing the stands behind them complementing its visual image with a verbal countdown, counting off the seconds, *"ten . . . nine . . . eight . . . seven . . . six . . . five . . . four . . . three . . .*

"Two . . . one . . ."

Silence.

Then, in utter quiet, orange-red flame spurted from the base of the shuttle, spreading out for a distance equal to half the height of the shuttle itself and billowing up around it. There was no movement of the vehicle in those first few seconds. Only the silent outburst of the flames.

Without warning, the craft was in motion. The first second of its movement had been imperceptible; but now, suddenly, it could be seen to move. It raised itself slowly, very slowly at first; but then, as it lifted, it began to move more and more swiftly. The flames spread out below and around it; and for the first time sound began to reach the ears of the watchers, a distant firecrackerlike popping.

Now it was lifting more swiftly, the flames behind it paling, going bright-transparent in the sunlight. Now, it was half its own height into the air, accelerating upward. The sound mounted; it came crashing around those watching, no longer in sharp snaps but as a rolling chain of heavy explosions that shook the air and sent ripples racing across the surface of the canal toward the bank on which they stood.

The earth and air were vibrating now with the sound and the movement of the shuttle. It was moving rapidly up into the cloudless sky. It had been able to fly after all; and now it was on its way. All at once they were all reacting. The tenseness and waiting, all the hushing of voices were over; and everybody was talking at the top of their voices, all around Jens.

"Did you see that? Did you see that?"

"Shit! Shit! Look at it go!"

"It's going—it's really going, it's going . . ."

Just in front of Jens the little Argentinian girl with the dark hair was pointing up into the sky with rigid arm and forefinger.

"*Mira!*" she was crying. "*Mira . . .*"

Jens himself watched it along with the rest until it curved away into the sky, became a point, and invisible. There was a moment of nothing, then a faint, faint down-range flare. The two massive solid propellant rockets had just burned empty and been jettisoned, for later ocean recovery. The orbiter was running on the liquid propellants in the even more massive tank attached to its belly. There was nothing to stop it now from reaching the Expedition spacecraft in orbit.

Jens turned from the water and the empty launch pad. He began drifting back with the rest of the crowd, back to the stands and Lin. He was coming down gradually from the excitement of the launch moment. He wondered how Lin had felt and it came to him that some time he should find out. It was one of the things he badly wanted to know about her.

The thought of the unmade appointments struck him like a blow. He found a phone in the stands and, as he had expected, was able to get through to Penny Welles and Wendy Hansard at Expedition Control. Both were evidently preoccupied—Jens could hear the drone of the controller's voices as they followed the ascent of the shuttle—but agreed on times to see Lin.

Lin seemed subdued when he rejoined her, and looked at him thoughtfully. He told her about the appointments.

She said, "It's good of you to have done that, and I should have known you would. That was . . . something, that launch, wasn't it?"

She had not said anything more about it, and in the bustle of getting back to town, he had not pressed her. Their afternoon—and, as it turned out, the evening and much of the night—was taken up with a post-launch party held at the home of a science fiction writer who lived in the Merritt Island area. Nearly all the people there that evening were professional writers who had been down with assignments of their own and press passes to the launch. Now, writers and photographers alike, they were back at the home of Mike Spelman, the local author, celebrating, watching the television coverage on the shuttle's trip to orbit and the subsequent delivery of the astronauts to the actual Mars Expedition ships, drinking, eating and talking—talking until Jens's own head began to spin with words and liquor, and he forgot to ask what it had been like for Lin at the moment of launch, after all . . .

Jens woke now to the undeniable fact that he was awake. His eyes were still closed. But his dream had run itself all the way into conscious memory, and he was once more aware that he was in his room. He opened his eyes and looked around him. The covers were thrown back on the other side of the bed and Lin was gone. Bright sunlight made radiant the drapes that were drawn across the window to keep the daylight outside.

Jens continued to lie still, waiting for his body to come to the moment of wanting to get up. He could think of nothing he needed to do; and after the pressure and hurry of the last week, a sort of delicious laziness held him where he was. Sooner or later he would feel like moving—and then he would get up.

While he still lay, thinking this, he heard a door shut in the sitting room of the motel suite, and steps coming briskly toward the bedroom. He closed his eyes again, quickly. As the steps came into the bedroom, they slowed and became more quiet. Suddenly, he felt guilty about pretending to be still asleep and opened his eyes.

"I'm awake," he said.

Lin was standing beside the vanity mirror on the wall across the room. She came over and sat down on the edge of the bed beside him, looking down at him.

"Where did you disappear to?" he asked.

"I had something to do," she said. "I thought you could use the sleep."

He stared up into her green eyes, which this close and from below looked enormous and brilliant. He felt a sudden, aching desire for her, but knew it was no use. Morning was always the quietest and best time for him. It was the time at which the world moved back into the distance. But for Lin it was the last thing at night, the end of the day, that was private and best. Now, without asking, without reaching for her, he knew that whether she would agree or not to come to him now, at best it could be only a divided time, in which they would not be fully together. She was wrapped around with her daytime armor. Her crisp clothes, the faint scent of cologne, the touch of lipstick on her lips, all held him at a distance.

"Do you still want to see the dragon?" he asked.

She smiled down at him.

"If it won't eat me."

"Not this dragon," he said. "All right, it's all set. Steve's going to lend me his runabout. I talked to him about it at the party last night."

"Which Steve was that?" she asked.

"Steve Fourmelle," Jens said. "He's not a writer. I mean he's not a free-lance writer. He works for one of the newspapers here in town. You were probably thinking about Steve Anjin. Anjin's in his sixties and he was writing fantasy for the pulp magazines back before World War II. Steve Fourmelle's about my age. Short, red hair."

She nodded.

"I remember him now," she said. "What kind of a boat do they call a runabout down here?"

"Just a small inboard," he answered. "Actually, I've never seen that one of Steve's, myself. Let me get dressed and get some breakfast and we'll drive down to the Eau Gallie Causeway and have a look at it."

They ate in the motel's coffee shop, which was still crowded, but nowhere nearly as much as it had been on launch days; then, one or two people had been standing and waiting for every one being served. In fact, in spite of the people who were still around, there was a feeling in the air as if the town of Merritt Island was already being deserted. Afterwards, they took Lin's rented car and Jens drove it to the Eau Gallie Causeway, a long stretch of bridge-highway across the shallow, extensive width of the Indian River that flowed down the eastern side of the finger of land that was Merritt Island.

The marina was larger than they expected and they had to locate the manager in order to find the boat they wanted. When they did get to him, however, they discovered that Steve Fourmelle had phoned ahead about their coming, and they were expected. The runabout turned out to be a twenty-foot green and white semi-cabin cruiser with a sixty-horsepower inboard engine and a draft of perhaps a foot and a half.

"Are you sure you can drive it?" asked Lin, as Jens standing below her, helped her down from the dock into the cockpit. She stepped carefully across the drainboards to sit down on the semicircular padded seat that filled the end of the cockpit.

"No problem," said Jens. "I've been handling boats like this since I was a kid. Remember I grew up in lake country—Minnesota."

He leaned forward to check out the controls. The manager of the marina was still standing on the dock, watching them. He leaned over to speak through one of the open windows of the half-cabin in which Jens now stood.

"The channel's straight out in the middle, here," he said, "you'll see the markers. Better follow them pretty close. This channel's been dredged ten-twelve feet, but the water'll get real shallow any place you're not inside the markers, right down to near the end of the island."

"Thanks," Jens said, over his shoulder.

He started the motor, backed the runabout out, turned it around and headed for the center of the broad expanse of blue-green water where the channel markers indicated passage. A few moments later, they had left the marina behind and were purring southward along the Indian River with the shore seemingly a long distance away on either side.

"We'll be going down the east side of Merritt Island, headed south." Jens called over his shoulder to Lin.

She came forward and perched on the pilot chair to his right in the cabin, looking out through the front windshield as he stood at the wheel.

"How far is it?" she asked.

"It's only a twenty-minute run," he said, "and twenty minutes back again."

"Does it smell this bad all the way down?" she asked, wrinkling her nose.

"No," he said, "we get away from that. They're tidal lagoons, actually, these Indian and Banana Rivers, more than they're anything else. There's a lot of silting up and decay of vegetable matter in the shallow water along the shores. Farther down, the bottom near shore gets rockier and deeper, as we come to the tip of the island."

"It seems to be getting better already. Did you spend some time down here when you were a boy?"

"No." Jens shook his head. "When we weren't out of the country altogether, the places we lived were mainly up north, and always were after dad became a senator. But we were down here at Kennedy sometimes, on trips for a day or two. He brought me down to some of the old Apollo launches— but I told you about all that, didn't I?"

He was conscious of her watching him, although he had to keep his eyes on the water ahead.

"Yes, you did," she said. "That's when you fell in love with all this, wasn't it?"

"You mean with the Space Center and the idea of space?" he said. "No. I was hooked before then. I can't really remember how much before. To tell the truth I can't remember when I wasn't in love with it."

"Was your father ever?" Lin asked.

Jens shook his head. Under his fingers, the wheel of the runabout resonated with the vibrations of the motor that was sending them steadily southward.

"No," he answered. "He was all for the idea of being in a race with Russia, the idea that started the first space push in the fifties that ended with landing a man on the moon. But anything beyond that sounded to him like a waste of money.

As far as he was concerned, the moon was just another rock and we had plenty of those down here on Earth already.''

"Maybe he was right," said Lin.

Jens shook his head again.

"No," he said. "He was a working politician. He ought to have realized that where there's competition for anything there's a need in common; and this time it was a need that'd been around since the beginning of civilization—the need to find a better way of surviving. There's all sorts of pressures pushing our frontiers out into space. Not just political ones, either."

"Yes, I've heard you on that," said Lin. He could feel her eyes watching him steadily, while his own gaze was still fixed on the water ahead. "All right. I can see it, too—technology and civilization pushing us out to the moon, and even to Mars. Only, I'm not so sure we ought to let technology and civilization do that to us, even if everybody for the last three years has been jumping on the bandwagon and saying what a great thing it is, talking about all the advantages in new engineering techniques and pure knowledge to be picked up by getting outside the environment of Earth's atmosphere. And I can see the bit about our learning more about this planet by getting outside it. I like the idea that now we've got better crop control and better weather control, and that we're beginning to handle our land and seas better because of being able to look at it from the outside. It's just that I wonder if the cost isn't too high."

He looked at her.

"That again?" he asked.

"I'm not convinced, that's all," she said. "I'm willing to be convinced."

"I can't convince you," he shook his head. "I've tried that. I believe, myself, because I believe in a number of factors that can't be measured exactly; and they convince me. You don't believe in those factors; and since neither of us can measure them exactly—there we are."

"I'd feel better," Lin said, "if I could believe it wasn't just a hangover from the stars in your eyes when you were young that makes you so sure of these unmeasurable factors you talk about."

"I don't know how to prove to you that's not the case, either,"said Jens. "Didn't you ever have stars in your eyes? And what makes you so sure that you haven't still got some, for something? How can anybody be sure of that?"

"I'm not. Of course, I'm not," Lin said. "But I can have a hangover of stars in the eyes and still want to be practical."

He looked again out at the water ahead.

"I don't know how to convince you," he said, half to himself.

"Try looking at it from the opposition's point of view, once, why don't you? Step off to one side and take a view of the whole project from a different angle."

"Damn it, that's what I do every day!" said Jens. "Do you think all the people around me are people who really believe in the space program? Do you think these other ministers for space believe in it the way I do? If they do, it's for entirely different reasons than mine. They're most of them hooked on the business of an immediate profit from it, or on some kind of an immediate personal or national benefit from it, just the way my father was! I spend ninety percent of my time trying to get a grip on their way of looking at it, so I can talk with them on grounds they understand. This whole business of too heavy an experimental load—" He broke off abruptly.

He waited for her to speak; but she said nothing. He turned his head from the water to stare at her.

"Believe me," he said, "the number of people in this thing who've got stars in their eyes is a lot less than other people think—a lot less among those with authority, anyway. And as for the nonstarry-eyed—they're all as practical and hardheaded as even you'd like. I'm talking about the mass of the NASA people involved, the engineers, the engineering companies themselves, the 'nauts and all the rest. They may have a dream or two but what they're actually doing is as straightforward and realistic as digging a ditch. And that attitude pays off for them eventually in exactly the same way that digging a ditch does. It gets the ditch done, and kicks out the knowledge and the skills to dig the next ditch better, to get more and better ditches dug in the future, so that we'll all be better off. Now, you ought to know that."

She sat without saying anything for a few seconds, not as if she had been impressed, but as if she were gathering together in her mind what she would say next.

"I've got one opinion about this expedition and the whole space effort," she said finally. "I've got another opinion about you. Right now, it's you I'm thinking about, and what all this is doing to you."

"It's not doing anything to me!"

"Whoa! Back up, Jens!" she said. "It's done plenty to you, already; and it's going to do more—and you know it!"

He took a deep breath, looking back out at the water.

"All right. It's doing a lot to me." The dazzle from the river surface ahead was abruptly in his eyes. He blinked. "There's got to be a line somewhere that we can agree on, something between being impractical and wanting to see something accomplished, some effort for something better that wins out."

He stopped speaking. For a long moment he steered the boat in silence, and Lin did not speak either. Then he opened his mouth again.

"We've gone around and around on this before," he said, "and we never get anywhere. The plain fact of the matter is you can always outargue me. But that doesn't make you right and me wrong."

There was a small, sharp, audible intake of breath from Lin. He waited, but she did not answer. He wanted to look at her but somehow could not make himself do so.

"Nothing more to say?" he asked, at last, still watching the river.

"No," she said, quietly. "At least, not about that. Tell me something about this dragon. What is it, the fossil of some dinosaur someone's found and mounted somewhere?"

"No, not that." He found himself grinning, quite lightheartedly, to his surprise.

"You're not trying to get me to think it's some kind of actual dragon, now?" she said. "You're not going to tell me that?"

"Well," he said, "I think of it as an actual dragon."

She got up, stepped over, and threw her arms around his waist from behind, digging her chin into his right shoulder.

"You would!" she growled in his ear. "You and a real dragon! Now there's a great combination!"

He felt the agreeable pressure of her body against his and the tight warmth of her arms around him. He was also aware that her right knee was pressing lightly against the inside of his own right knee and a simple yank backward by her, using her knee as a fulcrum, could put him on the deck.

"No tricks," he said.

She chuckled in his ear.

"What's the matter?" she asked. "Are there rocks in the channel?"

"Damn it, of course there aren't. But there're rights-of-way and we're not the only boat out here. We're not supposed to be straggling all over the place without a hand on the wheel."

"No spirit of adventure," she said. But her knee relaxed its pressure against the inside of his. "And you're the one who's taking me to see a dragon. I don't know where you get your suspicious mind, anyway."

"Experience," he said. "I know you, remember? As a matter of fact, take a look out to your left. The channel's moved closer in toward the land now that we're farther down the island. If you look out there, you'll see there are some rocks, though it'd take us a few minutes to get close enough to run up against them."

She stepped to the half-open window of the cabin.

"And the smell's gone. This is more like it. When did we get so close to the bank?"

"We've been moving in, all the way down along the river," he said.

He looked over and saw her fascinated by the shore. The scene here was entirely different. Alongside them, here and there through the trees there was a glimpse of riverside road— but only a glimpse. Most of the shore they were looking at consisted of a rocky rise of several feet, either with green, well-kept lawns coming down to it, or land simply grown over, with a path through it. But in each case either a path, a walk, or some stairs led down to a dock or a boathouse.

"It looks like the kind of a place I might like to have some time," said Lin. "How far to the dragon?"

"We're almost there," he answered. "Look ahead."

For a second, she said nothing, just peering ahead. Then she spoke.

"That? That right down there where the land ends?"

"What do you see?" he asked.

"It looks like a lump of something, right where the island ends."

"Does it look like a dragon?"

"No," she said.

"Now, turn around and don't look at it again until we're level with it," he told her. "I'll tell you when we're level and then I want you to look at it again."

She turned back. The boat rumbled on.

"Now!"

She turned quickly and looked out the window.

"Jens!" she said, her voice suddenly different. "It *is* a dragon! It's a real dragon!"

Jens killed the motor, went back to the stern and threw out the ship's anchor; the boat drifted forward a little bit as the rope snaked overboard; the rope stopped leaving the boat, tightened, lifted and held. He went back to join Lin, who had come out of the cabin and was looking across the low side of the cockpit at the dragon, now separated from them by less than fifty feet of water and seen in full relief against the far sky, side-on.

Lin was leaning half-over the side of the boat, her eyes brilliant, her lips parted. He stood back a few feet, watching her and feeling something that was almost an ache of pleasure inside him. When she was completely caught up in something, or specially happy, she radiated. She lit up like a five-hundred-watt light bulb.

He stood, watching her. She had fastened on the sight of the dragon with that remarkable sudden intensity that was part of her, like a powerful searchlight stopping on something it had hunted for a long time through vast darknesses. In fact, the dragon was not unworthy of that kind of attention. Someone had built it into the very structure of the point of land that was the southernmost tip of Merritt Island. Crouching, eight or ten feet above the water on a point of land like a rocky bowsprit, it was perhaps twenty-five feet in length, with a heavy threatening head in which the jaws were parted and the teeth showing. It was a marvelous construction.

"It's a Chinese dragon," Lin said. "Look, Jens, look at its head. Isn't it a Chinese dragon?"

"You're right," Jens said. "It certainly has a Chinese look up front. Would you believe me if I told you it could spout flames?"

"Flames?"

The single word was not a question from Lin, it was an exclamation of joy. He moved in to stand beside her, not quite touching her. It seemed to him that he could feel the heat of her. She swung suddenly, hugged and kissed him.

"Now, that's a dragon!" she said, leaning her head back to look into him, but still holding him around the waist. "You told me the truth!"

"Don't I always?" he asked.

She let him go and turned back to look at the dragon.

"Not like that," she said. "Tell me more. What do you know about it?"

Not much," he said. "Mike Spelman told me about it first. He'd heard about it from Steve Fourmelle and when I spoke to Steve, he said he'd lend me the runabout, here, to come down and look at it. Ready for a bottle of beer and a sandwich?"

She turned to look at him again.

"Beer and sandwich?" she repeated. "Now where did you get sandwiches and beer?"

"I asked Steve to put them on board," he said, enjoying this new, if smaller, surprise, reflected in her face and body. "It was part of the business of getting the runabout ready for us to use. How about it? Do you want some?"

"Picnic with a dragon—and the dragon's friend," she grinned at him. "Why not? It may be a little risky, but I'll chance it."

He got down on his knees to pull a styrofoam ice-chest out from under the circular seat that extended around the cockpit. As he was taking the plastic-wrapped sandwiches and a couple of bottles of beer off the ice inside, he felt a kiss on his neck and the next thing he knew she was kneeling beside him. Awkwardly, because of their positions on the hard drainboards, but none the less fervently, they held each other.

"When you're right, you're so right," she whispered, still kneeling and facing him. There was a sort of trembling in her and she felt very soft and yielding in his arms.

"You, too," he said.

"I'm going to stay on down here a few more days," she told him. "I'm going to take five days of my vacation time."

Joy flooded him.

"When did this happen?" he asked.

"I called back to the office this morning, when you were still sleeping," she said. "I'd asked them about it last month, before I came down here. I told them I'd call. I did, and now it's all set."

"I should bring you to see dragons more often," he said, holding her.

She clung hard to him again.

"You and dragons are all right," she said. "I love you and your dragons. Really, I do love your dragons. You know that, don't you?"

16

Walther Guenther walked heavily into the living room of his motel suite and dropped into an armchair beside the windows, but with its back turned to them. The Pan-European deputy minister was somewhat swollen about the eyes and he narrowed his gaze against the indirect late morning light coming through the windows behind him.

"Berthold!" he called, raising his voice as little as possible. "Where's that damned coffee and cognac?"

Berthold came from the bedroom door opposite the one through which Guenther had emerged. Guenther's secretary was a tall, studious-faced young man with narrow features under white-blond hair, surprisingly fragile in general appearance in spite of his height and breadth of shoulders.

"I'll check, sir."

He went out the door to the corridor; only a minute or two later, Guenther heard a key turn in the lock. Berthold came back in, holding a tray balanced expertly in one hand, and putting his suite key away with the other. He placed the tray, which held a coffee cup, glass coffee carafe, and a snifter glass with brown cognac in it, on an occasional table at Guenther's elbow. He poured from the carafe into the cup.

"It was just ready to be brought."

"Damn their slow souls to hell!"

"Yes, sir."

Guenther drank coffee and sipped brandy.

"Well?" he said, after a moment or two. "Where are the reports?"

"Right here, sir."

Berthold brought some typed sheets over from a nearby table.

"What are you looking so smug about?" growled Guenther.

"There might be a point of some interest in today's transcriptions of the Wylie conversations," Berthold said. "I've got the pertinent section on top."

"Oh?" Guenther straightened in his chair and shoved his coffee cup aside on the occasional table. He took the papers. "Who's this supposed to be talking now? Wylie and that girl of his?"

"Yes, sir."

Guenther read.

"I don't see any—" He broke off and continued to read in silence to the bottom of the page. Then his eye returned to its upper section.

"'Dragon'?" he said. "What dragon?"

"Exactly, sir."

"Wipe your nose!" said Guenther. "What're you thinking—that it's code of some kind? Just because it doesn't identify itself from the context, here?"

"Nothing in this set of transcriptions or any other references explains 'dragon' as far as I've been able to find out."

"Oh?"

"Yes. I've also checked the local zoo and nearby museums for anything like the lizard that's called the Komodo Dragon, or some particularly well-known piece of sculpture involving a dragon."

"And nothing?"

"No, sir."

Guenther finished his cognac and drank another cup of coffee, while he read the rest of the conversations recently transcribed from Jim Brille's laser tap on Jens's motel windows. He went back to the first page.

" 'When are you going to take me to the dragon again?' " Guenther read out loud. "And then Wylie answers her, 'He's not someone you can visit every day . . .' "

He became thoughtful.

"You remember our thought," Berthold said softly, "that it was just possible Alinde West could be some kind of contact for him, if indeed he were engaged in something more than he seemed to be."

"Yes . . ." murmured Guenther. He lifted his head abruptly. "That's right. Berthold, get me another cognac!"

"Sir, lunch is—"

"Another cognac! Bring it yourself."

Berthold went out. Guenther sat gazing at the typewritten pages in his lap until Berthold returned with the cognac.

"Of course," he said, taking the glass and drinking, then looking up over the rim of it, "you'll have to do a much more thorough job of checking. Motion pictures in the local theaters—newspaper advertisements—these eating places they build here with funny people, elves and animal statues outside them."

"Of course, sir, I was just waiting for permission."

"Right away, Berthold. Right away. By damn, if we've really got something here to show Wylie's something more than a stuffed toy, after all . . ."

It was still and hot in the cab of the battered pickup, even though it was parked with windows down in the shade of some trees. The thin, black man whom Gervais had set to watching the Kelly Estate drank from a two-liter bottle of Coca-Cola that was nearly empty.

"All the time, all the time . . ." he muttered out loud.

The phrase had originally been *All the time, all the time, it's me.* But a number of years in a number of different places, not the least of them being Willermore, which was a full-security rehabilitation center for the chronically criminal, had brought him to eliminate—at least aloud—the last two words. A car pulled out of the estate gateway and turned up-island on the road. A second later it went past the pickup. Inside it was the fat man with the few strands of hair plastered over his skull, who made notes in a book even when driving. The man in the pickup, whose name was DeMars, started his engine but let the other car go out of sight around a bend in the road farther up before pulling out to follow.

A half-mile or so down the road he caught sight of the car with the fat man and settled down to matching the other's speed at a block or two of distance. When they reached the business section of the upper island and turned onto a street with heavy traffic, DeMars closed up and stayed almost directly behind the other until he drove into the parking lot of a motel.

DeMars also parked, in another part of the lot, and watched the fat man go in. Through the glass front of the lobby he saw the other bypass the motel desk and go directly to the elevator. It opened to let riders out almost as he reached it, he stepped inside, and the doors closed behind him.

"All the time, all the time," muttered DeMars.

He sat, biting his lip for a minute, then got out of the cab, went into the lobby and turned immediately to the pay phones inside the entrance. He dialed the number of the Holiday Inn.

"Mr. Jackson," he told the hotel operator.

"One moment, please."

The line hummed; then Gervais's voice spoke.

"This is Jackson."

"This me," said DeMars. "He in the Bell Tower Inn—staying, look like."

"What he?"

"That perfesser."

"I gave you the right names. Use them."

"Willy Fesser," muttered DeMars.

"Go find out what room he's in, and what name he's staying under."

"All the time, all the time . . ." said DeMars under his breath.

"Did you hear me?"

"Can't," said DeMars softly, squirming a little as he stood at the phone. "Had a little trouble here, once. They know me. Man at the desk looking over at me, now."

"You're calling from that motel?"

"Nearest phone almost ten blocks—"

"Get out of there. I'll take care of it, then. Call me tomorrow."

"Yes," said DeMars, "sir."

"What?"

"Yessir. I'll call first thing, sir."

DeMars heard the phone click dead, hung up and stared at the instrument. For a second his face showed a weary lifetime of helplessness under pain, then it was merely dull again. He turned and went back out to his pickup.

At his desk, Gervais looked around to check that the security office was empty, then punched out a number on his phone. Its screen came alight with the image of a heavyset, middle-aged man with a police uniform jacket tight-buttoned about his upper body.

"Gervais!" said the man. "What all's new down your way?"

"Just a little something we need to check on, Sarge," said Gervais. "Could your people find out the name and room number used by a guest at the Bell Tower Inn? His real name's Willy Fesser—you won't find any record, I'd guess. We'd like to know whatever other name he might be using and his room number. I'll send a picture over."

"Well, I guess we can do that, all right. Looks like you federal troops can't do it all yourselves, after all. Can you now?"

"To be sure, Sarge," said Gervais. "We'd be helpless without the local police."

"Yeah, now. All right. I'll be looking for that picture and I'll call you when we find out something."

"Thanks, Sarge."

Sarge winked into the screen.

"Take care, now."

"Good-bye."

Gervais hung up, thinking. If Fesser was at that motel under a name other than his own, then he was certainly involved in something; and that something would certainly have to do with one or more of the ministers, because there was nothing else here right now to be involved in. He reached into the drawer of his desk, took out a paper with a list of names, and with his silver pen printed neatly after the typed name of Willy Fesser the words *Bell Tower Inn*.

17

Sir Geoffrey Mayence drove along a winding road toward the narrow seaward tip of Merritt Island. He was feeling particularly well. The early afternoon sun was interrupted by tall trees on each side of the road, the branches of which interwove overhead to dapple the asphalt beneath with cool shadow. Sir Geoffrey had managed to talk a local automobile collector into lending him a vintage Cadillac convertible out of the fifties. Now he was wheeling along with the top down, and the breeze of passage tossed his gray hair about. He zipped by the heavy stone archway that was the entrance to the Kelly Estate, and almost missed seeing it.

He put on the brakes, brought the Cadillac to a stop, and backed up carefully until he could turn in through the entrance. Ahead of him a beefy figure in white shirt, dark pants encircled by a gunbelt holding a revolver in a holster riding back and high on one meaty hip, stepped out of the bushes at the side of the road and waved to him to stop. Sir Geoffrey put on the brakes; and the guard, as he seemed to be, came up beside the car on the driver's side.

"Yes, sir," he said. "You looking for someone?"

"Sir Geoffrey Mayence!" barked Sir Geoffrey. "I'm here to see the Duchess Stensla."

"Yes, sir. Just a moment."

The guard unclipped from his belt a radio transceiver, walkie-talkie type, which was a counterweight to the revolver he wore on the other side of him, and repeated into it what Sir Geoffrey had just said. There was a slight pause and then the speaker of the walkie-talkie crackled with an answer, loud enough to reach Sir Geoffrey's ears.

"No appointment."

"Of course I haven't got an appointment, God damn it!" said Sir Geoffrey. "I'm here to surprise Clothilde!"

The gateman grinned down at Sir Geoffrey in a way that may have been intended to be reassuring, but which Sir Geoffrey found only irritating.

"Sorry. Guess you just have to phone in for an appointment."

"The hell I will!" said Sir Geoffrey. "You call in on that thingamajig and tell whoever it is on the other end that I'm coming in to surprise Clothilde."

The guard made no move to comply.

"You back out now and turn around," he said.

"Oh, don't be more of a bloody cretin than you were born to be!" said Sir Geoffrey.

He shoved the Cadillac into low gear and it leaped ahead. Behind him he heard a shout; and, looking in the rearview mirror, saw that the guard had pulled his gun and was waving it in the air. If he takes a shot at me with that thing, thought Sir Geoffrey grimly, I shall put this in reverse gear, back up, and mash him against a tree. However, just then, the narrow private road he was on took a turn to the right through some pines and the guard disappeared behind him without having used his weapon.

Sir Geoffrey drove on, cooling down a little. He came out after a bit in front of a large building and a large expanse of lawn before it. Sir Geoffrey ignored the parking area and pulled the Cadillac to the curb directly in front of the main door, got out and went up the steps.

He let himself in and almost stumbled over a man in white shirt and white pants.

"Hey, you!" said Sir Geoffrey.

The man, who had been headed away from him down the hall, turned around and came back.

"Go find the Duchess Stensla and tell her Sir Geoffrey Mayence is here," Sir Geoffrey said.

"Sir?" said the man. "What esay you?"

Sir Geoffrey repeated the sentence in passable Castilian Spanish.

"Si, señor," answered the man, and went off again.

Left alone in the large front hall, Sir Geoffrey wandered around trying doors and eventually found one that opened on some sort of library. Leaving the door ajar, so that Clothilde would have no trouble finding him, he went in. It was a pleasant, long, sunlit room, with a side table holding several cut-glass liquor decanters. However, these were empty. Turning about to examine the rest of the place, Sir Geoffrey caught sight for the first time of a man seated before a lit phone screen on a table by the window, with the control unit in his hand. The man was in his late forties or early fifties, balding and on the narrow line between being merely over-weight and outright fat. He was staring hard at Sir Geoffrey, the control unit apparently forgotten, as if he had been in mid-conversation when Sir Geoffrey had entered.

"Don't mind me," said Sir Geoffrey, amiably. "Go right ahead."

However, the other shut off the screen and put the unit firmly back down on the table.

"Sir Geoffrey Mayence," Sir Geoffrey introduced himself. He peered at the other man. "You look familiar. We've met, have we?"

"No," said the overweight man. His voice was slightly hoarse.

"Odd," said Sir Geoffrey. "I usually never forget a face."

He turned back to look wistfully at the decanters, as if they might have refilled themselves while his back was turned.

"Where could he have gone?" The Duchess's voice floated

in through the partially-open door. "Are you sure he said his name was Geoffrey Mayence?"

"I'm in here!" shouted Sir Geoffrey.

A second later the man in white shirt and slacks came through the door, closely followed by the Duchess.

"Is here," said the man, and went out again.

"Geoffrey, it really is you!" said the Duchess.

"Hello, Clo," said Sir Geoffrey.

The Duchess walked slowly and elegantly forward toward him. The material of her jade-green pantsuit rustled as she moved.

"Willy, dear boy," she said, looking past Geoffrey. "Weren't you wanted on another phone?"

"Yes," said the stout man. He got to his feet without looking at or speaking to Sir Geoffrey, went past the two of them and out the door, closing it softly but firmly behind him.

"Thought I'd drop by and surprise you," said Sir Geoffrey.

"Geoff!" said the Duchess. There was a clear fondness in her tone. "It's been fourteen years."

"No, it hasn't," said Sir Geoffrey.

"Fourteen years."

"That much? Well, well," Sir Geoffrey sighed. "Seems like just a few months."

Reaching out one of his enormously long arms, he slapped the ample seat of her green pants. The Duchess accepted the gesture with as much dignity as if he had kissed her hand.

"Come and sit down, Geoff," she said. "What do you want to drink?"

Sir Geoffrey cast an absentminded glance at the decanters on the sideboard, and thought a second.

"How about daiquiris?" he asked. "Why not make it a pitcher of daiquiris?"

The Duchess went over to the phone that the man called Willy had been holding earlier, lifted it, punched three numbers and spoke into the unlit screen.

"A pitcher of daiquiris. The Rose Room," she said, and hung up. She came back and sat down on the couch facing a tall gray overstuffed chair.

"Sit down, Geoff," she said. "Tell me what's been happening to you."

"Nothing to tell," said Sir Geoffrey, perching himself in the chair. "Lila died six years ago. I've just been rattling around, since."

"Lila! My dear, what happened?"

"Oh, you know. Heart," said Sir Geoffrey. He looked aside at the bright sunlight streaming through the windows and blinked. He cleared his throat. "Quite suddenly. We'd just come back from dinner and she said she felt a little queer. I went into the bathroom to get her some medicine the doctor had her on, came back, and that was it."

"Geoff," said the Duchess softly, putting a hand lightly on one of his bony knees.

"Well, there it is," said Sir Geoffrey, still looking at the sunlight. "How about yourself, Clo?"

"I've been all over the place, of course," said the Duchess. "Oh, and I've been married once, I think, since I saw you last. Nobody important. An Italian."

"Leave you any money?" Sir Geoffrey looked back at her.

"He's still alive. The settlement was quite nice, though." The Duchess smiled almost mischievously at Sir Geoffrey. "I did wonder why I wasn't running across you, now and then. I even began to wonder if you weren't possibly avoiding me."

"I? Avoiding you?" Sir Geoffrey snorted. "No. For the last six years, and most of the time before that, I've been taking posts off in some odd corner of the world or other—"

He broke off, as a different man in white shirt and pants came in bearing a tray with a pitcher of frothy amber liquid and two cocktail glasses. The man put the tray on the table and went out again without a word, at a nod from the Duchess. As the door closed behind him, Sir Geoffrey was already filling the two glasses from the pitcher.

"Well, now, that's good," he said, emptying his glass and refilling it. "Damned if I know why they always make daiquiris with white rum in this country. No taste. Now these are the way they should be."

The Duchess sipped lightly at her drink.

"Have you thought of marrying again, Geoff?" she asked.

"At my age?" Sir Geoffrey peered at her over the edge of his glass. "That's right, you're free now yourself, aren't you?"

"You know I didn't mean me," the Duchess said. "Not that I wouldn't like to have you around—but we both know damn well that I wouldn't have you around, would I? Besides, I'm past that now, in any real sense."

"Don't believe a word of it," said Sir Geoffrey.

"Well, you should. But it's different with you. You're male; and besides, you'll never grow up," she said. "But I'm more comfortable by myself nowadays. Besides, I'm ready to retire. That's what you should think of doing, Geoff. Get off and enjoy the years from now on."

"Get off what?" said Sir Geoffrey. "The world's still there."

"Our world isn't, dear," said the Duchess. "Haven't you noticed?"

"Come on, Clo," said Sir Geoffrey. "You can't tell me that. Here you are in the thick of things yourself, large house, Spanish servants and people like that Willy character who's just left, all over the place as usual."

"The shell's here," answered the Duchess. "But there's nothing really much inside it, lately. In a very real sense, my dear, I've been put out of work by computers. My house-guests never did really produce anything that was important; only paperwork to oil the machinery and make the other people feel they were dealing with the things under the table as well as on top of it. But computers can spew out more paperwork than my people can, any day, at less cost and at higher volume. No, it's time for me to retire. I'm planning on moving to the West Indies someplace. Probably St. Croix."

Sir Geoffrey refilled his glass for a third time and picked it up.

"Damn it, Clo," he said, "the world never changes. People go on being people. They just have new toys to play with. That's all this space shoot is, this Mars Expedition. Just another toy."

"That's the way you think?" said the Duchess, looking at

him closely. "I thought you were the boy who built rockets, working rockets I mean, when he was twelve years old?"

"Oh, Lord," said Sir Geoffrey. "I suppose I did. But that's the point. I was just playing games. Now we've got idiot governments playing games."

"Did they ever do anything else?" said the Duchess.

"I suppose not," said Sir Geoffrey. "Anyway, here we all are; you, me, people like Verigin, Ambedkar and all the rest, doing it again."

"There's nothing going on with my guests that has anything to do with you, dear," the Duchess said. "Otherwise, I'd have told you about it a long time ago."

"Didn't think there would be," Sir Geoffrey laughed, a short bark of a laugh. "They'd be God's own fools to try to pick up anything on me. There's that young Wylie though. Somebody'll be trying to play games with him, I expect."

"Nothing serious," the Duchess said. "Does he mean something to you, this Wylie?"

"Oh, he's a young fire-eater, the way I was," said Sir Geoffrey. "He takes all this too seriously, this business about spaceships and Mars. I'd hate to see him served up in a pudding, that's all."

"Maybe he's one of those who insists on serving himself up in a pudding," said the Duchess.

"You may be right," said Sir Geoffrey. "Still, that's how it is."

"If it turns nasty, of course," said the Duchess, "I can always let you know."

"Appreciated," Sir Geoffrey replied. "But what are we doing talking about all that? Be suckered if I don't think I proposed to you just now; and I think you turned me down."

"Geoff, you don't want me," said the Duchess. "If you want anybody at all, you want somebody young—like yourself."

"Like myself?"

"You know what I mean. You never really grew up. As long as you live you'll belong with the young people."

"Well, damn it, now!" said Sir Geoffrey. "There's a good many people in a number of governments that take me seriously, even if you don't!"

"They don't know you like I do," said the Duchess. "Seriously, Geoff, why don't you think about retiring, finding yourself somebody young and warm and settling down to enjoy the next dozen years or so?"

"The last dozen years, eh?"

"If it comes to that," said the Duchess calmly. "Or less, if necessary. Any time at all is a bonus at our ages, Geoff."

"Hell's bells! I don't want a wife!" said Sir Geoffrey. "I want somebody like you around I can talk to. Besides, you were just telling me I'm as old as Methuselah. Who'd have me, anyway?"

"*I'd* have you if I were twenty years younger," said the Duchess. "That's not the problem, and you know it."

Sir Geoffrey gloomily poured the last of the daiquiri from the pitcher into his own glass.

"This is nice!" he said. "I drop out here to surprise you after fourteen years; and all you do is lecture me about getting married to somebody else."

"I have to take advantage of the chance," said the Duchess. "Heaven knows when I'll see you again."

"Well, how about tomorrow night for dinner?" said Sir Geoffrey. "I don't know about everybody else on this thing, but I'm going to stick around for an extra week or two and soak up some sunshine. Unless you'll be leaving yourself, now that the launch is made."

"No, not quite that quickly." The Duchess examined him critically. "But I'm tied up for the next two or three days. How about an afternoon, say next Tuesday? We can go for a drive some place and come back here for dinner."

"Right on!" said Sir Geoffrey, lighting up. "There're no good restaurants around here anyway. At least, none to match what your staff could do, if you've still got the kind of staff you used to have."

"I always have the kind of staff I used to have," said the Duchess. She got to her feet, and Sir Geoffrey rose automatically, a split second behind her.

"You're busy now, then?" he said, wistfully.

"I'm afraid so, dear," the Duchess said. "After all, I really wasn't expecting you to drop in like this. Next Tuesday, then?"

"Yes, by all means, next Tuesday," said Sir Geoffrey. "I'll give you a ring."

They went to the door of the room and out into the hall and the Duchess accompanied Sir Geoffrey to the front door, standing on the steps while he went down and got into the convertible. He waved at her as he pulled away and drove the Cadillac back along the narrow private road.

As he pulled around the curve and out of the pines, he saw his old friend, the guard, who now smiled at him from perhaps a dozen feet of distance. Sir Geoffrey brought the car to a halt; and the man walked over to it, agreeably.

Sir Geoffrey opened the door and got out, enjoying the sudden widening of the guard's eyes as Sir Geoffrey's lanky length unfolded to tower over him.

"You wave that gun of yours at me another time," said Sir Geoffrey, "and I will personally shove it up your bloody ass!"

The guard's face set itself in an odd way. The whites of his eyes showed underneath the pupils balanced between puckered lids and fat wrinkled skin. His shoulders seemed to settle and hunch down and forward. He shrank in height and seemed to swell in the body, like some old bull in one corner of a private pasture catching a flicker of movement at the pasture's other end but within the rails that penned him. Sir Geoffrey went tight suddenly, bracing himself.

Then the moment passed. Neither the face nor the body of the man altered; but the moment was gone.

"Yes, sir," the guard said.

Sir Geoffrey got back in the Cadillac, put it in gear again and drove off, turning out at last onto the highway. He drove along for perhaps half a mile before his head started to clear and he began to realize that it might have been something besides his own anger and size which had stopped the guard from reacting to what he had said.

It was a sobering realization. Undoubtedly, the man had just wanted to keep that job of his, even at the cost of taking that kind of lip from someone like Sir Geoffrey. Sir Geoffrey felt suddenly desolate inside. Who the hell was he anyway, to be throwing his weight around, nowadays? There might have been a time when he could have done something with a fat pig-tender like that; but a lot of years had gone by since then. It was time to stop challenging younger men in any physical sense. It was time to back off on a lot of things, including the drinking and women. . . . Suddenly, inexplicably, his mood lightened. He laughed out loud.

"Well, by God!" he said to the day around him. "She has me thinking as if I had one foot in the grave already!"

Inexplicably, this little nugget of understanding made him feel better rather than worse. It opened up an unusual perception in him of the Duchess and how she felt for him. In return he felt a sudden tenderness toward her—the sort of warmth that really had not visited him since Lila had died.

He drove back to the motel, feeling—for him—quite humble, and happier than he had for some long time.

18

Day 2 on the spaceship (Day 1 being the day of the launch that had ended with the talk between Tad and Fedya and sleep for all six marsnauts) began, according to a clock set at Eastern Daylight Time, at six A.M. Tad woke with the feeling that he had had a succession of not too pleasant dreams and a restless night. It was a feeling he had been expecting, however. The first night in no-gravity or an abnormal gravity—and the ship's gravity, imparted by the spinning of the docked vessels, was about one-half normal g—tended to disturb sleep patterns. This had already been established by previous space flights and the extensive Skylab work by both Americans and Russians. If he adapted according to average human responses they had charted, Tad could expect to get back to sleeping normally in about a week. His thoughts went to the experiment load and to his talk the 'night' before with Fedya.

Fedya was silent for an extended moment.

"I'll keep that in mind," he said at last. "Let me do some thinking for a day or so."

"All right," said Tad.

"Good," said Fedya. "Then shall we check out these schedules?"

He spread the papers he had been carrying between the coffee containers on the table before him. It was a combined list—Tad had its duplicate in the record files on A Deck above—of experiments and their scheduling aboard both ships; plus bargraphs of the activities of the crewmen on each ship through the next thirty days of coast toward Mars orbit.

"Seventy-two experiments, total," said Fedya, "of which there's nine of particular importance during this first month's period, plus eight medical report-keeping experiments that are continuing—"

"Plus housekeeping and exercise," interrupted Tad. "You see what it's going to be like."

Fedya met his eyes.

"It will be busy, of course," said Fedya.

"Too busy—" Tad broke off. "Never mind. Forget it for now. Let's check the bargraphs out and make sure we both know what's going on on the other ship; and then get some sleep ourselves. We'll need it."

Fedya nodded. Together, they bent their heads over the bargraphs.

Now Tad sat up and glanced at the bargraphs for Phoenix One laid out on the table beside his bed.

He was scheduled for S/HK, Systems Housekeeping, immediately after breakfast; and both Bap and Anoshi were involved likewise in continuing duties until after lunch—at which time they would begin setting up the specific experiments in the various labs of the ship. He got to his feet with some little effort and headed for the waste management room.

From there, shaved and clean from the shower with its own recycling system, but still not yet really awake, he went to the mass measurement device. Its controls had not been adjusted to ignore the light pseudo-gravity provided by the docked and rotating ships, so there was that to be done before he could even fit himself into the horizontal chair. Then, his slide forward in the chair and the jerk of the braking system as it measured the force needed to stop him started a faint headache behind his forehead. He got out of the chair and read the result. Translated into pounds of body weight, the mass-force necessary to stop him read one hundred and seventy-nine. Three pounds less than he had weighed yesterday morning before the launch—which was ridiculous but undoubtedly correct. He entered the figure in the log that was part of the device and went into the wardroom.

He was the first one in. Bap and Anoshi had yet to take their turns at getting weighed no-gravity style. He inflated the pod about their dining area, and then stepped through the pod hatch to sit down at his place at the serving table and turned on the vacuum. There was a slight murmuring as the fans started to draw air through the filter in the pod wall and from the pod into the particle collector. There were as yet no floating food particles in the air of the pod for the collector to collect; but it was doing its duty nonetheless.

Tad punched for coffee, and a carefully measured amount poured into the container at his place. He lifted and sipped it, grateful this trip had been planned so that it was possible for him and the other two to avoid drinking from tubes while the artificial gravity was operating. Thank God attention had been paid to a few purely personal and emotional matters like the pleasure of taking a shower and of drinking hot coffee from a cup instead of from a tube. No, not merely thank God, thank the men in past tours in the Skylabs, who had proved the need for such things.

The bargraph for the day, which he knew by heart, floated before his mind's eye, as he considered what was to be done before the next sleep period. He found himself beginning to view the upcoming shipboard day with increasing enthusiasm.

The sticky sound of the entrance to the pod being unsealed brought his head around. Anoshi was climbing in, followed by Bap, who turned to reseal the entrance. They both sat down at the table; and Tad came fully awake, looking at them.

"How'd the sleep go?" he asked.

"Not bad," said Anoshi. Bap laughed. He was the one wearing spacesuit underwear today.

"I was being chased by elephants," he said. "And the lead elephant was being ridden by our noble Expedition Director, old Nick Henning."

"Did he catch you?" Anoshi asked, punching for a stream of hot tea into his own container.

"I am here to tell the tale," said Bap, waving his own container before he filled it. He looked around the pod and then at Tad. "Cosy little breakfast nook. I wonder if they had some ulterior motive in penning us up like this for meals, besides the collecting of floating particles of food from the air? The original Spacelab got along without this."

"And its crew inhaled a lot of stuff over a ninety-day period," Anoshi said. "Remember all the worry over 'space pneumonia' in men—"

"And women," said Bap.

"—and women who should have been free from virus infections?"

"Of course I remember," said Bap. "But I am also considering the effect that this enforced intimacy three times every twenty-four hours may have on the human mind."

He, like the other two, had been punching for heated, pre-packaged foodstuffs, which now emerged from the table slots before him. He opened the largest package and extracted a disposable plastic fork/knife.

"What if I become violent some breakfast and cut your throats?" he said.

"Then you'd have all the work to do by yourself from then on," said Tad. He changed to a more serious tone. "You're going to begin solar observations for flares in your first period after this meal?"

"Right away," said Bap. "I'll be using Numbers One and Two remote cameras as telescopes. Maybe I'll get some good pictures, if there's anything to take."

"Kennedy ought to warn us if a large flare crops up early in the flight, the way they've been predicting," Tad said. "It'd be something if we could spot it as soon as they do—or before."

"We will," Bap said. "I promise we will."

They finished their breakfast, reduced the pod, and Tad took the scraps of uneaten food, the packaging and the other discardables to the waste management room to be carefully weighed and disposed of. Just as the body wastes of the marsnauts had to be measured and weighed, so their food and liquid intake had to be measured and recorded with every meal. This was Medical Experiment 122 on the schedule. Then Bap went to his camera telescopes, Anoshi got out the aerosol collector to take a sample of the ship's air and discover what loose particles were afloat in it, in spite of the meal table pod, and Tad went to Systems/Housekeeping.

This early in the voyage, there was little housekeeping or equipment repairs to be made. Tad covered all four decks of the life zone of the ship within a short time, then went directly to the Master Log of Phoenix One.

The Master Log was pretty much what its name implied. It was to Phoenix One what a ship's log was to an ocean-going vessel, with the complication that it and the Phoenix Two's log as well, included not only the commander's record of the voyage, day by day, but all recordings of data made on that day, which he was able to review on a computer screen before him and correct or amend with a keyboard and a light-pencil. The records of Day One of the Expedition, launch-day, were now awaiting Tad's attention.

When he had disposed of the log, Tad went out to find Anoshi at work in the C Deck lab space that would be his for his astronomical records. Face bent over the forty-five-degree-angled viewing plate, Anoshi was studying one of the photos he had just taken of the solar corona. He was apparently too wrapped up in his work to notice Tad, who went on up across to the exercise section of C Deck to see Bap there, in full spacesuit, working at the taskboard in Mode C of the experiment dealing with daily physical exercise by each of them.

Mode C was constant physical exercise for twenty minutes wearing a spacesuit. Mode B was similar work without a suit; and Mode A was twenty energetic minutes on an exercycle or jogging treadmill. Spacelab experience had shown how necessary exercise was to the health of humans away from normal gravity. Not *absolutely* necessary, I hope, Tad thought grimly as he watched Bap, remembering his plans if Fedya should decide to cooperate. Bap, engrossed in the heavy work and the uncomfortable spacesuit, didn't notice Tad watching any more than had Anoshi.

Tad took the access tube and went up to B Deck. It would be time for lunch in less than half an hour.

". . . Our first piece of information today," said the NASA official on the TV screen, addressing the press conference, *"is that because of Nick Henning's illness, Bill Ward, here—"* he nodded to Bill, sitting upright beside him at the long table cluttered with microphones and close-up camera eyes *"—will be taking over as Expedition Director. You've all met Bill before—"*

"Have we?" asked Ahri Ambedkar of the others in English.

"You remember," said Jens Wylie. "Bill Ward was the man who came in after the marsnauts' luncheon to take us out to the shuttle launch pad."

"Ah, yes," said Ambedkar.

He, Jens, Sergei Verigin, and Walther Guenther were sitting in the lounge area of their quarters in the Merritt Island Holiday Inn, watching the daily NASA press conference on TV. It was just after they had finished lunch. Later that afternoon, they were scheduled to hold a conference of their own for the press.

". . . absolutely on schedule." Bill Ward was already answering a question from the floor. *"So far everything has gone exactly as expected. The ships are now docked and the marsnauts are now into their first rest period, according to the schedule. Yes?"*

He nodded, pointing at a different section of the press seats. A stocky, thin-haired young man stood up.

"Can you tell us—" His accent was French. *"—if there are any times when the schedule does not operate? Any holidays, or relaxation periods for the marsnauts? And if so, where are they at present on their schedule?"*

He sat down again.

"As far as we know, there aren't any holidays in space," said Bill. There was a small stir and sounds of chuckling among the press crowd. *"To answer your question, though,*

there's no period that isn't accounted for on the schedule, from the time the Expedition was launched to the time of its return to Earth orbit, three years from now. The schedule itself does call for open periods; both to relieve the marsnauts from routine, and to ensure that any overscheduling gets caught up with. There are no such open periods in this first thirty days, however. As you know, this is when ground communications with the two Expedition ships are at their best; and we want to take the maximum advantage of that. Yes? Next!"

The TV camera moved to focus on another questioner.

"It's like climbing a mountain, I suppose," said Verigin thoughtfully. "But, like climbing a big mountain, like that one in the Himalayas that is the highest in the world; and to climb it an expedition must take months. There may be days of occasional rest along the route. But any celebration, any vacation, must wait until the full job is done—"

He broke off. Sir Geoffrey, his face politely expressionless, had just joined them, taking a seat. His eyes moved over them, from Verigin to Guenther, to Ambedkar, to Jens and finally back to Verigin again.

"Not interrupting anything, am I?" he said. He looked at Verigin.

"Not at all," said the Russian deputy minister, reaching out to turn the voice volume down on the TV set.

"That's good," said Sir Geoffrey. He glanced again at Jens, then back to Verigin. "Wouldn't want to be the unwanted guest. We don't see much of you—ah—Wylie."

"Sorry," said Jens. "One of my special duties is to hassle with the press for the Administration. I have to keep running out on errands to do with that."

"Yes. Well, duty first," said Sir Geoffrey. "Wouldn't you say so, Sergei?" he went on, turning to Verigin.

"Oh yes, duty," said Verigin.

"And old Ahri, here," said Sir Geoffrey, turning to Ambedkar, who did not seem pleased by Sir Geoffrey's use of his first name. "You know what duty can be like, I think? You were with Sergei and me at the first Pan-European Conference—was that before your time, Walther?"

"No," said Guenther, with a small cough. "I was there.

I was pretty junior, then, though. The rest of you weren't likely to notice lower echelon types like myself.''

"Don't tell me you were caught up in that business when the French presidential motorcade got routed clear off on the road to Liège and came in three hours late?''

"Oh yes," said Guenther, laughing.

"Where were you when that was going on?" asked Verigin, looking interestedly at Sir Geoffrey.

"Sir Geoffrey was in the bar of the Number One hotel," said Ahri.

"Wasn't I?" said Sir Geoffrey, almost triumphantly. "I was there from one to nearly four, getting wound like an eight-day clock. I must have had fifteen manhattans—that bartender there had a special touch with manhattans. Which reminds me—what do you think of this newest trouble that was in the papers about President Fanzone and the labor unions, regarding this Shared-Management Consultation thing—"

"I've got a phone call I have to make," Jens interrupted hastily. "Forgive me, I just remembered it.''

He got up from his chair.

"Ah, well," said Sir Geoffrey, "see you a bit later on, then.''

He watched Jens move off down the corridor and step into his own suite of rooms.

"What's the latest you've heard?" Verigin asked him. "I don't mean about U.S. labor unions, of course.''

"Duchess Stensla says someone's following her guests when they drive off.''

"You've been talking to Stensla?" Guenther said.

"Known her for years!" barked Sir Geoffrey, staring directly at the Pan-European deputy minister. "Know her family well!''

"Local police, I assume," said Verigin.

"Not that," said Geoffrey. "She checked.''

For a second or two, no one said anything, then Ahri Ambedkar spoke.

"But what does this mean?" he asked. "I'm not sure I understand.''

"Something's on the fire, that's my judgment," Sir Geoffrey answered him. "Sounds like something's going down. Amateur illegals about; and what's around here for amateur illegals to be concerned about?"

"Except ourselves, you mean?" said Verigin, thoughtfully. "But why do you use the word amateur? Here we are on U.S. soil; the natural conclusion would be some U.S. agency—"

"Because it damn well *is* amateur. The Duchess knows that sort of difference."

"But that's ridiculous," said Ahri. "We're hardly likely to go spying on ourselves."

"There's Wylie . . ." said Guenther.

"I . . ." said Sir Geoffrey, spacing his words and making them clear and distinct while he looked at the Pan-European, "don't . . . think . . . so."

"You don't?" said Verigin, softly. "Then what?"

"What, indeed?" said Sir Geoffrey, getting to his feet. "Echo answers. Well, I must get back to my suite."

He went off, leaving a long silence behind him.

19

The fact that the Expedition was on U.S. Eastern Daylight Time made for coincidence. After the second meal period of Day Two aboard the spacecraft, probably while the Deputy Ministers back on Merritt Island were sitting back to sip on coffee following lunch, the marsnauts were finishing their lunches thousands of miles deep in space. Anoshi was scheduled for Systems/Housekeeping. Bap and Tad were due to go to work setting up experiments in the labs, including the atmosphere and null-atmosphere lab sections of the no-gravity pod between the two ships.

During the days just before the marsnauts had boarded

Phoenix One and Two, both ships had been on a standby basis as far as internal systems went—with a single exception in each ship, a sealed lab section on C Deck, within which atmosphere pressure and normal temperature had been maintained for the benefit of the so-called 'live' subjects—ranging from field mice down through brine shrimp, fruit flies and flatworms to simple molds and spores. The seal on this lab had been broken when the lab was opened during their first visual inspection of the ship after the marsnauts boarded and brought her up to working order. But the experimental subjects themselves had been left until now in the care of the automatic machinery that had kept them nourished and alive since they were put aboard by the supply and fitting crews.

Now, Tad and Bap left the majority of the subjects still in the formerly sealed lab. But certain of them were immediately to be transferred—to the plant genetics lab, the biomedical lab and the two sections of the pod. Tad and Bap worked together to set up the plant genetics and the biomedical lab sections; but when it came to the pod, while Bap could reach the inside section through the cryotex tube connecting with it and phoenix Two, Tad had to suit up and EVA, going outside the ship to the airless, cold part of the pod from the hatch opening to space that lay in the perpetual shadow between the two locked-together revolving ships.

The work was both difficult and clumsy in a spacesuit; but the spores and cultures which Tad carried to the outer pod were contained in trays that even heavy gloves could handle with some dexterity. One by one, Tad fitted these trays into the shelves and racks built into the airless section of the pod, working in the illumination from the pressurized section, showing through the milky, yielding cryotex wall between the two parts. The blurred shadow he saw coming and going beyond that wall as he worked would be Bap, at work there, Tad thought.

—Unless it was Dirk or Fedya from Phoenix Two. Each ship was due to supply some materials and live subjects to the pod experiments. Primarily, it was the U.S. experiments on cryogenics that would be taking up space in the pod compartments, although both the 'green-thumb' paranormal plant response tests of the English, and the biorhythyms experiments of the Japanese were represented here. In essence, these were experiments which had been pioneered in the Skylabs. But they would be taking place under different conditions here, in that they were both farther from the sun, and subject to a skidding, sideways motion that was caused by the two ships wheeling about their common center where the pod sections were.

Tad finished his work and left. So far, no one from Phoenix Two had showed up to bring that spacecraft's trays of experimental materials to the outer pod—which was a little strange. If Tad remembered the bargraphs for Phoenix Two correctly, someone from that ship ought to have been out here at the same time he was.

Tad returned to Phoenix One, emerged into A Deck and began desuiting. Anoshi was waiting for him, and helped him off with the suit.

"Bap's over in Phoenix Two," said Anoshi, as soon as Tad's helmet was off. "Fedya had an accident with some oxygen tanks toppling over in one of the labs. It seems he's hurt his left hand."

Lin, watching from the window of her room in the Peacock Motel, about half a mile from the Holiday Inn, had seen no blue rental Lancia that would be Jens's pull up to the entrance, and was startled when her phone buzzed. She punched on sound only.

"Yes?" she said.

"Lin?" said a voice she recognized. "It's me, Barney Winstrom. Jens got caught up in some official business all of a sudden. He said he'd phoned and your room didn't answer. I'm here to fill in for him as chauffeur."

"Oh. Yes, I just got back up from lunch downstairs. That's good of you, Barney. I'll be right down."

She snatched up her miniattaché, took a fast check of herself in the full-length mirror—the crisp skirt and blouse looked eminently suitable for the Hansard interview, businesslike but not severe—and went out, leaving the clutter of the room behind her. She had taken this place to give her room to work, and to stash the growing piles of reference material on her interviewees.

Barney was in the station wagon in which he had taken her to the launch. She went to it and he swung the door open for her. His smile greeted her.

"My word," she said, glancing into the back of the car, "what're all the papers for?"

"Just keeping up with what the foreign press is saying," he answered, lifting the car on its air-cushion and sliding it around the driveway into the street. "There's no regular outlet here for overseas reprintings. I had a batch of copies of the foreign newspapers sent up from Miami."

She was half-turned, reaching out with one arm to riffle the newspapers covering the half-moon curve of the car's lounge seat behind them.

"*La Prensa* . . . London *Times* . . . something in German—Barney! Japanese? You don't read Japanese?"

"Well enough to get through the papers," he said. "I like languages, and I had about twelve years in assorted countries overseas, some years back. I liked most of the countries too—except France. My wife liked France."

"What do they all say?" She turned around and faced forward in her seat again. "Oh—by the way, you do know where I'm going? I mean, you know how to get there?"

"Been to the Hansards' before," said Barney.

"But what do they say—all those other papers?"

"Pretty much what American papers say. It's all the same news."

"Why read them, then?"

"I'm a pro," said Barney. "It's my pleasure."

She studied his stubby profile, feeling a liking for him.

"What's your opinion," she asked, "about this space business, and expeditions to Mars?"

He shrugged.

"We'll get there some day."

"Not this time?"

He shrugged again.

"You don't think much of it either, then," she said. "I wish Jens would be a little more clear-headed about it."

"I didn't say I didn't think much of it," he said, keeping

his eyes on the road that was leading them now down a corridor between filling stations, and fast-food places. "I'm just
not one of your optimists in general, about anything. As for
Jens—maybe he's right."

"Right?" she said. "You think he's right to live in a
daydream that suddenly six men will land on Mars and a
new age is going to dawn where all problems will evaporate?"

"You're sure that's just the way he thinks of it?" said
Barney. He turned to his right, off on a sidestreet that curved
away between green trees. "I'd have put it a little differently.
He thinks it's our future. He thinks it's the only future we've
got—and maybe I agree with him on that—whether we're a
couple of people riding along in a hoverauto like this one, or
a couple of people with ropes of twisted bark around our hips,
watching the sky for a moment and hearing a supersonic pass
overhead, before we go back to looking for a grasshopper or
two to keep our stomachs from being pasted to our back-
bones."

"Well, well," said Lin.

"All right, lady," said Barney. "Have it your own way.
But people like Jens with their daydreams actually do make
the world move forward. I've seen it happen, and I believe
it."

"What happens when the daydream goes crunch up against
reality?"

"When that day comes, he might surprise you."

"No," said Lin, a little bleakly. "He won't. He won't
surprise me."

"Wait and see."

They had just come to the end of the street on which they
had been traveling. Barney turned left into another street,
slightly narrower. This was a pleasant, clean street. Jacaran-
das marched along the boulevards on either side, although
the flowers they showed were sparse. Lin fell silent; they
drove without talking until he pulled up in front of a large
brown house with its backyard sloping down to a man-made
canal.

"Here we are," he said.

Lin opened the door, swung her legs out, holding them

neatly together, knees and ankles. She looked back over her shoulder at him.

"You're not coming in with me?"

He grinned.

"You want an old hand like me sitting in and criticizing?" he said. "Come on, now. I'll pick you up in half an hour."

He leaned over to catch the door on her side and swing it back, shut. He waved and pulled away from the curb. She turned and went up the front walk, curving across the lawn to a small screened porch. The door was open behind the screen; and it was an ordinary, old-fashioned wire screen—nothing electronic—but the house was not an old or cheap one by any means. The lot on which it was built would probably run around sixty thousand dollars, according to the real estate guide she had been studying. Lin reached for the doorbell; but before she could touch it, the form of a woman loomed up out of the dimness beyond the screen and the door swung open.

"I'm sorry, I meant to be watching for you," said Wendy Hansard. "You're Ms. West, aren't you? Jens Wylie's talked about you, often. Come on in."

Lin smiled and entered. Her eyes adjusted quickly to the dimmer inside light and she saw she was standing at the edge of a wide, sunken-floored living room, more modern than the outside of the house would have indicated. There was no other sound of other voices. The Hansard children must be outside or away from the place. Lin looked at their mother.

Jens, she saw, had been wrong when he had said that she and Wendy looked alike. They had very little in common, really, except that they were both about the same height and had athletically good figures. Wendy's hair was a very light shade, not like Lin's own rich brown; and it was almost too fine, the sort that would tend to fluffiness and disorder. Otherwise, the best description for Wendy Hansard was that she looked a little soft-edged. Slightly worn. As if she had been just slightly overused by her children and husband during her years with them; so that there would be no going back for her to the real attractiveness she must have had in her early twenties. No, there was really no comparison between her and Lin, as far as appearance went. Jens had been quite wrong. She pressed the side of the miniattaché to start the recorder inside.

"It's good of you to see me on such short notice," Lin said, following her into the living room. They sat down on short couches facing each other before a large, empty fireplace of rough stone. A coffee pot and china cups were on the table between them. "Jens promised to speak to you about me, my first day down; but he didn't get it done until just after the launch."

Wendy laughed, picking up the coffee pot. "Everybody's so busy at launch time," she said. "You'll have coffee, won't you?"

"Thanks." Lin had learned that whether she wanted anything to drink or not, it relaxed those being interviewed and made them more communicative when they played host. "I really could use a cup."

"About the short notice—don't let it bother you at all," said Wendy. "It's part of our job, being interviewed. Everybody in the space effort gets used to it—even the children."

"I suppose you're right. They aren't here—your children, I mean?"

"They'll be along in about ten minutes. I knew you'd want to see them." Wendy handed over a full coffee cup to Lin. "You don't have a photographer with you, or coming, or anything like that?"

"I thought not for this," Lin said. *"New World* is the sort of magazine that likes to stay away from patterns; and it's my job to find out something different from the sort of story a few dozen other interviewers have written up about you."

"Isn't that hard?"

Lin sipped her coffee. It was good. It would be.

"I need to be lucky," Lin said, and they both laughed. "What I thought was that nearly everything that's been done on you and the other marsnauts' wives has been this sort of apple-pie, dab-of-flour-on-the-nose sort of thing. I was hoping we could get into some other areas."

Wendy smiled.

"I don't have time for much in the way of other areas," she said.

"I can imagine," said Lin. "But you have to have opinions on the larger implications of a space flight like this—six nations working together to make the first manned landing on another world. There's the matter of your own philosophy, and how being involved in this affects it."

"Philosophy's a pretty heavy word," said Wendy, smiling.

"But you do have a philosophy?"

"Oh, yes." Wendy put her cup down. "I don't mean like a philosophy at college—but that's beside the point. No, my own philosophy's about getting things done."

"Getting things done?" Lin sipped again at her coffee. It was also good not to be seen taking notes or wearing a wrist recorder during an interview. Which was why she had her recorder out of sight in her miniattaché.

"I mean," said Wendy, placing one word after the other like someone carefully making her way across a fallen log that bridged a creek, "I believe certain things have to be done. They have to be done, because they're needed. And the greatest use anyone can put oneself to is to do such things. I suppose you'd call it a sort of philosophy of use—an ethic of use."

She looked up from her cup and across the table at Lin.

"Maybe that sounds apple-pie and flour-on-the-nose after all, come to think of it?" she said.

"No, no," said Lin. "Not at all."

"But I mean it in relation to large things as well as small," said Wendy. "You can apply it to the way nations ought to act as well as to the way individuals ought to act. I mean, we give the children duties to do around the house so that they'll learn what it's like to have responsibilities. So they'll find out when a man or woman is grown up, he or she can't just let things slide that need to be done. Adults have to keep after themselves until they get the necessary things done. It's the same way with communities, or nations, or people in general. If there's something that it's time for them to do, then they have to go out and get busy and do it."

"And this Expedition to make a manned landing on Mars is something that the world has to get done, now—is that what you mean?" Lin asked. This Wendy Hansard was turning out to be a more promising subject than Lin had hoped.

"Yes," said Wendy. "I really believe that. The world's got no place to go, in a way, but to Mars. I mean, it's got no place to turn to but some effort like this, to prove people are capable of saving this planet and fulfilling the dreams that everybody's always had for life right here on Earth."

"That's very interesting," said Lin, leaning forward attentively.

A small shadow for a second seemed to pass behind Wendy's pale blue eyes.

"No, please go on," said Lin, quickly. "This is just the sort of thing our readers get so seldom—an idea of what's behind it all; the way someone like yourself, who's caught up in it, sees it. You do see a purpose to all this technological effort, then?"

"Of course there's a purpose!" said Wendy. "It's a lot larger thing than the practical results that they're always deviling the space effort to produce. We all have to keep growing—we can't help it. It's a basic, instinctive, necessary push for new territory and knowledge that's in all of us. It's not just the 'nauts; it's all of us."

"You feel you and the children are a part of it?" asked Lin.

"Necessarily," said Wendy.

"That's a very good point for *New World* readers," said Lin. "Very good. Would you say that, in a way, you and the children are as caught up in this Expedition as your husband is?"

Wendy went away. Lin could feel the psychic distance between them suddenly lengthen. Damn, she thought, we were doing just fine and I had to go hit something personal.

"What I mean is," she went on, quickly, hunting for something to bring the other back, "I've been struck in the many instances of people who are not only not 'nauts but never could be, getting caught up in the space effort, to the point that it seems to own them body and soul. Jens is like that, now. Though I suppose he'll get over it once he's back in Washington in a few weeks.''

"No," said Wendy. "I don't think he will."

Lin felt a chilliness, a strange anger along with the positiveness in her voice.

"Well, maybe not," she said, lightly. "We'll see. After all, he's still got to live here on Earth."

"That doesn't matter," said Wendy.

Behind Lin, there was the abrupt sound of the screen door slamming, and the clatter of shoes that stopped suddenly just inside the entrance. She turned and saw a girl of perhaps fourteen, and a tall, thin boy in his late teens.

She would never have imagined that she would feel so relieved to have them appear.

Seated in the first restaurant he had come to, with a cup of coffee he did not want cooling on the table before him, Barney plodded though the less-familiar languages of the newssheets in front of him. The single Russian copy that had been brought him, except for a brief summary of Day One events, might have been written two weeks before as far as the Expedition was concerned. But the English, European, Indian and Japanese papers all conformed to a remarkably similar pattern.

There was, in each case, a digest of information from Expedition Control on the actions of the marsnauts themselves. This was reechoed and amplified in almost every paper by an interpretive and imaginative description, that attempted to put the reader in the shoes of the marsnauts and fill the gap left by the colorless official account. But even these few pieces of news, put together, made up no more than a small fraction of the wordage dealing with the Expedition.

The overwhelming bulk of newsprint space was taken up with related stories and feature articles. There were accounts of important people from all over the world who had been present at Cape Canaveral for the launch. There were reports of speeches about the Expedition, and of comments within speeches, by political and scientific figures alike. There were prognostications of problems to be encountered during the three years of the voyage, background material on the NASA installation and hardware, photographs of the shuttle and the two Expedition spaceships prior to launch, and diagrams of how the booster shuttles had lifted them into the Mars-injection orbit and then separated from their mother ship. Finally, there was a welter of lightly-connected material, such as one story in an Italian paper, confiding that Merritt Island had become a new social center for the rich and famous personalities of the civilized world; and might in time become a cultural center.

Barney grinned a little, briefly, over that one, and then sobered. It was not true, but what it suggested was not far from the truth. For this first month at least, there would be a colony of newsworthy individuals around the Cape, clustered about the small enclave of international political and scientific people drawn there by the Expedition.

Which only served to point up what he had known would happen. The Expedition was being treated as the hardly-important excuse for an international fiesta. Taken entirely for granted was its eventual safe return, and the accomplishments it was being required to perform along the way. Taken for granted were the spacecraft, the marsnauts and all the highly technical work and effort, knowledge and skill of the six combined national space programs that had put Phoenix One and Two on the road to Mars.

The newssheet-reading public was being conditioned by omission to the idea that no accident could happen now, no unforeseen failure frustrate the Expedition. Let something go wrong in the face of that conditioning, and explaining it to the common citizens of the world would not be easy.

Barney stopped reading and glanced at his watch. It was ten to three—already past the time when he should have been back to pick up Lin. He gathered up his papers and left.

Tad and Fedya sat opposite each other at a wardroom table. This time it was the wardroom of Phoenix Two; and it was Tad who had brought the bargraphs that were spread out on its surface. Fedya's left hand, wrapped in gauze band-aging, rested upon some of these. Bern and Dirk had been with them up until a moment ago. Now, for the first time since Tad had come over from Phoenix One with the bargraphs, he and Fedya were alone. Tad glanced at the bandaged hand.

"How bad is it, actually?" he asked in a low voice.

"As I told you when you first came over," said Fedya, emotionlessly, "bruised, that's all."

Their eyes met.

Tad nodded.

"All right," he said, turning to the bargraphs and pushing a sheaf on them across the table to Fedya, who picked them up with his uninjured hand, "here's how I think we'd better handle it. One man takes care of the outside section of the pod and all EVA duties for both ships. I've juggled the other schedules to spread the work load out as a result of this; and the parts of your own schedule that you won't be able to do one-handed."

Fedya studied the bargraphs for several minutes while Tad sat in silence. Then he looked across the table at Tad.

"The work load is all right over here," he said. "But over on Phoenix One, you're the one who's picking up the extra work that I'm being relieved of."

"Not directly," said Tad.

"No," said Fedya, "not directly. But it amounts to two hours of work of which I'm relieved, and nearly an hour apiece off the schedules of Bern and Dirk. While over on Phoenix One, you pick up four extra hours of duties—and I mean *you* personally."

Tad looked grimly at him.

"As Expedition Commander," he said, "I've got more independent duties and more free time than anyone else. I'll be absorbing those four hours into that free time."

"You know," said Fedya, "that's not true—nor possible."

"It's possible," said Tad.

"How?"

Tad sat back in his chair.

"As you told me when I first came over," he said, coldly.

"Your hand's bruised, that's all. I won't ask you about it again."

Fedya sat for a long second without saying anything.

"All right," he said, then, "I won't ask how you plan to make this work. But what makes you think Expedition Control will accept it?"

He waved his right hand at the bargraphs and the penciled changes Tad had made upon them.

"They'll have to," Tad said. "They've got no choice now. Out here, if it really comes down to it, no one can give us orders but ourselves. And if they got excited about it, that would be bad publicity for the Expedition."

Fedya nodded slowly.

"But you'll need help," he said. "you can't do all that alone."

"No help," said Tad flatly. "And no discussion."

He reached out and swept the bargraphs back into a pile in the middle of the table.

"And I have no choice, either?" said Fedya.

"That's right," said Tad. He got to his feet, pushing back his chair from the table. "Don't spend your time thinking about me. You know we're all overscheduled, here. It may not seem so bad the first week or two. But by the third week, that lack of repair and down time is going to be piling up. You'll all five be putting three or four hours more a day than you're scheduled for. We both know that. I'm just taking on my extras hours now, in accordance with an amendment of the schedules."

"And a week and a half or two weeks before the rest of us," said Fedya, softly.

"I tell you, I can absorb most of that extra duty," said Tad. He still kept his voice pitched low. "I'll be in better shape than any of you, three weeks from today."

"You will not," said Fedya. "And that is something else we both know."

But, before Fedya could finish speaking, Tad had already turned and left the wardroom. Fedya heard him entering the access tube on his way back through the cryotex lane to Phoenix One. Soberly, Fedya rose, took the bargraphs from the table under his arm and headed toward his sleeping compartment.

20

"I don't like it," said Bill Ward on Day Sixteen.

"Don't like what part of it?" Nick Henning asked. He was sitting up in the bed of his private hospital room, looking as if the massive coronary attack he had had just eight days ago had never occurred, let alone like a man who was four days out of extensive heart surgery. Nevertheless in spite of the fact they were old friends, he was very conscious right at this moment, of the fact that Bill Ward had replaced him as Expedition Control Chief. Bill had just dropped in to visit him. The private room he inhabited was a pleasant one, looking East, and the flowers on the window-sill looked crisp and well watered.

". . . any part of it," Bill was saying, sitting stiffly upright in the sunlight on the visitor's chair by the bed, his face more irascible than usual under his close-cropped gray hair. "I didn't want your job in the first place, damn it!"

"I wasn't the one who stuck you with it," Nick said. "Washington thought you were the best bet to keep Tad in line, that's all."

"Keep him in line!" Bill made a small convulsive movement as if he wanted to get up and pace around the room, but would not indulge himself. "The fact a man's a friend doesn't mean you're going to have more luck keeping him in line—it means you're going to have less." He hesitated. "You don't know the worst of it. That Undersecretary of Science for the Space Effort—Jens Wylie—came to me more than two weeks ago, on the morning of Day One, before launch. He wanted me to do something personally about the work schedules for the 'nauts, aboard the ships.''

Nick frowned. "And you've never told anyone about this?''

"For God's sake!'' Bill exploded. "Isn't it enough of a mess already? We know those boys are overscheduled during this first thirty days. Washington knows it. Every involved government knows it; and we all sit here like the three monkeys—see no evil, hear no evil, tell nobody about the goddamn evil!''

"It's something that falls outside our area,'' said Nick.

"That's what everyone says. What it boils down to is nobody wants to be the one to tell the king the bad news.''

"The king?'' Nick stared at Bill.

"You know what I mean—the billions of so-called common people out there who're treating this thing as if it was a show put on for their benefit and a promise of an end forever to war and trouble and not enough to eat,'' said Bill. "Can't the damn fools see that the same old political backbiting and pulley-hauling is going on just the way it always did—only now it's centered around this Expedition? Anyway, I almost did what Wylie asked.''

Nick's eyelids came down to narrow his gaze and his eyes steadied on Bill.

"Good thing you didn't.''

"Good for who? For Tad—for those others up there?'' said Bill. "It's *not* good for them.''

"This is something that just happens to be bigger than just an ordinary space mission,'' said Nick. "It's tough on them, being out in the front trench; but they're just going to have to take it—there's no way we can help them.''

Bill flashed an angry look at him.

"You know what I mean!'' said Nick. He remembered suddenly that he was a sick man and made an effort to hold himself in calmness. "Our whole space program's at stake. It's been at stake ever since each country involved in this Expedition started loading it up with their pet experiments. Right from the beginning we've had the choice of giving the 'nauts more than they could handle or face the accusation that NASA was trying to hog the show. That's still the situation unless the 'nauts themselves, or someone else, speak up first."

He stopped speaking. Bill Ward sat scowling and silent.

"Don't tell me you're thinking of sticking the U.S.'s neck out on this?" Nick said slowly.

"Not yet," said Bill, still scowling. "But there was that accident on Day Two to Fedya's hand . . . all right, it turned out not to be anything important. But that's space out there; and things can happen when the men exposed to it get too tired or physically eroded. Remember the two Russian cosmonauts on the Soyuz mission who reached the ground dead because of a mechanical error that probably wouldn't have been made if they hadn't been suffering the effects of being too long in no-gravity without our present drugs or exercises?"

"But you aren't thinking of doing anything about this situation on your own hook, are you?" persisted Nick.

"Not yet," said Bill. "Not yet."

Day Twenty-two/Phoenix Two: Dirk Welles sat in his darkened cubicle, crosslegged on his bed with his back against the bulkhead behind him. He was too tired to sleep, but he knew that this was merely tension. If he stayed unmoving and simply let his thoughts run, soon he would let down in spite of himself and slumber would come. Meanwhile, sitting here alone like this was almost as good as sleep.

Privacy—some privacy at least—was one of his deep and secret needs. He could survive without it as long as things were going on—he could probably have survived this whole Expedition without it; but the hunger for it would always have been there and he was more healthy if he could have it, as now. It was strange how the two crews of the space vehicles differed on matters like this. Over here on Phoenix Two, he, Bern, and Fedya were all privacy people. On Phoenix One, they were all adventurers, the open ones.

From the beginning the world had never suspected this privacy need of his. Fate had been kind in its design of him. He had been grateful for needing to shave at twelve, for his big bones, his jutting jaw. These physical signals answered the immediate questions of other people as to what sort of person he was; that first curiosity satisfied, they looked no deeper, leaving him unsuspected in his inner self. At the core of that inner self was something quiet and personal, a place that had been open only to himself until Penny had come along. Now they occupied it together, while still giving each other the right to go one step deeper yet and be completely solitary for occasional brief moments. This worked with Penny, because she was the same sort of person he was.

What a miracle it had been, the two of them finding each other! He had never even guessed that there could be another like him in the world, let alone that that other could be a woman, someone like Penny with whom he could fall in love. Nor had she guessed there could be someone like him. They had never discussed this miracle in words but they both recognized it and had told each other about it in that special, wordless way in which they had been able to communicate from the first. From the beginning they had not needed to utter the words other people spoke to each other aloud.

Perhaps, perhaps it was something like that with Bern and his Joanna. Not the same thing, but something like it. It had been inconceivable to Dirk and Penny that any wife would not want to come to the launch of an Expedition like this, to be with her husband right up to the last moment. Of course, Anoshi's wife had not come, either; but there was something about the difference in cultures, the East and West of it, that seemed to make that not-coming appear more reasonable in Anoshi and Reiko's case. But Bern and Joanna had been married longer and had children.

Still, obviously Bern cared deeply for Joanna and she for him, as witness the daily letters and almost daily phone calls that had passed between them. So it stood to reason that they, too, must have their own mated, private togetherness—different from, but similar to, what Penny and he had.

Fedya . . . Fedya had no family any more, of course, and never talked about his dead wife and children. That was his particular inner privacy, and none of the rest of them would intrude there under any circumstances, naturally. So, the end result was that on this ship they were all alike in that one way; more private, more isolated one from another, than they were on Phoenix One.

The tension was beginning to leak out of Dirk's back and shoulders, now. He could feel it going. His thoughts turned back again to Penny and a warmth began to seep through his limbs and body. She was so dear. It was marvelous how she and he could still talk secretly together, even across the lasercom link and all these miles of space, how they could read behind each other's words and have as personal a conversation as they wished, even though their voice connection was as wide open as that between two radio stations. They could still reassure each other that they were well, and speak privately of their love, without anyone else knowing. Not that either the others aboard the two ships, or the people back at Expedition Control, would deliberately listen in—in fact, there was a particular effort made to ignore husband-and-wife conversations—but even if they had, with Dirk and Penny it would have made no difference. Because Dirk and Penny could carry on two conversations at once, one aloud and one in the silent channel that ran hidden behind their spoken words.

". . . I finally got interviewed by that magazine friend of Jens Wylie," Penny had said the last time they had talked.

"Oh?" he had said, asking—*did you mind it much?*

"Yes," Penny answered—*no, I didn't mind. I liked it.* "She's nice." *I like her. She could be a friend.*

"Well, that's good." *I'm glad you've found someone there you can make a friend of.* "What's she like?" *What makes you like her?*

"Well, she's very strong and independent." *She's solitary, like us.* "Good company, that sort of thing; and we get along." *She needs a friend, too—a female friend.*

"Well, I always liked Jens." *Is she the same sort of person he is?*

"They've known each other some time." *Yes, but there's a problem there.*

"Oh?" *What sort of problem?*

"She's really very interested in the way people think who're deeply into the space effort." *She's trying to understand space—and its relationship to Jens. She doesn't understand now.*

"I should think Jens could explain that sort of thing for

her." *What's the matter with him, that he hasn't done something about this himself?*

"Well, he's been busy, of course . . ." *He doesn't know how she's trying to understand.* "And of course, she is, too." *And she won't or can't tell him.*

"Seems to me a little digging would give her the answers." *You don't have to take on everybody else's problems.*

"Why, when I can give her most of them?" *It's not taking on problems. I want to do it, for both of them, and because I like her.*

"There's that, of course." *Whatever you want, love.*

"And it's no effort." *I know I can help her—help them both.* "Besides, it makes me feel useful." *We've been so lucky, so happy, you and I. I'd so like to help some other people to that same kind of happiness.*

"Charge ahead, then." *So would I, I suppose.* "With my blessings." *I love you, very much.*

"Blessings acknowledged." *And I love you, more than anything.* "I will then . . ."

Memory slowed. In the darkness of the cubicle, Dirk's eyelids fluttered and dropped. Sleep reached up with gentle, impalpable arms and pulled him down to the cot. Warmth was all through him. He sent his now-drowsy mind reaching out across the far, far emptiness to another mind, back there somewhere.

Good night, my love . . .

Good night. He seemed to just catch the distant answer. *Good night, good night, my dearest dear . . .*

Day Twenty-two/Phoenix One: Tad woke with a convulsive jerk; and lay in the dark, unable for the moment to remember where he was or what the time was now. His body ached for more sleep, yearned for it like some desiccated desert plant yearning for rain. For the moment he was aware of only two things—that deep, desperate need for sleep; and the fact that he was disoriented, lost in darkness with nothing to cling to but the grim urgency that had driven him out of the cave of slumber back to wakefulness, again.

Then it came back to him.

He looked at the illuminated face of the clock on his bed-side table. The hands stood at 2300 hours. Eleven P.M. Bap and Anoshi would be asleep by this time, sleeping the heavy drugged sleep of the exhausted. For him, after a two hour nap, there were his personal medical tests and the log book to deal with.

He lay still for a few moments in the darkness, gathering his will to rise. At first thought, the effort involved in getting up seemed impossible. He felt like someone chained hand and foot to the bed by fatigue; while before him, sensed but invisible, loomed the ever-growing stack of work to be done. Every day he attacked that stack, that mountain, with super-human efforts; but every day, at the end of the day, it was higher. A little more time had been lost from the overall schedule. One more impossibility had been added to those already required of him. And the next day another would be added.

He shoved the self-defeating image from him. Follow your nose, he told himself. Keep the eyes in close focus on the immediate grindstone. Look at the total of things and you'll never make it—besides, for him, the current day was not yet over. He had only allowed himself a two-hour nap while Anoshi and Bap dropped safely off to sleep. There were two more hours of work yet for him, before he could come back to this bed where he was now.

Up—he forced himself to throw back the single cover and sit up, swinging his legs over the edge of the bed. For a second he slumped there; then with another convulsive effort he was on his feet, headed toward the waste management room and the shower.

The shower was beautiful. He stood, leaning and braced against the metal walls of the narrow, upright cubicle, letting its endlessly recycled and filtered four gallons of water beat endlessly down upon his naked body, driving some heat and life into his bones. Bless the water that never quit. To heat it, he was burning ship's power for a period of time long beyond the normal interval, but to hell with that. They had power to spare and he was a piece of machinery that needed an infusion of energy to get it operating. Warmed at last to something like working temperature, he staggered out of the cubicle and headed back to his sleeping compartment to dress.

Dressed, he went into the wardroom and dropped down at the dining table, punching for a cup of coffee. Drinking it, he stared with unfocused eyes at the wardroom bulkhead opposite, where the dartboard hung, sprouting the feathered darts from the last game. Now that he was this far back into a waking mode, he did not really know how alert he was. Undoubtedly, he was tired, but all he felt, sitting at the wardroom table, was a sort of leaden brightness. The effective modes for him were no longer awake or asleep, but operative or inoperative.

It was, he thought as he sat drinking the coffee which was pleasant for its heat but no longer much use as a stimulant to him, a question of how far Anoshi and Bap had also descended down this road to exhaustion on which he himself was now far advanced. If he could not judge his own condition any more, it was certain that he could not trust himself to judge them. Of course, he had started to bear the work a good week and a half before the gradual accumulation of lost time on a too-crowded schedule had begun to drive them to extra hours of effort. From that, he should be able to count on their having reserves of energy still that he had already squandered. Of course, he would be going to work on the log in a minute and in the results of their daily physical checks, there should be some clue. But it was hard to be certain . . .

He would get to work any minute now. But first, one more cup of coffee . . .

. . . Ah-hah! Caught you at it, thought Tad, staring at his coffee container. His hand had just automatically reached out and refilled the container from the spout under his name on the wardroom wall against which the table faced. Thought you'd con me into sitting here while I drank a third cup, did you, he said to his hand. Well, it won't work.

Carefully, not spilling a drop, he poured the contents of the cup down between the bars of the drain under the spout, to be metered there also and deducted from the intake total the spout had been adding up for him in the log. He got up and went out of the wardroom.

He took the access tube to A Deck and went to the log console. Dropping heavily into the seat before it, he punched up the Day Twenty-two figures and began his study of them.

The recorded work schedule was already strongly at odds with the bargraphs of the projected work schedules aboard Phoenix One; and undoubtedly the same thing was true aboard Phoenix Two. Meal periods had shrunk to as little as fifteen minutes on occasion, and there were no open spaces between duties or experiments where one 'naut had a few minutes to wait until another could join him for a two-man activity. The Systems/Housekeeping periods were down to no more than five minutes. Finally, to top the matter off, the record showed the whole day running up to half an hour late into the normal beginning of the sleep period between 2100 and 2200 hours.

That much obvious increase of the work load and added use of time could stand in the official record. It was not an impossible situation, on paper—or rather, on the screen of the log here and back at Cape Kennedy. But on the other hand, it was not a true record of the situation, either.

What did not show on the record was the real trouble. For example, all three of them aboard Phoenix One had fallen into the habit of what they called "doing the chores": rising an hour and a half to two hours early to do any number of things that did not involve use of the recording equipment aboard and which consequently did not show up on the log.

Tad punched the log screen to focus in on the running physical statistics on the three of them aboard. The overwork was showing up as a weight loss for both Anoshi and Bap in the mass experiment—M149. Bap had lost eight pounds and Anoshi five as of Day Twenty-two's weighings. Neither of those was an unreasonable figure. Tad decided to leave them as they presently appeared on the record. Experiment M119 showed some calcium and nitrogen loss by both men; but again it was not so great a loss that it appeared threatening. M107—Negative Pressure, that experiment which required a 'naut to sit in a device covering him to the waist and fastened there with an airtight seal while air was exhausted below the ambient pressure of 5 psig, showed some cardiovascular changes that were not good.

Tad drummed his fingers on the lower edge of the console, debating with himself. It was one thing to stick his own neck out: but something entirely different to risk major damage to the other two. How many days were left? Eight, to finish the first thirty-day period; after which the schedule was to be cut almost in half. Risk it, he decided, with Bap and Anoshi, a few days longer. He left the M107 figures as entered.

He went on through the other checkpoints on the two men—heart rate, blood pressure, vectorcardiograms. The true figures on these would pass. The time and motion studies, on the other hand, showed Bap and Anoshi fallen off again; they had dropped sharply in performance in the last three days. In this case, Tad made slight corrections of the record, improving their marks slightly. So slightly, in fact that nothing was risked, either way; but enough of a change so that if, for any reason, he wished to improve the record of their performance tomorrow, it would not seem like a sudden change.

He left the log records dealing with Bap and Anoshi, then, and went to those dealing with himself.

For a moment he sat, merely staring at these. It had been a number of days since he had first begun to believe the evidence of his own physical deterioration as reflected in the records. Each day he corrected them to keep them in the same range as the records of his two crewmates; and each day the correction had become more unbelievable. It was true he was averaging no more than four to six hours of sleep out of the twenty-four and working at least two hours more than the others; but it was hard to credit that difference with causing him to fall apart as fast as the record showed.

Of course, he knew what the real reason was. He had known and figured on it before he ever spoke to Fedya about incapacitating himself. Tad's plan had been to use Fedya's injury as an excuse to juggle the work schedules of all six of them so that he himself would pick up a potential extra four hours of activities and each of the rest would have his load lightened by a potential forty-eight minutes apiece. One of the four extra hours Tad would eventually need to put in was to be an hour of activity after Bap and Anoshi were asleep;

and he had deliberately thrown his schedule out of phase with theirs to explain why they might wake to find him up and around when they were resting.

But the other three hours he had intended to save by simple cheating, by not doing certain scheduled activities in which he alone was concerned and faking the log records to show them as done. It had been a difficult problem to find three hours of personal activity that he felt could be eliminated without endangering the Expedition and his crewmates. But he had done it, thanks mainly to the eighty minutes he had saved by completely skipping his daily exercise period.

He could not have done this aboard Skylab. There, all such exercise required two men—the participator and the observer. But one of the points NASA had yielded on as the experiments piled up for the Expedition was the requirement that all exercise be observed. Tad had only needed to place his exercise period at the end of his day's schedule, after Bap and Anoshi were asleep, and then ignore it completely, except for recording fake evidence of it in the log.

It had been a calculated risk. Early in the period of manned spaceflight, it had been discovered that bodies designed for gravity deteriorated rapidly in a no-gravity situation. A few days without gravity were enough to do noticeable damage. The Skylabs, with their complete lack of gravity and long terms of duty by the men aboard them, had come up with an answer to this—daily exercise.

The two ships of the Mars Expedition, docked together and spinning, were not without gravity, even if it was a gravity less than half of normal. There had been evidence to show that a full gravity might not be what was necessary to keep the human body in normal good condition. Even a light gravity might be able to do it. Tad had gambled on this being so . . . but there was no denying the evidence he had been forced to correct daily for the last two weeks. Even in a light gravity, exercise was probably necessary. He had deliberately avoided exercise and the effects on his body were piling up.

But there was no going back, or no changing his plans, now even if he had wanted to. With a weary breath, he picked up a light pencil and began to correct his test figures to more healthy-looking ones . . .

"Yes," said the voice of Bap behind him. "You see, I was right."

Tad dropped the light pencil and spun about in the chair. He was braced to see Bap and Anoshi; but what he did see was worse.

The man with Bap was Fedya.

21

The Washington chief of Gervais's section, the tall, thin, half-balding man called Amory Hammond whom Albert Gervais no longer trusted, was a coffee spiller. He was also a coffee mopper-up. The two of them sat on opposite sides of a booth in the motel coffee shop after lunch, with Hammond drinking innumerable cups of coffee, spilling innumerable spills into his saucer, and adding paper napkins to soak them up.

Gervais sat watching him, without moving, behind the mask of his own face. Until he could get rid of Hammond, he was stuck with the man. The Air Force had charge of general Security in anything to do with the deputy ministers for space, for reasons that Gervais could not accept. This should have been a complete operation from the non-military side. This way, as it was, with his team on the bottom and the gold-braid characters up top, both sides were hampered; since he could not trust the Air Force to look the other way when he had to do something a little out of the ordinary; and naturally they were not going to trust him to look the other way if they had to sweep something under the rug. Since Hammond himself was not Air Force, but his immediate superior was, the partnership became uneasy at that point; and Hammond—as Gervais was now certain—did not have what it took to handle that uneasiness. He was showing visible signs of coming apart. Add the fact that he had been working with the Air Force so long that nobody in the home office really knew him any more; and in addition to not trusting him, as Gervais now did not, Gervais had always suspected him of lacking the guts to carry anything through—in spite of the good reports that Air Force was always sending over on him. Hammond and Gervais had known each other off and on over a period of nearly ten years now, and they were exactly the same age.

"No problems at all, then?" Hammond asked sucking at his coffee cup.

"Not so far," said Gervais evenly. He was perfectly polite. "All routine."

"And your crews all working well? You're satisfied with them all?"

"No complaints," said Gervais.

Hammond emptied the last of the coffee in his cup, finger-wagged at a passing waitress and waited until she brought the bulbous glass coffee pot, cleared the soggy papers from underneath his cup, and went away again.

"Some kid in town here got beaten up a few nights ago, pretty thoroughly, the local cops tell me," Hammond said, pouring large quantities of sugar in his cup and then adding cream. "Any time you get a lot of people together, like at one of these launches, there seem to be a few freaks among the rest."

He looked sharply back at Gervais over the edge of his cup as he lifted it. Gervais met his eyes calmly.

"I suppose," said Gervais.

"The local cops say they aren't surprised too much at anything that happens just before a launch," Hammond went on, dropping his gaze away again, lifting his brimful cup, spilling some of its contents into the saucer and drinking deeply before putting it down again, "but after the launch it goes back to being the same sleepy little neighborhood. Nothing much happens during ordinary times, they tell me."

"No," said Gervais. "No, I wouldn't expect anything freakish now that the crowd's clearing out. Of course, there has to be a certain amount of felonies in the ordinary course of things."

"As few as possible, we'd hope," muttered Hammond to his cup.

He reached over for one of the paper napkins, folded it, and put it in his saucer. The spilled coffee soaked into it and became a brown stain on the paper. He studied the stain, then looked up once more at Gervais.

"Did you hear?" he said. "They say there's been another fuss about some of the team people using ex-cons to do their dirty work for them."

"Is that so?" said Gervais. "I hadn't heard. What teams were they talking about?"

Hammond watched his coffee as he stirred it.

"Nobody seems to know for sure," he said. "But they seem to think it's teams on the non-military side."

He waited but Gervais said nothing.

"Well," Hammond went on, "it's probably no one we know, particularly no one in our outfit. Most of our people know the danger of anything like that getting in the papers."

"Yes," said Gervais. "I'd say you're right."

They sat there for a moment more of silence, while Hammond drank coffee. Gervais put his hands before him on the table and steepled the fingers together.

"You know the Duchess is out in the old mansion?" said Hammond. "If she's around, there must be a few things going on."

"That old bitch," said Gervais quietly, "was over the hill ten years ago. Before that she wasn't anything either, and the people she had around here weren't anything but playpretties."

"Tell me something I don't know," said Hammond. "This is still an international matter. All the foreign ministers will be around until the first month of the Expedition is over; and we're worried about the newspapers and other media."

"When weren't there newspapers to worry about?" Gervais said. "We just keep our heads down and do our job as usual."

"All right," said Hammond. "You know I trust you, Albert. I've always felt there was no one like you for a situation like this. All right, then. I'll see you in a couple of days when I get back from the home office."

His face twitched slightly. He stood up, picked up the checks for both their lunches and walked toward the cash register. Gervais sat still, looking after him, his own face perfectly steady. When Hammond had paid the checks and gone out into the hotel lobby, Gervais got to his feet and went, not to that door, but to the swinging doors through which the waitresses entered from the kitchen. He stepped through the right-hand door, circled the tables where the white-suited kitchen staff was at work and came to a flight of stairs. Four steps down he came to a fire door which let him into a corridor; and halfway down through the corridor, going through a door to his left, he stepped back into the office just off the lobby that was his own headquarters. The only one on duty there at the moment was Joe Kolin, a half-bald, kindly looking forty-year-old man, beginning to sag a little bit about the jowls, and wearing a cheap summerweight business suit that was a little too tight for him across the shoulders.

"Where's Brawley?" asked Gervais.

"Up in his room, catching some sleep, I think," said the man in the palm beach suit, "Want me to call him?"

He reached for the stud at the base of the picturephone on his desk.

"No," said Gervais, "I've got to go up anyway. I'll drop in on him."

"Is Hammond going to be staying around?" asked the other man.

"No. Going back," Gervais said.

"There's been talk that there's some kind of sticky business going on here, to bring him down," said the agent.

"There's always talk," said Gervais. "There's always some kind of business."

"Nothing to do with Kil?"

"I'm responsible for Kilmartin Brawley, not you," said Gervais. "But just to stop any rumors, the answer's no."

The other nodded slowly and sat back in his chair, picking up the paperback book he had been reading. Gervais went out into the lobby, across to the elevator, and took one of its cars up to the seventh floor where all of his own security team had their rooms. He went down the silent, carpeted corridor to room 743, and tapped on it with a fingernail.

"Yes?" said Kilmartin Brawley's voice, sounding close to the door on the inside.

"It's me," said Gervais.

The lock rattled and the door opened. Gervais stepped in, glancing around as Brawley closed the door and relocked it. Gervais's eye noted the rumpled bedspread and the tangle of Brawley's hair.

"What is it?" Brawley asked.

"You're not showing a lot of intelligence, Kil," said Gervais. "It's not smart to build a backfire against anything I might have to do to you over these little adventures of yours. Particularly, it's not smart to build a backfire by setting up the fact we're sweeping trouble under the rug down here. What made you talk to Hammond?"

Brawley's face twisted.

"Albert! Believe me, I wouldn't—I'd never do anything like that!"

"You're telling me the truth?" Gervais watched him closely.

"You know I'm telling the truth. I swear I'm telling the truth!"

"You lie to me," said Gervais, "and I'll see you in a straitjacket for the next sixty years. I'll lose you, Kil."

"I'm not lying."

"Hmm," Gervais stood a moment, thinking. "You know of anybody else on the team who might be carrying stories to higher-up?"

"Nobody," Brawley said. "They wouldn't do that, Albert, anymore than I would."

Gervais stood a second longer.

"It just may be something is actually going on," he said, finally. "So keep your eyes open; and tell the rest of the team to be particularly sharp—just in case."

He turned around, unlocked the door, and let himself out again, closing the door behind him. Kil had been telling the truth, that was plain. He did not have the guts for real game-playing, which was why he would never be anything more than one of the troops. Of course there was nothing real going on—outside of whatever game it was that he was beginning to zero in on, involving Willy Fesser and whoever Willy would be working for. If it was not for his need to do something about Hammond, he would let Fesser have that game of his, unmolested. But right now, it was just too useful to ignore. Not that whatever it was would stay secret anyway. Situations like those at this launch always took place in a fishbowl. Sooner or later, unless you were a veteran like himself, or someone like Mayence or Verigin, anything you did got found out.

Still caught in his own thoughts, he walked down the hall, put a key into the door of his own room, let himself in, and locked it behind him. He went to his bed, sat down beside the phone, flicked it on to copy, and then punched the three number code that he had inserted in there the night after meeting Arthur DeMars, the thin, black ex-con with the pickup whom he had put to work keeping an eye on the people at the Kelly estate. The phone buzzed its call in his ears, but the screen did not light and no voice answered.

He pressed a stud to leave an automatic message on the other unit he was calling and spoke into his own phone.

"This is Jackson. Get in touch with me just as soon as you can."

He flicked off the phone, got up and went over to sit down in an armchair near the window. The bright, hot daylight outside, dimmed by the light-responsive window, left him illuminated softly. There was certainly something going on—no doubt about that.

A cold anger at the whole weak and vacillating tribe of ordinary men formed inside him and began to rise as in a wave of sickness toward his throat. With the practice of long experience he willed it back down. The mirror across the room gave him back his own image, showing not the slightest change of expression; but when he was done conquering his anger, sweat stood out on his forehead.

The one bright spot was that he now had an almost good team—all except Kilmartin Brawley, of course. Kil was a sour apple who would have to go, just as Amory Hammond had to go. Outside of those two, however, the people on the scene from his outfit were good and reliable effectives. Even

Kil could be an effective while he was still around—as long as he was kept under control.

But before Gervais could take any real action, he needed to know who was doing what. The only game in town was the floor of ministers, upstairs; but there was literally nothing concerning them that was worth two cents to anyone; so why would anybody hire someone like Fesser to go to the trouble of breaking through the security on them? If there were something to be gained, it would be that much easier to figure out who was after it. As it was, whatever was going on was probably going on for some private reason or other. That meant it could be any one of the ministers themselves, and also any one of the other government outfits besides his own, or even some large commercial concern, like one of the engineering companies involved in the Expedition. What Gervais needed was something, anything, to go on, any kind of clue at all. Once he had that, it was just a matter of checking until he could zero in; and once he zeroed in it would be his pleasure to take care of whoever was causing the trouble . . . and at the same time wrap up people like Hammond and Kil.

Slowly and meticulously, in his own mind, Gervais began to go over everything that he had seen, felt, or learned, since he and the rest of the team had first arrived on the job a little over two weeks ago. As he thought, he opened the drawer in the desk beside him and got out a towel-wrapped bundle. He unwrapped it, and laid out on the desk top a heavy file, a small screw-on vise, and the other souvenir paper-knife he had bought at the Space Center Information Building. Still thinking, he fastened the vise in position on the edge of the table and clamped the knife in it, with its blade protruding.

He picked up the file and checked himself, abruptly, looking down at his hands. Together they held the file delicately but with the firm grip of practice, fingers gripping it expertly at each end.

He paused and breathed deeply, slowly. He shifted his fingers on the file. Now his hands held it roughly, clumsily, the way someone might hold it who had never used such a tool seriously before. Holding it so, he stroked at the softly rounded point of the knife, and the light metal there scraped away at his touch, becoming narrow and sharp.

22

"How long has this been going on?" asked Fedya, as he, Anoshi and Bap stood facing Tad, still seated before the log screen.

"What're you doing here?" demanded Tad.

Fedya ignored him. He took one long step forward to level with Tad's chair and looked down at the page of the log imaged on the screen.

"Hold on there—" Tad tried to spin around to face the console; but Feyda pushed him back again and Bap caught him, holding on. "What the hell—"

His voice was thick; and his legs, when he tried to get to his feet against Bap's arm, were without strength. Fedya stood looking past him at the log records for a long moment; then he stepped back and Bap let go of Tad.

"I'm senior—" Tad began. Fedya broke in on him.

"You are sick," he said, "a man who is seriously worn out and sick. Bap, take a look at the figures on him in the log."

Bap stepped past Fedya in his turn. This time, Tad made no attempt to stop the log from being seen. He sat in his chair, glaring at Fedya.

Bap said something softly but emphatically in a language Tad did not recognize, then stepped back from the console and turned to Tad, reaching out to close the fingers of his left hand upon the pulse in Tad's left wrist and gently lifting one of Tad's eyelids with the fingers of his right hand. Then he let go of the eyelid; and a moment later took his hand from the pulse.

"Tad," he said, looking down at Tad and shaking his head. "Tad!"

Tad glared up at them all like a cornered wild dog.

"Cut it out!" he said, harshly. "You're not going to do anything. You tell Expedition Control about me, and you'll blow everything wide open."

"Expedition Control's already concerned," said Fedya, "on the basis of the data on your vital signs during the monitoring period each day."

"But they don't know what's going on here; and they won't if we don't tell them!"

"That part's true enough," Bap said to the other two beside him. "But he can't go on like this."

"No," said Fedya. His dark eyes were boring into Tad. "So this was the way you thought you could get around the overload of activities? How could you try something so impossible?"

"Go to hell!" said Tad, savagely. "If the gravity had been enough, I'd have been all right. It's just the lack of exercise that's got to me."

Fedya glanced questioningly at Bap, who shrugged with his eyebrows.

"Probably," said Bap. He looked back at Tad. "Anyway, as the closest thing to a physician on this Expedition, I'm personally ordering you to bed until further notice."

"There's things to be done," said Tad. "Nobody but me can do them."

"They can wait ten hours," said Bap. "Even falsifying that record can wait ten hours."

"What'll you tell Expedition, when they ask to have it relayed to them tomorrow morning?"

"That they'll have to wait," said Fedya. "And meanwhile—" he turned and walked over to seat himself at the command console "—we'll put them on notice that our activities schedule has to be cut, immediately."

He flipped the communication switch and pushed the laser-com control buttons.

"This is Phoenix One," he said into the mike grid of the console before him. "Phoenix One. This is Fedya, for Mars

Expedition calling Expedition Control from Phoenix One. Come in, Kennedy.''

There was a perceptible delay. Already they were far enough from Earth for communication lag. The screen before him blurred with color and resolved itself into the features of a thin-faced communications engineer with the ranked consoles of Expedition Control at the Cape, behind him.

"This is Expedition Control," he said. "This is Expedition Control receiving you loud and clear, Phoenix One. What's up, Fedya?''

"I want to talk to the Expedition Director," Fedya said. "I must talk to Bill Ward, immediately . . .''

". . . left him there, locked in the closet." Sir Geoffrey wound up his story and the group about him laughed. One laugh in particular, that of the Duchess, rang clearly across neighboring conversations. Sir Geoffrey winked at her in appreciation, and instantly realized that once again he was sailing dangerously near his limit on drinks. It was a damned annoying thought for someone who used to be able to drink all night and the next day without showing it. He would just have to quit for the evening, even though there were at least a couple of hours more to go. Damn!

"But what happened to the man?" asked Bill Ward's wife, Jenna.

"Happened? Haven't any idea," said Sir Geoffrey. "May still be there in the closet, for all I know.''

More laughter. Bill felt a touch on his elbow. He turned, and it was Al Murgatroyd.

"Fedya wants to talk to you on the lasercom—right away."

"What about?''

"I don't know," Al said.

Bill hesitated and looked around him. Sir Geoffrey had just begun another story. Bill beckoned Jenna to join him and they walked off from the crowd.

Bill waited until they were well away from anyone who might overhear, before turning to Jenna.

"Nothing desperate," he said. "But the 'nauts want to talk to me about something. I'll have to run back to Expedition Control. Can you get a taxi home?''

"Oh, someone will give me a ride," she said. "Don't worry about me." She looked up at his tall, thick-waisted figure concernedly. "Don't forget you need your sleep."

"Of course, of course," Bill said. "Don't wait up for me, though."

He turned and walked swiftly off toward the hotel entrance next to the parking lot before she could give him any more good advice. She had fussed over him ever since Nick Henning's heart attack. He found his car in the parking lot and headed back to the Cape.

It took him nearly forty minutes to get there, in spite of the relatively empty, after-midnight highways. Ten minutes later he was talking to Fedya.

"Where's Tad?" asked Bill.

There was a delay, even at the light speed of the laser communication beam, before the lips of Fedya's face in the screen moved, and Fedya's voice was heard.

"He's asleep, and he has a tranquilizer in him. He can't talk to you now."

"There's something you're not telling me," said Bill.

"No," said Fedya. "What more do you need to know? The activity load is too heavy. All of us are worn down by it. Tad was so worn down he was ready to collapse."

Bill thumbed a pile of log duplicate sheets that had been brought to him while he had been talking.

"According to these, Tad—" he was beginning, when a thought woke in the back of his brain. Quietly, he pushed the sheets aside. "You're asking Expedition Control to cut the experiment list?"

"Yes. They can cut it," said Fedya. He paused. "Or they can face the fact that certain work will be left undone for lack of time in which to do it."

"How—" Bill's voice surprised him by its hoarseness. He cleared his throat and tried again. "How soon do you want an answer?"

"Twenty-four hours," said Fedya.

"Oh, now look here!" said Bill. "Cutting that list involves checking with various governments—your own for one. You can't mean twenty-four hours!"

"They can take as much time as they like," said Fedya.

"But starting immediately, on both ships, we will only do what there is time for us to do in a normal days' work-period."

"That's not—" began Bill, and broke off as a paper was pushed into his hand by someone standing nearby. He read it and laughed. He looked back into the screen at Fedya.

"Saved by the bell," he said. "Guess what? We've just got word of a solar flare that's due to hit you in five hours and thirty-eight minutes. Did you get that?"

"I heard you," said Fedya. "We copy. A solar flare is due to reach us in five hours and thirty-eight minutes. I assume you mean a flare large enough for us to run the laser-com tests."

"Of course," said Bill. "And running those tests means you drop everything else and concentrate on them. You'd better get started and put as much distance between the two ships as you can. Meanwhile, I'll pass along your request for a cut in the activities schedule."

"Good," said Fedya. "Phoenix Two will speak to you again just before breaking off to lock communications contact with Phoenix One for the duration of the LCO tests. Over and out."

"Over and out," said Bill. The screen went blank. Bill sat back in his chair, gazing at the unlit surface for a long moment before he seemed to shake himself out of his dark mood and look about for whomever had handed him the note about the flare.

"Who gave me that?" he asked. "And how bad's it going to be?"

"I did," said the communications engineer on duty, Mick Howard, leaning in toward him. "And it's going to be rough."

Tad leaped suddenly to full wakefulness out of deep sleep, as if someone had shot a cannon off at his bedside. He lay listening, but there was no sound. He felt light-headed but alert. Only his body was still numb with exhaustion. He forced it up into a sitting position on the edge of the bed . . . and floated off the bed surface entirely into the air.

There was no gravity.

Phoenix One and Phoenix Two were no longer docked together and rotating.

In that moment he heard it again—the noise that had roused him from sleep. It was the heavy clang of metal against metal, somewhere forward in the ship—it sounded as if it might be on A Deck almost directly over his head.

Tad jerked himself out of the bed; and pulled himself through the gravityless environment to the hatch of the access tube, then along the access tube up to A Deck, and out on to A Deck. He saw Bap and Anoshi manhandling thick metal sandwich panels into position about the control consoles. As he emerged from the access tube they finished locking the one they held into place against the line of panels already up to the left of the consoles; and Bap saw him.

"Awake, Tad?" Bap said. "I was just coming down to get you. We've got a solar flare coming. In fact, it's already here."

"A flare?" The information jolted out of Tad all the anger that had been building up in him at not being wakened before this. For a second his mind was full only of the situation that a large solar flare implied for Phoenix One and Two. Then his anger returned with a rush. "Why'd you let me sleep this long?"

"We were doing all right without you," said Anoshi. "The radiation index is already starting to rise; and we're all buttoned down outside, except for the lasercom—and that's now matched with the LCO mirror on Phoenix Two."

"Where is Phoenix Two?" Tad asked.

"Fedya's moved her a good hundred and forty kilometers off. We've both said our last words for the moment to Expedition Control. Now, as soon as we get the storm cellar set up here, we'll be ready to ride it out. You'd better get dressed."

"Dressed?" Tad recognized suddenly that he was wearing nothing but standard onboard duty clothes. Anoshi and Bap were dressed in the undersuiting that went with their spacesuits, including even biomedical sensors and the semi-bulky EMU urine collection systems about their crotches and waists. He looked at the new panel the two were now picking up— the last one to be put in place to surround the control system.

The panels made up a specially protected area which the 'nauts themselves referred to as "the storm cellar."

"How soon should we be inside?" Tad asked.

"The next fifteen minutes, to be amply safe," panted Bap. In no-gravity, the panels lacked normal weight; but their mass and inertia made them problems to handle.

"I'll be back up in ten," said Tad.

He turned and went hurriedly down the access tube to B Deck. He got into his undersuiting, swallowed a hot cup of coffee in the wardroom, made a hasty visit to the waste disposal room and was back up the access tube and into the storm cellar within the time limit he had given. He entered through the gap where the last panel of the cellar stood ajar; and he pulled it closed into its fitting with the adjoining panel behind him.

Bap and Anoshi were already on their acceleration couches, Tad pulled himself over to his and belted down. He was once again clear-headed; but the heavy sleep had reawakened his appreciation of what bodily tiredness meant. He was like a live mind in a nearly unconscious carcass.

"How long was I out?" he demanded.

"Nearly six hours," said Anoshi. "We got word of the flare when Fedya told Expedition Control about cutting the activities schedule, about an hour after Bap put you to bed."

"And Fedya took Phoenix Two off? We're still holding course?" Tad asked.

"Right. Right on both counts," said Anoshi.

"How intense a flare?"

"The forecast Kennedy gave us was upwards of twelve thousand BeV at Earthpoint," said Anoshi. "That should push it right up near the end of our scale."

He pointed at Phoenix One's outside counter. Twelve thousand billion electron volts was more than three-quarters of the way up its line of measurement. Right now the needle hung just above the bottom pin.

"Are we all buttoned up?" Tad said. "Did you get the live subjects from the labs into the safety room?"

"All of them, including the plants from the atmosphere section of the pod. All the films out of the outside cameras—everything's done. We didn't miss your presence at all."

"You hope!" snapped Tad. He was still fighting his exhaustion-deadened body; and Bap's usual humor irritated instead of amusing him. He turned to the communications section of his console and punched buttons to call Phoenix Two on the LCO.

Color swirled and became the face of Fedya. It was clear and sharp; but then it should be. To the laser beam carrying it between the outside copper mirror on Phoenix Two to the duplicate mirror on Phoenix One, a hundred and forty kilometers was no distance at all compared to the work it would finally be called on to do, in maintaining communications between Cape Canaveral and the Expedition, once it had arrived at Mars. Theoretically, even the billions of electron volts—the storm of proton and electron particles thrown off by the solar flare following its first burst of electromagnetic radiation—should not disturb it, at this short distance. But that was one of the matters that the Expedition was about to test. Both ships had aligned their outside laser mirrors on each other, putting them out of contact with Earth, except for radio communication; and radio communication was limited, even with the more powerful equipment aboard Phoenix One, which was to do the long-range tests once the Expedition reached Mars orbit.

"Fedya?" said Tad, the second Fedya's face was identifiable. "You did talk to Kennedy about cutting the schedule?"

"I spoke to Bill Ward," Fedya answered. "I told him that in any case, we could none of us do more than there was time to do in the normal waking hours, from now on."

"Good," said Tad. His mind jumped to another problem. "About the log—"

"I said nothing."

"Good. You had a last word with Expedition Control before realigning your LCO mirror?"

"Yes," said Fedya. "I called them to say we'd reached our distance of one-forty klicks from you; and that we would open communication again as soon as the particle storm was safely past its peak. Estimate is, that should be at least fifteen hours from the time of my last transmission to them."

"All right," said Tad. "How's everybody over there?"

"Just lovely," said the voice of Dirk, before Fedya could answer. "Snug as bugs in our storm cellar here."

Fedya smiled a little.

"You, too?" he asked Tad.

"Affirmative," said Tad. "We'll leave the communications channel open for metering purposes. Feel free to talk to us at any time."

"We will," said Fedya. "Over and not out."

"Over and not out to you," said Tad.

Fedya's face moved away from view of the screen on Phoenix Two, which now showed a portion of storm cellar paneling and the paneling overhead of A Deck. Tad leaned back on his couch against the pull of the strap.

"Maybe I'll take a nap," he said, "as long as there's nothing more we can do right now. Yes, I think I'll . . . take . . ."

And he began to dream almost immediately that Phoenix One had reached Mars. She was buried deep in sand; and the sand, despite all they could do, was finding small cracks and fissures in her hull, through which it came, silently and inexorably trickling into the ship . . .

There was no sound to the solar storm, raging through the vacuum about the ship, and even through the ship itself. There was no sound, vibration, color nor apparent motion. There was only the needle climbing on the BeV meter. It climbed slowly to twelve thousand billion electron volts . . . and continued upward while the three in the storm cellar of Phoenix One watched, and waited, and waited some more; talking back and forth occasionally with Phoenix Two.

"Look," said Anoshi, finally.

He was pointing at the BeV meter. The other two looked. It took a second to make sure that they were not seeing simply what they hoped to see.

"It's backed off, all right," Tad said. "Just barely. But it's backed off. Phoenix Two—"

He turned to the communications mike and the screen of the LCO. But the view of the panels and ceiling enclosing the command area of their sister ship was no longer showing on the screen. Instead, the screen showed a slowly drifting and changing pattern of random colors.

"Now what?" muttered Tad. His fingers went to the controls of the LCO, while he repeated himself into the mike grid. "Phoenix Two. Phoenix Two. Come in, please. Phoenix One calling Phoenix Two. Do you read me, Phoenix Two? Do you read me? Phoenix Two, this is Phoenix One. Come in, Phoenix Two . . ."

The colors continued to drift, unresolved. Tad reached out and turned the gain up on the console speaker; but all that resulted was a louder rush of background static.

"Either their LCO's out, or ours is," said Anoshi.

"Shouldn't go like that," said Tad, under his breath.

"What?" Anoshi asked.

"I said—" Tad raised his voice, harshly "—it shouldn't go like that—in just a minute, and completely out."

He turned and flipped back the cover of the recording strip on the LCO, pulling out a long tongue of paper with five parallel lines running lengthwise on it—running steadily until, some eight inches from where Tad's hand grasped it, the straight lines broke into a wild up-and-down marking that continued back into the recorder.

"Went out suddenly, a little over three minutes ago," Tad said. He looked at the others. "Were either of you watching the screen then?"

Bap and Anoshi both shook their heads, watching him.

"Well, it must be our unit," Tad said. "Either that, or Phoenix Two is deliberately transmitting nonsense. Now why would our LCO hold up beautifully all through the storm and then go on the blink the minute the storm started to back off?"

He looked at the BeV meter. The needle was now perceptibly down from the high peg against which it had been resting. Bap glanced up at the ship's chronometer, high on the console.

"The storm was stronger than they forecast," Bap said; "but it's slackening off before they forecast it to. We should have an hour or more of heavy particle bombardment to wait out yet."

"As long as the storm fades, I'm not going to ask why,"

said Tad; and was startled for a second by the near-anger in his voice. Get hold of yourself, he said, internally. You're becoming as touchy as nitroglycerine. Becoming? Or have you been like this these last couple of weeks and been too tired to realize how you were acting with Bap and Anoshi?

However, there was no time for emotional self-examination now. The point to concentrate on was that the LCO was malfunctioning. He looked once more at the BeV meter. There was a red line near the bottom of its scale; and a blue line below that. Once the indicator needle dropped below the blue at the bottom of the scale, it would be safe for a man in a spacesuit in EVA—extra-vehicular activity—outside the ship.

"As soon as we get below the red," he told the other two, "we can check everything right up to the point where the system goes out through the hull to the positioning controls of the mirror. Meanwhile, we can at least check the console part of the system. And I suppose we might try the radio—just for luck."

He reached out as he finished speaking; and keyed in the radio system to the mike and the speaker. But at the first touch of the volume control, the torrent of static that poured in on their ears ruled out any possibility of communication by radio with Phoenix Two.

"Long shot," he said, and made himself grin at Anoshi and Bap. "All right, give me a hand at getting the front panel of this console off and we'll start checking the LCO."

They went to work. But that part of the system which was reachable within the area of the storm cellar was relatively easy to check; and it was not long before they had proved that there was no malfunction in the system as far as they could reach it. They replaced the front panel of the console and Tad looked at the BeV meter. Its needle was already below the red line.

"Dropping beautifully," said Tad, getting to his feet. "All right, let's break out of this storm cellar and check the system as far as we can the rest of the way inside."

Bap and Anoshi also rose. But Anoshi was frowning at the BeV meter.

"I agree with you," sad Bap, although Anoshi had not

said anything. "It's not what they told us to expect—the storm dropping off this soon and this fast."

Tad felt the sudden gorge of his earlier irritation and rage boil up automatically like a sour vomit taste in his throat.

"Have you got some other suggestion for checking on the situation?" he asked Bap. "We can't raise Phoenix Two, let alone Expedition Control."

Bap merely frowned slightly, his dark brows joining in a single black line above his fatigue-darkened eyes, apparently more puzzled than provoked by Tad's words and the edge in Tad's voice.

"We could sit tight for a few more hours," he said. "Phoenix Two was the one who moved off from us. All we have to do is wait and she'll be rejoining us, if the storm's down and all communications are out."

"And what if she's in trouble on her own?" Tad demanded. "What if she's in worse trouble than we are; and needs us to contact her and get word back to Expedition Control?"

He did not wait for Bap to answer, but walked directly to the last panel that had been put in place to seal the storm cellar. He broke the seal loose and pushed the panel back, stepping into the open part of A Deck.

"All right," he said, heading for the access panel that would allow them to begin tracing the LCO system beyond the area that had been enclosed by the storm cellar. "Somewhere along here we'll find the malfunction."

23

However, when they got the last access plate off, the LCO wiring checked okay right up to the inner skin of the bird.

"That's it," said Tad, disconnecting the leads from the

test unit and fist-thumping the access plate back into its own tension-held position. "It's got to be in the positioning motor unit for the mirror outside, then, just the way I said. The storm was heavy enough to knock out any outside electronic components."

"The positioning drive is shielded," said Bap. "That whole housing below the mirror is shielded."

"Not enough," said Tad. "Not enough, goddamn it. Or maybe you think we overlooked something inside, and the trouble's not out there after all?"

He stared at Bap. Bap's dark face was honed now by tiredness to the sharpness of an axe blade chipped out of gray flint. There was little humor left in him. Anoshi was equally pared down, and silently watching them both.

"I mentioned the shielding only," Bap said. "Of course it must be outside."

"Right then," said Tad, his voice again impersonal. He turned and led the way toward the central ladder tube; and they went up the metal rungs to the Control Deck again. Tad checked the needle on the radiation graph. It was down now, on a good thirty-degree slope of fall; still above the blue line by an inch or so but plunging.

"All right," said Tad. He checked the radio; but only the mindless blare of static roared from the control console speaker. "I'll go EVA and have a look at the trouble outside where it lives."

"We're not in the blue, yet," said Bap. "And there's Expedition Control to check with before an EVA."

Tad looked at him again.

"No," said Anoshi. "Until the storm dies down there's no reaching Expedition Control on the radio. And you remember what we said—maybe Two's had the same trouble. Without a radio she can't reach us—or Kennedy. At least we have a chance of reaching Expedition by radio in a day or two—even if the LCO's are out for good, for both of us. We could lose Two, meanwhile."

"All right," said Bap, still standing, looking back at Tad. "But you're Commander, Tad. I'll go—or Anoshi."

"I'm Commander. I'm going," said Tad.

He headed toward the ladder tube.

"You're not in the blue yet," Bap said.

"I heard you the first time you said that," Tad answered without stopping, without turning. "But by the time I'm suited and ready, it'll be down. That's a classic curve for flare activity, there on the graph. Tell you what, though—" he had to turn to face the other two as he began to back down the ladder "—the sensor eyes are working all right. Keep the picture on by Hatch Three. I'll wait to go out until you tell me we're under the blue line. Okay?"

"Okay. Real fine," said Bap. "I'll keep the picture lit by Hatch Three and advise you on the blue line."

"Right," said Tad. "And keep a radio and LCO watch in case Two or Expedition comes back in again."

"Will do," said Anoshi.

Tad went on down the ladder, out of sight of the two still on the Control Deck.

Over in Phoenix Two, a check of the Laser Communications System was also in progress; but with different results.

"There could be trouble outside," Bern said.

Fedya merely shook his head. They were in the Control Area of Phoenix Two and while the other two stood behind him, Fedya was seated at the test board of the LCO.

"Not likely," said Dirk. "We'd have trouble lights somewhere. It's got to be the LCO over on One."

Fedya's long, thin fingers drummed thoughtfully on the edge of the test board. Of the three men on Phoenix Two, he showed his fatigue the least. Above his white coverall collar his grave, handsome face looked not so much tired as remote, considering, as if this were only another theoretical problem to be worked out on the finite squares of the chessboard.

"No radio," he said, turning the speaker sound up momentarily with its roar of static. "No LCO with One." He turned the speaker sound down again. "Very well. Let us see if we can make contact with Expedition Control. Contact will prove our LCO is operational; and we can get word about One to Control."

He looked up at Dirk.

"Dirk," he said. "You stay on the radio and try to raise One that way, while I work the LCO into contact with Kennedy."

At Merritt Island, the temperature was in the nineties. Tom and Cassy had wanted to go swimming at the tennis club pool. Wendy, thinking that Tad would have let them go, had given in, packed them bag lunches and seen them off on their bicycles. Left with the empty house and the endless whispering of the air conditioner, she had gravitated naturally to the garage and had ended up driving out to Expedition Control. There was nothing particularly alarming about the spacecraft passing through a solar storm. In the storm cellar on each ship the men would be as safe as if they were back on Earth. But her last LCO contact with Tad four days ago had left her uncomfortable. He was tired, that much was plain to see on his face in the viewscreen. When he was tired, things never went their best for him. It was when he was tired that he stubbed his toe and broke it, or dented a fender on the car, or got word that their real estate taxes had been raised.

When he was rested, it was just the opposite. Then the flow of luck seemed to reverse and everything went wonderfully. She had learned to trick him into lying down, sometimes, and then deliberately let him oversleep, once he did drop off. If he suspected what she was up to before he fell asleep he was furious with her and himself. But if he did not suspect until after he had slept, he was never angry over what she had done, no matter what the consequences of his oversleeping turned out to be.

"It'll be all right," he always said; and somehow it always was.

There was no way she could trick him into sleeping now, over a laser communications beam, across four million miles of empty space; but she wanted to feel herself in contact, sharing whatever it was, with him—as anyone might want to hold the hand of a loved one, even though he was unconscious, while sitting with him in an ambulance racing him to the hospital.

When she got to Expedition Control, the glassed-in observation booth was empty. But the gray skullcap of hair belonging to Bill Ward was visible among the heads down around the front consoles; and after awhile, glancing around, Bill saw her up there. A moment later, the Assistant Communications Engineer, a thin, brown-faced man named Ed Ciro, came up to the booth's speaker-mike.

"We're out of contact with both One and Two, right now," he told her. "The solar storm and the LCO in-flight tests between the ships could either one be the reasons. But both ought to be over by now. We should be making communications contact again inside of half an hour. How about some coffee?"

Wendy shook her head, no, staring down at Bill Ward and the others in the room of ranked consoles beyond the glass wall.

Tad was sweating by the time he was sealed into his spacesuit by the Hatch Three airlock on the bottom deck; and the suit temperature controls went automatically to work to dry him off; so that he felt hot and chilled at the same time—a feverish sort of feeling.

He remembered suddenly that he should have had Anoshi follow him down to check him out in the suit before he went EVA. He had not thought of it; and evidently it had not occurred to Anoshi, either. It was not really necessary; but the fact they had both forgotten was another symptom of the bone-tiredness that was afflicting them all when it should not—that, and the sweat he had worked up getting suited, were both warning signals from their body systems. That was one of the bad effects of fatigue—it not only impaired judgment and put your temper on hair-trigger, it walled you off from the people around you. You could not spare the energy to remember that they were as worn out, as mistake-prone as you were; and everything they did wrong irritated you. . . .

Tad suddenly realized he had been standing by Hatch Three for some little time, holding the test kit he would take outside to check the LCO. He spoke into his suit phone.

"Bap? You've got me on screen, haven't you?"

"On screen. Right," came back Bap's voice.

"What's the matter? Are we still above the blue line on the graph?"

There was a little silence before Bap answered.

"No. Just below, now. But the curve's flattening out a bit. I wanted to give you a bit of margin below the blue line."

"Never mind margin. The line *is* below the blue?"

"Below the blue. Right."

"Then I'm going out," said Tad. "Light up the outside sensor eye from Hatch Three, if you can, and keep me in sight. I'll stay on tether."

"Sorry, Tad. Hatch Three sensor not responding. Maybe you better keep talking and we'll record."

"Roger," said Tad. "I've already got the inner airlock door open on Hatch Three. . . . I'm in the airlock now and the inner door is closing. Evacuation of airlock . . . Do you read me?"

"Read you fine," Bap's voice said. "And we copy that."

"All right," said Tad. "Outer airlock door now opening. I'm on my way out, tether behind me. . . . All the way out, now. I'm pulling extra length of the tether out so I'll have plenty of line to let me reach the mirror."

"Okay. Copying," said Bap.

"I'm going to stop this conducted tour for a minute or two," Tad said, panting. "Running out of breath. I'll get back to chatting with you in a few minutes when I start down along the hull toward the mirror."

He fell silent, pulling out the last of the tether-cable that not only tied him securely to Hatch Three and the ship, but also contained his main primary air and phone lines. Damned mess, he thought, sweating inside his helmet. His magnetic shoe soles practically welded him to the skin of the spacecraft. His chances of getting separated from the ship were one in a million. So much easier if he had come out here untethered, simply with backpack oxygen for what would not be more than twenty or thirty minutes' work . . .

"Give us a word, Tad." It was Bap's voice sounding in his helmet. "Just so we know you're still with us."

"I'm here. Hold on. Talk to you shortly. . . ." Tad said.

He gathered up his tether and began the clumsy shuffle down along the hull toward the small upright, square shape of the LCO mirror, outlined by stars alone. He was in darkness—Bap had changed the attitude of One enough to put the slant bulk of the ship between him and the sun; and so give him that much extra protection against radiation.

All right, thought Tad, good enough. Play it safe if you like, Bap. The only problem might be uncovering the mirror mount and testing out its positioning motor's components in the dark. But he had the work light at his waist. Try it anyway, he thought.

"All right," he said aloud over his phone to the two inside the ship. "I've reached the mirror. Now I'll see about getting the cover off the motor mount."

"Reading you fine and clear," answered Bap's voice. "We copy that—you're going to take off the motor mount cover, now."

"Going to try," muttered Tad. Tensing his leg muscles, he pulled himself and the clumsy suit about him down on its knees before the motor mount. He switched on his belt light. The motor mount cover with its four recessed bolts appeared just before him.

He got the socket wrench from his tool belt and went to work to loosen the bolts.

"Talk," said Bap in his earphones. "Talk to us in here, Tad."

"Sorry . . ." Tad said, breathlessly. "Too much to do, here. I'll let you know, soon as I get something done."

He worked on. Eventually he got the bolts loosened and the cover off. Inside was the neat tangle of components and connections. He opened the test kit he had brought and his gloved fingers clumsily picked up the leads, one . . . then the other, and pulled them out to attach to the motor components.

"I've got the motor mount cover off," he said aloud, suddenly remembering Bap. "I'm starting to test now."

"We copy that," said Bap.

Time went by.

"Some news here for you," said Bap's voice, unexpectedly. "Phoenix Two's getting through to us a little on radio. Lots of static, but every so often they come through clear. I've been talking back to them on our radio, telling them about our LCO trouble, but they don't seem to read me too well."

"How's their communications?" asked Tad, working away.

"Say again?" Bap said.

"How's the LCO over on Two? Did it go out like ours did?"

"Negative," said Bap. "They're all right. They're trying to make LCO hookup back with Expedition Control. As I say, I've been trying to tell them what's happened to ours, but they aren't reading me too well—don't think they've got it, yet."

"Keep trying," said Tad.

"Roger," answered Bap.

Tad went on testing.

"Theres an AJK4191 out here," he said, "and both AJK60Ls acted like they were out at first, but they're both responding, now. It's the signal amplification that's gone out. The motor was getting the messages but it couldn't do anything with them. Also, an M84B connector, and an AJK4123 are out. Check stores will you; and make sure we've got replacements?"

"Roger. Will do," said Bap. "I copy, search stores for an AJK4191, M84B connector, an AJK4123. Anoshi's going to check. I'm still trying to get our story told over the radio to Two."

"Okay." Tad straightened up his cramped knees, rising erect in his suit, held by the soles of his feet firmly to the hull of the spacecraft. "I'll hold here while Anoshi looks at stores. Let me know what he finds."

"Roger," said Bap. "How are you feeling?"

"Like twenty hours' more sleep," answered Tad. "If you don't mind, I'll just hang here and take it easy until Anoshi gets back with the word on those replacements."

"You do that," said Bap. "The next voice you hear will be Anoshi's."

The suit phone went silent. Tad hung there weightless,

letting himself float in his suit, anchored by the magnetic soles. He was so weary he felt empty inside; but just for the moment not having to do anything was infinitely pleasurable; and on the heels of such pleasure came something like a moment of sanity.

He felt ashamed of the way he'd been chewing on Bap and Anoshi. It might have been unconscious reaction to fatigue on his part, but it had been hard on the other two men, nonetheless. Actually, he could see now, he had been indulging himself, like the selfish head of a family who says, "I'm important. I can take out my temper on you because I'm important. But you can't take out your temper on me."

I've got to quit this, he told himself, or we'll never finish the trip.

And Expedition Control, he thought, had better trim that priority list on the experiments, or I'll do it for them. We can't take it. None of us can take it.

And no reason we should. In fact, we've gone by the rules too long already. That's the difference between us and the rest of the world. We try to make things work even when it looks impossible—that's our instinct. The instinct of most of the rest of them back there seems to be to start looking for a way to duck out, the minute they hear what needs to be done. But we're out here now; and when you get right down to it, we're the ones who go and do. We listen to them when we're on the ground. We do everything they say. But out here, we're like fish in the water while they're back on dry land. In the long run we've got to tell ourselves what's best for us to do.

He thought of the fact that they were all alike, in a way—all six of them in the two ships. Never mind the fact they all came from different cultures, different languages. Out here it was so damn small, that kind of difference. Out here it was like the hunting party in strange territory—*really* strange territory. And they were all here because they wanted to be here—really wanted to be here. Not just like someone who thinks it'd be something special to go out into space.

That's why we're all alike, here, Tad thought, and all of us so different from those back there. We've got to be different if we're going to live. And they've got to be different back there, because they've never come out here to know what it's really like.

Tad hung in his suit and lifted his faceplate to the stars.

"All right," said Anoshi's voice in his helmet. "Tad, we've got the replacements. I've brought them to Hatch Three. You want to come back and get them? Or how about my going out and putting them in?"

Tad heard him; but his mind held the words off from registering for a moment while he looked at the stars. He would answer in a second; but just for the moment, he wanted to finish his look and his thought.

Oh, you beautiful, he said silently to the lights all around him, oh, you damn beautiful, beautiful universe. . . .

Ed Ciro, who had been talking to Wendy in the booth, broke off suddenly.

"They're calling me down," he said. "Maybe they've got LCO contact back. Just a minute—I'll be back."

He turned and went out of the booth, bounding down the steps to the forward communications consoles. In the first screen he saw the image of Fedya—a little wavery, but recognizable; and the voice that came through was only slightly mush-mouthed by uncertain beam linkage.

". . . had it over the radio, finally, from Bap," Fedya was saying.

"You mean now?" It was Bill Ward, pushed in beside the Communications Engineer for the Expedition. "You mean he went out there as soon as their meter went under the blue line?" Bill jerked his head aside to speak to one of the engineers standing about. *"Get me an estimate on that."* He turned back to the screen. "When did you hear, there on Two?"

There was the short wait as Bill's words, even at light speeds, traveled the distance to Phoenix Two.

"Radio contact has been bad until just now," Fedya said. "Evidently Bap was trying to tell me all along that their LCO motor control had been knocked out by the storm; but I didn't understand him until now. Evidently Tad went out as soon as their BeV showed it was safe to do so.''

''And he's been out since? Get on that radio!'' Ward said. ''Call One and tell Bap to get Tad back in there. There was a burp of increased flare activity only twenty minutes or so behind that first dip in radiation. Get on it!''

Bill stopped speaking. Before Fedya could answer, the engineer Bill had asked a moment before for an estimate came back with a piece of paper. Bill snatched it, glanced at it; and stepped back from the screen toward the outskirts of those standing nearby.

He looked up at the glass booth, then around him until his eyes fell on Ed Ciro. He reached out, hooked his finger in Ed's shirt pocket and drew Ed to him.

''That's Wendy up there, isn't it?'' he muttered. ''What did you say before you came down here, just now?''

''I? Nothing,'' said Ed. ''Just that I'd find out what was going on and come back up to tell her.'' He stared at Bill Ward. ''What is it?''

''Oh, Christ!'' said Bill. ''Christ!''

Grimacing, he stared at the paper in his hand, scratching at his chin with one finger, briefly and furiously.

''She would be here!'' Bill said. ''This, of all times!'' He looked at Ed. ''Tad went EVA to fix the LCO positioning motor controls on One—they'd been knocked out by the storm. Unless Fedya's got the facts wrong, Tad's been outside for nearly an hour. Neither One or Two was in contact with us here and we couldn't tell them to expect a sudden rise in radiation count after the first fadeoff. Fedya's passing the word to get Tad back in now; but what good's that going to be?''

Ed stared.

''You mean he's been burned?'' Ed asked. ''Bad?''

''Bad,'' said Bill. He stared at Ed for a second. ''Very bad. He's been too exposed. If he's been out there the way it sounds . . .''

His voice trailed off. He glanced back at the booth.

''And there's Wendy!'' he said. ''And Christ, Christ, I've got to go talk to her. I've got to tell her—that just while she was standing here, waiting to hear about him . . .''

He stopped speaking. His big hands fell limply to his sides, one of them still holding the paper.

24

Tad came in through Hatch Three to the airlock into the end of the access tube, down the tube and out onto Deck A. In the spacesuit, it was necessary to back onto A Deck through the hatch. When he turned around, he saw Bap facing him a few feet off; and holding a radiation counter.

"Get out of that suit as quick as you can, Tad," Bap's voice sounded in his earphones. "We've just got word from Kennedy, relayed by radio from Phoenix Two. Something went wrong—it was still hot outside, when you made the EVA. Strip and we'll get to work on you right away."

"Hot?" said Tad. He felt a little emptiness just behind his breastbone and noticed neither of the men was coming forward to help him off with his suit. "How hot? How hot am I now?" He began to struggle out of the spacesuit.

"Don't know what it was outside," Bap said. He looked at the counter in his hand and hesitated. "Hard to say about you. It's jumping around. Say . . . a hundred and eighty rem; probably most of that in your suit."

Tad got the helmet off and heard the soft buzzing of the radiation counter. He climbed out of the suit and dropped it at his feet, then stripped off everything else he was wearing.

"Right," said Bap. "Now, down to the shower."

Tad preceded him into the access tube and down to B Deck and into the waste management room.

"I contaminate this," he said, only half-jokingly as he stepped inside, "and you two may have to go dirty the rest of the Expedition."

"We can dump the water," said Bap. "Anyway, we'll see. Scrub off as much as you can."

Tad closed the shower door and turned on the water. He stayed under it until he heard Bap's voice calling him. He stepped out and put on the fresh on-board suit Bap had waiting for him.

"Now for the tough part," said Bap.

His voice was light; but Tad's fully alerted senses caught something different in the way he spoke; an almost gentleness that alarmed Tad even more. He did not have to ask what the tough part was. They had all been fully informed about procedures in case of radiation poisoning of any of them—whether from space or from some accident with the big nuclear engines in the shuttle that was to be their main drive once they reached Mars.

He went ahead of Bap down to the infirmary and stretched out on a table. A mass of clustered, red-filled tubes stood in a cradle beside the table. It was fresh, whole blood—thank God for recent improvements in flash freezing and cryogenic storage that made it possible for the spacecraft to carry supplies of fresh blood with them in the frozen state. Bap had probably started it quick-thawing with the deep-heaters before Tad had stepped out of the access tube onto the floor of A Deck.

Bap was looming above him, dressed now in special protective smock, mask and gloves, because now the time had come when he would actually have to touch Tad's body, itself undoubtedly radiating and dangerous. The wearing of the protective clothing was laid down strictly in the operating procedure, but still it made Bap look uncomfortably alien and unfamiliar. Tad felt the small pricking of needles as Bap hooked him up to the apparatus that would flush his present contaminated blood from his body and replace it with the clean blood in the tubes. Other pricks followed; and Tad felt the anxiety quieting in him. Bap must have given him some sort of tranquilizer. A drowsiness approached him. He closed his eyes. The surface of the table underneath him felt almost soft. . . .

* * *

"Will you have a cigarette?" Bill Ward's thick fingers trembled slightly as they offered Wendy the pack.

"No thanks. I don't smoke," said Wendy. After a second, she added, "You know that."

"Oh, yes," said Bill. He put the pack of cigarettes back in his pocket. "Of course."

She looked around the large, empty room from the conference table where they sat. It was the unfitted firing room in the Launch and Flight Control Center.

"I suppose you thought I'd be hysterical or some such thing," she said emptily. "That's why you brought me in here."

"I . . ." Bill shrugged his shoulders, helplessly. "I didn't know."

"I wouldn't have," Wendy said. "I've been expecting something like this, now, for a long time."

"Well," said Bill; and cleared his throat. But then he fell silent again. She looked at him suddenly with a gray face.

"It's really bad, isn't it?"

"No, no—" Bill began.

"Don't lie to me," she said. "That just makes it worse."

"I'm not lying!" Bill exploded. "I don't say how bad it is because I don't know. We don't know how much radiation he ran into. We just don't know. Nobody does. The chances are that it's light; and everybody on that ship knows what to do immediately something like this happens. In a day or two we'll probably know it wasn't anything."

She sat still in her chair, half-facing his, at the end of the conference table—still calling him a liar without saying a word.

"Look," he said. "There probably won't be any word for a while. But if you'd like to stay here, we can fix one of the offices up for you. I can phone and get someone to take over for you at your place with the kids."

She nodded, slowly.

"Yes, I'd like to stay close, here," she said. She got to her feet. "But I want to go home first. I want to tell the children about this myself before they hear about it some other way. Then I'll come back."

Bill was on his own feet.

"I'll drive you," he said.

She almost smiled at him.

"No," she said. "You know better than that. You've got to stay here. I've got the car downstairs. I can drive myself home and back here again without help."

Bill hesitated.

"I'll send someone with you, then," he said. "Now, I'm not going to argue about that. There's plenty of people here who can be spared. I'll send Ed Ciro."

"All right," she answered.

"Good," Bill said. "Now remember, no one knows anything is really bad. It may be days before we know."

They went back to the Flight Control Room and Bill spoke to Ed Ciro. Ed made a quick phone call to his own home to say he might be late getting off shift, and came down with Wendy to the parking lot.

"Want me to drive?" Ed asked.

"No. I'd rather be doing something."

They drove back to the Hansards' house and pulled in, stopping the car in the driveway short of the double garage. Ed followed Wendy in through the side door to the air-conditioned stillness of the house.

"Tom! Cassy!" called Wendy, as they passed the front door. But the house received her words emptily.

"Sit down, Ed," said Wendy. "I'll get you a beer."

He shook his head.

"No thanks."

"Of course you'll have one," she said.

"No. Really," he said. "Unless you want one—"

She shook her head.

"I want something hot," she said. "Coffee. But you can just as well have a beer. There's nothing for you to do until we go back to Flight Control."

"Really—"

"Don't fret me now," she said. "I have to pack a bag and phone around to get the children home so I can talk to them. I want you settled in a corner with your beer and out of my way. Sit down."

He sat. She brought him an uncapped bottle of beer; he stayed in one of the big living room chairs, slowly drinking it, while she went into a bedroom. He could hear her talking beyond its closed door.

After about ten minutes. she came out with a small, black overnight bag, which she put down just inside the side door.

"They'll be here soon," she said to Ed.

The youngest boy was the first to arrive, followed by the girl, and then the older boy, Tom—only a year younger than Ed's own son.

"Hi, Mr. Ciro," said Tom, in the semi-drawl that the kids were all using nowadays. "Something up?"

"Your mother's in her bedroom with your brother and sister," Ed said. "I think she wants to say something to you."

He had tried to keep his voice casual; but Tom's face sobered immediately, and he went quickly across the living room, down the hall and into the bedroom, so quickly that he swung the bedroom door not quite shut behind him. In his chair in the living room, with nowhere to go, Ed could not shut out Wendy's voice as it reached faintly but intelligibly to him.

"Come in, Tom, and sit down here with the others."

"What is it?" Tom asked.

"I've been telling Cassy and Jimmy," she said. "Dad's had an accident on the Expedition. He's feeling all right now, Bill Ward tells me; but I wanted to tell you three about it before it got into the news or you heard it from someone else."

There was a slight pause as if she was waiting for some word from one of the children; but none of them made a sound.

"Dad was caught in the radiation from a solar flare," Wendy said. "It happened at a time when the Expedition ships were out of communication with Expedition Control; and Expedition Control couldn't tell them it might be dangerous for Dad to go outside the ship. Bap helped to take care of him the minute he got back inside; and now Dad's resting while the others wait to see how he is. Nobody knows just how he is, right now. I want you to remember that. If you hear anyone making guesses about that, or anything else, just remember, no one really knows. As soon as anyone knows anything, they'll tell me first before anyone else, and I'll tell you. I'm going back to spend the night at Expedition Control so I'll be there if any news comes in. There'll be someone coming over to make dinner and stay the night with you; or I think the Swanns wouldn't mind if you'd like to go stay with them for a day or two the way we did during the launch. Would you like to go to the Swanns?"

"No," said Tom's voice quickly. "We'll stay here."

"All right," said Wendy, becoming brisk. "That's settled then. I'm going back with Mr. Ciro, now."

"Mom," said Tom.

"Yes?"

"It depends on how much radiation there was, doesn't it?" Tom said. "It could be bad, couldn't it?"

"Yes," said Wendy. "There's always danger. Nobody right now seems to think it could be bad; and we pray it won't. But the danger's always there."

"You'll call us as soon as you know—anything?" Tom said. "Like how much the radiation was, or anything like that?"

"I'll call you the minute I'm told anything myself," said Wendy. "Kiss me now; I've got to go."

A moment later, Wendy came out of the bedroom, followed by the three children. The little boy, Jimmy, had large, wondering eyes fastened on his mother and the girl caught and held him by the hand as he started to follow Wendy and Ed through the side door.

"We'll be all right," said Tom. "You call us."

The three of them stood in the side door, Cassy still holding tightly to the hand of the small boy, as Wendy backed the car down the driveway and turned away up the street.

Tad drifted back to wakefulness to find himself lying on the bed in his own sleeping compartment, with Bap standing beside him holding a hypodermic needle—putting it away on the bedside table, in fact. Tad had a vague memory of being helped back here from the infirmary compartment. He felt filled with lassitude, but otherwise very good—perhaps the hypodermic needle he had just seen had something to do with that.

"How am I?" he asked Bap.

"You're starting to be safe to touch." Bap smiled.

Tad came farther up the slope of wakefulness into an area of concern.

"How's the ship?" he asked. "How's everything? What's been happening?"

"Our LCO's still out," said Bap. "We've been talking to Phoenix Two by radio; and they've been talking to Expedition Control. Both ships got hit a lot harder by the storm than we thought. All sorts of systems are knocked out on both of us. We're all working to get things going again."

Tad rose on one elbow.

"I've got to get up," he said.

Bap pushed him back down.

"No," said Bap. "You're supposed to rest."

"At least get me a phone hookup down here, then," said Tad. "Patch me in with the communications system so I can talk to Fedya. I want to know what's going on."

"All right," said Bap. "We can do that much, I suppose."

He went out of the compartment. Some ten minutes later, the intercom unit by Tad's bed buzzed. He propped his pillow up against the bulkhead at the head of his bed and sat up against it. He leaned over to snap on the phone; and Anoshi's face took shape in its screen.

"We've got Fedya on the radio for you," said Anoshi. "Hang on, there . . ."

The hiss and crackle of static moved in over his voice. Anoshi's face stayed on the screen, but Fedya's voice came through.

"Tad?"

"It's me," said Tad. "Can you hear me?"

"I can hear you all right. Can you understand me?"

"You're a little blurred by static," Tad said. "But not enough to matter. Why haven't you got the Phoenix Two back docked with us by this time?"

"The storm . . ." A louder rush of static did, at the moment, wash out Fedya's words. ". . . control systems are out all over the ship. Our maneuvering thrusters are not responding properly. I was afraid we couldn't control any docking attempt. We have trouble enough right now without smashing the two ships together and damaging them. We don't even want to risk approaching you too closely."

"Maybe we can dock with you holding still, then," Tad said.

"Anoshi tells me your control systems on the Phoenix One are also unreliable," said Fedya.

The lips of Anoshi's image moved on the intercom screen beside the bed.

"That's right, Tad," Anoshi said.

"What's holding up getting them fixed—here as well as on Phoenix Two?"

"The extent of the damage." Fedya's voice cut across Anoshi's as Anoshi started to speak, then stopped. "And the shortage of repair parts."

Tad stared at the screen.

"Say that again?"

"I said the shortage of repair parts," Fedya's voice answered. "Both here and on Phoenix One. We do have undamaged parts and equipment to substitute; but not as much as we should. Remember, certain sections of both ships that were originally planned to hold reserve equipment and spare parts have been devoted instead to the loading of equipment required for the experiments."

Tad swung his legs abruptly over the edge of the bed and sat up facing the screen without benefit of pillow.

"So," he said, "now it pays off. They sent us out with not enough supplies and equipment for repair on either ship."

"Not necessarily," said Fedya. "What was sent was probably considered adequate. But they didn't foresee such extensive damage to both ships at the same time."

"That's not the point!" said Tad. "The point is, in order to get more experimental stuff on board, they shaved the repair margin too thin. Is that the situation, or isn't it?"

"You could put it in those terms," said Fedya.

"Have you talked to Expedition Control about this?"

"I gave them a brief report," Fedya said. "I was waiting until I had definite information on what we were short before I went into the matter more deeply with them."

"You've still got your LCO working?" Tad demanded.

"Voice only. The picture is out. But I've been in voice contact with Expedition Control ever since we realigned Phoenix Two's mirror with them after losing contact with Phoenix One."

"Patch me through to Bill Ward," said Tad.

Both Tad and Anoshi spoke at once; so that neither one was understandable. Anoshi's face moved out of the bedside screen and Bap's replaced it.

"Tad," said Bap, "you're in no shape to be talking to anyone."

"Yes, I am," said Tad. "I feel fine. Fedya, patch me through to Expedition Control."

The picture on the screen vanished. The sound of several voices speaking at once tangled together and then went silent. Tad got half out of bed, thinking he would go up to A Deck in person and force the issue. Then he sat back down again. They would not deliberately keep him from speaking to Expedition Control.

Sure enough, after several minutes, the screen lit up again with Anoshi's face and the speaker of the intercom hissed with radio static.

"All right, Tad," said Anoshi. "We're through to Expedition Control for you."

He stopped speaking; and a voice came through the static that Tad recognized.

"Tad?" it said. "Tad, Wendy's here. She's been here at Expedition Control since we heard about you."

"Wendy?" said Tad. He leaned convulsively toward the intercom. "Bill? That's you, Bill Ward, isn't it?"

"It's me," said Bill's voice. "Just a second—Wendy—"

"Tad!" It was Wendy's voice.

"Wendy, what're you doing there? Where are the kids?"

"At home. They're all right. Tad, how are you?"

"I'm fine!" he said. "Fine! I don't feel a thing different

from usual. Look, don't you hang around Expedition Control. There's no need to.''

"All right. Tad, honey, there's a doctor here that wants to talk to you."

"Wendy—" Tad began; but another voice was already speaking to him.

"Tad? This is Kim—Kim Sung. Can you hear me all right?"

"Read you fine, doctor," said Tad, impatiently. Dr. Kim Sung was one of the NASA physicians. "What is it?"

"I'd like you to answer some questions, Tad. How do you feel at the moment?"

"Fine, doctor."

"Any nausea, vomiting, diarrhea?"

"No—I told you."

"How about earlier. Did you have any upsets like that earlier?"

"After I came in and Bap pumped all the blood out of me and shot me full of someone else's blood and a lot of chemicals," said Tad. "I was a little nauseated, yes, and felt bad. But that all went away some time ago—look, Doc, don't let Wendy get away there, or Bill Ward. I've got things to talk about with them, and things to do."

"I think you'd better take it easy for the present, Tad," said Kim Sung. "How's your appetite?"

"I'm not too hungry—but then I just woke up," said Tad. "Honest, Doc, I'm fine. Got my hair still on my head, and everything."

"Tell me, when you first came in from being outside and exposed to the solar storm, did you feel at all warm and feverish . . . ?"

The questioning went on. Gradually, it began to register upon Tad that he was not going to be given the chance to talk over the repairs situation with Bill Ward, after all. Not merely that; but as the medical voice continued evoking answers from him, his concern for the Expedition began to move back in his mind and give way to a more personal attention. That touch of immediate emotion that had been like a small, cold finger touching behind his breastbone when Bap had first told him he had been exposed to the solar storm now returned; and this time it lingered.

25

The three of them sat in one of the hotel rooms occupied by Barney Winstrom's cable TV team. Equipment, papers, glasses, empty fast-food cardboard cartons made a small jungle around them. Barney was in an armchair, and Jens and Lin sat on a couch facing him. Lin was close to Jens, one of her arms through his and her hands together, so that—though loosely—she touched and held him.

"And you don't know anything more than that?" Jens was saying.

"No more than you do, Jens," Barney said. "I don't think there's any more to be known. Hansard got a dose. How big a dose, nobody knows."

"How is Wendy?" Lin asked.

Barney shrugged. "They've got her and the kids under security to keep the media away. There's no telling. But she's a level-headed lady. I'll bet she's handling it."

"They've got no idea at all—how much radiation?" Jens asked.

"They say not," Barney said.

"Then it could be all right."

"Maybe."

"You don't—" Jens looked at him. "You aren't sounding very reassuring."

"Who am I to tell?" Barney said.

"If you've got some reason for thinking it can't be all right and there's no hope, tell me."

"Nothing . . . hard," said Barney.

"Soft, then, damn it!"

"All right," said Barney. "It's just feel, and experience. I think if there was hope, they'd be coming down harder on the reassurance pedal. But they aren't. They're acting instead like a bunch of doctors who keep telling you you can't tell for sure until the tests come back from the lab; and you smell all the time that everything they've ever seen tells them they don't need to see the tests."

"Oh, my God!" said Lin, so softly that she barely breathed the words. Her hands closed on Jens's arm.

"Yes," said Jens. He felt bleak and cold inside. Even the living warmth of Lin beside him could not change that. "It was bound to happen."

"Can that!" said Barney. "Nothing's ever bound to happen."

"This was," said Jens. He heard his voice as if it came back to him from a little distance away. "They were sent out with too much to do, they got too tired, and they had an accident. It was bound to happen."

"Now," said Barney, slowly, staring at him, "that's why I don't like you starry-eyed believers. The minute anything goes wrong you think you see the inevitable at work."

"I'm something a little more than a starry-eyed believer, Barney." The words came out more harshly than he had intended.

"Jens!" said Lin swiftly. "Jens, he's trying to help."

"That's all right, Lin," said Barney.

Jens took two deep breaths.

"No, it's not all right," he said. "Sorry, Barney. It's the damn frustration of it all. It's beginning to get to me."

"It does that. But look, Jens, there's nothing you can do, nothing anyone can do right now, but sit tight and see how it works out."

"I guess you're right," said Jens. "Okay. I'll sit still, then—for now."

Wendy Hansard sat leaning back with her arms on the arm-rest of the chair in the glass cube at the back of the Expedition Control Room in the VAB. She was grateful that this was not Houston. Up until two years ago Expedition Control would have been in Houston, and she would have been sitting there now, separated from friends and everything that was familiar, including their home and possibly even the children. No, come to think of it, the children would have wanted to go and she would have given in. They at least would have been in Houston with her. But that would have simply meant that they all would have been away from home.

It was much better to face this at home, here, where things were ordinary and handleable. Nothing should go wrong, she told herself, curling her fingers around the end of the armrest, nothing should go wrong in this place where everything had always come out all right before.

She looked out and ahead down the sloping floor of the Expedition Control Center, past the consoles and screens at the small knots of men clustering around the one near the front where the screen was dark but where there was a murmur of voices. Up there they were communicating, but there was nothing in that communication to help her. They were checking the state of Phoenix Two with Feodor. If it happened that a transmission started to come through that concerned Tad, they would call her on the phone screen in front of her and key her in on it.

She breathed deeply, seeing the Expedition Control Room as a whole, not focusing on any part of it. She was alone in the glassed-in section right now. Earlier a number of other people had come and sat with her, until she told them that she really did not need or want company. She preferred to be alone with the room as a whole, whatever transmissions might come in, and her own thoughts.

Those thoughts were ranging, now. She remembered as a little girl, wondering how grown-ups could sit so still for so long without apparently having anything to occupy them, like reading, or praying. She had tried praying silently, here in this glass booth, as she had on the way here with Ed Ciro, and aloud at other times when she had been alone. But prayer, while soothing, was not what her mind sought at the present moment. What she wanted now had something to do with making everything all one piece, all one whole; and she had the feeling that if she could just let her mind wander, it would gather up all the loose ends and tie them together.

She went on thinking about how it had been when she was

young, when she had marveled at people, at adults, sitting so still. She remembered the time her oldest brother had scarlet fever and her mother sat up, unceasingly, it seemed, day and night with him for more than a week. Most of that time her mother had been doing nothing. Merely sitting as Wendy sat now, with her hands either in her lap or on the arms of a chair. Wendy had sat also and watched her mother until a worry had begun to creep into her mind. If her brother could die, perhaps her mother could die. Perhaps she could die even while you were sitting and watching her.

Finally, Wendy had gone across and touched her mother's arm. Her mother had looked at her.

"What is it, Wendy-baby?" her mother had asked.

Relieved that her mother was unchanged, and filled with a superstitious fear that if she mentioned the possibility of death it might happen, Wendy had fallen back on a question of her own.

"What were you thinking?" Wendy asked.

"Nothing . . ." her mother answered. "Nothing."

Now, years later, Wendy understood. Because now she, too, was thinking nothing. Well, perhaps not nothing, but thoughts that might as well be so, because they were nothing that could be told to anyone else. They were thoughts that had no real shape or value. In fact, she was not really thinking them. She was merely sitting, and letting them flow by themselves.

They slid through her mind like the passing cars of some endless train, going somewhere on a track with no end. The image was a familiar one. Her father had been an architect for a development company; and her family had been continually on the move from one part of the country to another. When she was younger, at each departure she had struggled with the unhappiness of leaving all her friends and the places she had grown familiar with. Later on she had learned to sit back on the train that carried them away each time, and just let it happen, let the past go and be only on the train going to some place new, as if continually starting over and over again was a natural way of life.

In the end she had simply let the train carry her away each time to wherever it wished. There was a relief in facing the fact that she had no control over what was happening to her, a relief in just letting it happen. But for all that, somewhere inside her there had always been a buried hunger for a place where she would be able to stay put, a place from which there would be no more moving.

It was a hunger that Tad had finally met, with a specific place, an anchorage, a home where she could put down roots. Unlike her, Tad had spent most of his growing years in one house. He put down roots himself as unthinkingly and instinctively as an oak, and like an oak, whose rough, warm bark felt good to hug when no one might be watching who would think you crazy for doing it, he was good for her to cling to. In the early years of their marriage her friends had wondered how she could stand being married to a test pilot. They could not see how she could bear the daily worry and the uncertainty, the ever-present danger of an accident.

What they did not understand was that, from her viewpoint, while an accident to Tad could rob her of him, it could never take away what he had given her, that immovable territory that now contained their home, their children, and their life together up to the present moment. It was not thinking small of Tad to acknowledge that she had gotten far more from their life together than she could be robbed of by his death.

Yet she had never really thought beyond that moment in which she might lose him. That far her thoughts had often gone, but no further. Nor did she think about it at this moment. Instead she let her thoughts run, like the train on the endless track, clickety-clacking forever, off into the distance. She did not, even now, feel that much separated from him. Partly, this was his own doing. He had talked to her for years of a time in which travel to the nearby planets and even to the nearby stars would loom no larger in people's minds than taking a jet plane from this city to another one. In fact, he had used that comparison in talking about space travel.

"Back a couple of hundred years ago," he had said, "if I'd left here for Washington, I couldn't have made the round trip in less than weeks or months and all sorts of things might have happened to me, or you and the kids, before I got back again. I might even not have got back. Nowadays I can go up there on the morning plane and be back by evening. A thousand years ago, even five hundred years ago, to go fifty miles to the next town was an expedition. Sometimes people didn't come back alive; and it wasn't just because of enemies along the road, either. There was natural accident, sickness and everything else. Nowadays, though, we don't think a thing of hopping back and forth across the ocean. And that's the way it's going to be, crossing space, for our great-great-grandchildren. Mars may turn out to be just a little old Sunday drive for them. So there's no place I'm likely to go that's really more than a Sunday drive, if you just put your mind ahead a bit."

She believed that. In the early days of their marriage, before the children came, she had faced up to the dangers of his life in her own way, by trying to be with him in mind and spirit, even though they were separated physically by space and occupation. She had asked for only one thing then, and that was to know immediately if something happened to him on his test flights. She had tried to tie a psychic cord between them, so that she need not sit and wonder and worry about possibilities—she would know immediately if anything happened. She would know it before anyone could come and tell her; and, knowing that she would know, she could go serenely about the business of waiting down here on the ground while he was up in the air taking chances with his life. With effort and practice, she thought, she had succeeded in this. It had seemed to her then that she could feel very clearly the invisible thread that bound them together, while she was down on the ground and he was away somewhere, up in a new, untried plane going several times the speed of sound.

The children had come; and with them around this connection had not exactly been forgotten or withered away, but it had moved into the background. She had not lost it, as far as she knew. It was just simply that she had not evoked it as often. For one thing she had the little ones on her mind, with all their growing up and all their sicknesses and all the concerns and fears that went with raising them from infants; and for another, Tad had left his test-piloting and become an astronaut; the danger did not seem so frequent, so immediate and sharp.

Now, sitting in her glass cage at the back of the Expedition Control Room, Wendy could not remember having felt anything at the moment at which Tad must have been exposed to the flare out there in space. But, she thought now, this might have been because he himself had felt nothing and had not even thought to worry until he came back and got the word from the others that he had been irradiated. Of course, since then, as at this moment, she had felt once more very closely in touch with him. In all that counted, she was there on Phoenix One with him. Only her body and mind were left behind here in the Expedition Control Room, sitting still and waiting, spinning their endless stream of thoughtless thoughts like a spider building an empty web.

But still it was not quite the same as it had been, back before the children, when he had been a test pilot. For if she and Tad had grown together over the years, they had also grown apart. In a sense, they had become two complete but separate beings, each one incorporating a part of the other. What Tad had of her she did not know exactly, but she could feel that he did have something. What she had of him was something of his strength, something of his calmness, something of that same ability to take root that she had missed earlier in her own life.

It was not all it should be, perhaps, but it was more than might have been—a good deal more. So now, there was only the waiting and she had finally learned how to wait.

"A shocking thing to happen so early in the expedition," said Ahri Ambedkar.

He and Walther Guenther were having drinks with Sergei Verigin in Verigin's hotel suite. In half an hour they were all scheduled for a semi-official dinner with businessmen and Disney Corporation people from the Disney World complex; but right now they had a moment to discuss the news of Tad Hansard's radiation sickness.

"It's not without risk, this going into space," said Guenther.

They were once more talking French. It had come to be a small tradition of these three-cornered chats they had been having lately. They sat in armchairs before the white-brick fireplace in the lounge of Verigin's suite, a fireplace in which there was no fire. Instead, the air conditioning hummed softly in the wall ventilators.

"Accidents," said Guenther, "of course, can happen at any time."

"It's unfortunate, nonetheless," said Ambedkar, sipping at the glass of grapefruit juice he held. "Coming so soon, this way, it gives the whole expedition a sort—how does one say it—ramshackle look."

"Oh, I don't think it does all that much damage," said Verigin. "And in compensation, it injects a note of high tragedy which should generally gain sympathy for all our people out there in space."

"There's that," observed Guenther. He was drinking a martini made with gin of which even Sir Geoffrey would have approved. "Still, as I say, it points up the risk. And the member nations in my area particularly are going to be thinking of the considerable financial investment."

"Come," said Ambedkar, "we are past the matter of investment, surely? What fills the newspapers around the world are stories of the human element. It makes bad press that young men should be sent out to die."

"Not at all," said Guenther. "That's their business, after all."

"True," replied Ambedkar. "Still . . ."

"I'm sure you are all aware," said Verigin, "that on any large project there is a built-in casualty rate. Take the construction of a large bridge, for example. Statistics will tell you that by the time the bridge is completed a certain percentage of the workers will have had accidents; and a few of those accidents, again by statistical prediction, will be fatal. This is all quite understandable. The main thing is that such statistics shouldn't be allowed to interfere with the advantageous attention that the international aspect of this expedition has been getting, and possibly may still get for some time yet."

"Indeed," said Ambedkar, "it's to the advantages of all nations to have this breathing space when public attention is focused off the earth. That's why I am concerned that the possible death of this Hansard might cause us all difficulties."

"One does not die quickly from radiation poisoning," put in Guenther. "At least, unless that poisoning is massive; and from what I've been able to gather, it probably isn't that massive in this case."

"That's my impression, too," said Verigin. "I do not think we should expect Colonel Hansard to die suddenly, gentlemen."

"And in fact, he may recover," said Ambedkar.

"My medical advice seems to cast doubt on that," said Guenther.

"I don't believe anyone really knows, surely?" asked Verigin. "The available information from Phoenix One is too limited."

"It's annoying to be in the dark," said Ambedkar.

"To say nothing of the fact," said Guenther, "that the first one to learn anything will undoubtedly be Wylie."

Aha, thought Verigin, pouncing mentally—caught you, Walther! Wylie will be not the first, but the last of us to know, of course, since he's only a straw man for the U.S. President. You are dragging a herring across the trail, aren't you—trying to throw the rest of us off the scent in case we've suspected anything? And your only reason for doing that can be that you are the one who's been playing around with this amateur spying Sir Geoffrey hinted at. Who were you spying on—Wylie? Now that you're beginning to suspect we suspect, you've just tried to give us a reason for any little games we might stumble upon. Verigin glanced across at Ambedkar briefly. Had that old fox also picked up on Guenther's self-betrayal? Yes, he had. It showed in the precisely judgmental way he held his glass of grapefruit juice.

"In any case," Verigin said aloud, "regrettable as it is that one of our marsnauts should pay with his life, that's often the cost of great expeditions; and, in fact, of progress in any field. I myself take the point of view that we simply must bear up under all situations, including the chance that he might not survive. We must keep our attention and our hopes concentrated on the other brave men who are still healthy and moving toward a truly international manned landing on our planetary neighbor.''

''You don't suppose there might be any thought of sending one of the ships back?'' said Ambedkar, ''I mean, so as to return Hansard to the better medical care available here?''

''Turn back one of the ships?'' said Guenther.

''If they can come back from Mars, certainly they can return from partway there?'' said Ambedkar.

''Oh, I know it's physically possible,'' said Guenther, a little irritably, ''I was thinking of the practicality of it.''

''Whether it's physically possible or not,'' said Verigin quietly, ''I should think it would be the highest order of impracticability to endanger the expedition by reducing it from two ships to one. The single ship going on alone would have no redundancy, no hope of assistance in case of trouble. I should think a concern for the lives of the three healthy men aboard Phoenix Two would outweigh the natural concern for the health and life of the one already ill man on Phoenix One.''

''Absolutely!'' said Guenther. ''Besides, the hopes of a world are tied to a successful journey of these two ships. They must both go on, no matter what the cost. If I'm asked, I shall put it in the strongest terms that there should be no turning back out of a misguided concern for Colonel Hansard. Don't you agree?''

''Indeed,'' said Ambedkar, ''three lives must always concern us more than one. I agree with you, Walther. I feel most strongly both ships should go on; and I'll say so also if I'm asked. How about you, Sergei? You agree to that, don't you?''

''Oh, of course,'' murmured Verigin. ''It begins more and more to look as if this Expedition was less well prepared than we thought. But of course there's nothing any of us can do about it, now. All we can hope is that the men on the ships will now make the proper effort to bring it through all right. I feel myself that both ships must continue, no matter what happens to Hansard. It's only reasonable to expect that they should.''

26

With two drinks in him, a perfect sense of contentment and well-being took charge of Del Terrence. He leaned against the soft cushioning of the booth restaurant, his right hand wrapped around his glass, his left holding Jonie Wextrum's right hand below the table top. He had the curious, almost light-headed feeling that he would like things to stay just as they were indefinitely; stay just as they were, with the restaurant never closing, time never advancing, night never giving way to day, and everything outside this dining room remaining nonexistent until further notice. He was almost awed at how touched he was that she had set up this surprise birthday dinner for him.

"But you look so tired," Jonie was saying. "You don't have to work that hard."

"I do, though," he answered her, almost absently.

"No, you don't," said Jonie. "Are you ready to order dinner now?"

"I guess so," he said and reached out to pick up the two large folded menus of dark blue cardboard. He passed one to Jonie and unfolded the other.

"Why don't you have—why don't we have the rack of lamb for two?" Jonie said. "You'll like it."

"I will?" He put the menu down and looked at her. "You wouldn't have ordered it already?"

"You'll like it. Wait and see," said Jonie.

He laughed.

"All right," he said. "Did you set this whole dinner up in advance?"

"Well, I wanted to be sure it'd be done right."

The waiter, caught by Jonie's eye this time, was already approaching the edge of their table.

"You can go ahead now," Jonie told him.

"Yes, ma'am."

The first thing he brought them was two large crabmeat cocktails. Tasting his, Del found himself suddenly ravenous, and remembered that he had had nothing but a sandwich at about eleven o'clock unless he counted a dozen or so cups of coffee. For a little while he forgot about anything but eating. The rack of lamb turned out to be as good as Jonie said it would be, and the champagne was superb. Eventually, Del sat back, stuffed, comfortable and sleepy.

"Dessert?" asked Jonie.

"Let's have a cup of coffee first."

With the coffee before them, Jonie came back again to the topic of his working too hard.

"I have to," he told her. "I was the one who told Al that the slop in the system just before launch wasn't important. Now the system's gone out on Phoenix One. Maybe it isn't our fault, but . . ."

"Someone like Al has to understand how you could make an honest mistake," said Jonie.

"Oh, he understands," Del said. "But the fact remains that if it's an area of responsibility that belongs to you, you've got to make good. That holds true for me just like it holds true for him, and everybody else right up to the 'nauts off on Phoenix One and Two. Besides, it's not just how he feels about it; it's how everybody out there feels."

"Well, he's the only one you're responsible to, isn't he?"

"No," said Del, slowly, "that isn't quite right either. Actually, I'm responsible to the whole space program."

"That's an exaggeration and you know it," said Jonie. "Of course, everybody there's responsible to the whole program; but right now you're acting as if there was some kind of special personal responsibility between you and it. Killing yourself doesn't prove anything."

He did not want to argue with her, particularly at this moment; but he did want her to understand. He launched into a long description of how every element in the hardware of the launch interacted, and how all the work of those concerned with that hardware had to interact as well. She listened, but he felt that he was not reaching her. She was simply sitting there and storing ammunition with which to debate him. He found himself looking away from her steady gaze, staring uncomfortably out through the openwork, at the bar and the TV screen. He broke off suddenly.

"What is it?" asked Jonie.

"Jack!" he muttered. "Jack Sharney. My boss. What the hell?"

He slid around on the seat cushion, got up and went into the bar. The TV was on a shelf too high above the floor for him to reach and the sound was off. He turned to the bartender polishing glasses behind the bar.

"Turn up the sound, will you?" he asked.

"Why, sure," the bartender said.

He put down glass and towel, walked a few steps up the bar and reached underneath it. The sound came on, not all the way, but loud enough to hear from where Del stood.

By this time, however, the face on the screen had changed. It was no longer Jack Sharney's; it was the relaxed face and professional voice of some announcer.

". . . following the statement read by John Sharney, vice-president of Laserkind, Mr. Sharney was asked if the statement meant that the laser communications aboard Phoenix One were still operable, but that other systems had broken down and were preventing the lasercom from working. . . ."

Abruptly, Jack was back on the screen. His voice came clearly to Del's ears.

"Of course," he said, "we've no way of knowing, with communications out, exactly where the difficulty lies. However, tests of our system both on the ground and in orbit just before both ships left on their way to Mars showed the system was functioning perfectly. We had a representative on hand during the launch to make sure our equipment worked; and in this case he reported to us that the system was performing exactly as it should."

"But, Mr. Sharney," said a voice from off screen. "Couldn't the radiation from the solar flare have interfered with the working of the lasercom?"

"In the absence of complete data, of course anything is possible," Jack said. "However, in the opinion of our people on the spot the lasercom was responding perfectly right up to the moment of the flare; and we know of no way that even massive radiation could affect our controls directly. As I emphasized in my statement, the natural assumption is that Phoenix One is not getting orientation on the broadcast antenna for the system—and orientation can be critical in the matter of communication by laser. That orientation is effected by a mechanical process that should not be disrupted by radiation. On the other hand if power isn't getting to the system, because of the solar flare—if some electronic components that deliver power to that system have broken down—then the system's not going to work. But the components delivering power to the orientation process were not of our manufacture—"

"What the hell are they doing to me?" breathed Del. "Jack, what the hell are you doing?"

He felt an arm slip into his arm. Glancing to his right, he saw Jonie standing beside him, holding onto him.

"What's wrong, Del?"

"Those bastards!" he muttered between teeth clenched so tightly they ached. "Those complete bastards! Listen to what they're saying!"

However, by the time he had finished speaking Jack Sharney was no longer on the screen. The announcer was talking once more, and the image was of a kitten, perched on the top of a telephone pole, with two fire department rigs trying to rescue it. Del turned and led the way back to their booth.

"What is it? What did they do?" asked Jonie, as they sat down.

"You heard," said Del.

"Yes, but I didn't understand."

"What the hell wasn't there to understand? You saw Jack—holding a press conference and answering questions and telling the world that there's nothing wrong with our equipment on Phoenix One!" Del gulped the half glass of champagne that was still sitting in front of him. "Nothing wrong! And here I am knocking myself silly to try to find out why it's not working—and half the Expedition Control crew trying right along with me!''

"Why would he do that?'' Jonie asked.

"He did it because somebody told him to,'' Del said. "And I know just who the damn hell that somebody was, too—our beloved president Walter Kind himself. Old Walter, beating NASA to the punch before they can start asking why our equipment's no good!''

He was aware of Jonie staring at him.

"But—'' Jonie struggled with her words "—don't they—doesn't Jack and Walter Kind know it's not true, what they're saying?''

"Hell, yes, they know it's not true. But it's the big lie, don't you understand? Yell first and loud enough that it wasn't your fault; and some of the public's going to believe you—and even those who don't aren't going to be sure until it's all checked out, and that could be two years from now when the whole story's stale news!''

"But why'd they do something like this without telling you first?''

"So I couldn't trip them up, of course! So they can sit back there on the West Coast and lie safely, knowing I'm the one who'll have to face people like Al, who'll know the truth and think I was behind all this—this coverup!''

"You mean they're deliberately putting the blame on you?'' Jonie's face was pale.

"That's it,'' said Del. "The idea's to clear Laserkind's skirts, at any cost. Oh, Al and the others out at the Space Center are going to love this!''

"Well, why don't you go tell Al then?'' said Jonie. "Tell him you didn't know anything about it. In fact, tell him what they tried to do to you—and then quit. Tell everybody it wasn't your idea and that it wasn't your fault. Call a press conference of your own.''

The heat of anger inside Del cooled unexpectedly. He hesitated.

"I couldn't cut Laserkind's throat that way,'' he said.

"They're cutting your throat, aren't they?'' said Jonie. He looked at her and found her expression absolutely ruthless.

"No,'' he said. "I wouldn't do that—to anyone.''

He started to get out of the booth.

"But I'll tell you what I am going to do, though," he said. "I'm going to call Walter Kind now."

He was halfway to the door of the restaurant when he realized that Jonie was not behind him. He turned around and went back and found her standing by the booth.

"I'll get the check. Just a minute. I'll be right with you," said Jonie.

"Sorry. I didn't think," he said.

"Never mind."

The waiter came with the check. Jonie paid him and they went up to his room. Jonie perched on the armchair by the window while Del sat down on the bed by the phone on the nightstand. He punched the access code for long distance and the number of Walter Kind's home in Downey, California. There was a pause and then a woman's voice spoke from a still blank screen.

"Hello?"

"Mrs. Kind?" said Del. "This is Del Terrence, the company rep at Kennedy Space Center. Could I talk to Walt?"

The screen lit up, showing the pleasant soft face of a woman in her mid-fifties.

"Oh, Del," she said. "Well . . . just a minute. I'll see if he's here."

The face of Mrs. Kind moved off the screen to the right, but the screen itself remained lit. Del waited.

"Come on, come on," he said after a bit, through his teeth. "Don't tell me he isn't home, Lauretta, or I'm going to get a little impolite. I know he's home. He'll be sitting there having his first drink before dinner, right now."

A few more minutes went by. The lean face of a man in full middle age, wearing large, black-rimmed glasses, slid onto the screen.

"Well, Del," the face said. "How's it going over there?"

"Not so good, Walt," said Del. "We're still not locating what's wrong with the system. By the way, I just heard Jack's press conference on network TV here."

"That so?" said Walt Kind.

"Yes," Del said, "that's so. It came at a bad time, Walt. I thought I'd phone and tell you that."

"At a bad time?" Walt's eyebrows lifted on his high forehead. "I don't see how that could be, Del. If there's any danger one of our systems is going to be misunderstood by the general public the sooner we get to that public with the correct answers the better."

"That's right," said Del, "provided they're the right answers. Only, I think a few of Jack's answers may have been wrong."

"Wrong?"

"Yes," Del said. "Wrong. Damned wrong. Upside down wrong, in fact."

"Del . . ." Walt peered at him from the screen. "You've been working pretty hard at finding what the problem is that's interfering with communications out there, haven't you? Maybe you've been overdoing it. You know, you can't carry the load all by yourself. There's a lot of other people out there at Kennedy who have just as much responsibility for what's going on as you have—and more."

"I don't think so, Walt," said Del. "And I don't think it's somebody's system that's fouling ours up. I should have listened to Al Murgatroyd when he told me that up there in the parking orbit he was getting more slop than he got down here on the ground. I think it's our own system that's broken down and I think it's up to us to find it—not to put out smoke screens implying the trouble's some place else."

"Well, you're the man on deck," Walt said. "And we always want to listen to your opinion, Del. But you know from back here it's necessary to look at the overall situation. We've got a little more distance on this thing, seeing it from the West Coast; and of course we've got a duty to protect ourselves in case it is some other outfit's system that's messing up ours. That's all Jack was thinking of, I'm sure."

Del stared into the screen unbelievingly.

"Walt?" he said. "Walt, aren't I getting my point across? That TV broadcast just now is going to raise bloody hell here! Up until now we've had the NASA people on our side. Sure, maybe our system broke down, but that sort of thing happens and we've been trying our damnedest to find and fix it. I've been trying the best I can to fix it. But now, all of a sudden, we've gone to the public with a statement that the communication problem's not our fault—and these people here at Kennedy know damn well it's our fault!''

"Just a minute, Del," said Walt. "We can't be sure of that. They can't be, either.''

"They're sure enough, for God's sake!" said Del raggedly. "Walt, that broadcast cut our throats out here. It cut my throat. None of the people like Al Murgatroyd are going to give me the time of day when they hear about what Jack said! And I've got to work with them!''

Walt did not say anything for a moment. His face on the screen seemed to settle in on itself, and when he spoke again his voice was a little remote.

"Exactly what would you like us to do about it, Del?''

"There's only one thing you can do," Del said, leaning into the screen, holding on hard to the table where the phone unit sat. "Let me call Al, and maybe some others, right now and tell them that that TV broadcast was unauthorized, that it was an error. Let me tell them you'll be following this up with a letter, but you wanted me to get the word to them right away!''

"I don't think we can do anything like that," said Walter. His voice was even more remote.

"You've got to, Walt," Del said.

"No," Walt said, almost as if Del had not spoke, "I don't see how we can do anything like that, Del. Why don't you get a good night's sleep and simply go on with your work out there as usual? Let us worry about anything that comes from here.''

"Walt!" Del stared into the screen. "How can I go on as usual, *now*?''

"To be frank with you, Del," said Walt, "I don't see any real difficulty or problem for you in that. Now if you actually feel there is a problem, maybe you'd better think it through, get it down in detail, and then call me back. We don't want you working against your own grain, there, whether there's really anything to worry about or not.''

There was another silence; this time it stretched out for more than a second or two. Del found himself waiting for Walt to say something more, but Walt said nothing.

"All right, Walt," Del said at last, hoarsely. "Maybe I will get some sleep."

"You do that, Del," said Walt. "Sleep's a great thing, you know. Very often things look entirely different in the morning. But call me any time, Del. So long."

The screen went blank. Del looked across the room and met Jonie's unmoving gaze.

"Jesus," he said. "I feel like I'm working for a bunch of cockroaches. They're great survivors, roaches, but being around them makes you feel . . ." He could not go on.

She came over and put her arms around him.

27

The press conference was held in that same hotel where the Deputy Ministers of Science of the countries cooperating in the Expedition were still quartered, including Jens. No place else was large enough for it except the enlarged press stands out at the Cape, and it was awkward to get all the newspeople there.

The fact was, as Jens had noticed, that the press corps in the Cape area, instead of declining in numbers after the launch, had in fact grown as the feature writers moved in. Now there had been a sudden added influx of men and women with orange badges as word escaped of the solar storm, the damage to the two spacecrafts and Tad's accident.

The ballroom was equipped with high balconies at the back, overlooking the floor where folding chairs had been set up. These balconies gave an opportunity to seat a few groups of non-newspeople who were nevertheless concerned or interested in the news conference. One of these groups was made up of all the Deputy Ministers of Science for the International Development of Space, including Jens.

"Shame about that young man of yours," said Sir Geoffrey, gruffly, sitting down next to Jens.

Jens nodded.

"Yes," he said. He felt that he ought to find something more to answer; but no words came to him. He gave up and leaned forward to see the Expedition Control people filing onto the platform at the far end of the room and taking seats behind the long table on it. There were five of them, one brown-faced and oriental-looking; but the only one Jens recognized was Bill Ward, who seated himself in the center.

There was a moment of fiddling with the pencil microphones among the water glasses on the table in front of the five, then Bill Ward cleared his throat.

"All right," he said; his amplified voice boomed out through the room. "We might as well get started here. I'm going to give you a short statement to begin with, then we can have questions."

He cleared his throat again, and glanced down at some papers he had spread out before him on the table.

"At twenty-three hundred hours, twenty-six minutes of Day Twenty-two of the Mars Expedition," he read, "Expedition Control received from Spacelab Two a prediction of a strong solar flare, which prediction was communicated to the Mars Expedition spacecraft with the information that the Expedition had approximately five hours in which to undock and separate the spacecraft in order that experiment S082, a test of laser communication between the ships during a solar storm, could be performed—"

He coughed, interrupting himself; and then went on.

"The two spacecraft," he said, "accordingly undocked and separated a distance of one hundred and forty kilometers, while the crews aboard both ships erected the protective panels to create the storm cellar, so-called, as described in Experiment M199. The estimate of the duration of their stay in the storm cellar was placed by Expedition Control at approximately fifteen hours, during which time, because of the alignment of their LCO mirrors on each other, neither craft was in communication with Expedition Control."

He paused and took a sip of water from a glass before him.

"At approximately seventeen hours, forty-one minutes of

Day Twenty-three,'' he continued, ''the crew of Phoenix One observed that their LCO was no longer communicating with Phoenix Two. They checked for malfunction within the area of the storm cellar and found nothing. At this time, the meter reading the external radiation of the solar storm was beginning to show an apparent reduction in that radiation. The meter showed a continuing reduction; and at the point where it showed that all danger was passed for the marsnauts in movement within the spacecraft, the crew of Phoenix One left their storm cellar and traced the malfunctioning LCO system to the point at which it went through the hull to the drive unit that positioned the laser mirror outside the ship.

''It was evident that the malfunction was outside the ship, rather than in. Radio communication being still impossible under the solar storm conditions, Senior Mission Commander Tadell Hansard, fearing that the LCO on Phoenix Two might also be malfunctioning, decided on an EVA to inspect the drive unit and the mirror outside the hull.

''He accordingly suited up and made the EVA, unaware that radiation outside the ship was still at danger levels. The force of the solar storm had been greater than predicted; and, in fact, great enough to overload Phoenix One's radiation meter, with the result that it had falsely showed the radiation reducing more rapidly than was actually the case.

''As a result, Colonel Hansard suffered a presently unknown degree of radiation poisoning. Luckily, the LCO of Phoenix Two had not been affected by the solar storm; and finding herself out of contact with Phoenix One by that means, she contacted Expedition Control by LCO and Phoenix One by radio—the storm having decreased enough to make this possible. As a result, she was able to convey a warning about the dangerous level of radiation into which Colonel Hansard had EVAed; and as soon as Colonel Hansard returned to the interior of Phoenix One, his crewmates took steps to decontaminate him and offset the effects of the radiation.

''He is now resting comfortably, according to our last word from Phoenix One. However, both ships have suffered extensive damage to their electronic control systems as a result of the unexpected severity of the solar storm; and the crews of both ships are busy checking systems and putting them back into operation."

Bill ceased talking, shuffled his papers together and looked out at the crowd.

"Copies of this release are available on tables at the back of the room," he said. "Now, let's get to the question period."

A woman was standing in the front row before he had quite finished speaking. Behind her, several other people who had been a second too slow sat down again.

"There is speculation—" Her voice was so faint that it was barely audible up on the balcony where Jens was; then a seeking microphone picked her up and the rest of her words blasted from the wall speakers. "—that the U.S. marsnaut, Tadell Hansard, has actually received a lethal amount of radiation. Could you tell us if that is indeed the fact?"

She sat down again. Bill bent his head toward the oriental-featured man on his right.

"Kim? Do you want to take that?" he said. Jens's lagging memory supplied the full name of the man addressed. Dr. Kim Sung, one of the NASA physicians. Kim Sung was leaning toward his own pencil mike.

"I'm afraid we have no idea how much radiation Tad received," Kim said. "We have no means of knowing what the radiation was outside Phoenix One at the time he was exposed; and we would have no way of determining the extent of the damage to him, physically, otherwise, at this time. I might say, though, that to assume that any dose of radiation poisoning is necessarily a lethal one would be to fall into a pretty serious error."

Several other of the newspeople were now on their feet; but the woman in the front row persisted.

"But you would not completely rule out the possibility that he had received a lethal dose of radiation, Doctor?"

"In the absence of sufficient facts, all possibilities have to be considered, certainly," said Kim. "But we aren't spending a great deal of our time on that particular one."

"Next," said Bill Ward firmly, as the woman opened her mouth again. She sat down. A man several rows back with a

European accent Jens could not pin down found himself chosen by Bill's pointing finger.

"Have you any idea of the extent of the damage to the two spacecraft, sir?" he called. "And if so—"

"No. No knowledge whatsoever, yet," said Bill. His finger moved on. "Sorry to cut you off. But we've got a large group here and we'd better limit it to a single question apiece. Next!"

"Would you tell us—" It was another woman speaking. "—if radiation damage to electronic systems alone would be enough to permanently disable a spacecraft like Phoenix One or Phoenix Two?"

"Jim?" Bill turned his head, passing the question along to a balding, round-faced man on his right.

"Theoretically," James Howell, systems engineer for the Expedition answered her, "if enough systems were knocked out at once abroad her, one of the Phoenix craft could be completely disabled. However, she'd remain disabled only until her crew could repair the damage and replace the necessary parts to get her working again, which is what the crews of Phoenix One and Two tell us they're presently doing."

"Next!" said Bill.

"Assuming Tad Hansard is seriously ill from the radiation—or worse," asked a black-skinned, turbaned man standing among the rows of seats close to the wall on the right side of the room, "how will this hamper the continuance of the Expedition?"

"The Expedition," said Bill Ward, "is already redundant in the fact that it consists of two identical ships, each of which is capable of making the Expedition by itself. If Tad's going to be laid up for a while, of course, that will require some readjustment of work schedules aboard at least Phoenix One, and possibly aboard both ships."

"Can you tell us," called another woman toward the rear of the room, "if it is correct that the crews of Phoenix One and Two had already requested a readjustment of the experiment priorities before the present emergency happened?"

"The matter had come up for discussion, yes," said Bill, harshly. "Both the marsnauts and Expedition Control are constantly evaluating and reevaluating the elements of the

Expedition for maximum performance. But of course anything like this has to take a back seat now to the larger matter of getting the spacecraft back to full performance. Next!''

"Assuming the death of Colonel Hansard as a result of this radiation poisoning . . ." began a man near the front.

Jens felt a sudden wave of nausea. It came on him so suddenly that it was as sharp as an unexpected pain. He clutched reflexively at the arm of the chair in which he sat, pushed himself to his feet and stumbled unsteadily back through a curtain and a door beyond into the silence of the wide, carpeted corridor behind the balconies.

He was abruptly aware that someone had followed him. It was Sir Geoffrey, and the tall old man had a grip on his elbow, steadying him.

"Little shaky, there?" muttered Sir Geoffrey in his ear. "You need a drink. Come along."

He steered Jens down the corridor with a clutch that was surprisingly powerful for someone of his apparent age. They entered an elevator, descended to the second floor lobby, and went into a large, dim bar with overstuffed furniture and one waitress. Sir Geoffrey piloted Jens to a booth against a wall opposite the bar, and pushed him into a seat there, sitting down opposite him. The waitress came over.

"What would you like?" she asked.

"What's the specialty of the house?" Sir Geoffrey asked her.

"The special drink?" she said. "The shamrock. That's the name of the bar—the Shamrock Lounge."

"Shamrock? Irish whiskey, isn't it? All right," said Sir Geoffrey. "Bring him one."

"Nothing for you?" she asked.

"No. I—well, damn it, give me one, too."

"Two shamrocks," she said, and went off.

"Always order the special," said Sir Geoffrey looking across the table of the booth at Jens. "Get more for your money; and the chances are better than even that the drink'll be made right, too."

Jens felt he ought to say something but the effort was too much.

"That's right," said Sir Geoffrey, encouragingly, "you

just sit there. As soon as you get a drink or two into you, you'll feel better. Alcohol, coffee and iodine—cure anything in the world, one of the three. Anyone who's had malaria might want to add atabrine, perhaps. But we're not in a malarial area, are we?''

There was a little pause. The waitress came back with the two large cocktail glasses, green liquid lapping at their rims, and set them down carefully in front of Jens and the other man.

"Drink it, now," said Sir Geoffrey when the waitress had gone. "Pour it down, if you're up to that. Most irritating thing in the world, buy somebody a drink to help their nerves and they sit there and play with it. Women do that a lot. Here, I'll show you how."

He drank from his own cocktail glass. Jens reached out and lifted the one in front of him to his lips. In the moment before he sipped at it, he thought he could not drink anything. Then it was in his mouth, and the taste was minty and not unpleasant.

"That's better," said Sir Geoffrey. "Let it hit bottom now, and you're halfway back to health. Upset about Hansard, were you? You shouldn't be in this kind of work. Bloody amateur—oh, I know that's what your government wanted to prop up in the shoes you're wearing; but it's sickening all the same. Waitress, two more."

"No, one's plenty—" Jens began, but the waitress was already giving the order to the bartender.

"What you've got to face," said Sir Geoffrey, "is that somebody's always bound to get hurt in things like this. That's the way international politics is. That's why you need professionals who know someone always gets caught in the machinery. Can't do without the machinery, either. We'd be back hitting each other over the heads with stone clubs. So, where are you? Drink up the second one now, Wylie. Just like you did the first."

Jens was, in fact, beginning to feel, if not better, at least anesthetized to a small extent. He picked up the second drink.

"It's always a mess," Sir Geoffrey said firmly. "Always. You've got to learn to expect that and let it happen—"

"And to hell with everybody, I suppose?" Jens was a little

surprised to hear himself say it. The first drink was already beginning to work on him.

"Not to hell with everybody!" said Sir Geoffrey, irritated. "To hell with the situation and anyone who's so tangled up in it they can't get loose. You're a piece of the machinery yourself if you're good at this work. You don't smash yourself on the first problem that comes along; you keep yourself in working order so you can be used again—and again."

"How about smashing the machinery instead?"

Sir Geoffrey looked at him.

"Now, you aren't going to go smashing any machinery," he said. "Even if you could."

"This Expedition—" said Jens, a little thickly, and was surprised to see that his second cocktail glass was empty. Sir Geoffrey was already wagging a long forefinger in signal to the bartender. "This Expedition was sabotaged before the 'nauts even got into the shuttle and left the ground."

"No doubt," said Sir Geoffrey. "And you knew that and did nothing about it. Nothing that made any difference, that is."

"Yes," said Jens, sickening again inside at the thought of Tad Hansard.

"And you're not going to do anything now or later, take my word for it," said Sir Geoffrey. "Now drink up, brace up to the facts of life, and let's get back to that balcony before the press conference ends and anyone notices we've been gone—anyone important, I mean to say. Our fellow workers in the vineyard don't count."

Fedya stood in his spacesuit on the hull of Phoenix Two. Half a kilometer away, the lighted part of the hull of Phoenix One looked like a lopsided rectangle in the illumination of the raw sunlight. A wire from a spool clamped to the hull of Phoenix Two by her Hatch Three led to Fedya's belt; and an individual propulsion pack was strapped to the shoulders of his suit.

Keeping his eye on the reflection of the distant spacecraft hull, he rose on his toes, flexing his bootsoles to cut off their magnetic attraction to the metal of the hull beneath them, and sprang outward from the ship. It felt as if nothing had happened. There was no sensation of movement; but then, extending his legs, he found no solid surface with them, and turning, he saw the hull of Phoenix Two now something like his own length from him.

He turned back to locate the hull of Phoenix One with his eyes, raised his gloved hand to the chest of his suit and activated the propulsion pack.

Cold gasses spurted from the two thrusters at the tips of the twin arms extending from the pack. Still, there was no feeling of movement toward Phoenix One; but when he looked back again, he saw Phoenix Two visibly receding from him, the bright, thin line of the wire from the slowly unreeling spool in a catenary curve between himself and the ship he had just left. He turned back to concentrate on the lighted section of the hull of Phoenix One, toward which he flew.

For some time, it was hard to see any change in it. But gradually he became aware that the rectangle was apparently growing out toward his right and shrinking in to his left. He was headed off at an angle that would take him past the other spacecraft on his right, unless he corrected.

He corrected, gradually adding pressure to his right thruster until the rectangle ceased to grow in the manner it had been growing.

He traveled on through space. There was no pull at all that he could feel from the wire attached to the heavy belt at his waist. He noticed abruptly that the rectangle was once again changing on him. Now it was narrowing—narrowing rather rapidly, so he must be getting close to Phoenix One. Getting close and sliding away at an angle above it. He corrected again.

The rectangle broadened once more. He was now close enough to see, within its lit area, the erect shape of the copper LCO mirror and a corner of Phoenix One's Hatch Three.

Fedya was correcting constantly now, as he zeroed in on the other spacecraft. His target was no longer just the hull itself, but that same Hatch Three. Playing with the controls of his propulsion pack, he drifted toward it. Abruptly, he found the need to decelerate was upon him. The hull and the hatch were growing in size swiftly before him. He rotated the handle on his chest that turned the nozzles of the thrusters a hundred and eighty degrees, and opened their valves full.

Once more, there were moments in which it seemed what he had done was having no effect whatsoever. The hull continued to swell toward him; and he drew up his feet instinctively to take the shock of a hard landing. But then the swelling slowed, slowed . . . and he awoke suddenly, only a few meters from his destination to discover that he had now reversed his movement; and was in fact drifting back, away from Phoenix One.

He cut off the valves completely, reversed the nozzles of the thrusters again; and with weak jets of gas began to work his way back toward the hull. It was a good five minutes, more, however, before his feet at last touched down and the magnetics of his bootsoles gripped the stranger hull.

He clumped over to Hatch Three and the bit which had been welded beside the hatch to secure the end of the wire he had carried over from Phoenix Two. As he was detaching it from his belt and securing it, the cover of Hatch Three opened; and, moving as ponderously as some medieval armored knight, another spacesuited figure emerged to help him tie down the wire to the bit, and connect it to the end of another wire waiting there, before following him back down inside Phoenix One.

The manner of the other figure's movement identified the man within its suit. It was Anoshi. At another time there would have been something cheerful said between the two of them over the suit phones as they met. Now, however, they went in silence together back inside the ship, through the airlock at the end of its access tube and on to A Deck where they removed their suits.

Desuited, finally, Fedya turned to face not only Anoshi, but Bap and Tad. Tad was not even sitting down. He was standing by his control console. Fedya went over to him and gripped his hand.

"How are you feeling?" Fedya asked.

"Fine," Tad said. "I'm feeling up to anything and just fine."

Fedya smiled at him. But Tad was not looking fine. He was looking . . . different. There was no greatly visible change, but his face seemed more bony and pale than Fedya had ever seen it before. For a moment, Fedya was baffled as to why it gave that impression; then he realized that Tad had already lost some of his hair. He had worn it cut short always, so that the difference was not remarkable; but now his hairline had gone back and scalp was quite visible under what remained. Also, there was an air of strain about him, a little tension, as if he were trying to be polite at a social occasion when flu, or a bad cold, was making him long to be at home, in bed.

28

The afternoon sun was reduced to kindness by the reacting tint of the floor-to-ceiling polychromic windows. The small, square, walnut-colored table between the two chairs seemed to glow with a golden hue in a dining room draped with nets that held tridents, seashells, and other salt water artifacts.

"Very pleasant to get off by ourselves," said Ahri Ambedkar, glancing around him. He and Sergei Verigin sat almost alone in one corner of the dining room. "They say the shrimp in particular are very good here."

"So I hear," agreed Verigin.

The restaurant in which they had chosen to have a late and private lunch was the upper floor of a wood frame establishment that gave the impression of projecting its top level out over a flat, slow-moving Florida river. At the foot of the building was what seemed to be a small marina, filled with a number of pleasure boats of all sizes from cabin outboards to large and expensive ChrisCraft cruisers; and the impression given was that a good percentage of the diners had come by water. Verigin and Ambedkar, however, had been chauffeured out here and dropped off. The driver was due to pick them up again in two hours.

"Do you have any tea?" Ambedkar was asking the waitress who had just appeared.

"I don't know. I'll see," she said. She smiled at them both, a gentle-faced, somewhat raw-boned woman in her forties. "And you, sir?"

"I think I'll have cognac," said Verigin. "Do you have Cordon Bleu?"

"Yes, I'm sure," said the waitress. "Do you want that on the rocks?"

Verigin shuddered.

"No. No ice. Just in a wine glass, please."

"And what luck have you had in the case of your little dog?" asked Ambedkar, as the waitress went off.

Verigin brightened.

"That expedition director—Bill Ward," he said, "was kind enough to get in touch with a brother of his, who's on the staff of the veterinary school at the University of Minnesota. It seems his brother knows of another staff member who has a great deal of experience with the kind of paralysis that Chupchik's suffering. The other staff member's gone on a sabbatical, right now, but apparently he's due back in a week or so. Ward's brother says that he'll have this other staff member get in touch with me. It sounds as if I might be able to get the answer I need for poor Chupchik's sake. I've written the good news to my wife."

"Fortunate," said Ambedkar.

They chatted of inconsequential and personal things until the end of their meal. Then they got around to more important topics.

"You heard, I suppose," Verigin said, "that there's some speculation the experiment load may indeed have been a little too heavy; that this may have contributed to a certain inefficiency on the part of the marsnauts, and this inefficiency in turn may have led to the accident of Tadell Hansard?"

"Yes," said Ambedkar. He sipped at a cup of tea the waitress had just brought. Verigin drank cognac out of a very small snifter glass.

"You and I know, of course," said Verigin, "that the

Americans saw this expedition as a chance for them to gain what they call good publicity—extra international goodwill to counteract the effect of the Shared-Management System, which so recently quadrupled their gross national product and once again favored them with a chance advantage over the rest of us. We who work for the future with our diversification and cottage industries know that such publicity is unimportant, not to say ephemeral. On the other hand, national reputation does have some importance, looked at from the standpoint of the immediate moment.''

"Oh, yes," said Ambedkar. "You're referring, I suppose, to our earlier insistence on the maximum experimental program for the expedition? You think that could now return to haunt us?"

Verigin gestured with the hand that held the snifter glass.

"Not haunt, exactly," he said. "It might be noticeable, that's all."

"I don't really see what we might do about it now, however," said Ambedkar. "Our earlier attitudes are on the record, and, of course, we acted on the instructions of our governments."

"Naturally," said Verigin. "But that alone shouldn't cause too much trouble. After all, the Americans also strongly pushed for their full share of the experiment program. On the other hand, we might keep a weather eye out to see that nothing crops up to connect with and complicate our earlier attitude. I mean, of course, that it would be a good thing not to do anything that might irritate such potentially irritable situations.

"You're right," said Ambedkar. "That's only common sense. As we both know."

"To be sure." Verigin sighed. "Experience teaches that perhaps the greatest art is the art of doing nothing. Particularly in the area of international politics."

"Yes." Ambedkar sipped once more at his teacup and put it back down on its saucer. "It's a shame it takes the younger people so long to learn that."

"Some, like Wylie," said Verigin, "probably never will learn. But then, in my judgment, Wylie is not cut out for politics at this level—as you and I, my friend, are. Others, perhaps, may learn it, but have not yet.''

"You mean Guenther," Ambedkar said.

"I'm afraid so," said Verigin.

"It really is a pity," murmured Ambedkar to his teacup. "I don't believe Guenther realizes the risks he runs sometimes."

"I agree," Verigin said. "I gather then that you have a fairly clear picture of what seems to be going on?"

"Well, one gathers some things, inevitably," said Ambedkar carefully. "Naturally, in a situation such as this, the ideal is one in which nothing out of the ordinary happens. On the other hand, when one is younger, like Guenther, there is perhaps a tendency to worry unduly about how one will look in competition with older hands like ourselves, if nothing at all happens. There is occasionally a desire to justify inactivity by showing a certain amount of energy expended."

"Quite true. And a perfectly harmless reaction under ordinary conditions," said Verigin. "Up to the point, that is, where there is suspicion that the activity has come to the attention of those affected by such activity, to the point where it may become a matter of interdepartmental concern for them."

Ambedkar raised his eyebrows slightly.

"Oh?" he said. "I hadn't realized it had gone that far."

"I'm not sure that it has," said Verigin. "Of course, it's only conjecture based on experience in such matters."

"Of course. But experienced conjecture should not be taken lightly."

"Thank you. Still, even that could be relatively harmless, as I say," Verigin went on. "But when accident takes a hand—as in the case of this solar flare—bringing a possibly fatal injury to one of the marsnauts, such activity on the part of someone in accredited position runs the risk of eventually becoming a matter for attention by the press. Particularly under conditions such as we have at the moment."

"Ah," said Ambedkar, "you mean this excessive, popular reaction to the fact that Hansard may have been fatally injured? I've been studying the newsfax reports, from around the world. How curious that one man, who by his own inadvertence has put himself in the position to be perhaps fatally injured, should create such a wave of concern from people of all cultures.''

"Exactly," said Verigin. "Publics are always sentimental.''

"When they can afford sentiment," said Ambedkar. "I'm afraid this worldwide sympathy for Colonel Hansard will make difficult any attempt to be realistic about the wisdom of another attempt at this Expedition.''

"Of course it will," said Verigin. "Therefore, it's to our own interest to understand exactly what brings about such a popular reaction. Consider it from the point of view of one of the world's masses. It costs him nothing to grieve and fear for the handsome marsnaut struck down by an unearthly force while engaged in a high adventure on behalf of the human race. The point is, however, that it may be remembered that we resisted cutting the experiment load—and that this may have been a contributing factor to fatigue in the marsnauts, that may in turn have blunted Hansard's ordinary good judgment about going outside the ship while radiation was still high. In addition, it may be remembered, when word of his accident first came we went on record—not publicly, of course—as feeling that the expedition to Mars should continue in spite of the state of his health.''

"Yes. I see," said Ambedkar thoughtfully. "Ordinarily something like that might easily be forgotten. However, with this emotional reaction the question is bound to arise, with regard to Colonel Hansard, of 'what went wrong?' And, of course, the next question after that must necessarily be 'whose fault was it?' I'm not suggesting that these questions can't be properly answered, of course. It's merely that in the process of answering them, control over another attempt at the Expedition may slip out of governmental hands into those of the popular press. Particularly since the public desire to see the Expedition completed still remains.''

"Outweighed, now," Verigin replied, "by a more sensible perception of the situation on the part of us who are close to the matter. My government feels strongly now that for humanitarian reasons, as well as for the reason that more damage may have been sustained by the spacecraft than we know, that this attempt at the Expedition should be ended and another attempt be very seriously investigated before it is considered. As you point out, there will be a good deal of public attention to the matter to begin with; and this will necessitate finding answers to those questions you raise—particularly the matter of discovering who was responsible—''

He broke off and eyed Ambedkar keenly. Ambedkar nodded slightly.

"If this can be done expeditiously," Verigin said, "it may well be that much of what was originally envisioned in the way of focusing public, and newspaper, attention off-Earth, may still be won from this same present public attitude during the months that follow the return of the marsnauts, the healthy ones in particular. Of course, this abort of the Expedition will merely be until a new expedition can be tried."

Ambedkar frowned across the table at his lunch partner.

"You don't seriously think . . ."

"Oh, of course not!" Verigin drank from his snifter glass. "Such a concentration of political and public attention as was required to produce effort one isn't likely to occur again for a number of years, at least. It took a great deal of luck just to make it conceivable in the first place. But if we can make good use out of the canceling of this one, we may in the long run be further ahead. After all, the important areas of space are those beyond our own atmosphere. As long as we have room for our working—and other—satellites, what do we need with more planets? We're wiser than earlier generations, Ahri. They couldn't see that the vacuum outside our atmosphere was valuable for industrial and other activities which were impossible here on the surface. But by that same token, we're wise enough—I mean you, I, and other responsible people— to know when to stop. The other worlds of this solar system are mere rocks. It's inconceivable that they could ever have any real value."

"You reassure me," said Ambedkar. "If my government had thought that yours was at all serious about making another expedition—"

"Come now."

"Of course," said Ambedkar. "But to return to this small matter of the *sub rosa* activity here that you were talking about earlier. I'm sure that I, and my government, would feel that we would be best off disassociated from such a chain of situations."

"Of course," said Verigin. "On the other hand, one could say there might be a sort of community responsibility here. After all, sometimes we can best protect ourselves by operating within the areas of our own experience, but without going through a great deal of official machinery. A word of warning might be in order."

"Warning? Are you suggesting that I . . ." Ambedkar paused.

"Unfortunately," said Verigin, "our younger friend, because of the present international situation, may have a certain distrust of my advice. It would be more effective coming from someone else—someone without a geographical border in common, so to speak."

"Hmm," said Ambedkar.

"The alternative," went on Verigin, "would be to do nothing. In which case things might take any one of several natural courses."

"Yes," said Ambedkar, "we return to the golden rule that the preferable situation is one in which nothing at all happens."

"Exactly," said Verigin.

"Yes. Well, I shall certainly have to give the matter some thought," said Ambedkar.

Their driver came and they returned to the hotel, where they parted, each to his own suite. Stepping back into the sitting room of his suite, Verigin found himself suddenly weary. Things were no longer as easy for him as they had been. He dropped into an overstuffed chair in the empty suite and simply sat there, gazing at the walls around him.

In a little while, he told himself, he would get up and go in and take a nap before dinner; but right now he did not feel he had the energy even for that. He sat, he thought, like a run-down battery waiting to be recharged; and his mind drifted off aimlessly in a number of directions.

He became conscious after a bit that he was again thinking of the dogs—all of the dogs he had had over the years. After each one died there would be a period of silent internal mourning; and he would be resolved never to have another one. Then one day would find him walking through the Bird Market in Moscow, and looking once more. That particular flea market for pets was always full of dogs. Dogs of all sizes, all shapes, all varieties. In time, a puppy face would catch and hold him; he would stop to look, watch the small wriggling body, hear the faint squeaky puppy-barks and feel his fingers licked by a small pink tongue; and it would begin again.

His thoughts came back to Chupchik, and to his wife. He had tried not to sound triumphant in the letter he had written Elena Markovna. If he sounded too triumphant over the fact that Chupchik could be brought back to health, it might give that woman some ideas. She had been maintaining for some time now that the only thing to do with Chupchik was to have him killed.

Chupchik . . .

Verigin became aware that his left arm was dangling over the left armrest of the chair, his hand touching thin air. But he could almost feel that his fingers touched the crisp fur on the head of a ghost, the ghost of a small white dog.

"Chupchik," he murmured, his fingertips stroking the ghost head.

His thoughts wandered again. It was a bad place and a bad time. The younger people were always to be distrusted. If Elena Markovna had only been a real wife to him all these years, things might have been different. He had never really wanted to lose himself in his work. He had wanted to be an ordinary husband, an ordinary father along with being a good worker and a successful man. A man needed three things in order to be whole. He needed work, wife and children. Of those three, he had the work, but his children had been kept away from him by her almost from the time they had been born; and she had kept herself at arm's length. Consequently, where most men had three, he had had only one . . . and Chupchik. Chupchik, and the other dogs before Chupchik.

Of course, it had made him good at his work. There was no one here in any way compared to him—well, perhaps Sir Geoffrey. But the English were limited by nature and training. There was no real comparison. Not that that meant that it would ever be wise to ignore Sir Geoffrey. It was now clear that Sir Geoffrey's guarded hint to that idiot of a Guenther three weeks ago showed that he had had an inkling that Guenther was fooling around with private and personal spies long before Verigin himself had been aware of it. The incredible imbecility of someone like Guenther playing around at amateur espionage in a situation where there was nothing at all to be gained by such nonsense. . . !

But Ahri was reliable. There was no fear he would not speak to Guenther. It would be all right. . . .

Half thinking, half dreaming, Verigin fell asleep in the chair where he sat.

Meanwhile, Ambedkar, who had gone to his own suite, and sat for some little while thinking, was turning to the table beside him to punch out a call on his phone to Guenther's suite.

"May I drop in on you?" he asked in English, when he got the Pan-European Deputy Minister in communication.

"By all means. Come ahead!" Guenther's face was energetic and cheerful on the screen.

Ambedkar left his own suite and went down the hall to tap on the door to Guenther's. The door was opened by Berthold. Guenther himself was seated at a desk with some papers piled in front of him, but he got to his feet at the sight of Ambedkar.

"Reports. Reports . . ." he said in French, waving at the desk, and walked over to greet Ambedkar. "What might I offer you?"

"Nothing, thank you," said Ambedkar, still in English.

"Well, I'll have a beer!" Guenther humored his guest by moving to English also. He nodded at Berthold, who went out of the room. "Now tell me. What's the interesting news of the moment?"

The beer was brought in a tall, ample glass, and Guenther drank thirstily from it.

"Sergei and I have just been having lunch at the Three Anchors Inn," said Ambedkar. "Do you know it at all?"

"I don't think so," said Guenther. "Let me see . . . no,

I've never been there; but it seems to me someone mentioned it.''

"It's about twenty miles from here. A place overlooking a river. The seafood is excellent," said Ambedkar.

"So you had a good lunch?"

"A fine lunch," Ambedkar said. "Of course, Sergei is an enjoyable lunch companion."

"Indeed. Indeed!" said Guenther, nodding.

"In our occupation, as you know," said Ambedkar, "it's always difficult to maintain acquaintanceships. We're all at the beck and call of our governments. But I must say that over the years I have come to have a very high regard for Sergei."

"Yes, I too," said Guenther, "he knows his way around. No wonder he's lasted all these years."

"Experience, of course," said Ambedkar, in his precise, almost-rhythmic English, "is very certainly the key to everything. Naturally, we all have to think of our own jobs and our own governments. Nonetheless, I've found it pays to keep an ear open to people like Sergei who may sometimes have the advantage of a slightly different slant on the overall picture than I have myself."

"Yes," said Guenther. He sat, almost sprawled in his overstuffed chair, the still half-full glass of beer resting easily in one square hand. But his eyes had fastened on the face of Ambedkar. "An outside view to compare with is always damned valuable."

"Just the way I feel myself," said Ambedkar. "Which is why I thought I'd drop by and chat with you. Sergei seems disturbed about something—a minor thing, but perhaps you might be able to shed a little more light on it from your own point of view."

"Of course. Of course!" said Guenther. "We all have to help each other. Any way I can be useful . . ."

"It has to do with this distressing rumor that the press may be picking up."

"Rumor?"

"I assumed you had heard it," said Ambedkar. "I'm referring of course to this idea that some amateur surveillance has been going on in connection with our presence here."

"Oh, that?" said Guenther, thoughtfully. "Yes . . . come to think of it, I think I remember hearing something about it."

"Rumors like this are always around," Ambedkar said comfortably. "Whenever the representatives of more than one government begin to associate on any particularly important occasion. Or even without that much of an excuse. Of course, in this instance we have the Duchess—I assume you know about her—on the scene as well."

"Yes," said Guenther. "I've heard about her."

"At any rate," said Ambedkar, linking his fingers together before him, "it's the sort of thing we might have paid little attention to, but Sergei told me at lunch that he begins to get the impression that the press may have heard of it, and are trying to track it down."

"Oh?" Guenther was watching him closely again. "Just what exactly did Sergei say?"

"I'm afraid I can't remember exactly." Ahri unlocked his fingers and waved one hand gracefully. "In fact, my memory isn't quite what it used to be. I may not be reporting it exactly as the subject came up. But I do remember him saying something about the fact that something like this could be a concern to us all. You will recall how we all acted for our governments in negotiating an increased experiment load for the Expedition; and the press has been getting the notion that this experiment load may have been a factor in causing Tad Hansard to be overtired at the time of the flare, so that in a way our position may have been partially responsible for his accident."

"No," said Guenther. "I hadn't heard that."

"Well, now," said Ambedkar. "There is probably nothing to it, of course. Sergei's point, however, was that possibly we should all keep a weather eye on the situation. There's no telling where things will stop once the press finds something, or believes it has found something; and of course the business of Hansard receiving a possibly fatal dose of radiation is a highly emotional topic with which the press is likely to have a heyday for some time yet."

"Very true," said Guenther slowly. "But I'm most interested in why Sergei thinks the press may have concluded that there's some kind of surveillance going on. You're sure he wasn't more specific?''

"Oh, I hardly think he could be," said Ambedkar. "Undoubtedly he was speaking on the basis of something that just happened to come to his ear casually. But an old hand like Sergei tends to notice such things; and, as I say, I find myself that it pays to listen to him. After all, if you put talk of foreign spying together with the fact that an *American* was the one irradiated, particularly when the report is in an American newspaper . . .''

"I'm sure you and he are both right," said Guenther. "I feel inadequate, though. I wish I could be more help to you. The truth of the matter is I haven't heard any such thing myself.''

"Well, well," Ambedkar got to his feet. "It may be I'm concerning myself unduly. In fact, if my memory isn't tricking me—it really isn't too reliable these days—I think I remember Sergei saying something about how all of us here, with the exception of young Wylie, of course, would be entirely competent to take proper steps in dealing with such a situation if it ever should arise.''

"I'm sure of that." Guenther was on his feet too. He set the half-empty beer glass, from which he had not drunk during the last few minutes at all, carefully down on the coffee table. "If I were you I wouldn't worry. You also might suggest to Sergei that I think there's nothing to worry about. In fact, it seems to me I remember now hearing that whatever may have been going on has since been stopped and everything to do with it cleared away.''

"That would be a great relief, if we could depend on it," said Ambedkar. "Particularly if all loose ends are tucked away. Reporters are perfect demons for running down any untidinesses. For example, it's almost impossible to hide a person from them, nowadays, as you know.''

"A person?" Guenther asked.

"Why, yes." Ambedkar wandered toward the door and Guenther followed him. "People have a tendency to talk, when found. A distressing tendency. And, as Sergei and I were agreeing, the press is expert at finding such.''

"Of course. But I really can't conceive of anything like that happening," said Guenther.

"It does sound inconceivable, doesn't it?" said Ambedkar. "One would just like to be sure, that's all."

"Of course," said Guenther, opening the door for him. "But as I say, personally, I'm not the least bit worried."

"Excellent." Ambedkar smiled at him. "Good afternoon. We'll see you this evening at this Cocoa Beach affair?"

"I've been looking forward to it all day," Guenther said. "Outside of the reports, there's been nothing else on my mind."

"Well, then," said Ambedkar and went off.

Guenther closed the door behind him and turned back into the room. He walked slowly to the center of it, stopped and stood thinking for a second. Then he lifted his head and raised his voice, reverting to German.

"Dragons!" he snarled. "Bedamned dragons! Berthold, get in here!"

29

Willy Fesser sat in an armchair in his room at the Bell Tower Hotel, where he was registered under the name of Robert K. Larsen. He was thinking. In his lap lay an unmarked white envelope containing a sheaf of ten-dollar bills—Jim Brille's weekly pay, which Willy would be taking to the locker in the bus station shortly.

Willy was letting the present, overall situation run through his mind. A number of small things had been niggling at him lately; the general atmosphere, now that trouble had turned up with the Mars Expedition, the fact that Walther Guenther and that Berthold assistant of his had turned out to be more amateur than even he had guessed, and just recently, the information that some pickup truck had been following everybody leaving the Duchess's place.

Willy could not remember being followed; but—and he blamed himself for it—he had really not been paying proper attention. But then who would have expected such a daylight idiocy as someone tailing any of those who headquartered themselves on the Duchess? To begin with, there was no need to tail anyone like himself—since he would not be involved in anything important, anyway—and in the second place, who would be interested in doing so?

Unless, he thought now, there was something going on that he did not know about, so that somehow this Wylie business he was into tied into something bigger, something thoroughly professional?

Willy shivered a little at the thought. He wanted nothing to do with the professionals of the established agencies. They could get very real and very brutal with their wet work and their executive actions. If there was something going on that might involve that side of the business, it was high time he was disconnected and safely elsewhere.

On the other hand, the Pan-European was paying him eighteen hundred a week, and his only costs were his personal expenses, the regular small tab to the Duchess, and what he paid Jim. Discretion was always the better part of valor, but killing the goose that laid the golden eggs at the first ambiguous hint of danger was not the way to make a living in this line of work—

His phone rang.

Without moving his body as a whole, he reached out one arm to press the sound-on stud. The viewscreen did not light up, so whoever was at the other end of the connection was also not interested in face-to-face conversation; but a voice he recognized came from the unit. It was Berthold calling.

"Overseer Employment?" Berthold's voice was thinned by the electronic connection so that it sounded more English than Germanic.

"Yes," said Willy.

"This is Ace Architects. We're going out of business, so we won't be needing any more help supplied by you. As of now, that groundsman you sent us is discharged. He's no more concern of ours, but in view of the state of his health, you might want to see that he takes a long trip. We assume you or he will want to pick up his equipment without any delay. Undoubtedly, you'll be traveling, yourself, so—"

Willy picked up the envelope and took out the packet of ten-dollar bills, which he transferred to the money-thick wallet in the inside breast pocket of his own suitcoat. Then, with the phone still talking behind him, he got to his feet, went across the room and out the door of his room into the hotel corridor.

He took the elevator down to the lobby, nodded briefly to the desk clerk, who smiled at him as he passed, and went out the front door. There were a couple of cabs waiting there, and he got in the first one.

"Airport," he said. "Orlando."

He sat back as the cab pulled away from the hotel, feeling a twinge of regret for his gray tweed sportcoat, still hanging in the closet of his hotel room upstairs. But experience had taught him to make such departures as these without giving any sign that he was leaving. The most compact luggage in the world was a well-filled wallet; and the best use of time was always the putting of distance between oneself and one's former employer before that former employer realized one was gone.

Or one's employees discovered one was gone.

Berthold let himself back into Guenther's suite with his own key and closed the door behind him. He found Guenther sitting in a chair, staring hard at him.

"Well?" demanded Guenther.

"I got the security man at the Bell Tower Inn to let me in," said Berthold. "I didn't tell him who I was. I merely gave him a little money, and told him I was worried about my friend. Fesser wasn't there when we stepped inside. His clothes were, though."

"His clothes?" Guenther got to his feet and began to walk angrily back and forth across the room. "You think he's still around, then?"

"It's possible, sir," said Berthold, watching him.

"No. He's not a fool. He simply left without taking anything with him," said Guenther. "Was there any other sign?"

"His phone was still turned on. The channel was open," said Berthold. "I made my excuses to the security man and came back here."

"He's taken off all right," said Guenther, savagely. "Where does that leave us? What's the name of that man he had working for him?"

"I can look that up if you want, sir," said Berthold, "but it's probably not the correct name."

"No." Guenther stopped his pacing. "But if Fesser took off without telling us, it's certain he didn't take time to clean his man and that equipment out of that hotel room. It's just sitting there waiting to be found."

"Sir," said Berthold, "I could go over, possibly pick the lock, and clean the room out myself."

"Don't be a God damned fool!" said Guenther. "If you were found anywhere near that room, with what it has in it, and with your position on my staff, where do you think I'd be? Besides, the room's only part of it. If that spy of his doesn't hear from Willy, he may keep right on working; and I as good as told Ambedkar the whole business would be shut down!"

"The spy knows nothing about you, sir," Berthold said.

"That's something, at least," Guenther said, continuing to pace. "But he's got to stop, or be stopped. Damn it to hell! I should have known using that Fesser was too risky to be worthwhile! What in Christ's name can we do?"

"Well, sir," said Berthold, "we can always alert Security ourselves."

Guenther stopped pacing abruptly and looked at the younger man.

The phone on Albert Gervais's desk rang. He looked up from the report he was filling out and took off his reading glasses, laying them on the desk before him. He turned to the phone and punched it on. No face appeared on the screen, but a voice spoke.

"Is this the Security Office?"

"That's right," Gervais said. "Who's calling?"

"You might want to take a look in room fourteen twenty-two," the voice said, and the hum of a disconnected line came from the unit's receiver.

Gervais punched off thoughtfully. The voice had had an English accent with some other European accent underlying it—possibly an Austrian one. He was almost willing to bet he had heard it somewhere before. He sat for a moment thinking, then picked up his glasses, took the case for them from the inside of his coat, put the glasses carefully in the case, and tucked it back in his inside jacket pocket. He got to his feet.

"I'll be right back down," he said to Kilmartin Brawley, who was working at another desk across the room from his.

He went out across the lobby, and took the elevator up to room 1422. He tapped with his knuckle on the door and waited; but there was no answer. He reached into his pocket for a passkey, unlocked the door, and let himself in.

It was an ordinary room, with some clothes in the closet, a suitcase on the stand in the corner, and a tangle of equipment on the table next to the window. He closed the door behind him, walked quietly across the room and carefully examined the equipment without touching any of it. A slow, powerful feeling of triumph and satisfaction kindled and began to grow in him. After a moment he nodded to himself, turned around and went out again, carefully latching the door behind him.

He went upstairs to his own room, let himself in and opened the drawer of the desk there. The souvenir paper knife he had put there some days ago still lay there. He picked it up and put it in the inside pocket of his jacket next to the glasses in their case. Then he went back down to the registration desk in the lobby.

"Who's in room 1422?" he asked the short swarthy young desk clerk on duty. The desk clerk turned to look at the display board on the back of the pillar beside him, hidden from where Albert stood.

"Wilson Stang."

"Know what he looks like?" Gervais asked.

The clerk frowned, "I think so. . . ." he said slowly.

"Sort of a salesman type. Late thirties, early forties, kind of heavy, about as tall as you are."

"Color hair?" Gervais prodded gently.

"Brown . . . I think," said the clerk.

"Mustache? Beard? Wears glasses?"

"No, no beard or mustache. And I don't think he wears glasses."

"How long are you on duty here?" Gervais asked.

"Until seven."

"Let me know then, if you see him come in," said Gervais. "Try to hold him here, if you can, while you get word to me he's here. I'll be across in the office there; and if I'm not there, there'll be somebody there who knows how to find me."

"Sure," said the desk clerk.

Gervais looked closely at him.

"I mean that," he said softly. "The second he comes in, I want to know."

"Yes, sir," said the desk clerk. "Yes, sir."

The fried shrimp were very large and crisp. They seemed to break apart at the touch of a fork.

"Hey, these are good!" Jim Brille said.

"Billy's brother fishes them," Aletha said. "He catches for a number of eating places, but particularly for the Three Anchors, that place on the river outaways. You know it?"

"Yes," said Jim.

"Anyway, the Three Anchors is supposed to get the best, but Billy's cousin rakes over their load so that the best of the best comes here."

Jim chuckled. He and Aletha were seated on stiff, straw-bottomed wood chairs in a roadside restaurant so small that probably it could not have held more than thirty people at the most. A tiny, white-painted bar filled one corner.

"It pays to know your way around," he said.

"That's right," said Aletha. "I've been here all my life and I ought to. What did you think of Jake's Place?"

Aletha had been having some new points and a new condenser put into the motor of her car; and they had stopped to check it, on the way out to an early dinner before she was due to go on night duty at the bar. The car was being repaired at Jake's Place, a three-pump filling station with a small grocery store tacked onto one end of it, sitting on the corner between the highway and a side road. Jake himself, a slow-moving, stocky man in his early fifties, had struck Jim as knowing his way around car motors. The station was cluttered but everything was where it could be found. The little grocery store tacked on to it, on the other hand, looked fly-blown, run-down and dusty. It was apparently leased by Jake to a young couple who did not know much about running it.

"I like Jake," Jim said. "Those kids he's got in the store are trying to run it with one hand tied behind their back, though."

"That's what he thinks," said Aletha. "He's had a number of people running it, and he's getting tired of it. Matter of fact, he's getting a little tired of working on cars, too. He just inherited some money from a brother and he wants to buy himself a place on a river, back outaways, and just sit around from now on."

"Oh?" said Jim.

"Yes," Aletha said. "So all of the place he's got now is for sale."

Jim heard the words with a sort of slow, sad-happy twisting of his guts. He had been expecting something like this. He had never liked such moments; but this one in particular, he had found himself both looking forward to and dreading, out of all proportion to anything he had felt in such situations before.

"Sure," he said.

"No, I mean it," Aletha looked squarely at him. "That's a good-sized little lot there. For it and the filling station and everything else he's got on it Jake figures he'd need around thirty-two thousand. That means something like ten thousand down with a mortgage."

"Mortgages come from banks," said Jim Brille.

"I know that," said Aletha. "And I can get one. Also, I've got enough equity in my house now to raise the down payment."

"You figuring on hiring me for a mechanic?" Jim grinned.

"You know damn good and well what I'm saying," Aletha told him. "I want you to stay here permanently."

He reached across the table and touched her wrist with the ends of his fingers.

"Don't be stupid," he said.

"I'm not stupid," Aletha said. "I'm sharp. I know a good thing when I see it."

"Look," said Jim. "What do I know about running a mama-and-papa store?"

"It wouldn't be a mama-and-papa store," said Aletha. "You told me you could make a living fixing TVs if you wanted to. There's always TVs that need fixing. I saw what you did with my set. Run a TV repair shop out of the store front, and the filling station would pay the mortgage. I could still hold onto my job and help out around the place."

Jim shook his head.

"Leeth," he said. "If I had it in me to settle down, I'd have settled down before this."

"No, you wouldn't," said Aletha. "You wouldn't because you weren't ready. You've been a kid, still kicking around, wanting a high old night, every night. Now you're ready to settle down; and I want to see you settled down. I don't know what it is you've been doing here, but whatever it is, it isn't something that's good for you. You really want to get out of it; and this is the way you can."

Jim shook his head.

"It wouldn't work," he said.

"You think about it," said Aletha.

"It wouldn't work," said Jim again.

"Eat your shrimp before they get cold," said Aletha. They talked about other things through the rest of the meal and then Jim drove her to the Holiday Inn and let her off outside.

"Now you think about that," said Aletha, as she got out of the car.

"We'll see," said Jim.

She closed the door and he watched her go. As she approached the door leading directly from outside to the bar, it swung open, and was held for her by a tall, dark-haired man in his thirties. Jim squinted at the man. It looked like that Malcolm character she had been talking about, the one who'd been bugging her, off and on now, ever since before the launch. He was down here to buy a house because he was being transferred into the area.

As Aletha disappeared into the rectangle of inner darkness, the Malcolm figure turned, looked out at Jim's car and hesitated, still holding open the street door to the cocktail lounge.

Well, thought Jim, if you've got something to say to me, come on out here and say it.

The other man, however, continued merely to stand where he was, staring.

Maybe I should get out, Jim thought. He opened the door and emerged, standing up on his side of the car and looking back over its low roof directly at the man in the doorway. The other turned and went hastily into the lounge, closing the door behind him. Jim shrugged and got back behind the wheel. Aletha could take care of herself with anyone like that. As long as he was here, it would be a good time to check the equipment in the hotel room and put in some fresh tape units.

He put the car in gear, intending to drive around to the back of the hotel and park, then changed his mind. His money should be down in the bus-station locker by now. The thought of Jake's place was still sticking in his head. The possibility of settling down both enticed and appalled him. He had become almost superstitious about ceasing to be on the move; but somebody like Aletha was not easy to find and he was ready to quit traveling.

He put the car in gear and turned it to make the drive down to the bus station.

Malcolm followed the manager down a ground-floor corridor of the hotel. He had a warm, good feeling within him about what he had finally decided to do. He was not the sort, he told himself, to complain without reason. In fact, he had endured a good deal from this drifter who had been hanging around Aletha. All other considerations aside, society worked on the basis that those who were important in it deserved something more than those who were merely parasites upon it. After all, here he was, a responsible family and professional man, certainly deserving of a little relaxation, and here was this worthless fly-by-night whom a quiet word or two would remove. . . .

Once the drifter was out of the way, there was no doubt that Aletha should turn to him without too much trouble. He had had his successes that way before. If he had one virtue, he told himself, following the manager, it was that he knew the value of persistence with women like Aletha. After a while, you simply wore them down. They gave up. In essence, they knew that they were in no position to control their lives, and when someone with a strong hand came along and took charge, eventually they simply gave in.

The manager stopped at the door of a function room, turned, opened it, and held it open for Malcolm. Malcolm followed him in, and found the room had been turned into an office with a number of desks and various pieces of office equipment.

The only person already in the room was a slim, middle-aged black man with an authoritarian, aristocratic look that was not at all diluted by the fact that he was wearing half-lens spectacles. He looked up from one of the desks as Malcolm and the day manager came in.

"This is the gentleman I just called you about," the day manager said. "I'll leave him with you."

He went back out. Malcolm stepped to the desk and looked down at the man behind it.

"Are you the hotel detective?" he asked.

"Security is my job," said Gervais. "You were complaining about Mr. Stang?"

"Is that his name?" asked Malcolm. "I thought he might have a room here, but I didn't know his name. It *is* Stang?"

"What was the nature of your complaint?" Gervais said.

"Well, I'm not complaining personally," Malcolm said. He looked around the room. "I'm in the hotel business myself, but I've never seen a security setup this size before. I suppose you're something special set up because of the VIPs here for the Mars business?"

"If you'd rather not give me your complaint in person," Gervais said, "you can write a letter to the management of the hotel."

"No . . . no, it's not that important," Malcolm said. "I

mean, I just think something should be done about it. Being in the hotel business myself, I probably pay more attention to the problems of the employees than the average person does, and I thought someone ought to be told about this Stang. That's all.''

Gervais waited.

''Well, it's just that you might want to know he's been paying a lot of attention to the women working in the lounge— I mean, the bartenders—particularly the bartenders—and the waitresses and such. Of course, there's always a certain amount of that going on, but sometimes it goes past the bounds of good taste; and most managements I've been with have appreciated knowing about such things before they can get out of hand. I just thought I'd say a word to you quietly. I don't want to get involved, myself; but now that I've told you what's going on, you can suit yourself about whether you might want to look into it yourselves. . . .''

He let the sentence trail off.

''That's it then?'' Gervais said. ''That's what you wanted to tell us?''

''Well, yes. That's essentially it.''

''I see.'' Gervais picked up a sharp, plain, wooden pencil from the desk and made a brief scribble on a notepad, which Malcolm, looking at it upside down, was not able to decipher. ''Thank you.''

''Not at all.'' Malcolm lingered. ''You *are* going to do something about it, though? I should think—''

''Do you know anything about this man, personally?'' Gervais asked, still holding the pencil. ''Where he works— if he has family nearby?''

''Oh, I don't think he's got any family,'' Malcolm said quickly. ''I mean . . . I got the impression from one of the bartender ladies that he's just one of those salesmen types who move around all the time. I think she said he's out of work and looking for a job right now . . . I believe one of the other girls that work in the bar said something about that. And he's around at all hours. I don't see how he could do that if he had a regular job.''

Gervais made another minuscule note.

''Yes,'' he said. ''Very good. You've been very helpful.''

He looked up at Malcolm.

"Thank you," he said again.

"As I told you, not at all." Malcolm felt a twinge of annoyance. "You did say you were going to do something about him?"

Gervais smiled, momentarily, and—it seemed to Malcolm—a trifle coldly.

"We'll look into it."

"Yes. Well, I . . ." Malcolm shifted his weight from one foot to another. He began to feel slightly foolish, slightly schoolboyish, standing talking to this man who remained seated behind his desk. "All right, then. Good-by."

"Good day," said Gervais.

Malcolm turned and walked out, an undefined resentment beginning to seethe and burn inside him. He could at least have stood up to thank me, Malcolm told himself, as he let the door to the room swing close behind him. He headed back toward the lounge.

Driving down to the bus station, Jim let his mind play with the possibilities. If this nonsense business of bugging the room that Willy had him doing would keep up another week or two, he would have some cash in hand, himself. He already had eighteen hundred from the weeks past, since he had spent almost nothing, staying out at Aletha's. Twenty-five hundred, even three thousand would not bring him into what Aletha was suggesting, the way he should come in—as an equal partner; but at least he would be putting up enough to be useful and it would give him a leg for his self-respect to stand on.

He drove on, thinking, playing games with what he would do to Jake's Place if he actually took it over. Aletha was not wrong. The filling station could pay for itself, and then some. Jim was not the world's greatest auto mechanic; but he liked working at anything with his hands and he knew enough about engines to handle whatever might come in. Whatever the place was equipped to handle, that is. If something too big did come in, he could simply tell whoever brought it that there was no way to take care of it without more equipment than he had. As for the TV end of it, that would be a snap.

Six or seven hundred dollars would buy him all the tools he needed for the kind of thing he would be doing with that, and he had worked at something like that once before. He knew that he could hang onto most of the customers he got, and pick up new ones as fast as they might come in through the front door. Aletha was right; the thing would work—from the financial end, at least. Reaching the bus station, he parked and went inside to the locker. He tried his key in it and the door swung open.

The locker was empty.

Jim frowned. The locker was in the top row, just above his own eye level. He reached up and felt around inside it; but his fingers found nothing. There should have been a white business-size envelope filled with ten-dollar bills. It was the first time Willy had goofed up a payday.

Thoughtfully, Jim closed the locker once more and went over to the rack of phones along one wall of the station. He punched out the phone number of the Duchess, and waited. The phone rang at the other end, and a young, dark-skinned male face formed on the screen.

"Duchess Stensla's," said the face.

"Could I speak to Willy Fesser?" Jim asked.

"Moment, sir," said the face and disappeared from the screen. The face was gone more than one minute. Jim whistled silently to himself between his teeth as he waited; and finally the face came back.

"He not here," it said.

"Can I leave a message for him to call me?" Jim asked.

"With pleasure."

Jim gave the number of the pay phone he was at, punched off, sat back and waited.

Nothing happened during ten minutes. Jim got up at the end of that time and went over to a coffee machine to buy some coffee. He came back with the hot, full plastic cup and sat down again. From time to time someone passing by glanced curiously at the man sitting there with an inoperative phone, but no one stopped or commented.

30

Jim waited forty minutes before giving up. Among Willy's few virtues was the business virtue of responding to such calls immediately after he was told about them. Something had undoubtedly come up. In which case Willy would be getting in touch with Jim at the motel sooner or later.

Meanwhile, Jim thought, he might as well go back and put some new tape units in the equipment. He went back out to his car and drove at a moderate pace back to the Holiday Inn. When he got there he parked behind it, reached for the door handle to get out, and then stopped, taking his hand away again.

There was a touch of uneasiness inside him. Nothing great, but it was there. It was not like Willy to goof up a payday. It was not like Willy to be so far from the phone and from whatever message service he had set up that he would not be answering a call within half an hour at the outside.

Yet there had been no indication of any kind of trouble.

Jim sat a moment longer, then made up his mind. He got out of the car, went around and unlocked its trunk. There was some newspaper there, wrapped around an object about three feet long. He unwrapped the newspaper and took it out. It was a crowbar, entirely new, still encased in the brown paper the hardware store had taped around it, and with the sales slip still inside the wrapping paper, taped to the black metal.

Jim closed the trunk; and, carrying the still-wrapped crowbar as if it was a new purchase, he went in through a back door of the Holiday Inn, down a long, ground-floor corridor and stepped out of its far end into the lobby. He turned abruptly right to face the elevator and punched the *up* button.

"Mr. Stang?" The call came from some little distance behind his back. Jim stared at the up button. *"Mr. Stang!"*

Jim turned and saw the clerk from behind the registration counter coming toward him across the lobby, a piece of paper in his fingers.

"You're Mr. Stang, aren't you?" The clerk came up to him, smiling, and handed him a small slip of paper. "This phone call came in for you. They said it was important."

"Thanks," said Jim. Almost as an afterthought, he reached into his pocket, fumbled a dollar bill from his wallet without taking the wallet out and handed it over to the clerk.

"That's all right, sir."

"No. Take it," Jim said.

"Thank you, Mr. Stang," said the clerk. "Did you want to call from down here? I can plug you in from one of the house phones to the switchboard."

"No," said Jim. "I think I know what it is. It's not all that important. I'll call later."

"Yes, sir."

The room clerk turned and went back across the lobby. The elevator doors had just opened. Jim stepped in and punched for the 14th floor. After a long second, the doors closed again and he went up. In the elevator, alone, he looked at the slip. The phone number and name on it were unknown to him. The only person outside this hotel who knew the name of Mr. Stang was Willy; and Willy would never call for him here, under any name. Jim crumpled the call slip and dropped it as the elevator stopped at the 14th floor.

He reached room number 1422, unlocked its door and stepped inside. Within, the air was dead still and nothing was changed. He went over to the equipment and looked at it. Yes, the tape units would need replacing. But for some reason his fingers hesitated to act. He looked out the window, not exactly sure why he did so. It had been late afternoon when he had dropped off Aletha. It had been deep twilight when he had driven back here. Now, with the suddenness of the day-to-night change that comes in lands approaching the equator, it was already the beginning of starlit evening, with a few tiny points of light incredibly distant in the as yet imperfectly dark sky. Across the small open space between him and the tower section of the motel, the ground was in deep shadow.

He turned once more to the equipment to change the tape

units; but again his inner feeling stopped him. It did not feel right—just did not feel right. And there was that phone call memo, just now.

He took a step back from the table on which everything stood, turned and walked to the door. Before leaving, he took a handkerchief from his pocket and wiped off the inner door handle. He opened the door and looked out. Outside, the corridor was deserted and the air felt almost as still as it had been in the room. He went out, wiped the door handle and, using the handkerchief, latched it behind him again. A sense of urgency was suddenly strong in him. He did not even turn toward the elevators, but went instead toward the stairway entrance he had gone through once before. He stepped into it now and began to descend the stairs toward the main floor.

Two flights down, he thought he heard an echo to his footsteps on the concrete steps. He stopped, but there was no sound. He started up again, and once more he thought he heard the echo.

He was now, to all intents and purposes, certain. He began to go down the stairs more quickly and a little less quietly, but still without clatter. The echo above him, now clearly to be distinguished, kept pace with him. His eyes kept track of the black numerals painted on the stairside of the doors on each floor he passed. He went by them and they were left above him in slow descending order . . . 11 . . . 10 . . . 9 . . .

When he reached the number 2 he leaned heavily on the door on which it was marked and stepped quickly out onto the soft carpet of the second-floor corridor. It was deserted. He ran quickly toward the front of the building to the wide front stairs curving down to the lobby.

He checked his speed once he came to the top of the stairs and went down them at a more normal pace. The desk clerk who had come up to him with the call slip earlier was busy now with a couple of people and did not see him. He turned from the bottom of the stairs and stepped almost immediately out through the front entrance of the hotel, went right and around the corner of it, and walked rapidly toward the back of the hotel. The paper-wrapped crowbar was still in his hands. He had held to it instinctively all this time; and he now found it giving him a feeling of some security, as if it was an old friend—in spite of the fact that this particular tool was one he had never carried before.

He was not consciously thinking, at the moment. Later he could stop and take time to puzzle out what had gone wrong. But right now the only thing he was concerned with was the fact that his car was at the back of the motel parking lot, and that he must get in it and get away.

The wall of this side of the hotel seemed enormously long; but he came at last to the end of it, and was about to plunge across the parking lot when he checked instinctively. The broad-shouldered young man he had encountered when he had ventured one floor above the fourteenth floor the first time he had been in the hotel, and who had politely chased him back into the elevator and downstairs, stood in the middle of the lot, legs spread a little and hands clasped behind his back as if waiting.

Jim looked around. As long as the man was there, his car was out of reach. To go back toward the front of the hotel was no good. Undoubtedly by this time there would be someone waiting for him there, too. That left only one direction in which he could run, and that was to his left, across the narrow strip of parking lot there, continuing on foot until he could get someplace where he could call a cab. He turned and moved out between two of the cars parked up against the sidewalk that circled the motel. As he did, he thought he saw a figure come around the front corner of the hotel, the same corner he had turned a few moments before, but he did not wait to see who it might be. He kept moving, across the open space between the two rows of parked cars, past the cars in the far column, and over a concrete wall about four feet high.

He came down the other side in the undergrowth of a vacant lot. To his left were the backs of a row of small stores, blocking him off from access to the main street he wanted to reach. Straight ahead there was an alley leading into the parking area behind the storefronts.

He waded through the underbrush, made the parking area and started down the alley. Walking more quietly now that he was in the open, he heard a thud and then rustling behind him. Glancing back over his shoulder, he saw a dark figure just inside the concrete wall, silhouetted by the lights of the Holiday Inn behind it and running toward him.

He turned and broke into a run once more himself.

The alley was dark and not long. He reached its far end, saw a lamp-lit block leading left to the brightly lit street he needed to reach. He stopped. He could hear the pounding footsteps of the man chasing him, growing rapidly louder as he stood there. Ahead, there was what seemed to be a small park, perhaps a block square in area, studded with flower-erbeds, bushes and small trees. He ran across the street and into it, feeling the yielding grass and earth suddenly under-foot. There was a chance he could get away from his pursuers among the growth there and the shadows; and, once free, he could then finally get to the bright lights of the main street and find a phone booth from which to call a cab.

He was winded now. He crossed the street and entered the park, slipping behind the first large bush he found. Hidden, he turned and peered through its branches. The alley mouth he had just left seemed empty and silent. For a moment hope moved in him that his pursuer had given up. Then, a figure took shape in the darkness he watched. It was the black man who had been standing by the desk that first day when Jim had followed the tall girl to the dining room door, to make it seem as if his interest was only in her. Now, after all his visits to the motel, Jim knew who the other was—Albert Gervais, the security agent about whom Willy had warned him.

In the alley mouth, now, Gervais stopped as Jim had stopped. He stood still for a moment, looking into the park. He might, Jim thought, merely be catching his breath, as Jim had done—but something in Jim doubted it. Gervais was plainly in a lot better physical shape than Jim; and he was probably five to ten years younger, as well. Jim faded back into the park.

Farther in the light was less, but Jim's eyes were adjusting to the night. The light from the nearest lamp, nearly half a block away, filtered among the growth and was reinforced by the more distant glow of two street lamps on the far side of the small park. It occurred to him that he could start working toward the front of the park as well as putting distance be-tween himself and Albert Gervais.

He began to move cautiously in that direction, slipping

from bush to tree, and as he did so a memory came to lighten his tension. He suddenly recalled that when Albert Gervais had stood at the end of the alley he had not seemed to be carrying any kind of a weapon with him. Of course, he might well have a handgun out of sight; and, being who he was, Gervais must also be good with his hands. But if it was only hands—those against a crowbar were hardly an even match, particularly with somebody like Jim who had weight, as well as some muscle for club-using. More to the point, though, thought Jim, moving quietly through the shadows, was the fact that Gervais's empty-handedness could mean that he had no real hope of stopping or arresting Jim—that maybe all the security man had hoped for was to get a good look at whoever had been the Mr. Stang in Room 1422.

Less than thirty yards from the main street end of the park, Jim paused to look and listen from behind an Australian pine. But, gazing through the fringe of needles on the tips of its lower branches, he saw and heard nothing. He was just about to move toward the lights of the main street, when there was a sound like a branch breaking—directly ahead of him, between him and his goal.

Jim froze. All he wanted, he told himself, was to get away; and this Gervais must know it. But for some strange reason the other insisted on following him. Now the security agent was between him and the lighted street that was his one road to escape.

Then the anger passed. The other was probably just bucking for a promotion. That would be exactly the way Jim's usual luck would run. He felt a touch of wry humor. It was something like this that had always been his problem; the fact that even in emergencies he could not work up a good head of steam and hold it for more than a few seconds. He had been born easygoing, and that fact had made his life what it was. Now he could not even stay worked up about the man who was chasing him. Gervais was between him and the street; that was all there was to it. There was obviously no point in going on that way; he would have to keep moving in some other direction.

He turned once more to his right, to the way he had been traveling ever since he had left the hotel. Ahead of him through the small stretch of park that remained, and across a narrow, residential street, was another row of houses.

To leave the park and cross the street ahead was to expose himself to Gervais. Possibly he could lose himself between the farther houses and so get away; but on the other hand he might just as likely find himself trapped among backyard fences. He wished the other would get tired and give up.

To give himself time to think Jim retreated toward the back of the park, away from the lights of the main street. He heard no more sounds from in front of him but an inner, animal sense left him sure that Gervais was closing in on him.

Why back off like this? Jim asked himself. Why not just let him catch up with me and then scare him off? I've got the crowbar and he's got nothing. So why not let him catch up with me? The answer came immediately from the back of his head. Because then you might have to hurt him, you damn fool, and that's the last thing you want. You know that.

He retreated farther, to the shelter of a fairly large bush whose flowers were invisible in the gloom, but which was filling the night air with heavy perfume. The gentle, warm, moist darkness seemed to wrap about him and insist that what was going on was unreal, could not be real. He peered quickly in that same darkness. He could not simply go on backing up like this. He would be at the back edge of the park in another thirty or forty steps.

He looked once more over at the houses opposite; and for the first time saw a gap between them, the entrance of another alley. He had not expected to find anything like that this far down toward the end of the block. He looked toward the other row of houses at the bottom of the park. Here also was the bare street; and beyond it, other back yards in which he could possibly be trapped. If he waited here much longer he would have to back up farther and eventually he would not even have a choice of ways to go. While he still had a choice he had better try the alley-mouth opposite.

He bent low, taking advantage of what cover there was, and ran as softly as possible through the park, across the asphalt surface of the roadway, past the sidewalk and into the darkness that was the alley opening. Once safely in its deep shadow, he stopped and turned, looking out into the park. He waited. The seconds went by. But there was neither sound nor movement within the park, no indication that Gervais was even still there.

Briefly, the thought crossed Jim's mind that he could wait here for a safe time—four, five minutes or even longer, possibly even ten minutes—and when there was no sign of movement from the park, simply come out and walk up the block to the light and escape. There would be nothing to it, that way, he thought. Then common sense returned to sober him. It would be the easiest thing in the world for the man in the park to outwait him. Perhaps Gervais knew where the alley now behind Jim led to? There was no telling whether he did or not. And even if he did not know, but still wanted to follow, he would come after Jim into this farther alley, sooner or later.

On the other hand he might know that this alley led to a dead end. In which case the reason he was still waiting out there was for Jim to go into it, and trap himself certainly. However, if the alley did not lead to a dead end . . .

There were too many question marks. Jim felt a sudden weariness of the whole business. He was sick of running—but not sick enough so that he was ready yet to go out and challenge Gervais, and put himself in a position where he would have to use the crowbar. He was only weary enough so that he did not want to stand puzzling any longer. If the alley was a trap, it was a trap. He would go in, and if Gervais came after him, what would happen to him would be his own fault.

Jim turned and went deeper into the alley.

The light was dimmer there. Only the starlit sky above, and some house lights, enabled Jim to move without feeling his way. Once more, his eyes began to adjust, picking out here a lightness in the darkness, a greyishness that on closer approach turned out to be a garbage can, or the white wall of a picket fence. He went on, not hearing anything or anyone behind him. After a while he came out into an open parking area like that he had crossed at the rear of the storefronts next to the Holiday Inn.

Here, lighted windows from what looked like a small apartment building shone down in the clearing with an illumination like bright moonlight. It was possible to see clear across the parking lot; and Jim saw his earlier fear had been correct. This alley came to a dead end, completely walled-in by buildings.

He stopped, turned, and listened.

He heard nothing and saw no one coming after him down the alley. But then, from where he stood in the light, what he could see of the alley now was no more than an aperture of darkness. Still, a feeling of relief began to stir inside him. At least, it was finally settled, one way or another. There was no way out but back. He took a first step to go back the way he had come, down the alley and out to the street.

At that moment he saw, or felt, a movement in the alley darkness.

In that first second it was feeling as much as sight. His senses merely registered that something was moving out of the alley into the parking area. Then it stepped clear into the light and he saw it—saw his pursuer. It was Albert Gervais; and Gervais, having stepped into the light, stopped where he stood, still wearing his business suit and looking calm, almost indifferent.

The feeling of relief was still with Jim. Things had finally come down to a simple matter of doing, or not doing. He spread his hands apart on the paper-wrapped crowbar, holding it pointed horizontally forward before him at belt level, crook end in advance, right hand near the back end, left hand three quarters of the length up toward the crook. He began to walk steadily toward Gervais.

Gervais's right arm moved up from his side. But his hand did not lift to reach in his coat and come out with a gun, which was the one thing Jim had really feared. Instead, it came up as high as his waist, before him, holding something bright and not more than a few inches long. The bright length projected from his fist, pointed toward Jim.

Jim stopped. The relief was still with him, but now he also felt a faint disgust. He had never liked knifefighters, though he had never really been afraid of them. A knife had to reach you to do any damage; and with something like a club or a crowbar there was a reach advantage; and in this case, he had a weight advantage as well. Besides he knew how to use a crowbar. You did not swing with it, you smashed it straight out in a line. No knife was in it with that.

"I don't want to break your arm," he said to Gervais. "Just let me by."

Gervais stood where he was. The light falling on his face from the apartment windows was enough so that Jim could read its expression clearly, and there was no expression on it. Gervais was merely waiting.

Again, a sudden sense of all this as being ridiculous, a sudden urge to break into slightly crazy laughter, swept through Jim. It had to be insane that this security man should have chased him all this distance, and now was seriously proposing to face him with a four-inch knife blade. It just did not make sense. The only reasonable explanation had to be that Gervais had not realized he did not have a gun with him—and, having come this far and now discovered it, was now trying to bluff Jim out with some sort of pocket knife. In which case, all that it would take for Jim to get away clean would be to be firm about going forward, and using the crowbar if he had to.

Still—something about the immobility of Gervais's face left a little doubt in Jim about his reasonable adding-up of the situation. He could still not see any expression but, watching the other man closely, Jim got the strong impression of a powerful effort of concentration in the other. At the same time, the possibility of a government agent seriously using a knife on a fugitive was so unbelievable that it trampled down the impression made by Gervais's face and manner.

Jim walked forward.

"Just let me by, now," he said, almost soothingly, as if he was talking to a young child.

But as he got two steps from Gervais, Jim's instincts shouted a warning. The other man was too still, he was holding the knife too steadily. There was no one thing about him— it was all of him that screamed *danger*.

Reflexively, Jim lunged with the crowbar. He had been pushing with his right hand and pulling back with his left, so there was muscle tension behind the sudden flicking out of the crowbar's forward end, as his left hand let go of it. The crook end drove forward in a line that should have ended under Gervais's chin; but Gervais had flowed backward one step and aside; and the weight of the crowbar caused it to drive on with its momentum, wide of its target.

There was suddenly a cold stink in Jim's nostrils, which he recognized—not as fear, but as something very close to it. Inside him, there was the complete understanding now that the man he faced was here to kill him. But at the same time another part of himself, that part of himself that had never been able to do things right, that had never taken life seriously enough, could not take even this seriously. The alerted part of him raged at the unserious part of himself, telling it for once to realize that it had to fight for its life, that it had to want to win. But the unserious part would not change; and there was no time now to change, after a lifetime of being the way he was.

At full extension of his arm, he jerked the curved end of the crowbar back to hook and tear Gervais's arm, but Gervais was already flowing forward, inside the reach of the bar. The crowbar followed him, but it touched nothing. It was as if Gervais was made of smoke and the crowbar could not catch him. Jim saw the other loom close, almost body to body, felt something like a light punch just below his breastbone; and, unexpectedly, the world changed. Without quite realizing what had happened, he no longer saw Gervais but only the sky and stars. He was looking straight up, not horizontally. He was lying on his back in the alley with the tall figure of Gervais standing mile-high over him.

"Why . . . ?" he said. "Why . . ."

"Because I need a dead," came the savage whisper from the figure over him.

The answer made no sense. A feeling of incredulity flooded Jim for a brief moment; and then even the sky and the stars faded, into full dark.

31

Tad was not fine. This was the second day now since the return of the nausea and the general feeling of malaise that he had felt a little after Bap had changed his blood, when he had first come back into the ship after being exposed to the radiation. Also, the drugs had him feeling fuzzy-minded and unnatural. Now as then, he was determined to hide the way he felt; only it was hard to tell how well he was succeeding. The 'nauts had lived together too closely, too long, to be easily fooled.

Fedya, Tad saw, certainly suspected. And Fedya was a problem, since he represented what Tad feared most—that Expedition Control might take command of the Expedition away from him. From the moment he had returned inside the ship after being exposed to the solar storm, he had not forced his authority upon the other 'nauts; and neither Bap nor Anoshi, at least, had challenged the fact that he still had it.

Fedya, however, as junior co-commander of the Expedition might just be the one who would challenge that authority—with the result that Tad might lose it. And he could not afford to lose it. He trusted none of the others to take the necessary action with respect to himself, when the time came; and the time would come soon now. He turned from Fedya to Anoshi.

"Connected?" he asked.

Anoshi nodded.

"We're tied in by direct line now with the Phoenix Two LCO," Anoshi said. He glanced at Fedya. "I take it for granted Phoenix Two had the other end of the wire already spliced to its LCO?"

"It's spliced in," said Fedya. "Why don't you call Expedition Control and say we're ready here any time Bill Ward is ready?"

"I'll do that," said Tad.

He turned about and sat down at his control console. It was a little strange, after these several days of always going to the radio for outside communication, to be punching the buttons of the LCO as if the copper mirror outside the hull of Phoenix Two was still capable of being aligned properly. It almost seemed as if the picture and the voice that came in over the wire to the LCO and mirror of Phoenix Two ought to have some noticeably different quality. But the image of Ed Ciro's face and the sound of his voice that the console produced was the same as it had been in past days before the solar storm.

"Phoenix One and Two calling Expedition Control," said Tad into the mike grid. "Do you read me?"

Ed's lips moved on the screen a moment later, and his voice answered.

"Read you perfectly," he said. "You did get a cable connection between the two craft then?"

"Fedya just did," said Tad. "So now we can shift supplies between ships without docking." He was about to say more but a wave of nausea stopped him. "I'll . . . pass you over to Fedya." He got up, stepping away from the console so that he stood with his face turned away from the others, waiting for the feeling of sickness to pass.

"Hello, Ed," he heard Fedya saying behind him. "I'm on Phoenix One. Any time Bill Ward is ready to talk to us, we're available."

"He'll be with you in a moment, Fedya. He's on the phone just at the moment—here he comes now."

Bill saw Ed Ciro standing to one side of the Communications Console in Expedition Control, and waiting. He walked over, feeling the weight of his years upon him. He had lain awake most of the night rehearsing the words in which he would be speaking to the 'nauts and had finally fallen asleep about five A.M., his brain spinning with speeches, none of which was any good. Now he felt dull and heavy, like a man carrying his own mass in dead weight—and he still did not know how he would say what he had to say.

He reached the console and sat down before it.

"Hello, Phoenix One and Two," he said. He looked into the

face of Fedya, with the faces of Tad, Bap and Anoshi behind him at Phoenix One communications. "Look, we've gone over the data on both ships that you've been feeding us during the last few days. As far as we can see, it boils down to this—"

He glanced down at some papers he was carrying in his hand; but it was an action of pure reflex. He did not have to refresh his memory as to what their text told him.

"Both ships," he said into the silence from the screen, "are operable with some limits. Both have suffered some damage to their electronic systems, particularly the control components of their communication systems—as a result of radiation from the solar storm. Some of the damage can be repaired by pooling spare parts from both ships. But among the important systems which can't be repaired is the LOC of Phoenix One—which means Phoenix One is now dependent upon a radio or wired link to Phoenix Two, and only Phoenix Two has LCO with us here at Control. Also, there's damage to the main engines of the shuttle module of Phoenix Two, of which only two out of five will fire. In addition, you don't expect to be able to repair your attitude controls well enough to redock the two craft together. Am I right?"

He waited for the little time lag that would precede the answer.

"Right," said Fedya.

Tad moved forward a little in the screen, almost as if Fedya's speaking had triggered his recollection that he was in command of the Expedition. His face, under the illumination of the screen, looked gaunt and aged. Bill looked away from him, glancing back down at the papers whose contents he knew by heart.

"All right," Bill went on slowly, "it seems to us that the possibilities add up like this: There's two practical choices. One, both craft can continue on the Expedition together but un-docked, coasting to orbit around Mars. However, with only two main engines on her shuttle module and other damage, Phoenix Two will not be able to depart Mars orbit; so at the time of departure, all personnel will have to shift themselves and nec-essary supplies aboard Phoenix One, to return in a single ship."

He paused to give them time to absorb what he had just said.

"Go on," said Tad, harshly.

"Two," continued Bill, "we'll compute retro-fire figures now, and both ships will fire to an Earth-reinjection orbit, aborting this attempt at the Expedition and looking forward to repairing both craft once they're back in Earth parking orbit and a new window for a second try at the Expedition can be chosen from available launch dates."

He paused again. There was that momentary pause of transmission and response time; and then all the figures in the screen moved slightly.

"No," said Fedya.

"Just a minute, Fedya," said Tad. He looked over Fedya's head, out of the screen, directly at Bill. "You're saying there's no doubt that the Expedition'll be on again, once the ships are fixed and ready to go a second time?"

"Of course there's no doubt," said Bill.

"No," said Bap. "Fedya's right."

"I don't think we believe you, Bill," said Tad, grimly. "All the international business that made this trip possible isn't going to be something you can turn on again when you want to. I think we vote to keep going."

Bill pressed his back against the support of his chair.

"I suppose," he said, making his voice deliberately grim and harsh. "Very well, here it is, then. There's a lot of public interest back here in seeing this Expedition completed; and I didn't need to guess at what you all would prefer to do. But you've got two crippled vehicles and one sick crew member. Back here, we have to think in terms of the whole Expedition, the whole space program, not just this one try at getting there. Frankly, we'd be tempted to risk your continuing on toward Mars if it weren't for two things. One, you've got Tad aboard, and he needs the kind of medical attention you can't give him there. Two, you aren't able to redock. We can't risk your doing without at least some form of substitute gravity for the length of time yet ahead of you. You've got most of three years yet to go. So—sorry, gentlemen—but the decision back here is that the present situation calls for an abort. So if you'll start making ready at your end, we'll start here working up the figures for your burn to an injection orbit that will bring you to rendezvous with Earth in about thirteen days."

"No," began Bap again. Tad leaned forward over Fedya's shoulder, interrupting.

"Excuse me, Fedya," he said.

The picture disappeared from the screen. The red light on Bill's console, that signaled an interruption in communication, came on.

"What?" said Bill, staring at the console.

"It was cut from their end," said Ed Ciro.

"I know that, damn it!" said Bill. "What'd they do that for? What's going on out there?"

"Shall I signal with the radio that we're out of contact?" Ed asked.

"Of course. Of course!" Bill fumed. Ed sat down at the adjoining console and became busy. Bill stayed where he was, his mind in a whirl, staring at the dead screen before him. These men were officers in the armed services, used to following orders whether they approved of them or not—not only that, but everything coming and going over the communications link, every word, gesture and happening on it became a matter of record. . . .

The screen lit up again.

"Sorry about the interruption, Bill," Tad said. "I guess I leaned on the keyboard down there by mistake. Now, where were we?"

"How soon can you get both ships ready to fire?" asked Bill, bluntly.

"Well, that's a question," said Tad, thoughtfully. None of them, Bill saw, had changed position. Tad was still standing behind Fedya, who was seated at the console, but all of them now seemed to be content to let Tad do the talking. "We've got a problem we haven't brought you up to date on. Phoenix One is going to have to make it in small jumps. With everything else that's been happening, I didn't get it logged, but when I was EVA on duty about a week and a half ago, I was checking the control leads from the Expedition module to the shuttle module. I'd gone in through Hatch Four; and I took the shielding off the leads for the check. The shielding floated away out the hatch, and I was so woozy from lack of sleep that I forgot all about the chance of a solar storm and didn't make a hard enough try to catch it. So those connections went unshielded during the storm. I sneaked down and checked them yesterday before I was supposed to be up and around; and while all five engines on the shuttle module here on Phoenix One still respond to controls, there's just one deficiency. The steering engine won't lock in position during a burn. If we have to burn those engines, that steering nozzle is going to creep out of proper alignment and we'll fall off course. That means that the only safe way to get Phoenix One back to Earth orbit isn't with one long burn, but with a number of small burns, each one corrected for the creeping of the steering nozzle on the previous burn until a correct velocity and direction can be built up.''

He paused and took a breath.

"You see what it means,'' he said. "We may need five or six burns. Expedition Control will have to figure a fresh position for Phoenix One after each burn and give a corrected figure for the next burn. And the only way that information for each new burn can reach Phoenix One is through the LCO on Phoenix Two and then from Phoenix Two by radio to Phoenix One.''

Bill sat motionless in the screen—for a longer time than the delay in transmission required. When he did speak again his voice came heavily on their ears, saying only what was in all their minds.

"Phoenix Two can't fire to an Earth reinjection orbit with only two shuttle engines.''

"That's right,'' said Tad. "You'll need one man aboard her when the Phoenix One is firing to relay information from Expedition Control. Me.''

Bill's face stared at him from the screen. Behind Tad, none of the others said anything; but there was a feeling of negation from them that he could feel like a static discharge against the short hairs remaining at the back of his head.

"You're sick,'' said Bill, after a moment. "You're not fit—even if we were considering something like that.''

"I'm fit enough,'' said Tad. "But I'm the most expendable. I got a real dose during that storm. But there's more than that. There's a gamble to it. I'm a real spacecraft pilot— the only one on board besides Fedya. I can fire those two shuttle engines into as close to an Earth-injection orbit as possible. Maybe close enough so that some support shuttles can come out and find me, in time. Nobody else but Fedya could make the most of that chance; and you'll want him in Phoenix One to see that the majority of the crew get home safe—particularly with that unreliable steering engine."

Bill still sat, staring out from the screen at them. Finally he sat forward.

"I can't agree to anything like that," he said.

"Of course you can't," said Tad. "But go back and talk it over there at Expedition Control. Then let us know. I'm not worried. There's only one way you can decide; because you've got an obligation to save as many of the Expedition crew as you can. So, talk it over and decide. Only, don't take too long. I'm in fine shape now, as I say, but I may not last forever."

He stopped speaking. Bill, however, still stayed where he was.

"Over and out," said Tad.

Bill stirred himself.

"Over and out," he echoed heavily.

On Phoenix One, the screen went blank. Tad leaned on the back of the console seat, slumping a little.

"You are a liar," said the voice of Bap, beside him. "You feel much worse then you pretend, Tad."

"Go to hell," said Tad gently, without turning to face the other man. For a moment, geared up by his talk with Bill, he had forgotten how his body felt. But now the feeling of malaise came back on him. He closed his eyes, letting the sickness run about his body and limbs. "Go to hell, all of you. It's on the ground that they'll have to decide; and as I said, they've got no choice."

"All the same," said Anoshi. "I'm going to check on that steering motor, right now; and see if it's crippled the way you say."

"Go ahead," said Tad, "you'll find it like I said. But look if you want. It won't make any difference."

The phone rang in the darkness.

For a moment Jens merely lay on his bed listening to it. He had been dreaming—about what he could not remember, some sort of semi-unpleasant dream of struggling with some duty in which other people would not cooperate—and for a moment, still wrapped in the shreds of the dream, he confused the sound of the phone with the imaginary situation he had just left.

Then he came fully awake and reached out for the instrument through the dark, fumbling for the *on* button, finally finding and punching it.

The screen sprang to colorful life and the image on it resolved it into the face of Bill Ward.

"Mr. Wylie?" Bill said, squinting on the screen. "Have I reached Mr. Wylie? I can't see any image."

"You've reached me," said Jens, thickly. He struggled up on one elbow and punched on the bedside table light.

"There you are," said Bill. "I'm sorry to call you at four A.M. like this, but something important's come up with the Expedition and I need your help."

"My help?" Still groggy from slumber, Jens turned the two words over in his mind, trying to make sense out of them; but remained baffled. "Me? What can I do?"

"I'm down in the lobby of your hotel," said Bill. "Can I come up and talk to you? The security guard here says you'll have to talk to him."

"Put him on." Jens yawned. A face he did not recognize came on the screen.

"It's all right," Jens told it. "Mr. Ward is personally known to me. You can believe whatever identification he showed you. Let him come up, would you please?"

"All right, Mr. Wylie."

The guard's face vanished. The screen went blank. Jens punched off the phone, got heavily up out of bed and put on a bathrobe. A few minutes later the doorbell of his suite chimed.

He went to the door and let in Bill Ward, thanking the security man who had brought him up.

"What can I do for you?" Jens asked, closing the door. "I can call down for coffee. Or maybe you'd rather have a drink."

"Nothing, thanks," said Bill, seating himself in an armchair as Jens sat down opposite him. Bill's thick fingers drummed on the end table by his chair. "Yes . . . a drink."

"Coffee for me," said Jens.

He turned to the phone unit on his own chairside table and

punched for room service. A slow voice—another security voice, regular room service was long since in bed itself—answered.

"This is Jens Wylie," said Jens. "Forgive me for asking you this, but I've just had an unexpected visitor on an emergency matter. There isn't any coffee available down there, is there?"

"Yes, sir," said the security voice. "I'll get some up to you right away. How many are there?"

"Just one coffee will do."

"I'll send up a cup and a pot," said the voice. "Will that be all? I could probably manage a sandwich—"

"No, thanks. Just coffee. And thanks again. Good-by."

"Good-by, sir."

Jens punched off and looked back at Bill.

"I don't understand this," he said. "You said you needed my help with something about the Expedition. . . ." A sudden fear moved in him. He pushed it from him, forcing himself up out of his chair and over to the little bar in the corner of the sitting room of the suite.

"Bourbon?" he said. "Soda?"

"Water," he heard Bill Ward say behind him. "I didn't know who to turn to besides you. I've just been talking to the 'nauts on the LCO. I had to break the news to them that we'd decided to abort the Expedition."

"Abort?" Jens hands stilled on the glass with bourbon and ice cubes into which he was about to pour water.

"Abort this attempt at it," said Bill, stiffly. "We have to get the vehicles back, get Tad off and get the damage repaired. Then, as soon as we can get another date set up, we'll be going again, naturally."

Jens forced his hands to move. He poured water into the glass and carried it to Bill Ward, sitting down opposite him. Feeling the other man's eyes, he suddenly read in them an almost abject, silent plea for understanding.

"It may not be that easy to get the Expedition going a second time," Jens said slowly. "From the political standpoint alone."

"That's . . . nonsense," said Bill. His voice firmed. "Nonsense. We've got the hardware already, there's windows available all through the next two years. Of course, people will be disappointed. So were the 'nauts. In fact, that's why I'm here. . . ."

His voice slowed and became unsure again. He swallowed part of his drink.

"I shouldn't be doing this," he said, miserably. "I should be going through channels. But Tad and the others didn't like the idea of aborting, at all—"

"Good for them," said Jens.

"No . . . not so good," said Bill, jerkily. "We've got a space program that's bigger than just this one Expedition. I don't know—I got the impression . . . well, let me tell you about my talk with them."

"You see," he said, when he was through, "it's the most far-fetched thing in the world. It may be all in my imagination. But I can't help worrying that they might do something, try something that might really damage the program . . . because they want to continue, so badly. I thought the word had to be passed to . . . to whomever might need to know. . . ."

"You mean the President."

"Yes." Bill nodded. The ice tinkled in his glass.

"What could he do?" Jens asked.

"I don't know. I can't imagine," said Bill. "But even if it's the most remote chance in the world—we've struggled all these years to keep the program alive . . . at any rate, I thought you might be able to pass the word along, quietly, just in case."

Jens nodded.

"Well, I can do that," he said.

"I mean, now," said Bill, watching him. "I mean right away."

"It's pretty late to be calling Washington."

"I know that," said Bill. "But I think—I *know*—it ought to be done."

Jens nodded, slowly weighing the need Bill had made clear against what this call might cost him. "All right."

It took Jens a few minutes to get through to Selden Rethe at his home.

"Sorry to call at this hour, Sel," he said. "But something's come up."

After he finished, there was a short pause at the other end of the line. Then Selden spoke.

"Stay there," he said. "Both you and Ward stay right where you are—you're in your hotel room, right, Jens? I'll get back to you. Don't go any place until I do. It might take two minutes or it might take ten hours—but sit tight."

He broke the connection.

"I can't stay here ten hours—" Bill said aghast.

"It won't be ten hours," said Jens. "Fanzone's in Washington and Sel can get him on the phone in three minutes if he wants. Sit back. Have another drink."

"No. Well, yes," said Bill.

Jens got up, took the other man's glass and carried it over to the bar. He had made the drink and was just about to bring it back, when his phone sounded.

He came quickly from the bar, set down the drink in front of Bill, and keyed the phone on. Selden Rethe's face filled the screen.

"He wants to talk to you both, face-to-face—and right away," Selden said. "I'll set up transportation. Go down now to the front of your hotel. By the time you get there, your motor pool should have a car ready and waiting to take you to the airport."

32

The motors of the Vertical Takeoff and Landing Craft muttered on a bass note that set Jens's ears ringing, as the plane slowly sank level, and in a straight line like an elevator, from two thousand feet to the landing pad behind the White House. Rain drummed on the window beside Jens. The sky to the east was beginning to lighten with dawn.

They touched down and the door opened. Filing out, he

and Bill were met by Selden Rethe, ducking under an umbrella held by somebody who was undoubtedly a White House security man.

"Come on!" said Selden.

He led the way at a trot to a side door of a building that might or might not have been a part of the White House structure—it was impossible to tell in the dark that was intensified by the glare of lights about the landing pad. A moment later they were indoors, walking down a narrow, but thickly carpeted corridor. They stopped after a distance before a pair of doors that opened to expose an elevator.

"Wait here, will you, Jens?" said Selden.

He got in the elevator with Bill Ward, and the doors shut on them. Jens stood fidgeting in the corridor. A few minutes later, the elevator opened and Selden stepped out alone, then put a friendly hand on Jens's arm.

"Come on," he said.

He led the way down the corridor a little farther and then at right angles through a larger hallway to a door opening on a large, comfortable-looking office-library.

"Sit down," he said, waving Jens into one of the deep armchairs. "What would you like? Something to eat."

"Coffee," said Jens; and grinned a little. "I live on coffee."

"So do I," said Selden. He punched on a phone that sat on a desk and spoke to it, then dropped into a chair opposite Jens. "Now, tell me more about this."

"I don't know any more," said Jens. "Bill Ward just told me the same thing he told you when I got you on the phone. I don't think he knows any more himself—just what the 'nauts told him over the LCO."

"What's LCO stand for again?"

"Laser Communications System," said Jens. "Kennedy and the spacecraft talk to each other over a beam of coherent light. They even get picture as well as voice over it."

"I see," said Selden. "However, I don't think you and Mr. Ward know what it's like to wake up a president. And to wake him with bad news . . ." He broke off, biting his lower lip. "The hard part is having to take everything these space people say on faith. I don't get it, myself. They've been gone over four weeks. How is it they can come home in thirteen days, or whatever?''

Jens blinked at the other.

"You don't understand that?'' he said.

Selden looked at him, frowning.

"That's what I said. What's so surprising about that?'' he answered. "Most of the world is going to be asking that same question once word of this gets out—that and other questions that make less sense.''

"But—'' began Jens, and then stopped. For a moment he had been ready to believe that Selden was not serious in what he asked. Now he realized that Selden was serious; and the realization of what that meant was a jolt. It was like a door on what you had assumed to be a small closet opening to reveal a vast and echoing darkness of unknown dimensions. That any intelligent, well-educated man today should show such an area of ignorance was bad enough. That the man who did was private secretary to the President of the United States and the man who had effectively been the means of getting Jens his undersecretaryship to the space effort—that was incredible.

"There's been diagrams in all the papers for the last six months,'' Jens said. "You must have seen them.''

"Seen diagrams?'' said Selden. "Oh, you mean about the orbits the spaceships take, and the planets and so on. Of course I saw them, Jens. But I didn't have time to study them, naturally. I think you know what Washington is like. How much time do I have to study space-flight diagrams while I hold this job?''

"But you want to know now.''

"Now I have to know!'' Selden got up quickly from his chair as a knock came at the door. He walked to it, opened it, and said a few words and closed it again. He came back with a tray holding a coffee pot, cups, spoons, cream and sugar. Dropping it on the desk, he poured the dark, steaming liquid into a couple of the cups.

"Sugar?'' he said to Jens. "Cream?''

"Black,'' said Jens. Selden handed him one of the filled cups.

"I have to know now,'' said Selden, more quietly, sitting down again facing Jens. "Because I'm going to have to start explaining it to a lot of other people—our man upstairs to begin with. So—'' he glanced at Jens ''—I ask you. If it takes them three weeks and more to get where they are, how can they get back in thirteen days?''

Jens sipped at his coffee, watching the other man over the rim. There was a curious sort of chemistry going on inside him that he had never expected could take place in someone like himself. He had, he realized with a sudden, summer-lighting flash of clarity, been put down by experts all his life—starting with his senatorial father. After that there had been a sequence of experts to look down their noses at him and treat him as someone who knew nothing. The older newspaper people on his father's paper, the statehouse legislators, the experienced hands on the news bureau in Washington when he was transferred there. Then there had been the politicians on Capitol Hill and here at the White House, and finally the deputy ministers of science like Sir Geoffrey and Verigin. Even Lin had once treated him like someone who needed the guiding hand of a more experienced and knowledgeable person; and, with a sudden stark insight, he recognized that more than half the fault had been his. With all these people, he had invited their superiority, adopting without question his own role as inferior.

He had played the inferior to Selden Rethe, in just that automatic fashion. Now, in unexpected shock he realized that it was to him as an authority that Selden was turning, for comfort, information and help; and that all along, underneath, Selden had known him to be the stronger and more expert.

With a start, Jens realized that the other man was still waiting for an answer. Jens fumbled in his inside suitcoat pocket and came out with a card case and a ballpoint pen. He made three dots on a blank card and drew circles connecting the outer two.

''Not diagrams again!'' said Selden. ''Can't you simply explain it to me in plain English?''

''All right.'' Jens put the card away. ''It's not really an accurate comparison; but suppose you and I start out from New York in cars going a hundred miles an hour. I'm headed for Los Angeles, and you want to go to Seattle. Say that I, in my car, am Earth; you and your car are the two spacecraft on the Mars

Expedition; and our speed is continuous. After a few days on the road, we're still level with each other, but spread apart. You're west of Chicago, while I'm in Des Moines, Iowa."

He paused and looked at Selden to see if the other man was following him. Selden nodded.

"At that point," Jens went on, "something goes wrong and you decide to join up with me, again, on the road to Los Angeles. You can't simply turn and drive south towards Des Moines, because I'm still traveling toward L.A. at a hundred miles an hour. I'd be gone when you got there. In the same way, Phoenix One or Two can't simply turn and fire their engines toward Earth where it is now. By the time they got here, Earth would have moved ahead, since it's continually traveling in orbit around the sun. So, you in your car would head southwest, figuring out speed and distance so that you aim at someplace ahead of where my car is now—say, Rapid City, South Dakota—planning to reach it at the same time I'm due to arrive there also."

He paused again.

"All right," said Selden. "I'm with you so far. What's the point?"

"The point," Jens said, "is that from just west of Chicago to Rapid City, South Dakota, isn't as far as the distance from New York to just west of Chicago. In other words, our two cars have been separated for maybe two days, but it'll only take a little more than half a day to get us back together again."

Selden nodded again—and while he was still nodding the phone on his desk buzzed. He got up and punched on the set. A voice said something Jens could not quite catch.

"Yes, sir," said Selden. He punched off and turned back to Jens.

"We're wanted upstairs," he said.

Jens rose and followed him out of the room. As they went, it occurred to him that possibly even Paul Fanzone—the President of the U.S., himself—might at the moment be in Selden Rethe's position of needing answers, rather than the position of giving them.

The room Jens and Selden came to two floors up was another office, a much larger and more luxuriously furnished one. Bill Ward was seated stiffly in a black overstuffed arm-chair and Fanzone was pacing up and down the carpet.

"Come in. Sit down." Fanzone pointed them to chairs as they came in. Jens and Selden took seats near Bill Ward.

"Listen, now," said Fanzone, turning to Bill Ward abruptly. "You did the right thing—when I say you, I mean all of you down there at the Cape. You were right to come to me quietly this way. It'll be better if it's not generally known that your suspicions came to me directly. Let those who want to guess as much as they want. The point is, they mustn't know certainly. I want you and Jens here to go back to Florida, immediately. Sel?"

"Sir?"

"Is there still a plane out there for them to go back in?"

"Standing by," said Selden.

"Good. Now, Bill, I want you to talk to the marsnauts again, as privately as you can. You can do that, can't you?"

"There's no way anyone can intercept laser communication," Bill said. "It's not like radio."

"Then talk to them. Don't tell them you've seen me, or talked to me. Just say you passed the matter on to your superiors in the Space Agency; and it turns out the official decision of the abort has to be delayed until the governments participating in the Mars Expedition are at least notified; and there may be some little delay because of that. But probably not more than twenty-four hours. Can you do that?"

"Yes, sir," said Bill. "Only—"

"Never mind anything else," Fanzone said. "You do it, just as I said. You, Jens!"

"Yes, sir?" said Jens.

"We're going to have to give you some more authority than you've had up until now," Fanzone said. "I want you, as soon as you get back, to do two things. One is to get the deputy ministers of science for the various other countries together with you and say that I asked you, personally, to tell them, privately, about the decision to abort. Then do it—just give them the hard information about the damage to the ships; don't hint that anything more is involved, or that there's been any special contact between you and me, except that I called you early this morning and asked you to talk to them. You can do that?"

"Yes," said Jens.

"The second thing I want you to do, after that—note, *after* you've given the complete story to the deputy ministers and they've had an hour or two to contact their governments—is hold a press conference. You can handle a press conference on your own, of course? Can't he, Sel?"

"Yes, sir. He can," Selden said.

"Again, you tell the press nothing about the White House in connection with this, except that it was suggested you were the one to break the news to the world, as our government's formal representative on the spot. You tell them what there is to tell about the marsnauts and their situation, except what you've been told not to tell. Say the decision to abort is still up in the air, but it looks likely. Sel will call you shortly after you're back down in Florida, and let you know what we don't want given to the press right now. That's all—except after both the ministers' meeting and the press conference, you call Sel on scramble circuit and give him a report of what the reactions were. Is all that understood, now?"

"Yes, Mr. President," said Jens. "No mention of what Mr. Ward—"

"No. Sel, take them back to their plane, now." The three other men rose and started to the door. "And Sel—"

"Yes, sir?" Selden stopped and turned.

"As soon as they're off, get back up here," said Fanzone. "We're going to have to throw today's schedule into the wastebasket and make up one that's altogether different."

Bill Ward sat hunched before the LCO screen, talking to Tad.

"The foreign representatives, those deputy ministers of science, got briefed this morning by Jens Wylie," Bill said. "Wylie also had a press conference for the news people to pass the word to them, after lunch. So things are moving."

"Just so they keep moving," said Tad. "You said twenty-four hours?"

"Yes. It might be quicker, though."

"It needs to be quicker," said Tad. He no longer had any hair visible on his head as Bill viewed him in the LCO screen; and his face seemed to have fallen in until he had almost a skull-like look that the bald head reinforced.

"By the way," said Bill. "How're you feeling?"

"Fine," said Tad. "I'm just fine."

Jens Wylie sat in the sitting room of his hotel suite with copies of nearly a dozen newspaper printouts in various languages spread out on the rug in front of his chair. He had done his best; but the headlines, as usual, had gone for the worst.

CATASTROPHE FRAPPE LE VOL MARTIEN read the one next to his right toe. SPACECRAFT BOTH FAIL read the next nearest one, and so on from around the world.

Maybe, he told himself, in its own way, it was a good thing, this jumping to announce tragedy. Then, if they managed to save five of the six marsnauts . . . he wished Lin was back. He needed her to talk with.

But no matter what course events took, sooner or later would come the witch-hunters, looking for someone to blame for the failure of artificially high hopes.

Masahura Tatsukichi, the Japanese deputy minister of space, sat talking to Anoshi. Each of the deputy ministers had asked to speak to the marsnaut from his own country; and although on Phoenix One and Two they were still busy transferring repair parts, short interviews had been set up. Guenther had already talked to Bern, and Ambedkar to Bap.

"Regrettable," said Masahura to Anoshi, now, "that such high hopes should end in tragedy."

"Regrettable for all," replied Anoshi.

"Of course," said Masahura, "but I have been aware of your own strong desire to accomplish the completed Expedition; and so I offer my sympathy on a personal level."

"I deeply appreciate it," said Anoshi. "Personal regrets, however, are nothing when weighed in the balance against the greater loss. . . ."

Verigin spoke to Fedya.

"All that can be done on both ships is being done, then?"

"Yes."

Verigin leaned forward to examine Fedya's image in the screen more closely; and his tone gentled.

"My boy," he said, "you look thin. Quite thin and pale. You haven't been exposed to anything like radiation yourself, have you?"

"No," said Fedya. "I am only tired. As we all are."

Tad floated half-asleep in a fog of discomfort. He was too exhausted to stay awake but physically too miserable to fall completely into slumber. Vague thoughts and half-dreams chased through his head. Most of the repairs that could be made on the two ships had been made. This was the fourth day since Bill Ward had told them of the decision to abort; and still there was no word to go ahead with it from Expedition Control. Jens, whom he had spoken to last when the deputy ministers were being allowed to speak to the marsnauts of their respective nationalities, had fumbled, trying to answer Tad's direct questions as to why there should be any delay at all.

"Each government wants to consider the decision," Jens said. "Each wants to make sure it isn't just rubber-stamping a decision it'll regret later—"

"What happened to us had nothing to do with governments!" Tad snapped. "It was an overloaded schedule and a solar storm!"

"I know," said Jens unhappily. "And I know it is hard to wait. But . . ."

But, thought Tad, drifting in his mist of discomfort, Phoenix One and Two could not wait forever. He, for one, could not wait; there was more riding on an immediate movement than Jens or anyone back on the ground realized—

He roused to recognize the figure of Bap, which had loomed up in the darkness by his bed. Bap was smiling and carrying a hypodermic syringe.

"Something new the docs down at Expedition Control just suggested to keep you perky," Bap said.

"What is it . . ." Tad started to ask; but Bap was already giving him the shot and it really did not matter. Whatever it was, it worked quickly. The needle had hardly been withdrawn from his arm before the sickness trembling all through his body and limbs began to quiet and diminish. The feeling of malaise faded; and his overwhelming tiredness claimed him.

"Working" he mumbled to Bap, who still stood by the bed. "working fine. That's good. I'll need my rest."

"Yes, you will," said Bap.

Bap continued to stand by the bed until Tad's breathing became slow and deep. Then he went back out and up the access tube to A Deck. Anoshi was there, with Fedya, Dirk and Bern.

"He's asleep," Bap said, as he came out of the access tube hatch. "It's fairly short-action, though. He shouldn't be out more than three or four hours."

"Good," said Fedya. "I'll get going, then."

Dirk and Bern helped him into his spacesuit.

"What if Expedition Control just delays in giving you the figures for our first burn?" Bap asked.

"Then you'll make the first burn on our own figures," Fedya said. "And I say that to you as an order, since I'm in command, now."

"Yes, sir," said Bap. But the smile that went with his words faded almost immediately. Bern and Dirk were fitting on Fedya's helmet now. As soon as they were done and had stepped back, Bap held out his hand.

Fedya shook it. They did not say anything. Turning slowly and clumsily about in a near circle, Fedya shook hands in turn with Anoshi, Bern and Dirk. Then he turned and left them, pulling himself into the access tube and along the tube to the airlock at the end of it leading to Hatch Three.

He emerged from Hatch Three into the unchanging lights and dark of space. The propulsion pack was already in place on his shoulders; but this time he would not have to rely on it alone to cross the void between him and Phoenix Two. He reached for a meter-long tether connected to the tool belt around the waist of his suit, and clipped the metal loop at the free end of it over the wire that now connected the two ships. Pushing off from the hull of Phoenix One, he activated the propulsion pack and slid along the line of the wire toward the other spacecraft.

At the far end, he detached his tether. He reached for the wire where it was wound around its bit, then changed his mind. With the inertia of Phoenix Two to hold it in place, the first thrust of Phoenix One's engines would snap the wire like a thread. He went down alone into Phoenix Two's A Deck and took off his suit.

He sat at his control console and sent a call on the LCO to Expedition Control.

"There's been a slight change in plans, here," Fedya said to the communications engineer on duty who answered. "We can't wait any longer to start Phoenix toward Earth; and we will start with our own figures for the first burn unless we get others from you in four hours' time."

"Just a minute!" said the communications engineer. "This is all over my head. Bill Ward's at home. Let me get him here to talk to you."

Fedya shook his head.

"There's nothing to talk about," he said. "We're not asking Expedition Control for permission to move. We're telling Expedition Control that we are moving—now. We'll be following the plan outlined by Tad in which one man stays aboard Phoenix Two to handle transmission of data to Phoenix One, while the other five travel in Phoenix One. The only change will be in the places of the pilots. Tad will pilot Phoenix One. I will stay aboard Phoenix Two."

"Wait," said the engineer. "Phoenix Two, wait. Let me talk to Tad."

"You cannot talk to Tad," said Fedya. "He's resting before the work of bringing Phoenix One in. In any case, he is no longer in command of the Expedition. Because of his illness, he has been relieved of his command; and I, as second officer, have taken over."

The engineer stared out of the screen at Fedya.

"I'll get Bill Ward," he said, finally.

"By all means," said Fedya. "Get anyone you like. But also get us the figures for the first burn in four hours or we will proceed on our own."

33

Tad woke from the deepest sleep he had had in days to find Bap shaking him.

"What is it?" he asked thickly.

"I'm sorry, Tad," said Bap, "but you'll have to get up. Fedya's taken command of the Expedition and he's staying aboard Phoenix Two, alone. You and I, and Anoshi, Dirk, and Bern are all here on Phoenix One."

Tad stared up at him blearily.

"Taken . . ." he muttered. "No, he can't."

"I'm afraid he has," said Bap. "Listen. He left this tape for you. Listen."

Bap reached out and pushed the record button at the base of the phone by Tad's bed. There was a second of silence and then the sound of Fedya's voice, speaking in the room.

"Forgive me, Tad," it said. "You did very well at hiding the way you've been feeling; but we all know you too well. It was plain that you are less strong and more sick than you wished us to think. But time is running out without the go-ahead from Expedition Control and we—both of us, you and I—have to think of the Expedition first and the chance of saving the larger part of the crews. It's true that handling Phoenix One down through a series of burns needs a man with your experience. But in a pinch, Anoshi or one of the others could at least attempt it, and probably get close enough to Earth orbit to be found by shuttles sent out to find Phoenix One. But what if you were alone on Phoenix Two and your illness got to the point where you could not transmit the necessary information from Expedition Control on to Phoenix One?"

There was a pause in the tape. Then Fedya's voice took up again.

"You see, Tad," he said. "The Expedition cannot afford to have anyone but a well man on the LCO of Phoenix Two. Forgive me, as I say—and believe me—I would not have taken this from you for any lesser reason than the good of the greatest number."

"Damn his eyes!" mumbled Tad. Then, slowly he shook his head. "No, it's true. He wouldn't have, either."

"Either—what?" asked Bap, looking down at him with strange curiosity.

"Get me upstairs. Get me to A Deck," said Tad, trying to stand up. Bap caught his arm and helped him to his feet. "I suspected something like this might happen. Has Kennedy given us the word to go and the first burn figures?"

"Yes," said Bap, helping him out of the room and through the hatch into the access tube. "Fedya told them that if we didn't have burn figures from them in four hours, we'd go on our own figures. They just sent their figures through. There's a permanent patch from the Phoenix Two LCO to its radio. We pick up everything that Expedition Control sends him by voice, as well as what Fedya says to us. . . ."

As Bap talked, he was guiding Tad up the tube and out on to A Deck. Tad dropped at last heavily into his usual seat, the acceleration couch in its chair position before the control console.

He leaned toward the console, lifted his hand toward its controls, then dropped it again, leaning back in his seat.

"Bap," he said. "I need something. You must have some kind of stimulant among those drugs of yours."

"You don't want anything like that," said Bap. "It'd give you a lift for a short while, but then you'd feel even worse."

"Get it for me," Tad said.

"Tad, listen to me—"

"Get it for me," repeated Tad. "I'm no good this way. Give me something to get my motor started turning over, and maybe I can keep it going myself."

Bap turned and went off. He came back with a yellow pill and a glass of water. Tad washed the pill down his throat and lay back, panting.

After a few minutes, his panting slowed and, with an effort, he sat up to the controls again. He punched communications.

"Fedya," he said. "Phoenix One to Phoenix Two."

"I'm right here, Tad," Fedya's voice came back immediately. "And, as I said to you on the tape, forgive me."

"Nothing," said Tad, rubbing the back of his hand across his dry lips. "You did the right thing. Bap said Expedition Control had already sent through the burn figures."

"You've got them on printout in the console."

Tad looked down and punched for course data printout. A tongue of paper darkened with figures marched slowly out of the slot into his hands. He tore it off and studied it. After a few minutes, he raised his head. He was sitting a little straighter now as the stimulant took hold; and his eyes were brighter.

"Fedya," he said, "let me talk to Expedition Control."

"We're right here, too, Phoenix One," answered Bill Ward's voice after a short pause. "Fedya has us patched in on his radio to you."

"Is this all there is to the first burn?" Tad asked. "These figures?"

"That's right," said Bill. "Fedya's got his own set, of course, for all the burn he can get at once, since he's only going to have one to get as much course change and velocity as he can before those two motors burn out. But what we thought would be best for Phoenix One would be to space out a number of small burns at first, to see if we couldn't figure out some kind of pattern to the way that steering engine of yours will creep. If we can figure out a pattern, then we can try to allow for it in the later burns at the same time as we're trying to straighten out your course."

"Good." Tad nodded.

"Let us know how it feels to you when the burn's on."

"Right," said Tad.

"Let us know when you're ready to go, then," said Bill. "We'll give you a firing time and an update of the figures to then."

"Let's get settled here, first," said Tad. He turned to look around at the other four men. "Bap and Anoshi, you'd better take your seats in couch position. Dirk, Bern—you two had better head down to B Deck and take a bed apiece, there. This isn't going to be much of a burn; but there's no point in taking chances."

Bern and Dirk disappeared into the access tube as Anoshi and Bap took their control seats, laying them back into the couch position.

"Fire!" echoed Tad, pressing the firing button. Vibration and sudden weight took them all aboard Phoenix One for the first time since she had been booted from Earth orbit.

But this was only a lesser and shorter version of the three-gravity thrust that the spacecraft had felt then. The firing was over, it seemed to Tad, almost before it had begun. But he had felt—he was positive he had felt—the direction of the change of angle of thrust as the steering motor crept off course even in that short time. He began checking his instruments eagerly, to see what they could tell him about the error the steering jet's movement would have caused.

"Phoenix Two! Phoenix Two, this is Expedition Control!" the radio speaker was saying. "Fedya, we were in communication all through that firing period, and we're in communication now, as far as we can tell. Come in, Fedya!"

"Phoenix Two," said Fedya's voice. "We're in communication."

"What happened, Phoenix Two? Didn't you fire? If you'd moved we would be out of communication now until the LCO could realign between us."

"No," said Fedya; and Tad stopped checking his instruments, abruptly to listen. "I didn't fire. There seems to be some malfunction in the controls. It doesn't look serious. I'll get down and check it. I can fire any time, of course."

"We'll give you an update on your own figures, to the next firing time of Phoenix One," said Expedition Control. "Let us know about that malfunction as soon as you establish what it is."

"Will do," said Fedya.

"Good. Phoenix One—Phoenix One—this is Expedition Control. How did the burn go with you?"

"Fine," said Tad. "There was a creep, all right. I'll let you know as soon as I get what information I have on it. When is our next firing time?"

"As soon as we pinpoint your present position," said Expedition Control, "and decide on the details of the next burn.

Estimate, twelve to sixteen hours. Without the LCO on Phoenix Two alongside you, we're going to have to hunt for you."

"Good hunting," said Tad.

He leaned back in the acceleration couch. He had meant to make some more energetic answer, perhaps some joke about little black sheep who had lost their way; but he did not have the energy.

Strapped in his couch, Bern gazed at the softly-lit cubicle around him and let his thoughts run. It was almost disloyal to the rest of them to think it, but now that they were irrevocably headed back toward Earth, he could not deny a small reeling of joy inside him.

He had wanted more than anything else to be on this Expedition and to approach Mars, even if he were for some reason prevented from setting foot on it. But at the same time he felt a very strong pull back to home, the strong pull of the *foyer*, leading him back to Joanna and the children. None of the others would have understood this, exactly as it was. The Pan-European representative, Walther Guenther, had not understood it at all in his brief talk with Bern over the LOC, along with the other national representatives speaking to their own marsnauts.

"We'll arrange to have your wife and children flown in so that they will be here when you land," he had told Bern.

"Please, don't bother," Bern had answered. "We have a picture, Joanna and I, of my coming back to our front door, opening it, and finding her and the children waiting for me there."

Guenther had not understood. He had been even a little offended that what he had proposed as a kindness should be rejected for this bizarre reason. We are both Europeans, Bern thought now, gazing at the cubicle, but he is not a real European. I am.

It is the family that counts. The family—primarily the children. Always the children. The next generation is the important one, whoever and whenever the generation may be. We who are adults have ceased to be a hope and become a reality. That does not make us less important, but it does make us less valuable.

Much as he had wanted to set foot on Mars, it had been

very much for Joanna and the children that he had wanted to do so. Now he never would. Others would. There was no doubt—and that was what people like Guenther and all the host, the multitude of individuals back on Earth who had not understood and who by mismanagement had caused this accident and return to be—did not understand. The Expedition was not halted. They only thought it was halted. The human race would go on and stand on Mars and on Venus eventually, and on all the other planets of the Solar System, and on worlds around many other suns. There was no stopping it. As we had come out of the sea, crawling amphibians, as we had taken over the land, as we had built our homes everywhere from pole to pole, so we would go on and build our homes and have our families throughout the universe, as far as the eye of the human imagination could see.

All that had been lost, from his individual point of view, was a little thing compared to that large future. He, himself, would not be one of those to go. That was a sad thought. But on its heels came a bright one. He was turned back to his own hearthfire, to his own promise of that future, that shone from the faces of his own children. He, alone and privately now, was disappointed but content.

"You understand," said Vassily Zacharin, "we must ask for a thorough examination and explanation of this."

Vassily Zacharin was the Soviet Ambassador to the United States of America. He and Verigin sat now in the office of Paul Fanzone; and Paul Fanzone himself, sitting behind his desk with Selden Rethe standing behind him, nodded agreeably.

"I do understand," said Fanzone gently. "I've had several of the representatives of the other powers involved with us in this space effort call on me today. Of course it's a great shock to us all that an Expedition that meant so much to the world should find itself frustrated in this tragic way."

"It's true, Mr. President," said Zacharin, "that we are very concerned with the failure of the Mars Expedition itself. But more important to the Soviet people is an answer to the question of why Feodor Aleksandrovich Asturnov should be the one of six marsnauts to give his life that the others may live."

"He hasn't given it yet," said Fanzone drily.

"We understand," said Zacharin, "that the chances of his bringing Phoenix Two close enough to Earth to be found and rescued are so small as to hardly be worth computing. You understand me, Mr. President, Feodor Aleksandrovich is a brave man and we do not doubt that he would not hesitate to offer to help his comrades even at the cost of his almost certain death. It is simply that we understand that your marsnaut Tadell Hansard first informed Expedition Control that he was to be the one to stay on Phoenix Two, since he was already dying from a lethal exposure to radiation—"

"Tadell Hansard isn't dead yet, either," said Fanzone. "And our doctors say no one will know whether he had a lethal dose or not until they get him back here and examine him."

"Undoubtedly," said Zacharin. "It is expected that physicians wish to be absolutely certain before making any pronouncement. But your doctors, like ours, like those of the rest of the world, can hardly avoid seeing the information of Colonel Hansard's steady deterioration as pointing to anything but one overwhelming probability. In short, few people qualified to interpret the symptoms doubt that he is a dying man. The question therefore arises in the minds of the peoples of the world—not just in the Soviet Union—why a dying man is being brought back to Earth, while a completely well man throws his life away in the dying man's place."

"I can't really answer that question any better than anyone else, including yourselves," said Fanzone. "Your marsnaut has told us that he took over command from Tad Hansard and made the change of ships between the two of them on his own authority. We have the tape of his telling Expedition Control so; and I believe you've heard it played. Presumably you understand one of your own nationals better than we do. Perhaps you can tell me why he did it."

"We have no idea, of course, Mr. President," said Zacharin, the even tenor of his voice monotonously unchanging. "We only point out that the question exists; and that since it was the marsnaut of your country that was favored at the expense of ours, we would like to be satisfied that the urgency to discover an explanation—a thoroughly impartial explanation, without partisanship toward any member of the

Expedition—burns as strongly in the minds of your people as it does in ours.''

"You can be certain of that," said Fanzone. "We would very much like to know why Colonel Asturnov deposed the established senior commander of the Expedition without authority. Also, why he took matters into his own hands, even to the point of threatening to risk the lives of other members of the Expedition on a burn from incomplete information, unless Expedition Control gave him the necessary data.''

"I'm sure, Mr. President," Zacharin said after a pause, "you do not mean to imply some sort of accusation against Colonel Asturnov?''

"Of course not," said Fanzone. "We are just, like your government, very desirous of finding out just what caused things to happen as they have. I think all of the world's people who supplied marsnauts to this Expedition have a common interest in that.''

"I agree with you," said Zacharin, inclining his head.

"Then we'll all look forward to getting the Phoenix One and Two back, so we can satisfy our interest," said Fanzone, briskly.

"Yes indeed, Mr. President. You've been most kind. If you'll excuse us, then?" Zacharin raised his eyebrows.

"Very good of you and Deputy Minister Verigin to come and see us," said Fanzone, rising behind the desk. Zacharin and Verigin were already on their feet.

"I will be informing my government immediately about your equal interest in this matter," said Zacharin.

"Thank you. Good afternoon," said Fanzone.

"Good afternoon, Mr. President.''

The two men went out. Fanzone, still standing, turned and looked at Selden Rethe.

"Now the rock-throwing starts," said Fanzone. "The public is hungry, Sel. Not just our public, but the public all over the world. The hopes they all had for the Expedition as a symbol of world cooperation were just too damn high. Someone's going to have to be hung at high noon for this, or governments all over the world are going to be shaken up. Any idea who could fill the role of scapegoat, Sel?''

"No, sir," said Selden. He looked at Fanzone curiously, and added, "Do you?"

"Yes," said Fanzone, bleakly, "the marsnauts, themselves, of course. This business of theirs of moving without authority will tie in nicely. But in any case, it'd have had to have been them. Nothing or no one else is big enough in this case to feed the wolves."

"Phoenix One, ready for your fourth burn?" asked Expedition Control.

"Ready," said Tad, coming awake in the control seat with a snap. Now, after three burns and more than six days, he had become conditioned to the sound of the voice of Expedition Control over the speaker. Since that first burn he had not needed again the stimulant he had demanded that Bap supply him. At the word that a burn was imminent, his body chemistry had leaped into high gear, repressing for the moment not only the vomiting and diarrhea, but the feelings of nausea and spasm, and the half-unreal sensation of waking dreams that made him doubt at times that he was actually seated at the control console on the Phoenix One. There had been other moments recently, when he could have sworn he was back at home, doing some painting on the house, or at the beach with Wendy and the children. He had told Bap about them, and Bap had blamed them on the drugs; but privately Tad had wondered if they were not a product of something deeper and more true at work within him in this final hour.

"Phoenix Two, how about you?" Expedition Control was demanding. "Are you ready to fire this time?"

"I am afraid not," Fedya's voice said. Six days plus had separated the two spacecraft enough now so a little static washed out his words, now and then. "I haven't been able to track down the trouble, yet; but I should find it soon. I'm not going away, Expedition Control. I'll have my chance to fire later."

"Better sooner than later, Phoenix Two," said Expedition Control. "See if you can't find it before the next burn time. Phoenix One, have you got your figures for the burns?"

"I'll read them back to you," said Tad. Since the first burn, when Phoenix One had still been in wired connection with Phoenix Two, a printout of the burn figures had been impossible. The only way they could be transmitted to Tad was for Expedition Control to read them to him over the radio patch from Phoenix Two; and the only check on the accuracy of their transmission was to have Tad read them back.

He began to read.

34

Lin had gone up to New York and was not back yet. Jens took time out from the business of following the situation aboard Phoenix One and Two to get together with Barney about three o'clock in the afternoon. They sat together in a booth down near one end of the bar that was almost empty. There was only one other drinker there, except for the female bartender and a tallish, thirty year old man with black hair, and a heavy, dark look to his clothes, as if he came from a more northern territory. He sat on a stool down at the same end of the bar as the booth in which Barney and Jens were seated. The bartender brought their drinks around to them.

"Ah, thank you, nurse," cooed Barney as she came up. "Just what we needed."

She gave him a brief smile, took the two glasses from her tray and set them down on the table of the booth. Then she turned and went back toward the bar.

"Wait," said Jens, suddenly, looking after her, "you made a mistake—"

He broke off at the touch of Barney's hand on his arm. He looked over and saw the other shaking his head.

"Let it go," Barney said. "If you don't want it, just sit a bit and then I'll go up to the bar and order what you want and bring it back myself."

"But she—"

"She's not feeling too good," Barney said. "That guy

who got knifed to death here week before last was somebody she knew.''

"Oh."

Jens looked after her. She was just then going around the end of the bar. As she went down behind it past the man sitting on the stool, he said something to her in a tone too low to be heard. She shook her head without looking at him and went on up the bar to its farthest end and began to work there. The man stared after her.

"Asshole!" said Barney, under his breath, staring at the man. "Excuse me a minute, Jens."

He got up and crossed the dozen feet that separated their booth from the man on the stool. Barney threw a hip on an adjoining stool and stared at the other, who turned to face him.

"Hi, there," Jens heard Barney say cheerfully, "I've seen you around here quite a bit."

"Oh? Yes, I've seen you around here too." The man's eyes for a second showed an unusual amount of white, almost flashing in the gloom of the bar.

"Sure," said Barney. "Isn't it about time you gave the wife and kids a ring?"

The white in the other's eyes showed again.

"What?"

"I said," Barney said, speaking softly still, but raising his voice slightly—although not enough to do more than carry to the far end of the bar, where the bartender now stood—"isn't it about time you called the wife and kids?"

He smiled into the man's face again.

"I don't have any kids," the other said.

"Then it's about time you called your wife, isn't it? Sitting around there with no kids, she'll be lonely. She'll be worrying about you. Isn't it about time you called her?"

The man stared at Barney for a long moment.

"What are you really," he said, almost whispering, so that Jens barely caught the words, "some sort of private detective?"

"Phones are out in the lobby," said Barney.

The man got off his stool, leaving his drink where it was. He went hastily across the bar lounge and out through the glass door into the lobby. Barney came back and sat down once more opposite Jens. The lines in his face were deeper and his face seemed to have squared.

"That bastard's been bothering her a couple of weeks now, ever since before the launch," Barney said. "You'd think he'd have sense enough to lay off."

"How'd you know he had a wife?" Jens asked.

"I can spot those bastards a mile off," said Barney.

Jens picked up the martini that had been brought him instead of the scotch and soda he had asked for. He sipped at it, giving Barney a little space of time to cool down; and found it tasted better than he expected. He did not ordinarily care for martinis; but he had found that drinking what the people with him liked could make unattractive drinks less so.

"Wouldn't she be better off at home?" Jens asked, finally.

"She feels better being busy. You know how it is," said Barney.

"You say somebody she knew got knifed?" Jens asked.

"Sure. Didn't you hear about it? Ten days or so ago."

"With all this business about Tad I haven't had time to look at the papers, lately."

"Some salesman between jobs. They found him in a sort of alley behind an apartment building. No telling how he got there. And Aletha, up there, doesn't seem to want to talk about it—just as well, probably. Anyway, he'd been knifed and rolled. Probably some kid. It was one of the Space Center souvenir paperknives. They found it still stuck in him. Somebody had hacked at it with a file a few times to put some sort of point on it—that's why they think it was a kid that killed him. Sheer luck anything only four inches long, even with a sharp point, killing a man dead like that, in one stab. The kid's probably still running."

Barney's gaze went past Jens to the far end of the bar where Aletha still worked, her head down.

"Forget it," he said, gently. "It's just part of the damn hell of life, anyway. They were going together, I think; but God alone knows what he was to her. Never mind." He looked back at Jens. "Good to have a chance to sit down with you once again, old buddy."

"Yes," said Jens, sipping again at the martini. "It's good. I meant to break loose and talk to you before this; but what with the accident on Phoenix One, there just hasn't been any time.''

''Come on, now,'' said Barney. ''You just had better company than me. Admit it.''

Jens laughed.

''You mean Lin,'' he said.

''Who else? She's a good lady.''

''You're right, Barney.'' Jens sobered. ''Very right. I admit it. She's better company than you. She's better company than anybody.''

Barney looked at him with crinkled brows.

''You had to get serious some day,'' Barney said.

Jens looked down at his drink.

''I suppose so,'' he said slowly. ''It's the craziest thing, Barney. I met her about four years ago when I first went to Washington to work for the news agency. I ran into her at one of those parties the Swedish Embassy used to give. And the minute I met her I liked her; but you know then I just couldn't see anything permanent ever in it for the two of us. She had too high-powered an engine. And you know me— everybody says I was born with stars in my eyes and I'll never get them out. It's true. If it wasn't the space program, there'd be something else that I was geared on.''

''So you ought to quit and become a free-lance writer,'' Barney said. ''I told you that before. Particularly after you get out of this political job you're in now. What you ought to write is good non-fiction books. We've got lots of non-fiction, but most of it's crap.''

''Funny. Lin said the same thing.''

''Of course. Because it's what you ought to be doing. You've got a newspaperman's nose; and you're interested in more than the immediate story.'' Barney stared at him over his martini. ''Marry this Lin and settle down. Hell, let her keep her job and support you while you're getting started. Then she can quit and you keep her in luxury for the rest of her life.''

Jens laughed.

''I couldn't do that.''

''How do you know?'' Barney said. ''Ever tried?''

''I mean, I couldn't ask Lin to support me while I was getting going. Anyway, she wouldn't.''

"How do you know?" Barney said. "Ever ask her?"

Jens laughed again, but a little uncertainly this time. He lifted his glass to his lips, and to his surprise found it empty.

"Here, give it to me," said Barney, standing up. "I'll go up to the bar and get them. What was it you wanted—Scotch and soda?"

"Please," said Jens. "The martini didn't taste all that bad; but if I drink those all afternoon I'm going to be knocked out by dinner time. I'm not like you."

"Damn few are." Barney took the empty glasses off to the bar.

He came back with a full martini glass, and a Scotch highball which he put before Jens, as he sat down.

"That character at the bar never came back." Jens nodded at the empty stool and the unfinished drink abandoned before it.

"Want to bet he doesn't, either?" said Barney. "He thought I was some sort of detective. He's called home by this time and his wife won't be used to his doing that. She'll be curious why he called; and that'll make him nervous and guilty. He won't be back—today anyway. But how about it, you going to let this Lin support you and make you both happy?"

"You know I can't do that, Barney," Jens smiled. "But I'd like to work out something. As I said, when I first met her I didn't think the two of us could ever stand a steady diet of each other. But you know, just during the launch things have changed. I don't know what happened. But now we seem to be thinking on the same track nearly all the time. It's weird."

"Nothing weird about it," said Barney. "People either grow together or grow apart when they're rubbed up against each other long enough. Maybe I ought to say people grow like each other or else find out how they're different, if they're boxed up together long enough. That's what happened to me when I was married. Wilma and I found out how different we were from each other. But I've seen other people find out how much alike they were. Sounds like it's that way with you and Lin."

"I'd like to think so," said Jens slowly. "I guess . . . I do think so. She went up to New York four days ago and she'd due back any time now. In fact, I thought she'd be in early today—she's taken a room here again. You know, it's not easy for me to judge, Barney. Everything's been happening all at once, lately. If the Phoenix One and Two ever get safely back, repaired and headed back out to Mars, properly, then maybe I can sit down and get my head straight about where Lin and I stand.''

"Don't wait for that," said Barney. "That's going to be never."

"Hey," Jens said, "but that's just this attempt at the Expedition that's being aborted. They'll be trying again in about six months, as soon as they can choose a new window for the launch."

"Come on now," said Barney. "You know better than that. And what about the inquiry? You heard the announcement about it on the noon news yesterday."

Jens frowned.

"No. No, I hadn't," he said. "What inquiry? And what's it got to do with a new window for the Expedition in six months?"

"Wake the hell up," said Barney. "I never saw it to fail. Take the best newsman in the world, put him in the spotlight and all of a sudden he doesn't hear and he doesn't think. What do you think the point of an inquiry is—an inquiry into what happened to the spaceships as a result of the solar storm?"

"Oh, that kind of inquiry."

"Not *that* kind of inquiry, at all," Barney said. "They aren't interested in the nuts-and-bolts answers. The point is to cool down public opinion on another try at the Expedition."

"How do you get that?" Jens stared at Barney.

"Open your eyes and ears. It stands to reason—and even if it didn't, six different governments can't keep a secret. The word is in the air clear around the world. The inquiry is to lay the blame for things breaking down on the 'nauts. To take some of the glitter off them—and so some of the glitter off another try."

Jens's lips felt stiff and cold.

"Barney," he said, "you're crazy!"

"Crazy, hell! If you weren't all wrapped ten inches deep in your diplomatic blanket, you'd have seen it yourself by this time. It was a nice game, but the international politicians have lost interest. They want to cash in their chips and go to something else."

"Barney—Barney, I tell you, you're crazy," Jens said. "I'm right in the middle of it with the other national reps. The minute they heard about Tad's accident, their reaction was that the Expedition should go on no matter what was going to happen to Tad. They didn't even want to consider sending him back to Earth on one of the ships."

"That may be the way they felt then," said Barney. "I'm just telling you what the news is. From where I sit, a change of your representatives' attitudes from what you say to what the present rumor says isn't surprising. This isn't the politician's kind of game, this Expedition. You ought to know that, Jens."

"I don't follow you."

"Why, I mean something like this Mars Expedition belongs to people like you, Jens," Barney said, "the nutty ones with stars in their eyes—all the damn idealists and the wonderful-tomorrows people. It doesn't really have much to do with people like Verigin and Guenther and the rest of them, to say nothing of everyone back home in their governments. Those kind of people can get attracted to something like a Mars Expedition for a little while, because it's like something pretty to eat that they think they're going to like. But after they bite into it they find out it's not their dish at all. Their kind of diet is whatever can be turned to their advantage at the moment—and that means turned one way today and another way tomorrow. Being one-way idealistic for months on end is too much of a strain for the political crowd."

"I don't believe it," Jens said. "Barney, I tell you I don't believe it."

Barney shrugged.

"Go make a phone call. Check."

"I will. I'll find out," said Jens. He pushed his drink away from him. "Stay here. I'll phone Sir Geoffrey. If there's anything like that really going on, he'll tell me."

"Good luck," Barney said.

In the lobby, Jens found a house phone, punched it on and put in a call to Sir Geoffrey's suite. There was a second's delay, then the screen lit up with a face—but not Sir Geoffrey's. It was the face of the officer of the day on their security floors.

"Yes?" the O.D. said. "Oh, Mr. Wylie. What can I do for you, sir?"

"I was calling Sir Geoffrey Mayence," Jens said. "But there wasn't any answer. Do you have another number where I can reach him?"

"Just a second, Mr. Wylie."

The O.D. disappeared from the screen momentarily, then returned. "Sir Geoffrey can be reached at 41-832-5909."

"Thanks," said Jens. He reached into his suitcoat pocket for his electropencil, to make a note of the number on the notepad screen below the phone.

"I can put you through to an outside line, sir," said the officer. "Would you like me to get Sir Geoffrey for you, Mr. Wylie?"

"Oh—yes. Thanks," said Jens. "I'd appreciate that."

The screen before him cleared. He waited. Half a minute later it abruptly lit up again with the face of a smiling young man wearing an open-necked white shirt.

"Sir?" said the young man. He had a strong Castilian accent. "Sir Geoffrey for you on the line in just a minute."

"Thanks," said Jens.

There was another short wait and the craggy features of Sir Geoffrey appeared on the screen.

"That you, Wylie?" said Sir Geoffrey. "What is it?"

"Hello," Jens said. Abruptly, he felt awkward. "I had a question to ask but maybe I shouldn't be asking it on the phone. When could I talk to you?"

"I'm going to be out here all day—" Sir Geoffrey broke off and stared off to one side out of the screen. "What, Clo?"

He looked back into the screen and at Jens. "Why don't you come out here?" he said. "I'm spending the day visiting the Duchess Stensla. She just invited you. Come along, and we can talk here, private as you wish."

"Well, thanks," said Jens. "That's good of her—and you. When should I come?"

"Come along right away, why don't you? It's only a twenty-minute drive, down toward the end of the island. You turn left as you leave the Holiday Inn there and—oh, hell! Just ask the officer of the day to have somebody at the motor pool give you directions, or give you a driver. It's the old Kelly mansion, tell them."

"All right. I will," said Jens. "I'll come right out."

"See you shortly," said Sir Geoffrey. "Good-by."

The officer of the day made arrangements to provide a car and a driver for Jens. The driver had the directions from the driver and the car that had taken Sir Geoffrey out to the Duchess's place earlier. It was, as Sir Geoffrey had predicted, a twenty-minute drive along a winding asphalt road turning finally through a heavy gate and a little patch of orange grove. A different white-shirted servant from the one he had talked to on the phone met him at the door, and took him inside to a small but comfortable sitting room on the second floor where he found both Sir Geoffrey and the Duchess.

"Oh, there you are," said Sir Geoffrey, getting up as Jens was ushered in. "Clothilde, this is the U.S. Undersecretary for the Development of Space, Mr. Jens Wylie. Wylie, this is the Duchess Stensla."

"Geoffrey calls me Clothilde, and you should too," said the Duchess, deeply, giving Jens a firm hand in greeting. "Can we give you something to drink, Mr. Wylie?"

"Oh, I guess not," Jens said.

"Come now," Sir Geoffrey said. "You need something. Clo, make him take something."

"Well," said Jens, "perhaps a scotch and soda."

"I'll have one, too," said Sir Geoffrey. "Maybe they could send up a bottle, a siphon and some ice, Clo?"

"I'll see it's sent along," the Duchess said, moving toward the door. "And I'll leave you two to talk."

"Please," said Jens. "Don't let me interrupt—"

"I have things to do," the Duchess said. "You and I can talk later, perhaps, Jens."

She went out.

"Well!" said Sir Geoffrey, dropping into an armchair. "Sit down, sit down. What's this you want to talk to me about?"

"I just heard from a cable TV newsman, a friend of mine," Jens said. "He was telling me that there's going to be an inquiry into things that went wrong aboard Phoenix One and Two."

"Yes. Announced it yesterday, I think," said Sir Geoffrey.

"I missed it," Jens said, slowly. "At any rate, what he was telling me was that there was a rumor that the aim of the inquiry was to put the blame on the 'nauts for the accidents and the abort of the Expedition."

Sir Geoffrey's thick gray eyebrows drew together in a frown.

"I just wondered if you knew anything about that," said Jens.

"Know?" barked Sir Geoffrey. "Know? Do you suppose anything like that gets written down like an Order of the Day, and sent off to everyone concerned?"

"I mean," said Jens, "is it true? Is that the real purpose behind the inquiry?"

"Look here, Wylie, damn it!" said Sir Geoffrey. "Something like this Expedition doesn't just happen in a vacuum, you know. There's a lot of other things right here on Earth that tie into it, in the case of every country involved. The wind blew one way for quite a while. Now it's blowing the other way, that's all."

"Then it's true."

"True? Who's to say what's true? We don't deal in truth, you and I. We deal in what seems to be going down at the moment. It was one thing yesterday, today it's something else entirely."

"How do you feel about it?" Jens persisted.

"I? I'm not to have opinions of my own," said Sir Geoffrey. "None of us are. You aren't, if it comes to that."

"I don't agree," said Jens. He felt strangely bleak inside. "I've got a right to my own opinion."

Sir Geoffrey grunted. At that moment, the door opened and one of the white-shirted servants came in with a tray holding a bottle of White Horse, two large bottles of soda water and a pair of tall tumblers.

"Here, sir?" the servant asked Sir Geoffrey, hovering over a coffee table nearby.

"Yes, yes. Thanks," Sir Geoffrey said.

The servant put the tray down, picked up the bottle and began to open it.

"You can leave that," said Sir Geoffrey. "We'll serve ourselves."

"Yes, sir." The servant went out.

As the man disappeared, Sir Geoffrey got up, opened the bottle, and poured the two glasses each a third full of the liquor. Then he hesitated.

"Damn!" he said. "I don't take ice in whisky and they've forgotten to bring you any."

"That's all right," said Jens, looking uneasily at the level of liquor in both glasses. "It doesn't matter, and I like a lot of soda anyway."

"Oh. Very well." Sir Geoffrey splashed a small amount of soda into his own glass. "Perhaps you'd like to fix your own, then."

Jens filled his glass with soda.

"Those men," he said, "tried to do the impossible under conditions that were deliberately made impossible. Now, to crucify them when they fail . . ."

His throat hurt.

"I just can't believe it," he said. "For that matter I can't believe the governments involved making such a shift in attitude."

"That's because you're such a bloody amateur," grumbled Sir Geoffrey, stretching out his long legs. "I think I said something to you about that. Damn it—you, I, everybody else like us, are each out on the end of a string. We dance the way they tell us, and if that means doing a right-about-face twice a day, then we do a right-about-face twice a day."

"I'm not talking about us," Jens said. "It's doing a right-about-face on the very thing that's most necessary to the world that's got me. What's wrong with Russia and Pan-Europe and the rest that they can't see what they're throwing out the window by killing the chances of this Expedition ever coming off?"

"How about your own government?" barked Sir Geoffrey over the rim of his glass. "It's not only that they're as ready as the rest to turn it round. They were the ones who moved first to set this inquiry going."

Jens stared at him.

"What did you say?"

"I said," Sir Geoffrey repeated, "that it was your government that moved first to set up this inquiry. If you're after who threw the first stone at your 'nauts, that's who it was."

"They wouldn't do anything like that!"

"Of course they did! That's to say," Sir Geoffrey said testily, "they haven't done it *yet*. It's what they're *going* to do. There's got to be some explanation, somebody to carry the can when a big show like this goes down in flames. Oh, I don't mean courts-martial or any nonsense like that. It's just that the inquiry will turn up the fact that the 'nauts were the immediate cause of things going wrong. Not that anything will be done to them. It'll be made perfectly clear they were under an unusual strain, dead tired, and all that. But the end result will be that they'll be shown to be just human after all—not quite the supermen they've been thought of as, up 'til now. And at the same time there'll be talk of how much the whole business cost, and the loss and expense and so forth."

"But that's just the sort of thing to put going into space seriously back fifty years!" Jens said.

"Well, there it is," said Sir Geoffrey. "What's that old saying about you can't make an omelet without breaking eggs?"

"But they can't get away with that," said Jens. He took a large swallow unthinkingly from his glass, choked on the strong mixture, then managed to swallow it without coughing. "The record will show that whatever happened to the marsnauts happened because they were worn out from trying to keep up with too heavy a load of experiments. And the fact that the load of experiments was too heavy was the fault of the governments that sent them out there."

"Ah, yes," said Sir Geoffrey, "But who's going to be pointing at that particular part of the record? Oh, if somebody stood up in public and accused the marsnauts of not doing their job properly, people might go back and look at the evidence. But it won't be anything like that. Also . . ."

Sir Geoffrey paused and cocked an eye at Jens.

"Also," he said, "the process isn't going to be as cruel as you think. It'll be just a small hint here and there, so that the people who were disappointed not seeing man land on Mars will believe the reasons for it not happening tie up to the marsnauts, even while they go right on feeling sorry for the 'nauts as individuals."

"Then somebody ought to tell them," Jens said savagely. "Somebody ought to tell them, even if I have to do it myself."

"You? Don't be a fool," said Sir Geoffrey. "They'd throw you in jail in two seconds."

Jens sat in silent bitterness.

"Drink your drink," Sir Geoffrey told him. "I said you were an amateur. This proves it. It's not your fault, of course, but people like you shouldn't be allowed within five miles of anything governmental. Governments are pieces of machinery, Wylie. It's no use expecting them to be kind, or considerate, or even to make much sense in the ordinary way of things. But we've got to have them. Without them everybody'd go their own damn way and then where would we be? Since we've got to have them, we've got to learn to put up with them. That's what you've got to do."

"Maybe," said Jens.

"Now, there you go," said Sir Geoffrey. "Next thing you'll be telling me that you're going to start a bloody revolution. Do that, and set everything right. Well, it wouldn't, even if you did. And you won't. You've got too much sense."

"Something," said Jens, "has to be done to save the space effort. It nearly went down the drain for twenty years. Then the governments woke up to the fact that there was energy and power and wealth to be had by going into space and the whole thing changed. For the first time in a while, we had a chance; and out of that came this Mars Expedition—the necessary next step, even if it didn't promise immediate power or energy or wealth. And now it's all to go down the drain simply because some governments don't want to be embarrassed; and so they're willing to make scapegoats out of the best people they had to send out there."

Jens stared at Sir Geoffrey. There was a pause. Beneath the thick, fierce thicket of the gray eyebrows in the large, bony face, he thought he saw something in Sir Geoffrey's eyes that almost startled him—a fugitive glitter, the kind of eager excitement that might have come into the eyes of Don Quixote de la Mancha on seeing the windmill, or Alexander of Macedon on looking eastward into Persia. Then it was gone again. The old man was as frosty as ever.

"Now you have it," he said, drily, "and high time, too!"

35

As Jens drove away from the old Kelly estate, Lin had just been picked up at the Orlando airport by Penny Welles.

"It's good of you to come," Lin said. "I could have gotten a cab, or—"

"No, I'm glad to. And anyway," said Penny, "it gives me something to do. It's quite tense, waiting."

As Penny pulled the car smoothly out on to the highway and found her lane, then put the vehicle on autopilot, Lin felt the other woman's eyes on her.

"Some trouble up in New York?" Penny asked.

"No," said Lin. "No."

She looked ahead out through the windshield, and shook her head.

"I really didn't need to go," she said. "I just wanted to get off by myself for a day or two."

Penny said nothing; and Lin was grateful for the silence. One of the good things about Penny was her patience and her refusal to intrude. They slid down the highway without speaking for several minutes, and the quiet was soothing. Lin felt the turmoil inside her subsiding.

"You know," Lin said, still watching the road ahead, "I never was one for making friends. I never felt I was in love with anyone until Jens."

"Me, too," said Penny. "Well, I mean, I wasn't the sort to make friends at school; and I never thought I'd ever have anything to do with a man, until Dirk appeared. I didn't see how I could."

"But now it's different?" said Lin.

Penny laughed.

"It's absolutely the other way around with everything,"

she said. "But you wouldn't have liked me in school. I was the kind who sat in a corner and everybody thought was too nose-in-the-air to make friends, when the truth was, I didn't know how."

"You wouldn't have liked *me,*" said Lin. "I didn't have any friends either. I was too busy pushing everybody else around."

"Well, then," Penny said. "We've both changed."

"Yes—" said Lin, and caught her breath.

They drove a little farther in silence.

"Would you like me to ask?" Penny said, finally.

"Oh, it's all turned around!" Lin burst out. She was still staring at the roadway and the loudness of her own voice in the small space of the car interior shocked her. "Everything I'd got all figured out goes the other way. I understood Jens completely. He was completely impractical. All the things he got wound up with weren't real, or important. I was the one who was tied into real things. I was the one who had my head on straight and knew what had meaning and what didn't!"

She stopped.

"And now?" said Penny, after a second.

"And now, it's the other way around!" Lin said. She was suddenly conscious she had her hands locked together in her lap, and made herself relax them. "All of a sudden, it's just the opposite. The things I thought were important aren't important at all. But the nonsense things Jens was so woolly-headed about—it turns out *they're* important, they're the real things!"

She turned to stare at Penny.

"That's why I had to get away! Everything's gone—*shift*—under my feet. Black's white. White's black. Could I be that wrong? Was I that far off all my life?"

"I don't know," said Penny, thoughtfully, staring ahead out the windshield herself, now. "No, I don't think you were. I know I wasn't. It was just that, after Dirk, the world got wider, sort of; and because it was wider, the values of everything had to be shifted around and something that was—expensive, say—wasn't what you'd call expensive any more;

and something that I hadn't thought was valuable became precious, and . . . well, like that. . . . ''

"But now I think he's right," said Lin. "I *know* he's right. All these stars, all these dragons he believes in—they *are* the real things. And job, and income, and success and security and making your mark in the world are still there—but they don't count the way the principles and the dreams do. How can you live like that, Penny? If they're the important things, and they're made out of moonbeams and thin air, then where can you anchor yourself? How can you put down a foundation and build four solid walls and a roof to keep out the weather when you're floating among the clouds? Penny?''

"I don't know," said Penny. "The way you put it, I can't answer you. But you do, you know. And, too, it's beside the point, your worrying about it, because you wouldn't be here now if you weren't already hooked. You'd have cut out and left a long time ago—left Jens, I mean.''

"Yes," said Lin under her breath. Ahead of them the double lane of roadway ran perfectly straight and level and without a turnoff until it was lost to sight.

"So," said Penny. "What you're really telling me is that you've made up your mind.''

Slowly, still staring at the eternal road before her, Lin found herself nodding.

Back at the hotel, Jens detoured on his way across the lobby to look once more into the lounge. There was an emptiness inside him; and he had been hoping that Barney was still there, and that he could talk to him. He needed to talk to somebody. But Barney was gone. There were four or five people in there he did not recognize and the bartender was busy. He closed the glass door. He had left the key to his suite at the desk. He went back and asked for it.

"Here you are, sir," said the room clerk. He turned to the pigeonhole behind him, took a slip of paper and turned back to pass it across to Jens. "This message was just left for you.''

Jens took the piece of paper. It was a standard hotel message form and on it were written the words: *I just got in. I'm in Room 219. Lin.*

Jens shoved his own key absently into his pocket, and still holding the note went to the elevators. He rode up to the second floor, discovered a sign on the wall that told him room 219 was among the rooms to his right and went down to the corridor to them.

He knocked and the door was opened almost immediately by Lin. He reached for her.

"What is it?" she asked, after she had kissed him, pushing herself back to full arm's-length to look up into his face. "You look like an elephant stepped on your toe."

"They're going to hold an inquiry," Jens said. "And blame the 'nauts for the fact it didn't go."

She was looking very steadily at him.

"Come on in," she said, pulling him through the door and shutting it behind him. "Sit down and tell me about it."

She led him across the room to one of the two armchairs, pushed him into that and sat down in the one opposite.

"When did you hear all this?" she said. "What happened?"

He told her all he had heard, from the rumor Barney had mentioned to Sir Geoffrey's caution not to start any revolutions.

"You aren't, are you?" she asked, when he was done.

"I don't know," he said wearily. "I've got to do something."

"Like talk to the President?"

He laughed, shaking his head.

"They're not interested in listening to my opinion," he said. "I had that made clear to me not only from the start, but half a dozen times since."

"Well then, Sir Geoffrey's right," she said. "You might as well relax and face the fact that you're . . ."

"I've got to do something about it, I tell you!"

The anger in his voice jarred him.

"If you can't, you can't, Jens."

He hardly heard her. His mind was chewing at the problem as reflexively as a rat gnawing its way out of a cage.

"I need to tell everybody to look at the record," he said. "If they'll look at what was done with the experimental load, there's no way the 'nauts can be blamed."

He chuckled a little grimly.

"Maybe I should take a full-page ad in the newspaper," he said.

"Jens," said Lin in a level voice, "just exactly what could they do to you if you made any kind of public announcement about this?"

He glanced at her.

"That was Sir Geoffrey's point," he said. "Only I think what he was saying was, what wouldn't they do to me?"

"I'm asking seriously," Lin said.

"Well, I took a loyalty oath and signed my life away to get this job," said Jens. "I'm liable to fine and imprisonment, if I violate it. Quite a lot of imprisonment—if I do anything that can be considered treasonable, or if I go against the orders of my superior, who in this case happens to be the President of the United States, and it's his orders I'd be going against."

"You were given an order not to speak up about something like this?"

"I wasn't given authority *to* speak up," Jens said. "Anything not authorized is forbidden. Lin—what's the difference? I'm not concerned about what they can do to me. I'm concerned about what I ought to do."

"You ought to figure first if it's going to do any good," Lin said. "If it's not to do any good, then getting yourself thrown in jail for years is hardly worthwhile, is it?"

"Oh, it's worthwhile all right," Jens said. "Just the chance that it might do some good makes it worthwhile."

He stopped talking and sat for a moment without saying anything. Then he looked at her again.

"I don't know why I'm dodging all around the point this way," he said. "I know what I've got to do. I knew it from the minute I told Sir Geoffrey that I ought to do something. I'll hold a press conference and simply tell the newspeople what the truth is. After that, there's no way they can sit on the information."

He realized suddenly, looking at her really now for the first time since she had let him in, how pale her face had become.

* * *

"Well, Phoenix One," said Expedition Control, "I think we may have some good news for you."

Tad woke with a start, came back from some strange, delirious dream, the details of which evaporated even as he tried to remember them.

"What—" he started to say; but the word was only a dry husk of sound. He tried to clear his throat, but it would not clear. A hand offered him a cup of water and he took it gratefully. He saw that it was Anoshi standing over him; there was always one of the others with him when he was at the control console.

The water moistened his throat, and he could speak aloud.

"What day is this?" he asked Anoshi. "How many burns so far?"

"Tenth day. Seventh burn coming up."

"Did you hear me, Phoenix One?" Expedition Control said. Relayed from the now-distant Phoenix Two, the radio was thin and scratchy with static. "I was saying we may have some good news for you, after all."

"I hear you," said Tad to the mike grid. "What is it?"

"Well, for one thing, you must be getting close. We're starting to pick up that radio signal of yours. We can't understand you on radio, yet, but we're beginning to bring you in. We'll be talking directly to you, soon as we can get a real directional fix on you." Expedition Control paused. "That's one thing. The other thing is, we think we've got the pattern of that creep in your steering motor figured out; so we can correct for it in the next burn. If we're right, it won't take more than one—maybe two—more burns to bring you home."

Tad nodded. It did not occur to him to answer, until Anoshi leaned forward to the mike grid.

"That's wonderful, Expedition Control," said Anoshi, "you're wonderful."

"Thank you, Phoenix One. The compliment is returned— is this someone else speaking?"

"This is Anoshi. Tad just had a frog in his throat for a minute."

"I'm all right now, Expedition Control," said Tad. "You've got some burn figures for us, then?"

"That's right," said Expedition Control. "Got them for

Phoenix Two, as well. You're going to go this time, aren't you, Phoenix Two?''

There was a perceptible pause before radio waves brought Fedya's answer to the speaker of the console on Phoenix One, and Fedya's voice, like Expedition Control's, was now dimmed by distance and static.

"Is this my last chance, Expedition Control?"

"Either your last or your next-to-last, Phoenix Two."

"Do not worry, then," said Fedya. "This time I'll fire."

"All right, then, Phoenix One and Two. Here's your data."

Jens, Lin, Barney, and Sir Geoffrey sat in Lin's room at the Holiday Inn.

"You're crazy, Jens," Barney was saying. "You're crazy even to have thought of this. You tell him, Sir Geoffrey."

"Absolutely crazy," said Sir Geoffrey. "Insane."

"Give up," said Jens. "You aren't going to talk me out of it. Anyway, that's not why I got in touch with the two of you. I told you, Barney, I wanted you to spread the word I'd be holding a press conference in the Tudor Room, downstairs at three P.M.—"

"And I did," said Barney. "I did everything but announce it on the air, and that's what you didn't want."

"—but I also wanted at least one news representative at the conference I could count on to report what I say the way I mean it. Just as I wanted you—" Jens turned to Sir Geoffrey "—there to get it straight for the diplomatic area."

"No harm in my doing that, of course," said Sir Geoffrey. But there was an almost wistful note in his voice; and for a second Jens thought he saw again the gleam of excitement that had seemed visible momentarily in Sir Geoffrey's eyes out at the Kelly estate. "If I was a younger man—but of course, I'm not. I'm not."

"Then we're all set," said Jens. "I want as many news people there as possible. But I can't risk being stopped—and one official phone call to Gervais or the Air Force people here could shut me down before I start."

"You'll make it," Barney said. "The wheels of official-dom grind slow, even when they know what's going on, and

I'm willing to bet no one that matters has heard anything about this, yet. You know as well as I do what happens when you're media and you hear something. You may tell a close friend or two in the business, but you don't start publishing until you've got the story."

"We hope," said Lin.

"Anyway," said Jens, glancing at her briefly, and then back to Barney, "now I'm going to need a lawyer."

"You want Paula Anisha, that's who you want," said Barney. "You have your dues still paid up in the Guild?"

"Of course," Jens said.

"Then hold this thing off until I can get Paula Anisha, or one of her legal team down here. I'll bet one of them could be down here in four hours. You're going to need all the protection you can get and the Newsworkers Guild—"

"—has muscle, but not as much as the U.S. government," said Jens. "No thanks, Barney. I don't dare wait. You must know some local lawyer."

"All right," said Barney.

He moved over to the phone and began punching out a number.

"This is Barney Winstrom," he said to the smiling woman who answered. "Is Tom around?"

Jens, Lin, Sir Geoffrey, and Tom Haley the lawyer Barney had contacted—a tall, powerful, cheerful man with white hair cut to a one-inch stubble—came into the Tudor Room, one of the function rooms of the Holiday Inn, just before the announced three o'clock time for the press conference. Barney was already there, seated in the middle of the first row of seats. The other four walked down the side of the room to the platform at one end with its long table and microphones. The ranks of folding chairs that filled the rest of the room had only a sprinkling of people already in them, but more were coming in.

"Well, well," said Tom Haley, looking them over, "not much of a gathering to hear a man accuse the leading governments of the world. Are you sure you're going to need me, Jens? I could have stayed at my office and got partway caught up on my work."

"There may not be many of them here," said Jens, "but the ones that are here have large ears, and their papers or stations or networks have large mouths. I'll need you, all right."

He went toward the center of the table.

"Aren't you going to wait?" Lin asked. "There's a stream of people still coming in."

"Maybe you're right." Then, abruptly, Jens started toward the chair at the center of the table. "No. See that gray-haired woman coming down the side aisle? She's the day manager of the Inn. Tom, will you try to stall her as long as you can?"

"No, no. You stick with him, Haley—and you, too, Miss West," said Sir Geoffrey—and there was no mistaking the note of excitement in his voice now. "He may need you beside him. Let me handle the manager. She's not going to get past me—"

Without waiting for agreement, he turned, and went toward that end of the platform that met the bottom of the side aisle Jens had indicated. Jens seated himself at the table, tapped the pencil microphone before him to make sure it was live, and spoke.

"Sorry to start while some of you are still coming in," he said. "But my time may be limited. As most of you may know, I'm Jens Wylie, U.S. Undersecretary of Science for the Development of Space, and former newsman myself."

Out of the corner of his eye he could see that the hotel manager had reached the edge of the platform and was halted there, facing Sir Geoffrey, who was looming impressively over her.

"What I have to say won't take long in any case," he said, "because I'm not going to give you information so much as put you on the track of finding it yourselves. As you know, the two spacecraft of the Mars Expedition had been disabled by a solar storm—Expedition Control is trying to bring them back to Earth orbit right now—and Tad Hansard, one of the marsnauts, has suffered some bad effects from radiation during the storm. You've also heard that very soon now, an investigation will be started into what factors were involved in the failure of this attempt at the Expedition."

The manager was still held up at the edge of the platform,

her way barred by Sir Geoffrey. But now, a heavy, middle-aged man wearing the uniform of a hotel security guard was standing beside her.

"There may be some voices raised to suggest that the cause of failure lay in the 'nauts themselves," Jens went on, rapidly. "In connection with that I want to suggest that you investigate the following possible chain of events. That the publics of the various nations and nation-groups involved in this Expedition competed against each other for the time and effort that the 'nauts would have to spare for scientific experiment and testing on the Expedition. That the result of this competition was that the 'nauts were given an experimental schedule too heavy for them to handle in the time available. That the 'nauts tried to handle this impossible work load, regardless, with the result that fatigue from overwork caused errors of judgment that led directly to the radiation damage to Tad Hansard and both ships."

The uniformed guard tried to go around Sir Geoffrey.

"Stop that!" barked Sir Geoffrey, loud enough to be heard over the public address system. Some heads turned to look at him.

"The necessary information to check this is already in your hands," Jens was saying, "and in the hands of the public you inform. I suggest you check the bargraphs of the 'nauts' schedules to establish whether the work required of them could reasonably be accomplished in the overall time available, unless all activities aboard the ship were miraculously free of any delay and time loss. I ask you to examine the reports so far released of events on both Phoenix One and Two; and decide for yourselves and your readers whether it was the demands of the Expedition or the marsnauts who are responsible for the failures. And now—" said Jens, hastily pushing back his chair and rising "—I must go."

"Just a minute," a voice called. "One question!"

Other voices joined in, already calling questions. Jens ignored them, hastily leaving the stage by the short flight of stairs at its far end, just as the hotel manager ducked under Sir Geoffrey's arm and began to come on stage. Jens ran up the opposite side of the room and escaped through the door of the entrance.

To his surprise he had got away. Peeking back through the door, he saw that Sir Geoffrey had followed the manager on stage and they had become entangled in a crowd of newspeople apparently eager to question them. Lin and Tom, now ignored, were coming up the center aisle.

Jens closed the door again, and waited. After a second or two, Lin and Tom came out and saw him.

"Better move while you can," said Tom.

They left the hotel for Tom's car, which was parked in the hotel parking lot outside.

"Where to?" the lawyer asked as they slipped out into the traffic of the street.

"Let's go back to my room and think," said Lin. She looked at Jens. "We should have thought about the next move before you got up to talk."

But Jens was supremely happy.

"Doesn't matter," he said. "They'll catch up with me sooner or later. But meanwhile I might as well enjoy life."

"You'd better simmer down," said Lin.

"That's not bad advice," said Tom. His car was the largest model air-cushion vehicle being made for private use, and he slid it through the traffic with absent-minded skill. "Everyone who's come after you so far hasn't had any arrest powers. When someone like that actually shows up, though, all Lin and I are going to be able to do for you is advise you to go quietly."

They came finally to the Holiday Inn. The phone within Lin's room was ringing as she unlocked the door, and she ran inside to answer it.

Jens and the lawyer followed, and heard her talking to someone at the far end of the line.

"Yes, I'll be right out," she was saying. She punched off and turned to them. "That was Penny Welles. She's out at Expedition Control and she says they finally figured out the creeping of that steering engine on Phoenix One. The last burn put the ship right where they expected her to be. One more will bring them in—and they can talk directly to Tad by radio, now, without going through LCO to Phoenix Two!"

"Thank God," said Jens.

"She says if we want to come out, she can get us into the

observation room and you might be safer there for a while than you would be here—I phoned her while you were in the bathroom, just before we went down from the press conference."

"All right." Jens checked suddenly and looked back at Tom Haley. "That's right, you won't be able to go in with us. Wait, you can wear my press pass and see how far you can get, if you like."

"I've got a press vehicle pass for our car and passengers," said Lin. "Unless they stop him inside the Flight Control building, he'll be all right."

"Do you want to go?" Jens asked the lawyer.

"I like to see things through," said Tom. "And as soon as word gets around you're there, somebody'll be tapping on your shoulder inside fifteen minutes. I'll stick with you as long I can."

"Good," said Jens.

They took Lin's rented car. The roads to the Cape were almost deserted in the brilliant, late afternoon sunlight. As Lin had guessed, the guard on the gate did not question Tom; and they pulled into the parking lot beside the Flight Control building. Inside, on the main floor, they hurried past another guard who was talking on the telephone in the lobby and did not see them pass.

The elevator took them up to the floor where the Flight Control room was. But there was a third guard on duty at the door of the room and this time Tom was stopped.

"I'll try to get someone to phone Security for you," said Jens. He and Lin went on into the glassed-in observation room, at the back of the sloping floor with its rows of consoles. The room was all but filled with members of the marsnauts' families and other observers. Penny was up front and they did not try to make their way through to her. Wendy Hansard was seated at one of the consoles, apparently having just finished talking with Tad. A speaker inside the observation room sounded with Tad's voice, over a background of light static.

". . . give me a time check."

His voice was heavy, blurred and slow, like the voice of a man under drugs or just awakened.

"Time is four minutes, thirty-seven seconds to burn," answered an Expedition Control voice. "Four thirty-six . . . four thirty-five . . . four thirty-four . . ."

"Copy," said Tad's voice. "Okay. Our time checks. You've got a perceptible disk, seen from here."

"Glad to hear it," said Expedition Control. "Are you all set with the figures for the final burn?"

"All set. All ready here. Just waiting it out," said Tad's voice, slowly.

"Phoenix Two, how about you?" asked Expedition Control. The light sound of static ceased, but there was no other response. "Phoenix Two. Come in, Phoenix Two. We're not reading you."

There was a faint murmur that swelled up clearly and loudly, suddenly, with no static to be heard at all.

". . . said that the LCO here seems to be fading in and out on transmission for me," said Fedya's voice. "Can you read me now, Expedition Control? Can you read me?"

"Roger. We read you now, Phoenix Two. We read you clear and loud," said Expedition Control. "You were out there for a few minutes again, then you faded back in all of a sudden. Is your reception of us or of Phoenix One fading likewise?"

"No. No fade from you. I'm receiving Phoenix One now through you. Too much static on radio direct from Tad now. Let me know if I fade out again."

"Are you set for burn, Phoenix Two? Have you got your figures?"

"I have the figures. Thank you, Expedition Control."

"Will you make the burn all right this time, do you think?"

There was a movement beside Jens, and he glanced aside briefly to see Tom, now with a badge, slip into the room beside him and stand listening. "If we lose contact with you through the LCO, we won't be able to keep updating your burn figures. You've got to go, this time."

"I intend to go," said the voice of Fedya. "Never mind me, Expedition Control. Concentrate on getting Phoenix One home safe."

"What is it?" Tom asked Jens. Unnecessarily, here he spoke in a whisper. "That business about his going?"

"He's been having trouble, getting the two working engines he's got to burn at all," Jens said. "He hasn't been able to fire at the same time as Phoenix One on any of the burns since the two ships were together—"

He broke off. Expedition Control was talking to Tad again.

". . . two shuttles," Expedition Control was saying. "One will stand off when they meet you. The other will come close enough to get a line to your Number Three hatch. We'll send a pilot across to bring Phoenix One in the rest of the way to orbit, and all of you will transfer over to the shuttle. Understood?"

"Understood," said Tad. "How soon after we finish burn should we rendezvous?"

"The shuttle should meet you in four hours ten minutes after you finish your burn," Expedition Control said. "That's provided you end up where you're supposed to. The shuttles are already on the way to that point, as we told you earlier today."

"Copy," said Tad. "Four hours ten minutes after end burn."

His voice was slowing even more as he talked, like a record on an antique phonograph that had been underwound.

"Tad," said Expedition Control. "Tad, why don't you let Anoshi or one of the others take over for this last burn? It's all cut and dried, now."

"Hell with that . . ." Tad's voice slurred drunkenly. "Took her out—bring'er back. Fedya!"

"I'm listening, Tad." Fedya's voice over the LCO was so clear, alert and free of background noise in comparison to Tad's that Jens almost started. It was almost as if Fedya had spoken behind Jens and Tom in the observation room.

"Good hunting, partner."

"Thank you . . . partner," said Fedya. "And I wish . . ."

His voice faded once more, suddenly, into nothingness.

"Fedya?" said Tad, after a moment.

There was no answer.

"Phoenix Two's LCO is malfunctioning," Expedition Control said. "We don't receive Fedya either, Tad."

Tad's voice muttered something unintelligible.

"One minute and counting," said Expedition Control.

"Ready for countdown, Phoenix One, Phoenix Two. Fifty-six seconds . . . fifty-five . . . fifty-four . . ."

"You mean," Tom Haley whispered in Jens's ear, "the other spaceship hasn't even started to come toward Earth?"

"Yes," said Jens. He was hardly listening. His attention was all on Wendy, standing by the console with her back turned to the end of the room. Her arms were at her side, and her hands were clenched. There was no other sign of tension about her. Someone else came into the observation room behind Jens and Tom, but neither of them turned to look.

"Twenty seconds . . ."

"Good luck, Phoenix One," said the voice of Fedya, suddenly loud in the observation room, drowning out the voice of Expedition Control's counting.

"Six seconds . . . five seconds," said Expedition Control. "Four . . . three . . . two . . . one . . . fire!"

A sudden roar of static erupted from the speaker, and was hastily tuned down. It was silent in the observation room. No one moved down in the control room proper. Jens and Tom waited, breathing shallowly.

Finally, after a long time, the speaker came to life again with the faint background of static Jens had heard originally.

"Phoenix One," said Expedition Control. "Come in, Phoenix One."

"Read you, Expedition Control," answered Tad's voice suddenly. "All over. Burn went fine. Everything's fine."

"Roger, Phoenix One," said Expedition Control. "You are on target. Repeat, you are on target. We're just getting confirmation on that by the ATM in Skylab Two. Congratulations. The shuttles will be with you soon."

"Thanks to you, Expedition Control," said Tad. "I thank you, we all thank you . . ."

"Phoenix Two?" said Expedition Control. "Phoenix Two, come in. This is Expedition Control calling Phoenix Two. Do you read me?"

"I read you, Expedition Control." Fedya's voice swelled up in volume suddenly from the speaker. "Great, good work, Tad. My congratulations to all of you."

"Salute to you, Fedya," said Tad.

"Phoenix Two, this is Expedition Control. Did you accomplish burn? Repeat, did you accomplish burn this time."

"I am sorry, Expedition Control," said Fedya. "Very sorry. No, I did not burn. But then I was not trying. Forgive me for keeping you in the dark this long, but I wanted to leave your minds free to concentrate on getting Phoenix One home safely. I never intended to use the figures you gave me."

"Phoenix Two? Hello, Phoenix Two. We're reading you, but don't understand. Did you say you didn't intend to burn at any time? What about the malfunction of your two engines?"

"There was none," said Fedya. "As I say, Expedition Control, forgive me. If I had told you the truth to begin with, you would have wanted to argue with me. I did not want argument, particularly useless argument, once my mind was made up."

"Phoenix Two, I don't understand—" Expedition Control's voice suddenly broke off and was replaced by one Jens knew. "Phoenix Two, this is Bill Ward. Fedya, what are you talking about? Have you been deliberately choosing to keep Phoenix Two as she is? Why, in God's name?"

"Leave him alone." It was Tad's voice suddenly, breaking in. "We started out to go to Mars, Bill. If one man wants to complete that Expedition, he's got a right to. Anyway, what're you going to do about it?"

"But . . ." began Bill; and stopped again.

"Please, Bill," said Fedya. "No arguments. We all know that the Expedition has to be completed, if there are to be more missions after this one. This spacecraft is a small capsule of all our efforts since time began; and someone has to see it safely to its destination. We decided that when you announced the abort. If it had not been me here in Phoenix Two, it would have been one of the others—Dirk, Bern, Anoshi, Bap. One of us would have stayed with Phoenix Two."

"Hey," said Tad, thickly, "don't forget me, you damned mutineer. It was my idea."

"I don't forget you, Tad," said Fedya. "But it had to be a well man. One who could stay alive until Mars is reached, and even after. Someone who could keep records and even maintain as many of the experiments as possible, so that the data will be there when the next ships come. I know . . . I know what I did in taking this away from you, Tad. But we agreed, all the rest of us agreed, that it had to be done."

"Sure," said Tad. "Sure. If I'd been in shape to think straight I'd have realized that earlier myself."

He stopped talking. There was no sound.

"Fedya?" Tad said. "Fedya, you still reading me? Fedya?"

"Phoenix Two, come in," said Bill Ward. "Phoenix Two, this is Expedition Control. We do not read you. Phoenix Two, we've lost your transmission. Come in, Phoenix Two. Phoenix Two, come in. . . ."

He continued talking. There was no answer.

Someone had come into the observation room a moment ago, and stood just behind Jens. He stepped forward now and Jens turned to look at him. He was a stocky young man with blond hair who might have been a first cousin of Kilmartin Brawley.

"Undersecretary Wylie?" He had a slow, southern accent, and he was holding out a wallet, opened to show a card within bearing his photograph and several lines of information. "FBI, Mr. Wylie. You are under arrest, sir, on an open charge. Please come with me."

36

It was all very polite and almost pleasant. The man who had arrested Jens—his name was Morris J. Wello, according to the credentials which he earnestly requested that Jens read through carefully—took Jens by unmarked car to an office in downtown Cocoa Beach, where forms were filled out and the details from the papers sent over a computer terminal to a main office in Washington. Jens was required to sign the forms, which were in quintuplicate.

"So I'm a criminal now," he said as he put his name to the last paper.

Wello looked shocked.

"Not at all," he said. "This just confirms the emergency arrest action, and it's only good for twenty-four hours from the moment of arrest. It's impossible to get a regular order of arrest until you've been properly booked as a matter of public record and your counsel fully informed. Then an open hearing has to be held, and so on. Things have changed a lot in the last ten years; and I'm sure you'll find they've been changed for the better."

He opened a drawer and produced what looked like a wristwatch.

"For example," he said, holding it up. "Do you know about these?"

"It's that electronic handcuff thing, isn't it?"

"Well, I don't know if it's actually electronic—though I suppose in part it is," said Wello, strapping the metal strap of the device around Jen's naked left wrist. "I'm afraid I don't know as much about it as I should."

He laughed, cheerfully.

"Not too tight, is it?" he asked. "If you'll look at the dial there . . ."

Jens looked. What he saw was a glass-covered dial showing a scale marked from one to five hundred. A single needle rested on the zero mark.

"You see mine?" went on Wello, laying his own left hand and arm out on the desk before them. He wore his own version of the device with the dial part on the inside of his wrist instead of on the back of it as on the one strapped to Jens.

"Now, you see, I set mine . . ." His fingers turned the small knob on one side of the dial and the needle on his instrument climbed up the scale to the number fifteen. The needle on Jen's unit matches this movement.

"That's fifteen feet you and I can be separated, without your unit reacting—what we call walk-about distance," said Wello. He grinned at Jens. "Most local police offices will set it at about five feet and ask you to stand up and walk away from them, so you can feel what it's like when you go past the distance; your unit reacts, and you suddenly have trouble breathing; but with the caliber of people we usually end up escorting, we don't find that necessary. You're aware, I'm sure, that even if you do go over the line, the shortness of breath you feel won't be enough to be really dangerous. It's just enough to immobilize you.''

"I'd heard that,'' said Jens.

"Yes," said Wello, "it really is a most civilized improvement over old-fashioned handcuffs. For one thing I can let you go to the john by yourself. Also it's a lot easier for both of us if we're traveling together to have two hands apiece to do things with, like eat and pick our noses, than it is if we've three hands between the two of us. Then of course, there's always that unexpected emergency in which it becomes dangerous for two people to be chained together. This new version of cuffs gets around all that.''

"What if I get caught on a subway and you aren't able to get on?'' asked Jens. "I could become pretty uncomfortable for quite a while before somebody could get to me and disconnect me.''

"We're trained not to let that happen," said Wello, smiling again.

He reached into the middle drawer of a desk beside him and took out what looked like a heavy, wide-jawed pair of pliers. He fastened the jaws on the buckle of the metal strap that secured the electronic cuffs around Jen's wrist. There was a faint crackling sound. When he took the pliers away the buckle had been melted into a shapeless blob of metal.

Jens instinctively winced away from what he assumed must be the touch of now-hot metal against his skin. But to his surprise, the apparently melted buckle was as cool as it had been before.

"Another of the wonders of science," Wello said cheerfully. "Will you come with me now, Mr. Wylie?''

They left the office and drove to the Orlando airport. There, they picked up tickets that were waiting for them on a commercial jet headed for Washington. The jet turned out to be an all first-class flight, and they were given the first two seats on the right hand side of the plane. Wello chatted cheerfully throughout the flight. He was, it turned out, a booster of the space effort.

"It really jolted me," he said, "When I heard what you'd told those reporters. You mean those 'nauts were really given more to do than they could handle?"

"More than they could handle without becoming dangerously exhausted," said Jens.

Wello continued to ask questions. He was eager to hear as much as Jens could tell him about the details of the Expedition itself and everything connected with it. To these things he listened with the attention and enjoyment of a true enthusiast.

"If you feel that strongly about it," Jens said to him, finally, "why don't you speak up? The only thing that's going to save the Expedition—I don't mean this Expedition, but the idea of any expedition to Mars, once this has gone down the tube—will be a large percentage of the population insisting that we don't quit—here, at this point."

"Oh, well," said Wello. "The people in the space program and in Washington here do know a lot more about it than I do, after all. They must know what they're doing. But it's a shame to have it all come to an end, as you say. It's been fascinating to think of a frontier in space."

"Well, you could write a letter to your Representative and your Senator," said Jens.

Wello smiled.

"This job of mine's a little sensitive, that way," he answered.

They stopped talking. Eventually the jet landed and they were met by a green, unmarked car, which drove them to what seemed to be a large pleasant, resort hotel with a small golf course attached, out in the Arlington area. It was, indeed, very much like a hotel: Jens was asked to sign a register, and then a man uniformed quite like a bellman carried off his luggage, which had been packed for him and brought from the Holiday Inn.

"This way please, Mr. Wylie," said Wello.

He led Jens off across the ground floor, through an unmarked door and into another large office. Here there were more papers to fill out, after which Jens was taken back out and escorted by Wello up to a hotel-like room on an upper floor.

The next five days consisted of nothing at all. It was like being locked in a hotel room in any large, strange city. Meals came regularly, and he was able to call down to room service for reading material, snacks, even—he discovered—a discreet amount of alcoholic beverages. The TV provided him with the best holographic image he had ever seen on any such set. But he was locked in, and in the final essential his days and nights were as empty as any prisoner's.

An almost blessed interruption came at last on the morning of the sixth day, shortly after the ten A.M. news program. Wello appeared unexpectedly, knocking on the door and stepping in immediately afterwards, like a discreet chambermaid.

"You've got a couple of visitors," he said. "Your lawyer and a representative from the Newsworkers Guild."

"I still want to talk to a Miss Alinde West—"

"I'm trying to arrange that, Mr. Wylie," Wello said, "as I told you. If you'll come along with me now, though, both your lawyer and the Guild representative are downstairs."

They went down and Jens was led once more through the unmarked door on the lobby floor, through the office there and into a back room set up like a lounge. Inside, to his surprise, were Barney and a lean, tailored-looking woman in her fifties with startling black hair and dark eyes, and almost as tall as Jens himself.

"Jens," said Barney, "this is Paula Anisha, senior attorney for the Newsworkers Guild."

"Oh, yes," Jens said, shaking hands with her. "I've heard of you, of course, ever since I first started working on the newspaper back home."

"Well, I've been hearing about you, too, though not for quite that long," Paula Anisha said.

Jens felt a sudden small sense of incongruity. This lady, who had reputedly been a terror to anyone trying to tilt with the Guild for the last twenty years, had a warm, slightly hoarse voice that would have fitted better on the heroine of a television soap opera.

"You still do have your membership in the Guild?" she asked now.

"As a matter of fact, yes," Jens said. "I never did take

myself too seriously as a government figure. I always thought I'd get back to honest work one of these days.''

"Not that it matters," put in Barney.

"No," Paula said. "It doesn't matter. The Guild would be concerned in a case like yours, involving freedom of expression, in any case. Why don't we all sit down; and you go over the whole thing for me from the time when you started to hold this conference, and tell me exactly why you decided to hold it?"

They pulled three of the comfortable chairs in the lounge together and sat down. Jens found himself reaching back to the moment in which Tad Hansard had warned him during lunch that the experiment schedule for the two ships was too heavy, and moving on from there. It was not until he came to the account of his arrest that he realized he had been talking almost uninterruptedly for an hour and a half.

"Sorry," he said to them both, "I didn't mean to keep going like that."

"Not at all," said Paula. "That's exactly what I wanted, Jens."

She got to her feet.

"I've got it all here, recorded," she said, tapping the small purse fastened to her left wrist. "From now on you'll be dealing mainly with other members of my staff, since I've got my hands full ninety per cent of the time. But Jens, I think we've got a strong case—a very strong case."

Jens and Barney had both gotten to their feet in response. She shook hands with them both now.

"Just sit tight," she smiled at Jens. "We'll be in touch with you. And if you want to get in touch with the Guild, simply tell your switchboard here to get hold of us. They can't refuse to put you through to us by phone at any time of the day or night. You'll remember that?"

"Absolutely," said Jens.

Paula left.

"Sit down again," said Barney. "I've got some more things to talk to you about."

"I've got some things to ask you," said Jens. "How's Lin? How come she couldn't come and see me?"

"The government's doing its best to keep you completely

locked away from everybody,'' said Barney. ''But they can't keep out your attorneys, and they can't keep me out as long as I'm officially designated the representative from the News-workers Guild. We tried to get Lin in, too, but we couldn't. Sit down.''

Jens sat down again, and Barney sat down with him.

''To begin with, how are they treating you?''

''Fine,'' said Jens. ''Except that I'm about to go out of my skull with boredom. I'm not used to being locked up.''

''Not many people are,'' said Barney.

''Too much of this and you can begin to feel like you're invisible. Like nobody knows you're there or cares,'' said Jens.

''That's the idea, of course,'' Barney nodded. ''They don't miss a trick. But it could be worse, Jens. Believe me, it could be worse. As it is, that's the most they can do to you with the media keeping its eye on them.''

''I've been reading the papers and watching the news broadcasts,'' said Jens. ''I really did kick up a fuss, didn't I?''

''You did that,'' said Barney.

''I couldn't bring myself to ask Paula,'' Jens said. ''But what does it look like they can do to me?''

''They can lock you up, all right,'' said Barney. ''It's just as well you didn't ask Paula. She doesn't have all the answers at this stage of the game and all she could have done would be to talk around the subject. But I can tell you—yes, they can lock you up.''

''And what else?''

''Well,'' said Barney, ''if you're thinking about things like electroshock treatment and things like that—no, they're not going to be able to get away with anything like that in your case. Yes, they'll send you to a therapy center, just as if you'd robbed a bank. But, no, they won't be able to play games with your head, via the drug route or special therapy, or anything else. All they'll be able to do is earnestly exhort you to mend your ways. In fact, they'll even have to be a little careful how they do that.''

''I feel a little guilty,'' said Jens, ''getting this sort of V.I.P. treatment simply because I know a few people.''

''Come off it,'' said Barney. ''If you weren't the kind of person who knew people, you wouldn't have been this nation's representative to the Expedition. If you hadn't been that, you wouldn't have stuck your neck out the way you did and got into this mess. It all hangs together. Now you're a small ant that a big government wants to step on. But a big newsworkers' organization, with connections to all the other newsworkers' organizations around the world is going to make sure it keeps its feet inside the legal lines. That's all."

Jens shivered. "To tell the truth," he said, staring at the wall of the lounge opposite, "it's good to hear that. I've picked up my share of horror stories about the present decriminalization process over the last few years."

"Some of them aren't horror stories," said Barney, without lowering his voice. In fact, it seemed to Jens that he spoke if anything a little more loudly than he had been talking earlier. "The point is that nothing like that's going to happen to you."

"Watch it, Barney," said Jens, with half a smile, "the room may be bugged."

"I know damn well it's bugged," said Barney, "and that's why I want to make sure they've got me on record. It was a good trick, this closing down the jails and sending everybody in them to therapy centers. But any system can develop a bad side—and there's a bad side there, too, with people who end up in padded cells or straightjackets for the rest of their lives. There are other people who get their brains cooked with drugs or electronic treatments, or even brainwashed without a finger being laid on them. The point is, nothing like that is going to happen to you or the Newsworkers Guild is going to be upset. *Very* upset."

Jens looked across at Barney and saw that his face was set and grim. The shiver he had felt earlier came back, followed by a warm surge of gratitude toward Barney and people like him.

"What would I do without you?" he said.

"You'd still do pretty well." The anger had gone out of Barney's face and voice. "There's the political system, too, to consider. Being the Undersecretary for the Development of Space, even for a short while, you got to be a little too noticeable to be filed away and forgotten. Even if the rest of us weren't around, it'd be sticky going outside the acceptable limits with someone like you. But it doesn't hurt to have us here, too."

"You can say that again," Jens said.

* * *

On the way back from Washington after seeing Jens, all the way on the taxi to the airport, on the flight down to Orlando, and driving his rental car from there back to Merritt Island, Barney had found himself prey to a disturbing, but not altogether uncomfortable, emotion. At first he could not put his finger on its exact nature. It was as if, somewhere inside him, a wall had gone down, letting a horde of unsuspected devils into the light of day, where they had shriveled and died in the sun. He felt somewhat disheveled internally from the crumbling of that part of his interior architecture, but at the same time very relieved that the devils—whose existence he had hardly suspected—were now taken care of.

It took him nearly three quarters of the trip before he began to be able to put a name to the devils and a label to the wall. The wall had been the cynicism he had chosen to hide behind ever since his marriage had broken up and the devils, quite simply, had been the fears and doubts about his own ineffectiveness as a man and as a human being that had followed upon experiencing that breakup.

He faced the fact that it was Jens's actions, Jens's almost romantic crusade on behalf of the astronauts, that had worked the cure in him. He had ended up wanting a piece of that action.

He suddenly knew he wanted to see Aletha again. For the first time he recognized something more where she was concerned than the deliberately casual interest he had taken in women ever since he had faced the fact that Wilma was gone for good. He saw now that he had deliberately steered clear of Aletha simply because she was the kind of person he could get serious about—and getting serious again, setting himself up for another human failure, was something that had terrified him.

Now that his mind had cleared, he saw a great deal more than he might have suspected earlier. For one thing he saw that Aletha herself labored under a burden of secret fear; only, in her case, the result had been that she had given in to life. He wondered whether that giving in had come on her at the time of her divorce, or had it been something that had trapped her earlier? At any rate, there was something in her that feared to take hold of any situation and try to make it go her own way, a sort of defeatism; and, contemplating his own recent escape from the cynicism that had held him so long, Barney felt very keenly that she did not really have to be afraid in that way, and he found himself searching for some way he could transfer the effect of his own recent experience with Jens to her, so that she, too, could break loose.

It was really a new feeling for him, this feeling he now had about her. There was an almost guilty aspect to it. What if he had discovered it in himself while that friend of hers—Jim Brille—had still been alive? What would he have done then? Would he have been able to square it with his new self that he could step in and compete with Jim for her? Or would the very fact that there was already somebody there before him have been enough to shock him back behind his wall again, to rebuild it and to hatch out new demons of self-doubt?

It was impossible to tell.

He reached the Holiday Inn and cruised the parking lot looking for an open space. It was just before the dinner hour and the lot was full. He finally found a spot on the far side of the motel from the cocktail lounge. He parked and went in the side entrance, crossed the lobby and stepped into the cocktail lounge through the door from the lobby.

He stood for a moment, adjusting his eyes to the dimness. As the lounge resolved out of the gloom, he saw that Aletha was apparently alone at the bar; and he was just about to go over to her when the outside door to the lounge opened and Malcolm Schroeder came in. There was a curious smugness visible upon his face as he entered. He came up to the bar like a cat approaching a dish of thick cream. Behind the bar, Aletha was working, with her head down. She did not raise it to look at Malcolm. There was a quickness and abruptness to her movements that was interestingly at odds with the slinking smoothness of Malcolm's approach—and, unexpectedly, hope kindled in Barney.

Instead of moving up to the bar himself, he stepped off to one side and sat down noiselessly at one of the tables back in the shadows. Malcolm sat down at the bar. Plainly neither he nor Aletha had seen Barney.

Malcolm Schroeder came into the bar lounge of the Holiday Inn and was pleased by what he saw. Aletha was back on her regular evening shift that began at four-thirty in the afternoon and ended when the bar closed at one o'clock in the morning. Right now, at quarter of five, she had just come on duty and was working behind a deserted bar, setting up; and there were only two other people in the room, up at the near end by the glass door, about as far from her as they could be and still be in the same room. Malcolm went down and took a seat opposite her.

"A Pabst," he said.

"Right."

Aletha finished washing the remaining glasses in the sink before her, set them to drain, dried her hands, and went to the bar to the beer cooler. She got out one of the squat brown bottles of beer, uncapped it, brought it back, and set it before him with a glass. She went back to washing more glasses. In all of this she had not once looked at him.

Malcolm poured the beer from the bottle into his glass. Originally she had done this for him. In fact, it seemed if he remembered rightly she had done this for him up until a couple of weeks ago, after her boyfriend had been killed. He had noticed that she did it for other people at the bar who ordered beer.

"How's it going?" he asked.

"Fine," she said.

She put the last of her glasses upside down on the drain-board of the bar sink, to dry and went down to the other end of the bar. Malcolm sat for a while watching her and then picked up his glass and beer bottle from the bar and started to go to her end. As he did, she came back down to the end he had just left.

He reversed himself and returned to take his original stool at the bar.

"Look," he said, "you'll be taking your dinner break around six-thirty, won't you? There's a little place a couple of blocks down the street here on the left."

"The Harmon House," said Aletha, not looking up. "I know it. No thanks, I'm going to be busy here."

"Don't be like that," said Malcolm. "You have a sandwich and a cup of coffee here every night. You've got to be getting tired of that."

"It suits me just fine."

"Come on, now. Anybody likes to eat out for a change. And you could stand the change. I didn't notice that friend of yours taking you out on your dinner hour all that often."

Aletha had begun to turn away. But now she turned back, reached for some lemons and began peeling them.

"I don't think you know any friends of mine," she said to the lemons.

Malcolm felt pleased. He had finally gotten her attention. A touch of humor, a little joking would do that sometimes.

"I know this one, all right," he said. "Or rather, I ought to say I knew him, since he ended up down at the morgue. You ought to be careful who you talk to in here. No telling what kind of business some of these people are in."

"Yes," said Aletha. The knife she was using to peel with dug as deeply into the lemon she was peeling as its inch and a half blade could manage on a slant.

"Yes," said Malcolm, wisely, "you can never tell what the people you run into in a bar like this are like. I'm sure you had no idea what that guy was like. But you can see it's just lucky that you didn't get into some kind of trouble with him."

He stopped and looked at her to see how she was taking this. She was simply continuing to work with her head down.

"Actually," he said, "what you really need is someone to take care of you. Now, as you know, I'm going to be moving down here just as soon as I buy a house. Of course I'm married, and I'd have to spend a fair amount of time at home with my wife; but there's no reason you and I—"

He broke off suddenly. Aletha was flourishing the little inch-and-a-half length of her paring knife only inches before his face.

"You get the hell out of here!" said Aletha. "You get the hell out of here and you get the hell away from me! You aren't fit to be in the same room where he was! Now you get the hell away from me and you stay away from me or I'll cut your balls off. And if you think I can't do it I'll get help!"

He stared at her, stupefied. Her voice had raised and he knew without looking that the other two people in the room must be staring at him. The little knife was almost touching his face and suddenly he was quite cold with fear.

He fell back off the bar and nearly went down. On his feet he turned and went blindly but hastily to his left, and out the door to the street into the open air. He was half way down the parking lot toward his car before he realized that he was running. He slowed down to a walk, glancing around to see if anybody had seen him come bolting out of the bar. However, no one was in sight. He walked on to his car, feeling shaky inside, but getting his breath and his self-control back as he went.

He reached the car, got inside and locked the doors all around once he was in. He sat for a few minutes, just catching his breath. Then he put the key in the ignition, backed out and drove off. It was not until he was actually out on the street headed down toward Melbourne that he could feel his pulse and his breathing getting back to normal. Gradually, however, a sense of relief began to flood him.

Thank God he had found out what she was like in time. His knees felt weak at the thought that he might have set up some kind of deal with her, and then had her explode like that after the house was bought and Myrt was down here. It was just his good luck to find out in time.

He drove along, his spirits rising. Yes, he was lucky in some ways. Probably the reason he hadn't gotten any farther with her during the past few weeks was because something inside him had instinctively realized what she was like. Her and that boyfriend of hers that got knifed were obviously two of a kind. Of course, she had certainly hidden that part of her well—for a moment he felt a twinge of regret, thinking of her body moving around behind the bar there. It would have been nice . . . but, no, it was much better this way. When you came to look at it, everything had turned out for the best—and why not, he thought? It was men like him, the solid ones, who always kept the world going—not trashy barmaids and flashy newspeople, and dumb spacemen who didn't have the sense to come in out of the sun. He chuckled at the joke, and made a note to tell it to Myrt, explaining it first. He drove on in the evening sunlight, reflecting that it was only fair that he be lucky, as well as four-square and hardworking. But it chilled him to think how she had looked there, when she was waving the knife in his face. And her language. God, what savages some women were!

* * *

Aletha had gone back to carving her lemons so fiercely that she had not seen Barney come up to the bar from the place in back where he had been seated. He sat down in front of her, and she jumped and looked up. Then, the tension leaked out of her at the sight of him.

"Oh, Barney!" she said. "It's you."

"Hey!" Barney said softly. "That was fine!"

She stared at him.

"You were here? You heard?"

"I walked in on it," said Barney. "Now, that was beautiful. See what happens when you pick life up by the ears and shake it?"

"I wasn't shaking life," she said in a voice that was not altogether steady, "I was shaking him."

"You were shaking something you didn't like—that's shaking him and everything else. That's taking charge of your own life, lady," Barney said. "You were magnificent!"

She looked at him and smiled, still a bit uncertainly. He smiled back. Their eyes held; and gradually the smiles became warmer and more firm. Her free hand made a little dabbing motion at the hair above her left ear and then went quickly down again.

"What would you like?" she said, then laughed. "What am I talking about? I know."

She turned away to go down the bar.

"No," he said quickly, "give me something else. Give me—a ginger ale."

She stopped and turned back at him.

"You don't mean that!"

"I do. I do," said Barney. "I want a ginger ale more than anything else in the world. Well, almost."

Verigin was lying on the bed in his suite, not sleeping, but resting, when he heard a knock on the door to the adjoining room. He waited to hear the sound of the door being opened, but he did not hear it and after a while there was the sound of the knock again.

Obviously, his aide had stepped out. Annoyed that he should be disturbed in this moment of mindless peace which he had just achieved after perhaps half an hour of staring at the ceiling, Verigin got creakily up from the bed and walked into the other room and up to the door there. Luckily, he had lain down fully dressed. He even had his shoes on.

"Who is it?" he called through the closed door.

"Ahri Ambedkar. Sergei, is that you?"

"Just a minute," said Verigin.

He fumbled with the lock of the door, unlatched it and opened the door. Ambedkar came in.

"I just got back to the motel here," he said, proffering an envelope. "When I picked up my key from the desk, they mentioned they had this letter for you. I knew you were waiting for news from your wife, so I thought I'd bring it up."

"Thank you. Thank you, my dear Ahri," said Sergei. "But come in. Sit down."

Verigin led the way to a couple of chairs and they seated themselves.

"Don't mind me," Ambedkar said. "Go ahead and open it, by all means."

"No, no." Verigin put the letter down on an endtable. "I can imagine what my wife has written."

The fact that Elena Markovna had taken nearly three weeks to answer could mean only one thing, that she was adjusting herself to this new defeat, the fact that he had found a way to help Chupchik after all. It was a triumph for him, and, as well as he liked Ambedkar, he preferred to savor it by himself. He would read the letter after Ahri had gone.

"In any case, a couple of minutes' delay won't do any harm," Verigin went on, "I do thank you for bringing it to me. It seems I heard you were leaving. Does that mean right away?"

"I'm afraid so." Ahri folded his hands before him. "My government wishes to rethink the situation with the Expedition, now that your Colonel Asturnov has chosen to continue alone in a single spacecraft toward Mars, after all. In connection with this, they've called me back to talk the matter over."

"I'm sorry to see you leave, of course," said Verigin. "But we'll be encountering each other fairly soon again, I imagine. Speaking for my government, we are, of course, very proud of Feodor Aleksandrovich Asturnov at taking such firm charge in an emergency. I'm sure your government, as all others, will realize that he did the only thing that was possible; and had we known the full facts of the situation, we would have urged him to do just what he did.''

''I'm not entirely sure my government shares that point of view,'' said Ambedkar. ''But then, I'll know more after I've got home and spoken with them. On a personal level, Sergei, it has been quite pleasant having you to talk with during these last few weeks.''

''I can only say that same thing about you, my dear fellow,'' said Verigin.

''Well, well, I must be going,'' said Ambedkar, getting to his feet. ''I understand that they've set an early trial date for Jens Wylie. *In camera* proceedings, all very neat and hush-hush.''

''Yes,'' said Sergei, also rising and following Ambedkar to the door. ''Even in the United States something had to be done after that press conference of his. No, I don't think we'll be seeing or hearing anything more of Mr. Wylie.''

''No.'' Ambedkar sighed, pausing at the door, which Verigin opened for him. ''Sergei, what's going to happen to the world after you and I and people like us retire? There'll be nothing but amateurs; and the mess will be frightful.''

Verigin nodded.

''I agree completely,'' he said, standing aside as Ambedkar passed out. ''Good-by.''

''Good-by.''

Shutting the door behind Ambedkar, Verigin turned back to the chair in which he had been sitting. He reseated himself and picked up the letter from Elena Markovna, savoring again his feeling of triumph.

As a matter of fact, things had turned out rather well all the way around. It was very good indeed that the Mars Expedition now consisted of one Russian and one spaceship going on to Mars. Whether young Asturnov would make it was immaterial. The point was that for the next five months the eyes of the world would be upon him and the possibilities for making use of his lonely voyage and adventure were unlimited. And, now to cap it all, a letter acknowledging defeat in the matter of Chupchik from Elena Markovna.

He ripped the envelope open and took the letter out. It consisted of three small pages covered with the thin, close spidery handwriting of his wife. It was a handwriting impossible to read without his glasses, and difficult even with them. He laid the pages down, went to get the glasses and came back, fitting them on his nose. He sat down, picked the letter up, and began to read.

> Dearest:
> I know how happy you must have been to find someone who could help your poor Chupchik. I, too, would feel happy for you if I could. Unfortunately, your letter came, literally, just a few moments too late. Earlier that same day I had been consulting with our veterinarian. Your poor Chupchik had had some sort of spasm of the hind legs and after talking it over with the veterinarian I could not feel it in my heart to prolong the painful life of the little creature any longer. Consequently, when your letter came, I had already taken Chupchik to the veterinarian—

The pages of the letter shook suddenly in Verigin's hand. His eyes filled with tears and his throat congested.

"Liar!" he cried out loud in a strangled voice. "Liar! Demon!"

The lines of handwriting swam before his eyes. He blinked hard and tried to focus.

> The veterinarian was most understanding, and your little Chupchik slept away his life quite peacefully under those good hands. I have had him buried with your other little pets in the back garden—

The welling moisture in his eyes made reading further impossible. Verigin crushed the pages in his fist and sat rigid in the chair, the tears streaming down his face, muttering between his teeth.

"Demon! Demon . . ."

37

Wendy Hansard came through the side entrance into the large, echoing employees' cafeteria on the ground floor of the Flight Control Center, and looked around for Bill Ward.

It took her a little time to find him, and then she spotted him sitting at one of the tables off near the corner to her right. She went toward him, and he got up as he saw her coming. His tray of goulash, salad, apple pie, milk and coffee was on the table in front of him.

"Can I go get you something?" he asked.

"No, I've eaten," she said. "Go right on with your lunch. I'll sit down and talk, if that's all right."

"Of course. It's good to see you," Bill said, as they sat. "You know I've been meaning to call, but with the way things have been . . ."

"I know," she said. "That's all right, Bill. I know you've had your hands full. We've all had our hands full, including the kids."

"Anyway," said Bill, "I should've checked with you some time ago to see what I could do for you. You shouldn't have to come hunting me."

"Actually," she said, "the reason I called up and wanted to catch you on your lunch hour like this doesn't have anything to do with the family. There's something that I'd like to do, and I don't know how to go about it. Maybe you can tell me how, or maybe you can even help me with it."

"What is it?" asked Bill.

"Jens Wylie. That press conference, knowing in advance they'd arrest him for it," said Wendy. "It was a brave thing to do. I want to get in touch with him, to thank him. But I can't seem to locate him or get to him in any way. Do you know how I can find him and talk to him, or write him?''

Bill pushed his empty lunch plate away and pulled his apple pie toward him. He picked up a fork.

"I don't know," he said, doubtfully. "Apparently the government wants him kept away from people, for the moment at least."

"But they can't just lock him up somewhere and throw away the key," said Wendy. "Legally, they can't do that."

"True." Bill took a forkful of apple pie. "You're quite right, of course. They can't. I can ask around and see what I can find out. But in any case, I'm sure he understands that you're grateful for what he did for Tad and the others."

"It's more than that, though," said Wendy. "That's why I want to talk to him myself, personally. It's not just what he did for Tad. It's what his speaking up did for me, for all of us."

Bill put his fork down and looked at her.

"I don't follow you," he said.

"His doing that meant something," Wendy said, "like Tad wishing Fedya good luck when he learned that Fedya had trapped him into coming back to Earth and Fedya was going on alone to Mars to try to complete the Expedition. Don't you see? Jens Wylie did the right thing, just like Tad and Fedya did the right thing. That's why I wanted to talk to him, to tell him that."

"I'll do the best I can to find out where he is," said Bill. He sighed, picked up his coffee cup and drank from it, then put it down again. "But the chances are it'll go for nothing; just like the chances are his holding that press conference'll go for nothing. That's the story of our life, here. We knock ourselves out and one way or another the rest of the world tends to waste it all. Did I tell you Del Terrence quit as factory rep with Laserkind over the breakdown of the lasercom on Phoenix One?"

"Del Terrence?" Wendy frowned. "I don't think I know him."

"Probably not, come to think of it," Bill said. "I forget you and the other wives don't know all the people around here the way the rest of us do. Anyway, he was a good man who couldn't stand for what his own outfit was doing. You know they went on TV with a statement that it wasn't their fault, almost within hours of our finding out that the lasercom had broken down?''

"And now this Del Terrence is out of a job because he spoke up, too? Is that it?'' asked Wendy.

"As a matter of fact, no.'' Bill chuckled. "He got a new job working for Disney World. Quality control engineer on the weather dome system they're putting up for EPCOT-Two.''

"EPCOT-Two?''

"Yes,'' said Bill. "Experimental Prototype City of To-morrow—number Two. You know, an updated version of the EPCOT they built in the seventies, but including all the new space-industries material and technologies. It's just like the first EPCOT, an actual working city, where people will live and work—''

"I knew about EPCOT,'' said Wendy. "I just didn't re-alize they were putting up a second one.''

"Oh, yes,'' Bill said, "it's been on the drawing board for three or four years now. At any rate, Del got a job with them; which worked out rather well, since it looks like he's going to get married to his girl friend here in town. But I'm getting off the subject.''

"Not really,'' said Wendy. "That's exactly what I was talking about—the people that go ahead and do what they know is right, in spite of all the other people who do the wrong things for their own reasons, selfish or otherwise. It means a lot to know that people like that exist. I said it wasn't just for Tad I wanted to thank Jens Wylie. It's for me, as well. Thanks to him, I think I'm going to go back to work.''

Bill stared at her.

"To work?'' he said.

"I don't mean for perhaps quite a while yet, but eventu-ally,'' said Wendy. "The immediate future all depends on the situation with Tad, of course.''

Her gaze darkened. She looked down at the table, then up again at Bill.

"I suppose,'' she said, "you know there isn't much hope.''

"I understood,'' said Bill, stiffly, "that nobody was sure about anything, about the extent of the damage that has been done him.''

"That's right,'' said Wendy. "No one really knows; and

we've got a right to go on hoping as long as we can. But I've had to look ahead and think about what might have to be done—by me and the kids, by everybody in the family.''

''But you won't need to work, surely?'' Bill said. ''I mean, what with the government pensions and all—''

''Of course I wouldn't,'' Wendy interrupted. ''We'd be more than well off enough for me to sit and be nothing but Tad's widow for the rest of my life. But living demands more of anyone than just existing as a symbol. I never realized that, really, until Jens Wylie stood up at that press conference and spoke out. Then I realized I'd been all ready to take the easy way if the worst happens. I'd been all set to be like one of those nineteenth-century widows who wore black for the rest of her life. That's not what Tad would ever want. It's not what he's lived for and what he may die for, for that matter. But it was easier to plan on that than to face up to the idea that I ought to go on living—not just survive, I mean, but go on living in an active sense, if I'm to be left without him.''

''But what kind of thing would you do?'' Bill asked.

She smiled a little.

''It happens that I've already been offered a job.''

He stared at her.

''From an old friend,'' Wendy continued, ''who thought I might want an excuse to get out of the house, where I'd be alone during the school hours now that the kids are all in school. I don't know if you know Mike Blaine? He's in real estate down in Cocoa. He said he could use me as a part-time office manager—or even full time, later on, if I wanted to put in the hours.''

''Office manager?'' Bill asked. ''Have you any idea—''

''Oh, indeed I do. That's what I was doing most of the time when Tad was in college, before he graduated and joined the Air Force. Of course, once he was in the service we were moving around too much and I had to give it up. But actually, I'm a good office manager.''

Bill looked at her with admiration.

''I'll bet you are,'' he said.

He drained the last of the coffee from his cup, almost as if he was drinking a toast.

''Yes,'' he said, musingly, ''that's very good. You're very

good, Wendy. You're remarkable. But you wouldn't be doing anything like that right away, would you?"

"Not for a year, anyway," she said. "We'll have to see how fast Tad gets better, or . . . but in any case, this was something I hadn't even the courage to think about—the possibilities of what I might do afterwards, I mean—until Jens Wylie spoke up; and I owe him thanks. So you will try to find him for me?"

"I will indeed," said Bill. "In fact, now that I stop to think of it, there's a word or two I'd like the chance to say to him, myself."

Amory Hammond picked up his cup to drink from it and then set it down again, spilling coffee down its side. He lifted the cup once more and added another napkin from the dispenser at his elbow to the stack already under the cup, soaking up the previously spilled coffee.

"It could be something of a mess," he said, judiciously.

Albert Gervais, sitting across the table from him in the Holiday Inn coffee shop, said nothing. Hammond was not talking about his table manners. The words lay there invisibly on the table between them. After a moment, Hammond spoke again, looking up at Gervais.

"You don't know what I'm talking about?" he asked.

"No."

"Well, here we are all ready to clean things up and get out of here," said Hammond. "And we learn through other agencies and the overseas grapevine that the Pan-European ambassador was indulging in a little private espionage here."

"Any details?" asked Gervais.

"Of course not," said Hammond. "The ones who leaked it to us just wanted to worry us. It could even be a lie."

"Probably not," said Gervais.

"He'd be using some free lance, of course," said Hammond. "Obviously, there's no harm done. But here we are ready to clean up and get out, and word like that is hanging around."

"Ignore it," Gervais said, watching him.

"You know I can't do that." Hammond drank from his cup. "And you know why."

"I do?"

"Of course you do," said Hammond, looking at him again. "There's that ridiculous business of that out-of-work salesman—probably some queer—that got knifed here in an alley. It couldn't have been worse. First the papers have to make a fuss over the fact of what the odds are on a little toy knife like that stopping a man dead; and making all sorts of guesses of how it had to have been an accident—and then this business about the Pan-European minister. The result is it doesn't take long for other agencies to start pointing out that it could be either a very lucky amateur or a very good professional. Now you tell me who the professionals were down here."

"Us," said Gervais.

"Exactly." Hammond drank some more coffee and spilled some more. This time he was too concerned to put down a fresh napkin. "It hasn't come to an order to me to investigate the thing yet, but that's what's next down the line unless I can lightning-rod it somehow."

"Well, perhaps you should," said Gervais.

"Are you crazy?" said Hammond. "Do you know what that would do to my record, even when we didn't turn up anyone? From then on I wouldn't be trusted with anything more sensitive than getting the groceries."

Gervais said nothing, and Hammond looked at him narrowly.

"You're acting pretty damned unconcerned about all this."

"Why shouldn't I?" said Gervais. "You're the man with the responsibility, and that's fine with me."

"It's your team, too, they're talking about," said Hammond. "You're the man in the field."

Gervais smiled thinly, feeling contempt.

"Yes," he said. "I'm the man in the field, and that's what I'm concerned with. From where I sit there's nothing but the field. The field is where it all happens and it's where all the responsibility comes home to roost, long before all the talk and paperwork begins up top. I've been settling problems before they were even noticed up top for twenty years now."

"You might give some thought to settling this one then," said Hammond. "If the local cops could only turn up whoever it was actually stuck the paperknife into that salesman-type . . ."

"Why?"

"Because then it'd be clear it wasn't one of our people!"

"You're sure it wasn't?"

Hammond, who was reaching for his cup, stopped. He gazed long and hard at Gervais.

"What are you trying to tell me?" he asked at last, in a lowered voice.

"I'm not trying to tell you anything," Gervais said.

"Oh, Christ!" breathed Hammond softly, staring down at his coffee cup. "Who was it?"

"How would I know?" Gervais said. "You're the man in charge. I didn't say it was anybody on our team. I just asked if you were sure—meaning that until we knew it could just as well be one of us as anyone else."

"God," said Hammond. "This could ruin me."

He reached absently for his cup and then shoved it away from him.

"Will you tell me who it is?" he demanded.

"I repeat," said Gervais clearly, meeting him eye to eye, "I didn't say it was anyone on our team."

"Damn well you didn't have to," said Hammond. "Now you tell me who it is!"

"No," answered Gervais, softly. The feeling of contempt was rising in him. "I don't have to wipe your ass for you. If you think it's somebody on the team, find him yourself."

"How am I supposed to do that? A man's discovered, dead in an alley—an alley, mind you. Who on the team's going to be running up and down alleys—" Hammond broke off suddenly and his face cleared.

His eyes met Gervais's above the table. He almost smiled.

"Oh, yes . . ." he breathed softly. "There're those punk kids that have been beaten up in alleys wherever your team was from time to time, aren't there?"

Gervais sat, watching the white face change.

"You know who's been doing that," Hammond said. "Suppose you tell me who he is. Is it who I think it is?"

"I don't have any hard knowledge," said Gervais, evenly.

"Brawley. Kilmartin Brawley." Hammond picked up his coffee cup and drank from it without spilling a drop. He put it back down in its napkin-laden saucer. "There's nothing in his record, though."

"That's right."

Hammond's eyes flickered across to Gervais's.

"You'll back me up on this?" he asked. There was a thin note of pleading in his voice.

"No," said Gervais.

They watched each other for a few seconds. The contempt he felt had risen within him until he could almost taste it.

"If he did," Hammond said, half to himself, "if he did, of course, it's not his fault. It'll be a psychological condition over which he probably has no control."

Gervais sat, saying nothing.

"And there's nothing in his papers. . . ."

Gervais continued to sit, waiting.

"We'll have to do it," Hammond muttered. "We'll have to take him in for a psychiatric check. It could be purely routine, of course. Yes."

"No reference to the knifing?" asked Gervais.

The relief that had begun to illuminate Hammond's face disappeared suddenly, like the light of a lamp turned off.

"God, no!"

"You might be able to handle it that way," said Gervais.

Hammond's face regained its look of relief.

"Yes," he said, "of course. There shouldn't be any need to get too specific and official—on paper, anyway. As far as the records go, they can just show that he was sent in for a routine psychiatric check-up. Meanwhile I'll pass the word privately . . . and then if they find something, some reason to hold him for a while . . ."

"A while?" Gervais said. Their eyes met.

"As long as necessary, of course," Hammond said sharply. Holding Gervais's eye, he repeated, slowly, "as . . . long . . . as . . . necessary."

Abruptly, he got to his feet.

"Stay here," he said. "I think I better make that phone call now."

He went out of the coffee shop toward the lounge, and the outside telephones. Gervais waited until he was out of sight, then got up and left, stopping to pay his bill on the way. He passed through the lobby unseen by Hammond, who stood talking earnestly into a pay phone. Gervais went on up to his room and sat down by the phone. He punched for the office downstairs.

"If Hammond comes in," he said to the face that answered, "tell him he can call me in my room, if he wants me."

Gervais punched off and reached into the drawer below the phone for notepaper and envelope. He laid out paper, envelope and stamp, and took the slim silver pen from his inside pocket. He put the date in the upper right-hand corner of the paper and began to write a letter.

Dear son:

I will be returning to Washington within the next week. Possibly, after a week or so there, I can get a few days off; in which case I will come down to see you and your grandmother and we can go to the Marine Museum.

I am glad to hear from your grandmother that you have brought your grade in history back up to an A level, along with the rest of your marks. There is no substitute for excellence and never any excuse for failure—

The phone buzzed, interrupting him. He laid his pen down and punched it on. The face of Hammond formed on the screen.

"Gervais, where the hell did you go to?" Hammond demanded. "I wanted to talk to you some more—"

"Where are you calling from?"

"From a pay phone in the lobby, of course!" Hammond said. "Listen, get your tail down here. We've got a lot more to talk about."

"I can't think of anything."

"You can't think of anything!" Hammond said in a raw whisper. "Look, this sweeps the situation here under the rug as far as the records go. But I'm still going to be tapped for not knowing there was somebody like Brawley on the team down here. I'm still going to be shoved off in a corner because they won't trust me. Come on down and help me figure a way out of that!"

"What way?" said Gervais. "There isn't one."

Hammond stared at him from the screen, for a long moment.

"No way? What do you mean?" His voice cracked. "No way?"

The contempt spilled at last into Gervais's voice.

"What do you think?" he said. "You've sent him in for a routine psychiatric investigation within days after you've started getting heat over that knifing. You think they don't read the papers and they can't put two and two together? Whether they get an admission to the knifing from him or not won't matter. If I were you, I'd resign."

He punched off the set, picked up his silver pen again and went back to the letter.

You will find that the world is divided into only two classes. Those who are inept and therefore let things happen to them, and those who are capable, who take charge and make things happen to others. If you do not put yourself into one class, you will fall into the other. Those who are inept and allow things to happen to them are better off dead, and it is most merciful then to put them out of their misery. I would allow no son of mine to ever be anything but one of those who take charge of life and of their fellow men.

Your loving Father

38

Fedya watched his hands entering the observational figures into the computer. He no longer consciously directed the movements of those fingers. Over the past six and a half months his body had reached the point where it did almost all things automatically. They worked the experiments, they kept the log, they did the housekeeping, all in all they took care of as much of what there was to be done as he was physically able to do.

He had long ago become aware that the duties—even the curtailed duties he had set himself to take care of aboard Phoenix Two—were too much for any individual. Somewhere after that some of the responsibilities had simply disappeared. He had not consciously dropped them; they had just somehow become eliminated from the day's tasks. He had not reported this to Expedition Control, because it had taken place after the lasercom and radio links aboard Phoenix Two had gone out in their turn. At least, he believed they had gone out. Either that or else he had deliberately stopped using them.

"You *were* the one who stopped using them," said the wraith of Mariya, his dead wife, "don't you remember?"

Mariya was not actually there of course. She, their four children who had died with her in the train wreck, and all the other marsnauts who had ridden with him at launch time, were present only in his mind. He was not deluded that they were actually there, for he was quite sane still, although surprisingly weak. No, he merely spoke out loud to them and imagined them answering as any other lonely, isolated man might talk to a cat or a picture and imagine it answering him, just to break the silence of his exile.

He remembered, now. It had been when he began to find himself breaking down physically that he had told himself that the communications with Expedition Control would no longer work. Of course, Kennedy was still getting certain monitoring readouts about his physical health transmitted automatically from the ship back to Earth. There was nothing he could do about that. But he could pretend conveniently that there was no way of talking back and forth; and so a great many of the little things that were happening to him need not be discussed or reported.

He was not even sure what was basically wrong with him. It was barely possible that he had had a touch of radiation also. But mainly the debilitation of his body seemed to be a matter of the bone loss and other troubles that had been expected to come to space voyagers in a confined enclosure who were not getting sufficient exercise.

He had tried to exercise, of course, but with the whole ship to handle, time and energy had been a problem. This, plus the loneliness, plus an odd sort of minor infection had weakened him.

"You're right, of course, Mariya," he said. He reached for the folder beside him in which he had carefully noted down his most recent symptoms, and once more entered them in the computer. Fever, cough, a general feeling of weakness. Once more the computer informed him that was being slowly poisoned by an excess of microquantities of zinc, normally a trace element in the human body. He had carefully checked the ship to see where such zinc poisoning could be coming from, but he had been able to find nothing.

In any case, the computer projection showed that this intoxication would not become incapacitating until well after he landed on Mars, and therefore it could be disregarded, as long as he could handle the slight lightheadedness and weariness that he felt all the time.

He got up to make his regular housekeeping tour of the spacecraft. As he went, not only Mariya and the children, but the other marsnauts as well, went with him. When he reached the galley, he sat down on one of the chairs by the table. He felt vaguely that something hot to drink would be pleasant, but it was too much effort to get up and get it. Besides, he had other important matters on his mind. He looked around at the imagined figures of Mariya, Iliusha, Kostya, Pavlushka, Vanya, Tad, Bap, Anoshi, Dirk, and Bern. They were all listening attentively, waiting for him to speak.

"It's only a little over forty-two days to Mars orbit, now," he said. "We're almost there."

He could feel that they were pleased, as pleased as he was himself. To the world of people behind him this might look like a historic voyage; but actually it was simply a matter of staying with things until they were accomplished. The greatness of it lay not in what it was, but in what it represented.

"Imagine the human race as one great animal," he told the assembled spirits now. "Think of it as a hill of ants in which all the ants are parts of one large living body; or a great mollusc in which the cells of the body are what we consider individuals. This great mollusc-like creature, which we call Man, evolved from a primitive ancestor, let us say, on the shores of a universal ocean. In the beginning, it may not even have had any consciousness of what it wanted, or where it wanted to go; but these things developed. Little by little it became aware that it had the gift of dreaming, of awareness.

"With this awareness, it begins to notice that where it touches barrenness, things grow. It begins to discover that it can grow and multiply and change the nature of the beach on which it finds itself. Gradually, it grows and develops until it is master of the little bay and the tidal pool in which it first came to consciousness.

"At this point it encounters a crisis. It has filled all available space in its immediate neighborhood. It looks beyond its bay, its warm, shallow, safely enclosed waters, at the rest of the beach and sees it stretching away to eternity in either direction, lifeless, barren, and frightening. Up until this moment, Man has paid very little attention to the rest of the endless beach of which its bay is a part. It has ignored the rest of the universe, in effect. But now, having looked around, it finds it impossible to return to its previous short-sighted, happy state in which it ignored everything but its own small area.

"And then an inner conflict develops. Part of Man wishes to move out, to explore and conquer the vast beaches beyond its own territory. But another part of it is frightened and wishes to stay where it is. *This little bay has always been secure and warm*, this second part of it argues. *Here, we know what the rules are, how things work. Out there the rules may not be the same. Perhaps there are unknown dangers. Certainly we see no other life but ourselves.*

"*But that is the glory of it*, says the first part. *All these infinite beaches lying there waiting for us to take for ourselves. Isn't it a noble thing to do? To go out and spread ourselves to eternity in both directions?*

"*But it may also be a painful thing to do*, replies the second, fearful part, *the adventuring may be hard. The cost may be high. What we win may be dearly bought.*

"*Nonetheless*, retorts the first part, *we are committed by what we are to exploring what we know is there.*

"So the creature debates within itself, fearful yet eager; until finally the part that wishes to experiment, that wishes to adventure, prevails so far that the creature determines to send out a pseudopod into the next bay—a slender tendril only, to adventure out across the dead and barren land where no life has ever been before. This way it will risk only a tiny part of itself, because the tendril is expendable.

"And, of course, this is its genius. In that expendability is the great virtue of the creature. Unlike any other creatures which may have tried to survive on the universal beach before and failed, it has survived because it is willing to sacrifice a part of itself in order to benefit the rest. So, hesitantly, it puts out its tendril—not far at first, only just over the small ridge between it and a small satellite bay, divided from it by the ridge.

"Even this is a great adventure, and a great struggle is made to accomplish it. But finally the tendril's end touches the alien soil of the satellite bay; and finds it cold, hard, alien—but obtainable.

"Then the long, eternal struggle begins in earnest, because the next step must be many times the trip to the satellite bay; it must be clear into a different part of the beach, a vast distance away. The conflict over whether this much greater trip should be made, goes back and forth. The creature is internally torn by it. Even when, at last, the decision is made to send the tendril all that inconceivable distance, to that strange and different place, the struggle still continues while the tendril is going out. Still—slowed, hampered by the division behind it, the tendril continues to move forward; and eventually it touches—touches what no part of the creature has ever touched before—a different bay, a part of the unending universe of the beach. And now, the die is cast. Even as triumph thrills through the creature at its success, it realizes it can never again be content to stay within its own small area. It has gone *outside* and will never endure to be *inside* again.

"And so," concluded Fedya, looking at all the ghosts around him, "you see everything is now accomplished. Because if the unknownness of the universal beach can be broken, can be violated, then *nothing* is unobtainable by the creature that is called Man. Anything that it can conceive can eventually be done; it knows that, now. All things are conquerable, even death itself."

He looked at Mariya and the children.

"And so, my dear ones—" he said to them. He looked over at Tad. "And so, my comrades—when the Lander from Phoenix Two touches down at last on Mars, your deaths cease to be, because you will then have traveled with me, in this spacecraft, to another part of the beach and into the larger universe in which all things exist forever, and life and work are eternal."

Fedya got up from his chair and moved on around the ship in his routine of housekeeping.

39

There was nothing resembling a manuscript-sized sheaf of typing paper on the desk at which Jens had been invited to sit in the Arlington, Virginia, Therapy Unit, Office Number Eight. Jens braced himself for a fight. He was not leaving without his writing.

"You'll find," said the U.S. Marshal behind the desk—he was a short, almost clerical looking man with gold-tinted contact lenses—"everything that was in your pockets at the time you entered legal custody is in this envelope. And if you'll just read and sign this last form . . ."

Jens, seated across from him, tore open the pink envelope and dumped change, watch, minicorder, and cardcase onto the desk top. He scooped the items into the pocket of his new civilian clothes and took up the form.

"What's this?" he said.

"Just your statement that you have no immediate complaints about your treatment while under sentence. It's not a blanket release for the government, of course. You have up to six months to file charges against any officials or personnel who, you believe, acted to you in an indecent, inhumane or illegal manner while you were under their authority."

"They were good enough," said Jens. He scrawled his signature.

"Very nice of you to say so, Mr. Wylie." The guard took it.

Jens grinned at him.

"Got my 'Mr.' back, have I?" he asked. "Nine months of being called by your first name can get you out of the habit."

"Yes, sir," said the marshal. "I can believe it. I understand there's quite a movement on now for Federal therapy units' personnel to be more formal and polite with their custodees.''

"Good," said Jens. "But prison's prison, no matter what you do about it." He opened the card case and saw it was empty. "My social security card?"

The marshal slid it across the desk to him. It was the same plastic card he had carried for years, but it was now a soft dove color, instead of its original white.

"Gray," said Jens, picking it up.

"Sorry, Mr. Wylie," said the marshal. "I understand there's a presidential pardon in the works for you. But until it's signed . . ."

"Don't let it worry you," said Jens. "As far as I'm concerned that gray's a battle award."

"Yes, sir," said the marshal.

"Tell me one thing, though," said Jens. "Do all Federal prisoners on their way out get treatment this polite? Or am I an exception?"

"All of them of course, Mr. Wylie." The marshal stood up and offered his hand.

Jens looked at it for a second.

"Where's my manuscript?" he demanded.

"Oh, sorry. I almost forgot." The marshal sat down again, reached down out of sight behind his desk and came up with two cardboard boxes that had once held blank typing paper, bound together with cord into a single package.

Jens's knees weakened with relief. But there was one more point.

"If you don't mind," he said, and began to untie the cord.

"Of course not. Would you like a knife?"

"No, thanks."

"A lot of us here'll be looking forward to reading it when it comes out," said the marshal, watching benignly as Jens untied the knots, opened the top box, and began to riffle through its contents. "My wife's been reading the articles you excerpted from it, and she says they're fascinating. She always was a bug on the space program. I'll probably wait until the movie comes, though. I'm not much for books, myself—well, you know. But my wife wanted me to ask you when will the full book be out?"

"I haven't got a publisher yet," said Jens. "I've got to finish the book first."

The manuscript pages were all there. Paula Anisha had told him that there was no way the government could withhold his writings permanently; but they might try legally to delay handing it over as long as possible, to slow down publication.

Jens became conscious that the marshal was once more holding his hand out across the desk top.

"What the hell," Jens said, and shook hands. "Good-by."

"Good-by, Mr. Wylie."

Jens stood up, holding his boxes.

"Which way out?"

"Let me take you," the marshal said.

He rose and came around the desk, revealing himself to be even smaller than he had appeared sitting down.

"This way, please."

He led Jens out of the office, down the corridor, around a corner and through a farther door into another office. A gray-looking man was sitting there; and he got to his feet as they came in.

"Sel!" said Jens. He stopped dead.

'Well, I'll leave you gentlemen."

The marshal went out.

"Hello, Jens," said Selden Rethe. Nine months did not seem to have changed as much about him as the knot of his tie. "I imagine you're eager to leave and find your two friends; but I'd appreciate it if you'd take a little run with me first to say a word with someone."

"Lin and Barney are waiting for me," Jens said. "Some other time, maybe."

"We've talked to them. This will just take twenty minutes or so. I'll bring you back here to meet them."

"Oh?" said Jens. "Just who is it you want me to see?"

Selden coughed.

"I don't think we should talk too much about that here," he answered. "He's an old friend who was around from the beginning of the matter that brought you here. He particularly wants to see you again, and talk to you."

Jens stared. "Are you telling me—"

Selden broke in. "Please, no names—out loud, anyway."

He shook his head, slowly. "Jens, I'm surprised at you. After all, you've been in the rooms of this establishment for nearly a year. Conversational privacy's not one of their attributes."

"No, that's right." Jens hesitated. "You say Lin and Barney know about this and they don't mind waiting?"

"They—I suppose I should say Ms. West, since she was the one who said it—was glad to hear you might be talking to our friend again."

"She did?" Jens thought for a second. "All right, then."

They went out of the office. Selden led them farther down the corridor by which Jens had come here, to a heavy door that slid lightly aside as they reached it, letting them into a sort of visitor's lounge with a farther glass wall containing a revolving door that let them out into a parking lot beyond. They took an anonymous-looking blue air-cushion car, which slid them softly above the pavement, out of the grounds of the Arlington Federal Therapy Unit on to a main surface route to Washington.

"I think I know what all this is about," Jens said, after they had reached cruising speed and traveled some distance without conversation. "The Administration wants me to sit on this book of mine. Well, the answer's no."

"You're jumping to conclusions, Jens."

"I don't think so, I don't think so at all, Sel. Let me tell you something. I was going to write the history of the space program the way it ought to be written, eight years ago. I should have written it in my spare time, two years ago. It took nine months of prison to make me understand you don't sit around waiting for the right time to get words on paper, you sit down anywhere without waiting and do it. Now, I've finally got it written—well, almost all written—and sections of it published. It happens that part of it deals with things that may be embarrassing to the Administration. Well, I can't help that. I set out to report a history, and that's part of it. But if you think anything short of death or hell itself, and I mean actual hell, is going to delay the publication of it by one hour longer than it physically takes to get it into print—"

Jens broke off. He had been growing angrier and angrier as he talked; and now he was beginning to hear his voice snarling in the enclosed, air-conditioned bubble of the car. The sound of it embarrassed him. He had not intended to rant, but to say clearly and unyieldingly what his beliefs and intentions were.

"Are you through, Jens?" asked Selden, in his unvarying voice, after several seconds of silence.

"For now," said Jens.

"Then let me repeat, you're jumping to conclusions. The Administration doesn't want you to do anything but publish your history, any way you see fit. That's why the President wants to speak to you. Far from wanting to put barriers in the way of its publication and success, I believe you'll find him offering you the government's support and wishes for your success."

Jens turned and stared at the other man's impassive profile.

"Sel," he said, after a pause, "you're lying to me. It won't do any good."

"I don't resent your saying that," said Selden. "I know you've been expecting opposition to the book's publication and the last nine months of your life would excuse any reaction on your part. However, I'm only telling you the truth."

"You can't be," said Jens. "Not after what I've been through."

"What you've been through is regrettable, of course," said Selden. "But it doesn't change the present situation, which is now a different situation than that of the time you were taken into custody for violating your responsibilities to your governmental position. I told you, and I believe other people told you, Jens, that you never would understand politics. Politics deals with human beings in mass, which are unpredictable quantities. It follows that the only plans of action which governments find workable are pragmatic ones. If the wind changes, and the opportunity occurs to take an improved course in a different direction, the government changes also, and moves on the new tack. That's one of the laws of the same history you're talking about."

"What's changed so much that now it makes my book something you all want?"

"We've got a responsible system in this society," said Selden. "Granted, it makes all kinds of mistakes from moment to moment, but overall it's committed to moving with its basic principles in the large sense. If it didn't it'd have gone down in ruins a long time since."

Jens glared at the other man. Abruptly, he realized his jaw muscles were aching. He had been holding his teeth so tightly clamped together in fierce suspicion that the muscles were beginning to cramp.

"You mean people have finally begun to believe what was done to the marsnauts—" he began.

"No," said Selden. "They would have learned that in the long run, under our system, eventually. You aren't the only fanatic after truth in the world, Jens. I mean that the situation now is different, as the result of a number of events, including Tad Hansard's death, Feodor Asturnov's going on alone to Mars, a certain indiscretion on the part of one of the national representatives to the launch and the Expedition, and the resulting unfortunate publicity surrounding the actions of a—well—psychotically unfortunate on our own governmental payroll—"

"What unfortunate?" asked Jens. "What accident?"

"Now," said Selden, "there's no need to go into that, Jens. Besides the young man is currently under therapy and there's strong hopes of reconstructing him, eventually—though it may take some years."

"Oh, I see," said Jens. "Another patsy like me."

"Not at all!" said Selden. "This fellow actually was criminally psychotic. The incident that caused him to be put under therapy wasn't his first—although it was the first fatal one."

"Well," said Jens, "even if that's true, it still sounds like a late night movie. If you knew all this, why was I in jail this last nine months?"

"The information was uncovered piece by piece," said Selden, "not all at once. It's only in the long run that there's no secrets in politics, Jens—that includes international politics, of course."

"And this new situation makes my book all right with the Administration?"

"Yes," said Selden. "The overall result of what's happened has focused the attention of both sides of the world very favorably on further space work, and particularly work with Mars. We may well now get a second expedition inside the next eight years or so; and both our side and the population-rich nations have adjusted to using that fact as a permanent talking point. So right now, and for the foreseeable future, national credibility is going to be of prime importance; and the honesty of your book is a great asset."

"I see," said Jens.

He felt scooped-out inside. He turned and stared through the one-way transparency of the side of the car, as the vehicle slipped along silently at high speed. He was pulling together the old memory of a story he had heard, or read, once, long ago—about a man who had rebelled against the fact that his people believed in wearing leg irons on their left legs. The man had reacted against the crippled and ulcerated limbs that resulted and taken a sword to find and kill whoever was responsible for the wearing.

Finally, after a long search he had been directed to the home of the demon responsible, who could only be destroyed if he was slain three times, thereby freeing the people. However, the man was warned, the demon could take many shapes. He must ignore whatever he saw and strike regardless. He went and did so, and found himself apparently forced to kill, in turn, his sister, father, and mother—all of whom pleaded with him to spare them.

Afterwards, he had left the home of the demon and returned to his own, where he found sister, father, and mother dead, slain in the manner in which he had slain their apparitions. But on the way home, everyone he had encountered along the road had been wearing leg irons on the opposite leg—the old way, they had told him, having been found to have been a superstition. . . .

Jens was not exactly sure why it should feel good to him to have recalled the story, but when at last he had the whole thing evoked to conscious memory, he felt oddly satisfied, in fact, almost comforted. He sat back in his seat.

Eventually, the car left the main route, and moved into a suburban area, stopping at last at a golf course. They left it for a golf cart; and Selden drove them out to the eleventh tee, where they found Paul Fanzone and his golfing partner, someone Jens did not recognize.

In contrast to Selden, Fanzone looked changed—older and more tired than Jens had seen him at the dinner in Merritt Island, just before the launch. He walked off aside with Jens, leaving Selden and the golfing partner patiently waiting. There were no other golfers Jens could see waiting, impatient to play through at this delay. Apparently such things did not happen when Presidents played.

"Jens," said Fanzone, when they stopped out of earshot of the other two and turned to face each other, "how are you?"

"I'm all right," said Jens.

"They treated you all right? I mean, no . . ."

"No straightjackets, drugs, or padded cells—no," said Jens. "It was the full country-club situation."

Fanzone sighed.

"Good," he said. "I want you to know I gave orders— quietly, of course. But my orders aren't always carried out in spirit as well as letter. I don't know what to say to you, Jens. I apologize, of course. I was wrong."

"Wrong?"

The verbal echo was jolted out of Jens by surprise. The last thing he had expected was Fanzone apologizing. Any apology was not only not necessary, it was completely gratuitous. Also, it had never occurred to Jens that presidents apologized—at least to ordinary citizens, like himself, and on unimportant matters.

He noticed again how old and tired Fanzone was looking; and a rush of his old admiration and affection for the man moved through him.

"Yes, of course," Fanzone said. "I didn't have the time to really look into what you were saying about the experimental load. So I took the words of other people—and they were wrong."

"It doesn't matter," said Jens.

"You'll be getting a pardon, of course. But how I can make up to you those nine months . . . only, once you were committed, it was politically impossible for me to reverse everything under the situation at the time. This is the first chance I've had to get you out."

"It really doesn't matter," said Jens. "In fact, it did me a favor. If I hadn't been locked up I'd probably have never gotten down to writing my book so soon."

"Yes, your book."

"Selden tells me I've got the approval of the Administration on it, now."

"Yes. Yes," said Fanzone. "In fact, any help we can give

you . . . I've read some of the magazine excerpts. You're a good writer. But we always knew that."

"Thanks," said Jens. "But it's just a solid news style paying off."

He waited. However, Fanzone did not say anything more for a moment. He seemed to be struggling with himself. He stared off at the trees that hid the fourteenth hole.

"Jens," he said, at last, turning abruptly to stand face to face, "we grind slow, that's all. But I'd like you to believe that in the end we grind fine. Most people—I mean most people, even people in power, everywhere—believe in civilization and have a stake in it. In the long run they do work for it. Otherwise we wouldn't have any civilization at all."

"I suppose so," said Jens. "All the same, any kind of progress we make seems to look more like a case of fumbling forward than anything else."

"Yes. Well . . . that, too." Abruptly, Fanzone held out his hand. "Will you keep in touch from time to time? I'd really like to know how things go with you."

"If you'd like," said Jens.

"I would. I'll be out of office in another year and a half. I don't think I'm up to more than that, anyhow. They tell you it's a big job in advance; but you can never believe how big until you get into it. Maybe, a few years from now, you and I can get together from time to time."

"All right," said Jens.

They shook hands.

"Well," said Fanzone, turning abruptly and starting again toward the tee. "I've got to get back to my game. I really don't like golf. It's the doctors make me play it."

Lin and Barney had been waiting a little more than an hour in the visitors' parking lot of the institution in which Jens had been an inmate for the last nine months. They were parked in one of the slots, sitting in Barney's personal two-door air cushion vehicle, Barney in the left of the two bucket seats up front and Lin sitting alone on the curving bench seat that filled the back.

"There he is," said Lin, suddenly. "Barney, pull out so they'll see us!"

Barney started the car. He backed out and around, so that

they were in the middle of the lane between the two rows of parked cars and headed toward the exit gate of the lot. A blue sedan which had just entered the lot swung in their direction, turned down the lane they were in and pulled up parallel to Barney's car.

"That's them," said Barney.

Jens opened the door to the blue sedan, turned his head to say a last word to Selden Rethe, and got out, closing the door behind him. Selden pulled off. Jens opened the door opposite Barney and climbed in, reaching out to shake hands with Barney, but continuing to the back, where Lin waited.

"Off we go," said Barney, putting the car in motion to-toward the exit and the road beyond. Lin caught Jens as he sat down beside her and held him fiercely, kissing him.

"Hello, love," said Jens softly, in her ear.

Lin began to tremble. Barney was pulling out of the exit and turning on to the road and she did not want to let go of Jens. She did not want to let go of him, ever. To her own great astonishment, she burst into tears.

"Baby," said Jens, stroking her hair.

"Hang on to me," she gasped. "Hold me!"

His arms tightened around her. She clung to him. She was not crying quietly at all. She was being very noisy about it and Jens was soothing her, and Barney was sitting there through all of it, only an arm's-length away, and she did not care.

She buried her face in the warm crook between Jens's shoulder and neck, and bawled.

40

They had to swing through downtown Washington to pick up Sir Geoffrey. He was standing just inside the front window of the liquor store he had specified, saw them as they pulled up at the curb and came out, clutching a package, which he handled tenderly as he climbed in to take the bucket seat beside Barney.

"What did you get?" Lin asked, after Sir Geoffrey had welcomed Jens back to the streets of freedom and Barney had once more pulled out into traffic.

"Oh? Wine," answered Sir Geoffrey, sliding the bucket seat back to its farthest position. "Just a very good champagne I think Clo might like. You can't get it anywhere else in this country."

"Only one bottle?" asked Lin, grinning.

"Well, it's just for the two of us, you know," said Sir Geoffrey seriously, "and Clo only sips, nowadays. Once on a time . . . but then, that was once on a time."

"Where are we going now?" Jens asked.

"To the airport and back to Merritt Island," said Lin. "There's a small celebration there, planned to mark your getting out. No," she added soothingly, as Jens stiffened, "nothing large. Just a bunch of local people—Bill Ward and some others. A couple of handfuls of people only."

"Good," said Jens, settling back. "Nine months in there quiets you down. I don't think I could take brass bands right away. Anyway, the thing to celebrate isn't me. It's Fedya riding Phoenix Two all the way to Mars, the way he has; and the fact that what he's done, and Tad's death, bought us a future in space."

"Got the papers, did you?" said Sir Geoffrey from the front seat.

"Oh, yes," said Jens. "I've been able to follow it all. All about the radio signals from Fedya's body sensors that could tell us he was still alive and active; the popular reaction all over the world, the blame for the Expedition's trouble finally getting pinned where it belonged, on politics-as-usual—"

He looked forward at Sir Geoffrey.

"No offense, in your case."

"Why not?" said Sir Geoffrey, cheerfully. "It was a good system. Politics as usual helped build the Earth. I was all for it, once. Not ashamed of the fact. But outside the Earth, evidently it's a clog, not a benefit. Right. Scrap it then. I have; and not ashamed of that, either."

"Geoff," said Lin, "was our strong right arm in getting

you loose this early, Jens. He was the man who knew just what strings to pull and just what buttons to push—and how.''

"That so?" said Jens to Sir Geoffrey. "What did the British government think of activity like that on your part?"

"Oh, Lord," said Sir Geoffrey, "I'm retired. I couldn't have done that sort of thing, otherwise. I quit right after that press conference of yours. Now that I have, I don't know why I didn't do it years ago. I can drink all I want now, whenever I want. Odd thing, I used to fear I'd end up one of those boozy old men that everybody dodges at parties. But not at all. After a bit I just get sleepy and doze off. Don't even snore, they tell me.''

He looked back over his shoulder, triumphantly, at Jens.

"What do you think of that?"

"Remarkable."

"Ah, well," said Sir Geoffrey, "it's just a natural talent, I suppose. But then, I've never been what you might call the average, ordinary sort of man.''

"The celebration at Merritt Island's for Fedya, too," said Lin. Jens turned back to face her. Beyond her profile there appeared the high acoustical wall guarding the concrete highway, a momentary blur of black color, warning of a housing area behind it, where quiet was required.

"They're not putting me in the same bag with Fedya!" said Jens.

"No, no. Not really," said Lin. "It's just that the two things happened at the same time. You were freed, and Fedya reached Mars ten days ago. If he's following the schedule they calculate for him, he's due to land on the surface today.''

"All that distance . . ." said Jens, half to himself, his eyes unfocusing on the concrete wall's blackness, like the darkness of airless space between the starpoints, spanning the highway on Earth to the rusty-colored crater-dust of the Martian soil. "All that distance . . ."

As Jens had said, nine months of semi-solitary living had had an effect on him. After an hour or so, he found the crowd, and the voices of the party, too much for him. He went looking for Lin, to whom in any case he wanted to talk privately and alone. He had not yet told her about the Administration's amazing about-face on his book. Something inside him had wanted to keep that for a surprise package in a private moment between the two of them.

It was mid-afternoon by this time. The party was being held at the home of the Duchess—which seemed to have unofficially become the home of Sir Geoffrey as well. It was not the same mansion she had occupied earlier, halfway down the length of Merritt Island; but a—for her—incredibly modest home about two miles away, which she had bought outright when, as Lin had told Jens, she had unexpectedly decided to settle down there, rather than in the West Indies.

The home was, therefore, nothing more than a modern, spacious, four-bedroom place with den, library, swimming pool, extensive grounds, private canal to the Banana River and a large boathouse and dock to which was tied a thirty-foot cabin cruiser with flying bridge. She and Sir Geoffrey used the boat frequently to go out by water for dinner. Most surprising, there were hardly any servants to speak of. The platoon of young men with strong Castillian accents had all gone home to Spain, and their only replacements had been a twice-a-week housekeeper and a once-a-week maintenance crew.

With all this, however, the house and grounds were large enough so that Jens had to hunt to find Lin. Right now, the rest of the guests were mainly outside around the swimming pool. He searched through the house and found her at last in the large and airy kitchen. She was with the Duchess, washing dishes in a sink below a wide window that looked out on the swimming pool and a cluster of deck chairs holding Sir Geoffrey and some other guests.

"Hi," said Jens, stepping into the kitchen. "The dishwasher break down?"

"It's full," said Lin, looking over her shoulder at him. "What are you doing in here?"

"I'm not as up to society yet as I thought," he said. "Is there anything I can do here?"

"You can take over for Clo," said Lin. She put down the dish she had just finished drying and reached over to untie the strings of the apron around the Duchess's waist. "Clo, go on out and be a hostess. We can take care of these."

"I'll just put away this glassware we've done, first, then," said the Duchess. Even in a kitchen setting she gave the impression of an international dealer in the fate of governments. She stepped around Lin, who began tying the apron on Jens, and started putting clean wine glasses back up into one of the kitchen's many cupboards.

Jens, harnessed for duty, put his hands in the sink full of warm soapy water, and found it comforting. From the window in front of him, the voice of Sir Geoffrey floated clearly into the kitchen.

"Sensitivity?" he said. "Fine for most, no doubt."

Jens looked out through the window and saw Sir Geoffrey talking with a tall, black-haired man in his mid-twenties and a small, very pretty girl of about the same age. His memory, searching, turned up the fact that they were Del Terrence and his wife Jonie—Del being the Laserkind factory representative who had quit his company over the lasercom failure on the spacecraft and now worked for Disney World.

"Never was sensitive myself," Sir Geoffrey was continuing, bending an intent eye on his two hearers. "Just not born that way. You'd always have to hit me over the head with a shovel first, to get my attention. Still once you'd done that, I usually tried to do the right thing. Just as when I lost my head and took young Wylie's side of it, after that press conference of his. . . ."

The Duchess chuckled.

"Dear Geoff," she said to Jens, "he really loves talking about that. Do you notice he gets to be a little more of the hero, and you get pushed more and more into the background every time he tells it?"

"Yes," said Jens. "But it doesn't matter. I like him; and he really did stick his neck out to help me, once the chips were down."

"True enough. Still," said the Duchess. "Geoff saw his chance to go out in a blaze of glory—honorable or dishonorable, it didn't matter—and took it. Listen to him!"

"So what could I do after all that? I mean, tripping up policemen, misdirecting FBI people, and everything else. I had to resign. But it's turned out all for the best. I'm free to sit around at things like this, now; and I can drink as much as I want without giving my government a black eye. Always looked forward to that—always dreaded it too. I was telling Wylie and Lin on the way here, it was a worry of mine. I mean ending up as a staggering old souse who can't say two words you can understand. But it turns out I'm all right after all. Once I've had one too many, or two, I simply need to take a little nap."

He settled himself deeper in his lawn chair.

"As now," he said, closing his eyes. Del and Jonie got up from their own lawn chairs and went away around the corner of the pool.

"Well, now," said the Duchess in a tone of satisfaction, closing the cupboard doors. "That takes care of those. Perhaps I *will* go and check up to see if anyone wants anything."

She went out. Jens looked after her.

"I'd never have pictured her here, like this," he said to Lin. "She seems happy as a clam."

"She is," said Lin.

"But, I mean it's something of a comedown after a mansion, and servants and international intrigue—if that's what she was really tied up in."

"I think she prefers Geoff to all of that. Don't be fooled by the way she talks about him."

"I suppose," said Jens, washing dishes. "He's certainly happy enough for ten. And I like that new wife of Barney's. What's her name, again?"

"Aletha."

Jens stopped washing, holding a dish in midair.

"That's who she is, then. She was the bartender at the Holiday Inn."

Lin looked at him curiously.

"You'd met her before?"

"Well, not exactly met her. I was in the bar there with Barney one day . . ."

Jens's voice trailed off. He looked at Lin with an enormous delight that had not so much to do with her, although she was part of it, as with—he had once again realized—threads; scarlet, gold and black, of no color and all colors, making up the tapestry that he had envisioned in that waking dream beside her months ago, just before the launch—a grand woven design that was this flawed, glorious, fallible, noble, selfish human enterprise.

Of course! This was the vision his book needed—the image

to pull it all together. Aletha would be one of the background threads, a thread which now made its pattern with the thread that was Barney's, changing both their destinies, and in some way affecting what would happen in decades and centuries to come, out in the dim reaches of the solar system and beyond. Just as there was this Del Terrence, whose gut-honesty had pushed him from Laserkind to Disney World, and so bound his skills to constructing models for a new human environment, even though he got his pay in the service of entertainers—another thread on its own changing way, diving and surfacing amidst the warp and woof of the background.

Every element of the design was around him, including those which had been obscure to him such as that of the security man, Albert Gervais. Gervais, for instance, must also have had his part in the pattern, a part that Jens would probably never know in full detail. He himself, Lin, Geoffrey, the Duchess, the 'nauts, Fedya out on Mars—they all went into it, they all were part of it. Without any one of them the whole pattern necessarily would be different. And without him, himself, Senator Wylie's son, the fake diplomat, the ex-newsman, it would have been very different. And by God, by the stars, by anything else the race would find itself swearing upon as it went on and out and out to the unending reaches of that great purposeful tapestry that unrolled before it to eternity, what he had made of it all would stand, would be the first and best explanation to the race of what it had all been about. This sudden explosion of understanding was so strong in him that he had to shake himself hard mentally to come back to the present, to the kitchen, where Lin stood staring at him curiously.

"What is it?" asked Lin.

He found he was not quite ready to tell her all about it now. He wanted to settle it in his own mind first. Tonight . . .

"I just remembered something," he said. "There's something I've been waiting to tell you. I wanted a moment when there weren't other people all around. You know Selden Rethe took me off to talk with Paul Fanzone before bringing me to meet you?"

"Sure."

"Well, Sel told me that the Administration isn't out to interfere with my getting the book published after all. Just the opposite. They're all for it. They want it. And Paul even offered me any help the government could give me in getting the facts."

"Hey!" said Lin. "How wonderful!"

He started to put his arms around her, realized they and his hands were dripping with soapsuds and dried them hastily on his apron before clutching her.

"Actually, even if they only half-deliver on that," he said, letting her go, "there's all sorts of material I'd feel shaky about using if I couldn't get the exact facts on it; and the rest of the book is loaded with nothing but stuff that needs to be checked for accuracy. Facts and figures—you know, conclusions aren't worth anything if the author, at least, doesn't know just what the facts and figures are backing them up—"

"Look," said Lin, pushing him toward the full dishrack, "if you're just going to stand there and talk, let me at the sink. At least half the job'll get done that way."

"Well . . ." Jens let himself be transferred. He picked up a dish and a dishtowel and started to dry it. "But you see what that means. The way things are now, it's only a matter of choosing between two publishers; and with the Administration okaying my access to the information I need, I can check everything out and come up with a finished, ready-to-go manuscript in three months. And whichever publisher I choose to bring the book out has been talking to me about the next one I'd do. You know what that means. Barney used to keep telling me to marry you and let you support me while I got the writing going. But the way it's turned out, I can marry you *and* support you while you're getting *your* writing going—"

"Are you telling me, or asking me?"

"What? Oh, sorry. Asking—you will, won't you?"

"Of course, you damn fool!"

"Isn't it something, though?" said Jens, after another small interruption in the business of getting the dishes washed and dried. "Isn't it amazing how things get accomplished? I told Fanzone I thought history was more like a case of fumbling forward—as in football—than anything else. And it's a fact. Look how in this instance everybody made mistakes and still things were done. Did you know I really wanted to be an astronaut, myself?"

"I guessed it," Lin answered.

"I mean literally. Oh, I knew it was an insane sort of hope. I knew better than almost anyone how many hundreds of thousands of men would be better qualified than I'd ever be. But I couldn't help dreaming about it, the way, at a football game, you can daydream that some miracle might happen, the star quarterback might somehow get taken out of the game; and you, the spectator, would for some freak reason be asked, out of all the stadium, out of the thousands of people there, to replace him. And you would. And it would work. So my dream was like that, and of course it never happened. But instead something just as crazy and impossible is going to happen in the real world, which is my getting this book done and published. It's going to be a good book, too, Lin."

"It's going to be one of the great books."

He stared at her. Slowly he became conscious of the fact he was still holding a dish and a dishtowel in his hands, doing nothing with either. He put them both down on the drainboard, and stepped to her. She was still facing the sink with both hands in the dishwater; but he put his arms around her from behind and held her, feeling how incredibly warm and alive she was.

She started to lift her hands out of the sink, then left them where they were and merely leaned her head back so her cheek was against his.

"You and your dragons," she said. Behind her, he thought he saw the ghost of the Senator, his father, looking at him with speculative, wary, but grudgingly impressed, eyes. There was a great deal in common between the Senator and Lin, he now recognized.

"Maybe," the Senator seemed to be saying. "Well, maybe . . ."

41

In his spacesuit, Fedya moved slowly and with great effort. He had controlled the Mars lander also slowly and with great effort—but precisely—down to a landing on the surface of Mars. He had redoubled his exercising in the past three months, he had even set up in the wardroom on B Deck the "squirrel cage," as the emergency centrifuge wheel was called; and spent two of his daily waking hours under its simulation of gravity. But the many months of slowly debilitating effect of almost no gravity and the strange illness in him had continued to weaken him.

From the moment he had reached Mars orbit his head had begun to clear of all dreams and fancies he had carried about with him aboard the spacecraft for the last half of the voyage. The imagined figures of his fellow marsnauts and of Mariya and the children were gone now; although they were always in the back of his mind. He was just terribly feverish and weak. The gravity of Mars, only three-fifths of Earth's, dragged him down and made his arms and legs as they moved above the controls feel as if they were hung with massive weights of lead.

Nonetheless a minimal amount of strength could be made to accomplish a great deal. With Phoenix Two in orbit around Mars, he had worked the Mars excursion module out of its storage compartment in the airless forward section of the spacecraft and readied it for a landing on the alien world below. He had entered it; and with a few touches on the position thrusters separated it from its mother craft.

The inboard computer of Phoenix Two had given him the figures he needed. He had retrofired the MEM's descent stage rocket motor for the descent, and fallen toward the surface. As they approached, the protective shroud and a portion of the heat shield was jettisoned—the latter an automatic action to allow use of the ascent stage of the MEM as an abort vehicle, unnecessary now; Fedya did not intend to return to Phoenix Two.

Close to the Mars surface, now—it seemed to swell away on all sides below him like a cratered surface of a larger moon—Fedya used the descent stage motor again for braking. His descent slowed, slowed, until he was finally hovering, just above the surface. Then he went down.

The jar of landing was slight. Fedya sat where he was at the controls, wrapped in silence. The weariness that dragged him down into apathy, urged him to stay where he was, comfortably seated, waiting for the final slowdown of his body into death that was not far off, now. But he had not come all this way to be found still encased in a vehicle, some yards above the Martian soil.

For a couple of hours he rested. Then, with great effort, he put himself into motion. It was an even slower business here, on the Martian surface, but he struggled, and rested, and struggled again.

Eventually, he was out of the MEM, and down its metal ladder to the surface, having carried out, one at a time, the few items he had determined to set up. One of these was the laser reflector. Another, the United Nations' flag, which he set up on the rubbled ground, together with smaller flags of the six governments who had combined in the Mars Expedition. With the colors of the artificially stiffened flags standing out in the light of the distance-shrunken sun, he turned to put up the locator beacon that would be activated by those who came after him, searching across the surface from their own touchdown location for the spot where he had landed.

With these two items out of the way, his duty tasks were done. He began to assemble the framework he had designed and built on board the Phoenix Two during the last two months. When it was done, it showed itself as a sort of standing support—half chair, half crutches. He had positioned it facing the sun; and when he backed into it, and relaxed, it held him facing the light.

He hung in the support he had created. It was not uncomfortable in Mars's light gravity; and now that he let go of the struggle to work and live, he could feel that the end, for him, was waiting very close.

He sighed a little inside the spacesuit. Sleep was pulling him down into silence and an end. Through weary eyes and the face-plate of the suit, he looked out, past the excursion module across the rubbled desertland of the Martian surface to the horizon. A fine, orange-red dust lay everywhere, drifted deep behind boulders and rocks. A memory of something Tad had mentioned once, a quotation about the "red sands of Mars" taken from some old book about the planet . . . was it one of the fictions of Edgar Rice Burroughs where the planet was called Barsoom, and fierce hordes of great, green four-armed swordsmen rode massive mounts across it? Fedya had never read any of the books Tad had talked about, and could not now remember if the quotation was from them, or from some other writing.

But this was the real Mars and he was here. Man was here. Beyond the horizon, everywhere, the atmosphere was full of a suspended dust, giving it a hazy look and scattering the light of a more distant sun until the whole sky was a bright orange pink—brighter than it should be if the dust had not been there and only the shrunken sun had been visible in a thin, blue sky. Outside his spacesuit the daytime temperature at this moment was minus fifty degrees centigrade. The Martian air was poisonous with carbon dioxide. From all these things, his life systems protected him; but that protection would be unnecessary soon, though it would continue for some time after he had no need of it.

Nonetheless, here he was. Here he would be, when those who would come after would arrive to find him. They would discover him, waiting, on his feet.

Far above him, in orbit, Phoenix Two faithfully continued to rebroadcast to Earth the body signals radio-relayed to it from the module and to the module from the sensors in Fedya's underclothing beneath the spacesuit. Those body signals were growing weaker, and at Kennedy, back on Earth, they would be able to note and record the moment in which the signals would stop entirely.

Before and after that moment, Phoenix Two would continue to fall endlessly about Mars in the orbit into which that world had captured her, rushing through space above the red planet, glinting in the light from the far-off sun, and waiting.

Waiting for the other men and women who would come before too long now. Who must come, since there was now no other choice. Because for human beings it had always been that way: The road led always forward—and there was no turning back.